THE
TRUTH
THAT
LIES
BETWEEN

THE
TRUTH
THAT
LIES
BETWEEN

a novel

W.D. McCOMB

TreaShore
PRESS

THE TRUTH THAT LIES BETWEEN.
Copyright © 2019 by W. D. McComb.

wdmccomb.com

All rights reserved. Published by TreaShore Press.

ISBN: 978-1-7340904-0-6 (hardcover)
ISBN: 978-1-7340904-1-3 (paperback)
ISBN: 978-1-7340904-2-0 (ebook)

First edition.

Printed in the United States of America.

DEDICATION

To...

The mothers:

The one who took me fishing, called me her little buddy, and cooked the best biscuits.

The one who stocked my bookshelves with *Hardy Boys* mysteries, insisted on proper manners, and clapped her hands when I showed up at her door during college.

The one who made sure Santa always brought me literature, taught me the worth of love and sentimentality, always had faith in my potential when I doubted whether anyone else did, and lest I forget, read more drafts of this book than she cares to remember.

And most importantly, the one who propped me up through exhausting years of engineering school, medical training, and building a practice, who told me to go for it when I first shared my idea of a crazy new pastime, patiently supported my long nights at our kitchen table, and lovingly endured all my quiet periods of preoccupation, and who believes in me and our children the way only a wife and mother can.

The fathers:

The two who happened to be both neighbors and friends, who wowed me with the war stories they would rather someone else tell, drove me countless times "to town for a Coke and a pack of Nabs," and let me shoot their shotguns and tangle their fishing reels.

The one who taught me—from wherever he happened to be: school, home, church, or even behind the wheel of whatever old Ford truck he got by with because money was tight—the value of hard work, the sanctity of integrity, and the importance of being tough enough to finish what I start.

The children:

The three who inspire me to strive for clean storytelling without sacrificing authenticity, to create something I can leave behind for them and their children long after I leave this world, and most importantly, to be a better person. And yes, without question all the "Dad, it's really good, when are you gonna publish that thing?" comments were helpful, too.

...This is for you. Thank you all.

PART ONE

"The highest compact we can make with our fellow, is, —
'Let there be truth between us two forevermore.'"
—Ralph Waldo Emerson

ONE

"HEY Bud, why don't you share the joke? Sure could use one."

I immediately recognize the voice, but I would have known it was Jack Masterson even if he communicated in Morse code. No one calls me "Bud" like he does. Most everyone else just calls me Case. I sneak a sideways frown at him. "Say what?"

"You're just staring off and smiling."

I glance back across the marble headstone-studded landscape and the last few lingerers from the meager assembly, but their somber looks, dark suits, and darker sunglasses under an ashen sky suggest nothing to smile about. Then I hear the popping sounds, probably some kid's firecrackers going off in the distance, and I realize Jack is right. I had been smiling. I shake my head. "Nah, don't know any good jokes. Just thinking."

"You always were a dreamer. Working on that book?" Jack knows I'm an English major. What he doesn't know is the novel I dreamed of writing as a kid now seems as likely to happen as a genie popping out of my coat pocket.

"*Me*—a dreamer? *You* were always the dreamer. And schemer."

Jack cuts his eyes at me. "Schemer? I'm just an optimist."

My grin returns. He's right about the optimist part. Such was always his nature—so long as life didn't force it out of him.

"Those firecrackers." I nod toward the sound. "Made me think about that time with the cap pistols. Your optimism could've gotten us killed."

His wink tells me he knows immediately what I'm talking about. When we were nine or ten, his sister Michelle told us a rumor about a homeless man lurking around town, maybe just sneaking in houses to steal food, maybe with other things on his mind. Jack convinced me we should sleep in the living room and scare him off with cap pistols if he showed up. Neither of us actually believed it would ever happen, but when the back door creaked open in the midst of a thunderstorm, our bravado proved as fleeting as the flash of lightning illuminating the figure looming in the doorway.

"I scared him off," Jack says. "Just like we planned."

"Like *you* planned. Except you shot on accident, peed your pants and ran to wake up Dad."

Jack shakes his head and finally shows a glimmer of a smile. "That was *you* with the wet crotch. But I'll give you credit. You did find the bullet he left."

"Not exactly what Michelle had us expecting from the Vagabond, huh?"

His expression darkens, and his eyes lock on mine, like he's searching. "Little did we know."

Little did we know we'd find that body later, and everything would go to crap. I want to say it, but I don't. I just nod and look away instead.

Havenrest Cemetery now appears devoid of people except two workers, dutifully shoveling earth into a hole six feet deep. One is a middle-aged black man and the other a scrawny white teenager, two or three years younger than us. Jack steps over and picks up a rose boutonniere lying on the grass adjacent to the mound of dirt, absently smells it, and tosses it underhand atop the partially covered casket. He stands up, opens his mouth to speak, then bites his lower lip and shakes his head. We both pretend to study an enormous flock of blackbirds, a sea of specks against the gray winter horizon. Their staccato calls, softened by the distance, pepper the awkward silence until I interrupt them.

"I'm sorry about Michelle. She'll be missed." I immediately hate the cliché but don't regret the effort.

Jack sighs heavily. "Wouldn't wish ovarian cancer on my worst enemy."

I pat him on the shoulder but still can't think of anything helpful to add, so I wait as he rocks back and forth on the balls of his feet. I can tell he wants to talk now.

"Sad thing is, she had really gotten her life back together." He stops abruptly and throws a glance my way without turning his head. "But after everything ... she started getting better. Kicked her habits, went back to school, to church. Got married. Said Ron was the first guy she'd ever been with who treated her right."

I can't help but wonder how Jack is really holding up. Physically, he seems fine. The wavy, brown hair, with a tinge of auburn when the light hits it just right, and his ruddy complexion haven't changed. And his muscular frame—up to six foot one and maintaining its two-inch advantage over mine—looks as robust as ever. But his usual disposition seems further away than the place smiles disappear with the death of a sister. I know it just by looking at him, the same way a flicker of facial expression conveys an emotional shift no painter could capture, but even a baby could identify.

We stand in silence, idly toeing blades of grass at our feet, hands in our suit pant pockets, shoulders hunched slightly against the icy breeze. "She's at peace now at least," I say.

"A hard thing to come by sometimes." Jack stands motionless for a time, then shrugs and bumps me gently with his elbow.

"What?"

He chuckles. "We sure had some good times, didn't we, Bud?"

"Are you … talking about before? Or after?"

Before and *after*— the two divisions in time by which all moments of our friendship are inevitably now distinguished. Jack knows this even better than I do. He stares at me hard before he answers, and I could kick myself for taking the conversation back there again. "Do you ever think about it anymore? You know, what happened?"

What happened. It suddenly occurs to me that within the tragedy of Michelle's death might lie an opportunity to extract something good, perhaps a new beginning. A dispatch of the *after*. Only Jack can decide.

"Do you?" Of course, I already know his answer.

TWO

Five years earlier — 1985

"SUCKERS! Y'all can't beat me!" Jet laughed as his three-wheeler skidded to a halt in Jack's driveway.

"Let Mr. Sissy ride with *you* next time," Jack shot back, "yap yap yapping in your ear to slow down the whole way through Papa Mac's farm, and see if you don't eat my dust."

I tried to trip Jack as he dismounted the Honda Big Red in front of me. "I'm not afraid of going fast. You just can't drive."

"Wusses and bad drivers got no hope keeping up with me," Jet said. "Speed is the name of my game."

Jack snorted. "The only thing you're fast at is getting to the refrigerator." He pinched Jet playfully where his belly protruded over his waistline just enough to make an easy target.

"Ow!" Jet yelped, swinging and missing Jack's back with his fist. "Punk."

Jack's eighteen-year-old sister Michelle leaned against her Toyota Celica, sucking on a cigarette. "Gonna get yourself killed riding like that," she drawled. "Y'all are all stupid."

I laughed to myself. While I supposed it possible that our reckless driving could get us hurt, and some might question the intelligence of Jack or me, the word "stupid" didn't belong in the same county, much less the same sentence, with a reference to John Edward Townsend. Jet's acronymic nickname might not be an apt description for his fleetness afoot—or lack thereof—but it just so

12

happened to be a perfect fit for his brain. My other best friend was incontrovertibly smart—freaky smart, we always said, his mind a whirlwind of facts, figures, theories, and words we had never heard of. He made straight As without a hint of effort, scarcely cracked a textbook because he was always reading something else, and completed school assignments absently while his mind sped off in myriad directions.

"Shut up, Michelle," Jack retorted. "Go smoke a doobie or something."

She glared at Jack and finished off her cigarette in one deep drag before putting it out against the car door and tossing it at his feet. Her pink halter top hung off her bony shoulders and chest in a revealing way that made me wonder whether the look was intentional or an unintended consequence of too many skipped meals. Either way, I suspected weed might not be the worst thing on her agenda.

"Hello, Michelle Masterson." I dragged the 'hello' out and emphasized each syllable in a mocking, yet playful, way. Troubled or not, she and I had always gotten along okay.

Her mouth curled at the corners ever-so-slightly. "Hello, Casey Reynolds," she drawled, mimicking my cadence. "Or should I say, Shaggy-Doo?"

Michelle was the only one who ever called me that, but that didn't mean I hadn't heard it a hundred times over the years. As a little kid, whenever American Top 40 with Casey Kasem came on the radio, I loved to remind people that my name was Casey, too. And most everyone ignored me—except Michelle, who pointed out that Kasem provided the voice for Shaggy, the inept, cowardly, dog biscuit-eating comic relief in the Scooby-Doo cartoons. An entertaining character to be sure, but not the image I was going for. Which is exactly why she called me Shaggy-Doo. I hated it, which made her love it even more.

The truth is, I was named after a knife. A knife brand, to be precise. My father and his before him both accumulated a collection of Case knives and believed a man should always have one in his pocket. At first, my mother wouldn't hear of her son being named after a pocketknife, but she eventually relented—with a compromise. So, the name on my birth certificate is Casey.

"Call me what you want," I said, "but you know you still love me."

She frowned. "I'd like you better if you hung out with someone besides my idiot brother."

Jack pretended to pick a booger and flick it on her as he walked by, darting beneath her attempt at a right hook. "Come inside, guys." He reached for the door. "I've got something serious to ask y'all."

Jet and I widened our eyes and together mouthed the word 'serious', mocking a look of worry about another scheme and its consequences. Jack rolled his eyes. "Oh, shut up and come on."

The blast of cool, conditioned air was a welcome change from the lingering smolder of a typical Mississippi September, almost as refreshing as the large glasses of sweet tea we poured. A note on the kitchen counter from Jack's mom said she was working late at the diner tonight, hot dogs were in the fridge.

Jet stretched his ample frame out on a brown plaid couch, and I plopped down in my favorite chair, a faded red leather piece that enveloped my body perfectly as the particles within it shifted to accommodate my shape. Jack's mom said it was called a Sacco, that Jack's father had ordered it years ago, before Jack was born, to bring some "Italian style" to their décor. She never particularly liked it, and now it was so worn it looked like it might fall apart, but she said she couldn't get rid of it. I figured it was because of the memories it carried but liked to think it was partly because it was my favorite.

Jack was, as usual, a nervous bundle of energy, pacing the linoleum floor that spread from the kitchen through the living room. "Okay, here's my idea. Let's build a cabin."

Jet leaned forward and placed his elbows on his knees. "A cabin? Where?"

"Where ya think? Duh. On Papa Mac's."

Hey, can we go to Papa Mac's?

The indelible echoes of that question from Jack or Jet were ever-present, a simple inquiry that had led to innumerable excursions onto what was a veritable paradise as far as we were concerned—a farm tucked precisely between my neighborhood and theirs, comprising everything we considered important. Fields and sloughs, hardwood bottoms and pine ridges, honeysuckle vines and blackberry thickets. Plenty of game to hunt, and a prime fishing hole we nicknamed Snake Lake, where the fish were big but our fear of the snakes was bigger. Best of all, though, was our campsite. A small clearing nestled within a copse of oaks, guarded by briars and hedge and hidden out of view from the field road, unless you knew where to look. Our three-wheelers could deliver every essential for an overnight stay, from firewood to boom boxes. It was our very own oasis, and we availed ourselves of its amenities almost as much as we fished and hunted the place.

I took a gulp of sweet tea and shot Jet a look while Jack anxiously tapped the linoleum kitchen countertop. "You're serious?" I asked Jack. "Build it on Papa Mac's?"

"Absolutely. Maybe not a cabin, but we can put *something* together. We'll call it the Hideaway."

Jet looked at me. "The Hideaway?"

Jack pressed on. "It's perfect. C'mon, maybe your dad could help us?"

Jet's father was a local contractor, but he had been having

difficulty finding enough work. So he most likely had some time on his hands, not to mention plenty of tools.

Jet didn't appear to take offense. "Dad might, but dude, it's not even our land."

Jack turned to me. "Whadda you think?" He began to pace, watching me, awaiting my opinion—my verdict. Papa Mac, the best friend of my late grandfather, had asked my father to keep an eye on the property. So it wouldn't happen without me, whether Jet was on board or not.

I smiled. "Let's do it."

Jack smiled back and pounded his fist in his hand. He continued pacing a moment, then spun toward us, speaking as he turned. "We have to keep it a secre—"

A low voice growled, "What secret? You *know* I don't like secrets."

THREE

STONE Perkins had somehow walked in without making a sound. He glared hard at Jack as if no one else was in the room, bloodshot eyes aflame and flickering. Jack had once told me he disliked his stepfather when he was sober but hated him when he was drunk. I had a feeling which version we were about to see.

He was only five-foot-nine but thick in the chest and thighs, like an athlete, although he clearly carried some extra weight in the midsection. Stone wore scuffed leather boots, faded blue jeans, and a short-sleeved, navy, button-up shirt that matched the dark circles around his eyes. A white patch on the left chest read S & S Heating/Cooling. I froze in my chair while he focused on Jack, ambling toward him a few steps before stopping right beside me.

"I asked you a question, boy." Stone pointed at Jack, who had stopped pacing and stood on the other side of the room.

"Why aren't you at work?" Jack was afraid of Stone, but lately he had begun to stand up to him more and more. I wasn't sure if it was because he had hit a growth spurt to five-foot-eight himself, had testosterone beginning to surge through his veins, or if he was just sick of it.

"Can't you see I've been at work? I don't just wear this shirt because I like the style."

From a foot away, it was easy to smell the alcohol. Was he drunk because he got sent home, or sent home because he was drunk? It didn't matter, the result for us was the same.

"I came home early today," he spat, "to spend quality time with you. Now tell me about your precious little secret before I squeeze it out of you."

"What's the matter with you?" Jack's tone was defiant, aimed to deflect the question about the secret. "Just get out of here and leave us alone. I don't have to tell you nothin'."

The secret wasn't much of a secret at this point, and it sure wasn't worth getting hit over. I knew that, and I knew Jack knew that. But I also knew Jack would never tell him at any cost. It was the principle of it. However minute, inconsequential, and undeveloped it was, it was *our* secret. Jack had some faults just like everyone else, but being disloyal was never one of them. There was very little I had not shared with him over the years, from girl problems to test answers, and never once had he divulged anything told in confidence.

Stone's forearm muscles tensed as he clenched his fists and teeth simultaneously. "You're gonna be sorry when I'm gone one day, but right now I've had it with your smart mouth." He started toward Jack.

I gulped. "Mr. Perkins, we, uh, weren't talking about nothin' important. I was gonna prank call a girl I been messin' with. Jack was just promising he would keep it a secret. You, uh, you chased the girls in your day, huh?"

Stone stopped and glared at me briefly before his face twisted into a roguish grin. "Yeah, you could say that." He glowered at Jack before meeting my gaze again. "Just don't be calling long distance, and don't say nothing stupid that gets somebody's daddy over here. I'd hate to have to rough somebody up."

Stone turned and walked toward his stepson. He appeared to look past Jack, like he wasn't even there, but my friend's eyes never wavered, staring him down. I thought their shoulders would bump as Stone walked by, but at the last second Jack flinched and stepped aside slightly. Stone stopped and faced Jack eye to eye, unblinking. Jack could not hold it. His eyes deflected toward the floor after a few seconds, and his shoulders slumped slightly. Stone turned and walked down the hall into the back of the house.

"Let's get out of here," Jack said, and Jet and I followed him outside. Michelle's car was gone.

We settled under a gigantic white oak tree in the vacant lot next to Jack's house, picking up the huge acorns that were beginning to fall and skipping them off the asphalt on the road. Jet bent and grabbed a particularly large one, displaying it like a piece of found treasure briefly before chunking it as far as he could. "Why does your mom put up with him?"

"Her excuse is always about Stone helping out after Dad got killed in Vietnam. Kept her from losing the house, blah, blah, blah. Now all I see is Stone telling her what to do and shutting her up if she questions him. Maybe he was decent at first, when I was little. Now he's just drunk half the time, mad *all* the time. Always coming and going, crazy hours, whispering in the phone, his panties all in a wad. I heard them yelling the other day about where his paycheck was."

"Maybe that's a good thing," I said. "If he quits bringing home a check, your mom might kick him out."

"What was that he said about missing him when he's gone one day?" Jet asked. "What's he implying?"

Jack snorted. "If you're asking what he meant, I dunno. He don't have any family anywhere. Parents died up in Pennsylvania. No brothers or sisters. I wish he *would* go."

As if on cue, Stone stomped out of the house, got in his truck, and drove away.

Jack spat in that direction. "Don't come back."

"Where'd he get his name anyway?" I asked. "Did he stay stoned in high school or something?"

Jack wasn't in a joking mood. "I don't know. He says he got it because he has fists of stone. My mother says it's from the Bible. Something about his real name, Peter."

"Ahh, the apostle Peter," Jet said. "You know, Saint Peter? His real name was Simon, but Jesus changed his name to Cephas, which means rock or stone in Aramaic. The New Testament was written in Greek, and the Greek form of Cephas is Petra, or Peter."

Jack grimaced. "If you say so. But I can tell you *he* ain't no saint." He nodded toward the road, where Stone's truck had reappeared and was pulling to the shoulder. "Why can't he leave us alone?"

Stone approached us with shoulders sagging slightly and four fingers buried in each front pocket of his jeans. He studied the ground and kicked at the leaves, his demeanor entirely different than before. He spoke slowly, slurring his words at times. "I been thinking. I just want you boys to know I meant no harm earlier. I can't tell you what all I'm having to deal with, but I'm under a lot of stress. It ain't no excuse, I know. I don't want you boys going home and telling your folks I'm some monster." He paused and looked at Jack. "I just want my family to be respectful. Sometimes they don't appreciate what all I do for 'em. I work hard and come home tired sometimes. That's all. Let me work out some things, and maybe we can all go fishing soon."

"Sir." Jet's voice was sincere as he gave a toothy grin. "You don't have to apologize to us. Sometimes life just makes you irascible and prone to imbibing. As for the local ichthyofauna, you know this convivial group would love to extricate some if there is more of a proclivity toward magnanimity."

I held my breath. I wasn't sure what Jet had said, but I had a pretty good idea as to the gist of it and wondered if he'd get slugged.

Jack's mouth dropped open, his eyes widened, and he coughed back a laugh.

Stone blinked vacantly then nodded. "Yeah, I agree ... okay." He reached out and tousled Jet's sandy brown hair. "You are a strange one, Townsend." He turned and walked back to his truck, got in, and drove off again.

"What the heck did you say to him?" Jack asked.

Jet smiled mischievously. "I told him he was a grouchy drunk, but we're fun-loving guys who'd love to go fishing if he'll be nice."

Jet, Jack, and I bounced around atop an upturned five-gallon bucket, an old tire, and a broken sheet of plywood propped on empty paint cans in the back of Jet's father's Chevy Silverado as we headed to Papa Mac's across town, just barely outside the city limits. Mr. Townsend had agreed to help us at the Hideaway—as Jack insisted we call it—but only on the condition that he spoke with Papa Mac first, and in person.

Jet's dog, Mutt, had insisted on coming too, and we laughed and dodged his slobber as he continuously ran back and forth, side to side, wagging his tongue in the wind. Mutt was what my grandfather called a "Heinz 57," mostly brown with no distinctive features of any particular breed, though Jet liked to say he had some shepherd in him, whatever that meant.

Papa Mac's farmhouse sat at the end of a short gravel driveway and desperately needed a coat or two of white paint. Otherwise it looked to be in decent condition. An aged barn, weathered and gray like the farmer who had built it two generations before, stood at an odd angle facing the back corner of the house, violated by a looming oak that had stabbed a limb through its metal roof. Various farming implements were scattered around the yard, and an ancient, battered, Ford truck, probably some shade of blue long ago, sat on blocks under a huge pecan tree to the side of house.

I had been there with my dad a few times over the years, and not much had changed; I didn't think the Ford was getting fixed any time soon. Papa Mac's two-tone truck was parked in front of the house, but I could see a black car I didn't recognize around back, opposite the barn. Only the back half was visible, but I knew my cars well enough to recognize a newer model Camaro. Its bright chrome wheels glimmered in the sun and were even more out of place than the car itself.

"Y'all stay in the truck and watch the dog." Mr. Townsend slid out and walked toward the house. He glanced back over his shoulder. "I'll call you over if I need you."

A group of birds darted and dove violently, their movements haphazard and random, dancing in continually mutating circles over the house.

Jet followed my gaze. "You know, everyone calls those chimney sweeps, but they're actually chimney swifts. They can't perch on a limb like other birds. Hang on to the inside of the chimney and fly, that's it. Even drink and bathe while they're flying."

I was about to ask for an explanation as to how something could bathe while flying through the air, but then Papa Mac emerged from the barn. He wiped his hands on a blue towel hanging from the front pocket of his overalls, shook Mr. Townsend's hand, and then lifted his cap to shield his eyes from the sun as he peered in our direction. He nodded, the equivalent of a smile for him.

Papa Mac seemed oddly out of place to me, here at his house instead of on his farm where we usually encountered him, cruising the fields in his 1969 two-tone green, long-wheel base, Ford F100 truck, with windows down, elbow on the windowsill, hand gripping the top of the door. Dust billows roiling behind him as he sees us and stops, opens the door with the outside handle, slides out, and shuffles over to where we stand in the shade. Inevitably wearing the same overalls, a tattered shirt with the sleeves rolled up, work boots, and a soiled cap with the logo obscured by layers of a working man's grime. Spitting tobacco juice in the dirt as he asks in a deep, unhurried drawl what us boys are up to on this fine day.

Jet scratched behind Mutt's ear, getting poked with a paw each time he stopped. "What you think he'll say?"

I shrugged and shook my head, feeling like our odds would have been better if I was let in on the discussion. It was my father, after all, who had been assigned responsibility to look after the place. And I knew Papa Mac better than Mr. Townsend did.

"Well it ain't like we're asking to build a high rise condo," Jack said.

"And, it looks like we have our answer," Jet said as his father shook hands again. Mr. Thompson headed toward us, smiling and giving a thumbs-up.

"You boys have fun and stay out of trouble," Papa Mac bellowed with a gesture that was half wave and half point of his index finger. Then he turned and walked back toward the barn.

Jet's father was about halfway back to the truck when I saw it. A flash of sunlight reflecting off of glass, then a glimpse of someone, face and torso obscured by the corner of the house, opening the back door to the Camaro. A blur of darkness poured from the car, and my heart skipped a beat when I realized what it was. An enormous black dog I immediately recognized as a Rottweiler barreled straight toward us, eyes fixed on Mr. Townsend, silent as an assassin.

FOUR

"RUN, Mr. Townsend!" I shouted. He smiled and shook his head. I frantically shouted again, pointing at the beast bearing down him. "No, I'm serious. Run!"

Jet's father was a tough, blue collar guy from the country, with thick forearms and callused hands the size of oven mitts, and I doubted he had run from many fights in his life. But on that particular day, at the moment he saw what was coming, I don't think he considered doing anything else.

Jet held Mutt by the collar as he thrashed about in the back of the truck, growling and barking and lunging. We all screamed at the top of our lungs, urging Mr. Townsend to run faster, but the massive Rottweiler was closing the gap far too quickly. With only fifteen feet to go but the dog right on his heels, the man's look of terror abruptly turned to one of resolution. He pulled up and stopped to face the beast.

Just as the Rottweiler leapt, a streak of brown intercepted it in midair, and two canine bodies crashed to the ground in a whirling tangle of fur and teeth and snarls. Mutt valiantly tried to slash while eluding the jaws of the larger brute, but the gravity of his peril was obvious. The Rottweiler outweighed him by at least 100 pounds, and Mutt was a family pet with some shepherd blood, not a guard dog.

Mr. Townsend yelled and tried to kick the black monster to no avail, as Mutt battled for his life. I grabbed a half-filled paint can and jumped out of the truck just as the Rottweiler crunched down on Mutt's front leg, lowered his shoulder, and forced the smaller dog to the ground. A sickening shriek pierced the air.

In one motion, I swung the paint can over my head and crashed it down on the black dog while also attempting to kick it. The effect of both efforts together was that neither was forceful, and I slipped and fell over the top of the dogs onto the dusty ground beyond them. It was enough to distract the Rottweiler from Mutt beneath him, but he turned his attention to me. I braced myself for his attack.

A loud explosion erupted to my left, and the Rottweiler wailed in pain, biting at his own hindquarters as he ran off toward the house.

Papa Mac stood ten feet away, shouldering a double-barreled shotgun. "Rock salt," he drawled matter-of-factly. "Kills a rat at five yards but won't hurt nothin' else. Not permanent, anyway."

"You shoulda used buckshot." Jet kneeled to gather a whimpering Mutt into his arms.

Papa Mac walked over, patted Jet on the head, bent down, and examined Mutt closely. "Got a broke leg, but he'll live." He looked at Mr. Townsend as he stood up. "Y'all shouldna brung your dog. Good way to stir up trouble at a strange house."

I was still sitting on my butt in the dirt, too stunned to move. Mr. Townsend reached down and grabbed my hand, pulling me up. His eyes scanned me quickly from head to toe, satisfying himself that I wasn't hurt. "I'm sorry we let him come, Mr. MacIntosh, and I do apologize. Didn't recall you had a dog like that or I wouldn't have."

"He ain't my dog. Belongs to my son, Vance. He's down from Memphis for a while visiting. Thought he had him put up."

"C'mon boys, let's get Mutt to the vet." Mr. Townsend helped situate Mutt on Jet's lap in the front seat of the truck, motioning for Jack and me to get in the back again.

Jack and I both started to speak, but Mr. Townsend shut us up with a hard glare. I could hardly contain myself, knowing what I'd seen at the back of the house, but I could tell he meant business. So I said nothing.

As the truck started slowly rolling to drive away, Mr. Townsend rolled down his window. "That dog was attacking me, not my dog."

Papa Mac nodded his head solemnly, but didn't say a word at first. As we pulled away, he called out, "Case, you and your friends go on ahead with your plan and build that hut or whatever it was you were talking about. Just be careful."

My mind raced as we drove away. Had anyone else seen what I had? Who let the dog out of the car? I assumed it was his son Vance. But why?

———

Two weeks later, the Hideaway was complete: an elevated ten-by-ten floor, three walls with double swinging doors spanning the front, and a metal roof stippled with dents and various shades of rust. The broad doors would be perfect when closed for fending off bitter winter winds or unbearable southern summer sun, ideal when open to let in the warmth of a campfire or a cool fall breeze. The Hideaway was primitive at best—it wasn't even critter-proof—but it would keep the rain and wind off us. And most importantly, it was all ours.

We told no one of what we were doing other than Mr. Townsend. Allowing even him to enter our sacred circle was an impropriety necessitated only by our self-imposed time constraints. Fall was prime time for camping and hunting, and we didn't want it to pass by without completing our plan.

Jack even insisted that Mr. Townsend take an oath of secrecy and goaded Jet into drafting a document for him to sign. Jet used his mother's typewriter and created two copies on her best stationary, and we presented it to Mr. Townsend one day as we worked.

> I, John Adams Townsend, before my family, friends, and Maker, do hereby solemnly swear and promise, under penalty of perpetual distrust, reproach, and opprobrium from said witnesses upon breech of this agreement, to keep confidential any and all facts and other information pertaining to the location, nature, and utilization of the area known as the Hideaway on the property of Paul MacIntosh, in Amberton, Mississippi, except as required by law or threat of bodily harm.

Jack read over it before passing it to Mr. Townsend. "Why didn't you just do it in Swahili?"

Jet's father studied it a moment. "Impressive, Jet. Sounds mighty lawyerly—you thinking about that instead of medicine?"

"No, it's still cardiovascular surgery for me," Jet responded. "I do like the way attorneys entangle you with the English language, but what they do is borrring. Are you gonna sign it?"

"C'mon, Mr. Townsend," Jack chimed in. "This is very important."

"Well, first I have a question. Why is it so important that I keep this a secret? It's not like someone can't just walk up in here."

"Because it's *our* spot. Case is the one who really has permission to be here, and if folks start busting up in here all the time, they'll ruin it for everyone. Plus, we have it hidden pretty good. Kinda gotta know it's here to find it."

"True…" He pursed his lips and tapped them with two fingers, indecisive. "I'm sorry, but I can't sign this."

"Why not?" I was unsure if he was serious or not.

"Because I have no idea what in the world op ... opprodi ... no, no ...." He paused to read again, carefully syllabifying the word. "No idea what op-prob-ri-um means."

"Dad." Jet swatted at him with a clipboard he was holding.

"Don't get mad at *him*." Jack countered. "No one else in the world knows what that word means except you and some guy named Webster."

"Okay, okay," Jet said. "It means dishonor, disgrace. You know, like the dude on that old Western—*Branded*—where they broke his saber, ripped off his epaulets, and kicked him out of the fort when they accused him of being a coward."

"Good grief, Jet." I shook my head. "Epaulets? Really? Only you would need an explanation to explain your explanation."

Mr. Townsend laughed and said he understood well enough, that we could trust him to take our secret to his grave. Unless of course, he said with a wink, Jet's mom wanted to sneak out here for a second honeymoon sometime.

We all pretended to gag. Mr. Townsend shook with a deep belly laugh, took the clipboard from Jet, and signed both copies of the agreement.

Jack produced an empty Folger's coffee can he had brought for the occasion, folded and rolled up one of the documents, and sealed the top. He lifted a loose floorboard in the back corner and hid it beneath, giving the other copy to Mr. Townsend.

"Mr. Townsend, can I ask you a question?" I said. He nodded. "The other day at Papa Mac's, with the dog. Why didn't you say more than you did? You know that dog was attacking you, not Mutt. And I know Jet has told you, I saw someone let that dog out of the car out back of the house. I wanted to tell Papa Mac, but you wouldn't let me say anything."

Mr. Townsend nodded. "Well, here's the deal. I don't know

why someone let that dog out on purpose, or even if they did. But you boys all need to learn something, and learn it good, right now. Family is everything. Folks start coming on another man's property and insulting him, his family—his dog, even—it's gonna be a bad outcome." He paused, like he wanted to say something else, then reconsidered. "Let me ask you this. You boys are kind of like a family yourselves. You love this here place, right? What would you be willing to do for each other to protect it, even if one of you was in the wrong?"

"Pretty much anything." I looked first at what we'd built, then toward Snake Lake and the creek bottom beyond it. *Pretty much anything.*

"I have one more surprise." When Jack said things like that I never knew whether excitement or dread was more appropriate. Both were often warranted before it was over. Nonetheless, one afternoon when Jack told us he had found a place named Hideaway Road on a map, it took all of about two minutes for us to plan our first camping trip since building the Hideaway. Yes, stealing a road sign was at best imprudent, but the idea of that sign hanging over the door was just too enticing to pass up.

Two-ten a.m. found us racing across Papa Mac's field from the Hideaway, navigating the ATVs around and through each familiar dip and turn as effortlessly as we would a stroll through our backyards. I rode with Jack so I could hold the sign on the way back, and Jet led the way since he was the one who had memorized the map.

We pulled onto MacIntosh Road, named generations ago when it was just a dirt trail bisecting what was once the MacIntosh Plantation, turned left on Lennox Drive for half a mile, then cut through the Birch Bend Golf and Country Club, pressing to the center of the course where no houses lined the fairways. Crossing the number eight fairway, we slipped through a gap in the fence and skirted around Amberton High School.

"Here's where it gets tricky," Jet hissed over the sound of the puttering engines. "Two miles down Vista Road, no side streets to escape on. I just don't know…"

"Don't be a wuss." Jack turned around looked at me.

"Ya'll both know I ain't no quitter."

Jet shrugged and shook his head but said nothing, zipped across the highway, and disappeared over the shoulder on the other side. Jack and I followed.

When Jet slowed suddenly in front of us, I realized a car was coming around the corner ahead. We tried to appear nonchalant as best we could while hiding our faces, as if teenagers on three-wheelers in the middle of the night were as normal on the road as a hungry 'possum. The car slowed but did not stop, and I breathed a sigh of relief as its taillights disappeared behind us.

"Okay, where is this Hideaway Road?" I asked Jet as he rolled to a stop in front of an abandoned warehouse a few minutes later.

He pointed to a narrow dirt path exiting Vista Road and disappearing into the trees behind the warehouse. "According to the map, this is it. It runs right down the side of the warehouse, then turns back west along the river for a half mile or so before it dead ends."

Two trips down Hideaway Road from one end to the other revealed nothing but unfettered roadside foliage supporting bridges of face-grabbing spider webs—certainly no road sign. I was afraid Jack would be more disappointed than he usually was when a plan failed, but he seemed to take it in stride.

"At least we tried," he said.

"Doubt there ever was a sign on that cattle trail." I stepped off the road to urinate into the waist-high weeds. As if on cue, I heard the unmistakable buzz of a jet of water hitting flat metal. I realized then my ankle was bumping against a metal pole, so I called Jet over excitedly. "Shine that flashlight down there." And there it was: the Hideaway Road sign, bent to the ground by some anonymous automobile in years gone by, now covered with grass and vines and mildew, but otherwise intact.

"Did you have to pee on it?" Jet asked minutes later, scowling as he knelt to tie the rope.

I chuckled. "That's my personal metal detector."

Jet rolled his eyes and grimaced as he groped in the foliage. "Okay, got it. Put it in low and ease out, Jack. See if we can pull it outta there."

The three-wheeler engine barely even roared before I saw blue lights whip around the corner off of Vista Road and speed straight toward us.

FIVE

SLOUCHING in the back seat of Sheriff Sykes Turner's Crown Victoria, I mulled how I could possibly feel such a powerful urge to urinate after doing so just ten minutes before. I had no idea what was happening outside to Jack and Jet, but the sheriff had barked out orders for me to get in the back, and I had not asked questions.

There had been no time to attempt escape and no need to explain. The scene of teenagers yanking on a street sign with ATVs near an abandoned warehouse in the middle of the night spoke for itself. We had all frozen and given our names on cue as the sheriff shined his flashlight in our faces, towering over us. His expression and the half step he took closer to me even before I said my name had told me he recognized me.

Shortly, my two friends pulled up on their three-wheelers and stopped in front of the patrol car, the dust from their rear tires rolling up over their backs like a dirty fog.

Sheriff Turner opened the driver's door and sat down. He didn't say a word for a few seconds, then growled, "Get your butt up here, Reynolds."

I scrambled out of the car and slid into the front seat beside the huge black man, noting his faded blue jeans, brown button-up shirt, and beige Stetson. I stared straight ahead and watched the dust settle around Jack and Jet, who remained motionless in the glare of headlights.

"Your daddy know where you are?" His deep voice reminded

me of James Earl Jones. I half-expected to hear some slow, mechanical breathing between phrases, but the pistol strapped to his side rather than a light saber reminded me that this was very real.

"No, sir." I tried to keep my voice from cracking. Dad had taught me to appear strong in the face of adversity, but I was certain this wasn't what he had in mind.

"Of course he don't. Your daddy would be ashamed of you right now. What you boys doin' out here stealing road signs?"

The thought of facing my father made me queasy. "It wasn't road *signs*, sir. It was just this one particular road sign."

He snorted. "Don't get smart with me."

Jack and Jet squinted nervously back over their shoulders, probably wondering what was happening in the car behind them. I wished I could trade places.

"I'm gonna tell you a story. You listen close, and don't interrupt." He abruptly got out of the car and spoke to Jack and Jet, gesturing and pointing down the road ahead of them. They began moving slowly in the direction from which we had come earlier. Turner got back in the car and spoke some police jargon into his radio, something about juveniles, a disturbance, and him patrolling awhile longer. "Let's see if those two jugheads can follow instructions." He adjusted his massive frame in the seat as he put the car in gear. "I was just a PE teacher," he began, "minding my own business, working toward retirement." He paused and looked at me hard to make sure I was paying attention.

What little I knew about Sykes Turner had come from conversations with my father, who told me Turner had been a coach at Kingston, which was the black school in town prior to the civil rights movement. When consolidation of the schools occurred, he moved to Amberton High where he had stopped coaching. I remembered Dad commenting when Turner took over as sheriff that he'd be fine if he was only half as tough on criminals as he had been on Amberton High's troublemakers. The memory of those words did not comfort me.

"Case, are you listening, boy?"

I gulped and nodded.

"A fellow by the name of Alton Hall was the sheriff. He was allowing a few dealers in the county to run free and extorting money from them—you know what that means? Getting them to pay him not to arrest them. Then he was arresting some other dealers and selling their dope back to the guys he was extorting from. Just a mess. But the feds finally busted him."

"Sheriff, I'm not sure—"

"I done told you to be quiet while I talk." Turner's voice rumbled like a charging locomotive, daring something to stand in its way. "Now, when Sheriff Hall resigned, it was up to the McKinley County Board of Supervisors to appoint his replacement until the next election rolled around, which was almost a year away. The black folk in the county were sick and tired of crooked white folk being in charge, and they asked me to throw my name in the hat. I ain't sure why that was. Maybe 'cause I had tore up enough of they tails with a paddle over the years for them to know I wouldn't take no mess off nobody. At first I said no way, I didn't want no part of being sheriff. But the more I looked at it, the madder I got.

"There was two other guys that wanted the sheriff's job—your daddy and a dude named Redmond Patridge, a deputy in the department. Your daddy was the person everyone thought would get it. He'd been chief investigator for several years and was deputy sheriff before that. Had the most experience. I didn't know neither of 'em, but for all I knew they both could be part of the problem, maybe in on it with Sheriff Hall."

"My father never—"

He silenced me this time with an authoritative point of his finger as we slowly cruised through the high school parking lot, following fifty feet behind Jack and Jet.

"Patridge saw Rex as his chief competition. I didn't know this until later, but he set out immediately to smear his name. It wasn't no elaborate plan, just everywhere you turned all of a sudden it was rumors that your daddy was in with Sheriff Hall or cheatin' on your momma or falsifying evidence, stuff like that. Nothing ever came of it as far as an investigation, 'cause there wasn't no evidence for it, but I believe Patridge hoped it would muddy the waters enough so's the supervisors would give him the job. Well, guess what?"

He paused like he wanted me to comment, but I thought better of it and said nothing.

Sheriff Turner muttered something under his breath about me not knowing when to talk and when to shut up, then continued. "The supervisors got sick of it just like the black folk in the county had. Something Patridge never considered happened—they hired lil' ol' me."

I fought back a grin for fear of what he might do to me, but the idea of Sheriff Turner being lil' ol' anything was comical. He was at least six feet four.

He pointed a massive index finger at the center of his chest and continued. "Me, the black PE teacher. Most folks thought I got the job *because* I was black rather than *despite* being black. Truth is, I didn't ask no questions, and I didn't care. I got the job and intended to do right by the folk that asked me to try it."

I sat speechless. I'd never heard the story from my father and had to admit it was compelling. But I couldn't understand what a few fourteen-year-olds stealing one measly street sign had to do with past controversies in the sheriff's department—or McKinley County race relations, for that matter.

Sheriff Turner was apparently just getting started. "I had no intentions of being a lame duck sheriff. I set out to clean things up. It didn't take long to figure out who was who and what was what. Patridge was nothin' but trouble. I suspected he was in on the drug stuff with Hall but couldn't prove it. What I could do was fire him, and I did. I worked hard to clean up the drug problems plaguing the county, and did a lotta good. Guess who helped me?"

He glanced at me but continued before I could decide whether to open my mouth or not. "You got it—yo' daddy. Turns out, he was one of the ones helped the feds bust Sheriff Hall in the first place. But he never batted an eye, never acted for one second like he resented me for getting the job instead of him. All those in the department who thought I'd be a nice little stooge and sit quietly on the office couch until the election while they ran their rackets? They tried to run me off, but guess who stood up to them? You got it—yo' daddy." He reached across the seat and rapped me firmly on the shoulder with the back of his hand. Not enough to hurt but enough to make sure I was getting the message. "You sensing a theme here, son?"

I nodded.

"A year later, I ran for sheriff, and I won. I expected Rex to run against me, but he didn't. He told me I had earned the right to be sheriff, and even though he wanted the job, it wasn't fair for me not to have the chance to finish the job I'd started. He stood up and helped me get elected, even though he had helped clean up the department at least as much as I did, truth be told."

We were now on MacIntosh Road, at the entrance to Papa Mac's farm, where we had exited earlier. There was a small turn-around there, and the two three-wheelers in front of the car had been sitting idle for several minutes. Jack and Jet were slowly easing away, toward the tree line between the road and the field.

Turner stopped talking and jumped out of the car. "I told you to stop when we got here! Move one more inch, and I'll blow the tires outta both three-wheelers with this .45, hope I don't hit you in the process, and if you live, haul you in and charge you with evading an officer of the law."

Both three-wheelers stopped, and I believe if a lightning bolt had stuck between them at that very moment, neither petrified rider would have flinched.

Turner collapsed back into the car and huffed. "I thought the Townsend boy was a superfreak brain or something, but he can't even follow directions. Now where was I? Oh, yeah. You can imagine my surprise earlier when I hear a call over the scanner in the middle o' the night that some juvenile delinquents are riding around, obviously up to no good. I take the call because I'm sitting up and can't sleep, and who do I find? Case Reynolds, only son of Rex Reynolds, my investigator. Out stealing street signs of all things."

"Sheriff, I—"

He banged the steering wheel with an open palm. "Dang it, boy. I didn't ask you to speak. So let me set the stage for you. I have twenty-five years in and plan to retire after this here year. Guess who I'll endorse for sheriff next election? You know the answer. Now I don't think his son stealing street signs is the kinda scandal that will cost him an election, but it won't win no votes neither. And I don't know what other nonsense you're involved in that *could* cost him. Right now, I don't wanna know. What I want you to do is keep yo' head down and yo' nose clean. So I ain't gonna tell Rex about this. Do not make me regret it."

Lightning flashed behind him, emphasizing his directive as if on cue. "Now get outta here, boy, it's about to hit." Thunder crashed upon us as he extended his hand to me with a hint of a smile. "You hear me?"

I gripped his hand firmly, apologized for his trouble, and affirmed that I had indeed heard him, loud and clear.

He unlocked the door so I could get out.

"Sheriff?" I paused with one foot on the ground, and one still in the car.

"Yeah?"

"Did Sheriff Hall go to jail?"

"No, he didn't live long enough. Suspicious hunting accident."

As soon as he said it, I remembered the news reports of the sheriff getting killed. I wasn't sure what he meant by suspicious, but I already had information overload and didn't think any other details were relevant to my life at that point. Maybe I would ask Dad sometime.

I stepped out of the car and was about to close the door when Turner stopped me. "Case."

"Yes, sir?"

It thundered again. "Redmond Patridge is bad news. I hope you never run into him, but I'm tellin' you, he's trouble. Supposedly he's sniffing around here again, working for some shady characters out of New Orleans."

I understood the implication. "Don't worry, Sheriff. We just wanted a sign for our camping spot. Ain't nothing else going on."

He nodded. "Get it from someplace legal, then."

I closed the door and walked to where my friends waited with the three-wheelers. Jet's had run out of gas, but he had not moved an inch.

"Let's get out of here." I gestured at Jet to get on Jack's three-wheeler with me.

"Next time I get a bright idea, tell me to shut up," Jack mumbled. Neither of us answered as we sped off, anxious to beat the storm but even more intent on getting as far away as possible from Sheriff Sykes Turner.

SIX

JET answered on the second ring. "Let's go wet a hook tomorrow," I said. "After dark, later when it's cooler. The Snake."

Jack, Jet, and I shared a few fishing holes, but none drew us in like Snake Lake, and not just because of the fish. Months before, we had scraped together just enough money for a battered twelve-foot aluminum rig, telling no one—not even our parents. With blood, sweat, tears, and a lot of curses we had carried and dragged it to the lake, where we hid it, chained it to a tree, and swore each other to secrecy. Who knew if anyone would have cared, but it was our little secret, and the conspiracy of it held a certain allure for sneaky fourteen-year-olds.

"I can't, dude," Jet said. "Going to Math Bowl, and I don't think we'll be back in time."

"On a Friday night?" I scowled into the phone. "You truly are a nerd, you know that?"

"Yeah, but nerds rule the world." Jet took that particular insult as a compliment, as always.

I dialed Jack's number, consoled by the notion that Jet's stupid plans just meant more fish for us. But Jack didn't answer.

Son of a gun. I slammed the phone down in frustration, flinching at the hollow ring of the handset hitting the housing.

"What's wrong?"

I flinched again at Mom's voice behind me and turned to see her eyeing the phone with a disapproving raise of one eyebrow. "Can't find anyone to fish with tomorrow, and weatherman says it's

39

supposed to be a 'Best' day." I had never seen much correlation between our local fishing forecast and actual results, but Mom didn't have to know that.

Her eyebrows flattened as she pondered. Then she grinned with a mischievous wink. "What about Abi?"

"You ready?"

Abi smiled, her teeth almost reflective in the headlight of the three-wheeler. "Hope you brought me a pole."

I tapped an assortment of rods and reels at my side on the three-wheeler. "Got you covered."

Abi Rossini was a couple of inches shorter than me, slender but not skinny, with a strong chin showing just a hint of a dimple. She had pulled her long, dark hair back into a ponytail like she usually did for warm weather or playing softball. It often showed highlights of deep brown when seen in the sunlight, but tonight it was jet black.

Her eyes were always her most striking feature, though, an electric blue that in the summertime seemed to burst from her bronzed skin. I was so enamored with her eye color that I had once dug under my bed to find my box of old Crayola crayons, to figure out the exact color. Blizzard Blue was the closest match I could find, but I thought it was oxymoronic—there was nothing cold about Abi Rossini's eyes.

For years she had been just another annoying girl in the neighborhood. Then we had gradually become fast friends, platonic but sometimes inseparable, especially at school. She had always been the second smartest person I knew, but in recent months something had changed. Abi had somehow morphed from a close confidant with whom I shared homework and occasional secrets into a creature that occupied my psyche like a hand inside a puppet. I had no idea if my mother knew that or not, but once she had suggested I call Abi, I couldn't get the idea out of my mind. And now here we were.

"Just you and me?" She looked around, her smile faltering.

I had not mentioned that part of the plan and hoped I hadn't blown it. "Thought Jack was coming, but guess not." Not a total lie.

She shrugged and swung onto the seat behind me. "His loss." She patted me on the shoulder as we sped toward Papa Mac's and Snake Lake. "Let's go catch some fish."

I sighed. What did her agreeing to go with me mean? Abi had been dating Lane Buckley, a sophomore two years older than us, off and on for several weeks. In fact, when Lane had begun calling her, I had somehow become a reluctant accomplice in his pursuit, encouraging her to give him a chance in the first place, be patient with him when he didn't call, forgive him when he was inconsiderate. Now I hated myself for it. I tried to tell myself I just wanted to see her happy, even if it wasn't with me.

But that couldn't be entirely true. Besides being too cowardly to tell her how I felt about her, my motives were selfish on some primal level: if and when I revealed my true feelings for her, perhaps my façade of selflessness would endear me to her.

I told myself not to expect too much from the evening, other than Lane wanting to kick my teeth in if he found out. Abi saw me as a friend, nothing more. That was enough, though. Spending time with her was enough. The night before, I had been obsessed with thoughts of catching big bass. Now those thoughts seemed a million miles away.

"You didn't say anything about a boat." Abi grabbed my arm

and hesitated as she caught sight of our prized possession. In the daylight, the upturned johnboat was hard to see lying in the tall grass, but in the beam of a light, innumerable scratches in the olive drab paint of the aluminum vessel shone like linear reflectors.

I gave her hand a gentle tug and started down the slope to the water's edge. "Since when is Amberton Country Club's finest lifeguard afraid of the water?"

"It's not the water. It's what's in it. I'm guessing y'all didn't name it Snake Lake for its pretty goldfish."

I swept the shoreline with my light to show the unbroken wall of cattails and briars. "If you want, I guess we can fish from the bank and hope we don't step on a gator." Abi didn't have to know there wasn't a gator within twenty miles of Papa Mac's.

She clapped her hands together softly and quickened her pace down toward me. "What a nice boat, Case. Let's try it out."

I unlocked the chain securing the boat to a willow tree and stuffed the key in my pocket. "It's plenty safe. A nice twelve-footer. Sometimes we fish three in it."

"You, Jack, and Jet?"

"Yep. But no one knows it's here but the three of us. Well... four now." I watched her for a reaction. After all, by being there, she was in a way entering—maybe even sharing— a sanctum of sorts. But she just stared at the boat, underwhelmed by the significance of the moment and more interested in what needed to be done next. I handed her my flashlight. "Help me watch for snakes while I turn this thing over." I grabbed the edge with both hands and jumped back as I flipped it quickly. For once, nothing slithered away.

"Why the secrecy?" Abi said. "Just for a boat?" So, she *was* paying attention.

"I guess it's not that big a deal, but we swore not to tell anyone.

So, uh, if you don't mind, don't tell Jack and Jet." I pushed against the bow of the boat and slid it stern-first into the water. "But it's not just the boat. It's this place. It's *our* place. I'll show you something else later, and you'll understand."

"Oo-ooh." She dragged the word out playfully into two syllables. "So mysterious."

"I'm serious, Abi. Don't tell anyone."

"You ashamed of me?" Her tone was suddenly terse.

"You know that's not it. Jack and Jet get weird about this thing, though. We made a pact."

She shook her head and smiled. "That is weird, but whatever. It'll be our secret." She moved to step in.

"Watch your step." I laughed and steadied her by her elbow as she tripped over a cypress root partially exposed by the summer sun's toll on the water level. She climbed in gingerly and carefully took the rods and reels from me as I slid the craft into the dark water.

Abi recoiled at a moccasin just off the bow, gliding through the water and unfazed by our presence. "Yep, just as I suspected. But at least it's not an alligator." Then she gestured at the rising yellow moon, cloned in the water's mirror. "It is pretty out here, though. Peaceful."

"Nothing else like it." I picked up a rod. "I'll set you up with a black plastic worm. And I'll try a topwater. See what's working."

"And remind me again why we are fishing at night?"

"Big fish are like predators. They hunt at night."

She swung her legs around and faced me, seemingly done with fishing talk for the moment. "What about you?"

"Me? What?"

"Are you hunting your prey tonight?" The curls of mischief in the corners of her eyes should have prepared me, but the thrust of her question still almost sent me overboard.

"Hunting? I, uh, well…"

Abi rescued me with a laugh. "I'm just playing. But I do want to know if you are coming to my birthday party next Friday."

I took a breath and gathered myself. Of course I would be there. *Play it cool.* I faked a conflicted look. "Friday? Yeah, maybe. I'll probably come by."

"What do you mean, 'I'll probably come by?' I told you about it over a week ago. You better be there, Case Reynolds."

In case you need my advice when you and Lane have a fight, is what I wanted to say. "So, you want me to be your date?" is what came out instead. *What was that?* Abi and I had never even joked about the possibility of us ever dating.

Her expression gave away nothing. "No, Lane will be there."

"Oh, uhh, I know. Now *I'm* just playing." My face burned, and perspiration wet my upper lip and forehead. *Stupid.*

She grabbed the pole I had set up and casted, more adept at it than I'd anticipated. After a few silent tosses, she tucked her chin and eyed me over her shoulder. "So you wouldn't be my date if I needed one?"

My heart tumbled once. "Yes, I wouldn't. I mean no, I would if you didn't. Wait, I mean, what? What's the question?" I wanted to crawl in the hole under my seat and stay a few days, until after the party. "Never mind. Sorry, I was just messing around when I said that."

She giggled. "So, you're messing around? I didn't realize we were talking about *that.*" She giggled again, clearly amused by both my fluster and her double entendre.

I was sweating profusely, and not from the humid night air. Did she somehow know how I felt about her? Was she leading me on for her personal entertainment, or was this just innocent chatting between good friends?

She grinned. "You never answered my question."

"Okay, what's the question again?" I knew what the question was, but I needed to stall.

"Would you be my date if I didn't have one?"

Now I was ready with an answer that made sense. "Okay, yeah, sure, I'd do that for you. What are friends for?"

She spun back around, rocking the boat slightly. Her grin had been replaced by a pensive frown. "One more question."

"Wow, you are full of questions. I don't recall you reading me my rights. Can what I say be used against me?"

"Ha ha ha. You know you can always trust me." She paused. "Here's my question: Would you be my date because you felt sorry for me, or because you *wanted* to be my date?"

Now every instinct told me to avoid, evade, deflect. *I object. Do not answer that question.* But then I remembered something Jet had talked about once on one of his ramblings, some Roman poet who wrote in Latin about living for the moment. *Carpe diem* was the term. Seize the day.

"I would go because I wanted to, Abi. I would most definitely *want* to."

"That's what I thought. Now let's fish."

"So, what do you think? Jack named it the Hideaway."

Abi stood with her hands on her hips, inspecting the building before us. I pictured the Hideaway Road sign nailed above the door until a vision of Sheriff Turner destroying it all with a sledge-hammer brought me back.

"Sounds like Jack," she said. "So *this* is what y'all have been doing the past couple of weeks."

"Cool, huh?" I said.

"If you say so," Abi laughed. "Y'all sure do love it out here don't you?"

I nodded. "I guess we're like family when we're here. Brothers from other mothers." *Ugh. Dumb.*

Thankfully, my corny rhyme didn't seem to bother Abi. She narrowed her eyes, trying to understand. "That's really awesome. Be careful out here, though."

I could tell that wasn't a random thought. "What do you mean?"

"I mean, my friend Rachel and I saw a guy the other day. We were walking around the neighborhood."

"Saw a guy?"

Abi frowned, then waved her hand dismissively. "It was nothing. That poor homeless man, you know the one we always see walking around town, usually half-dressed? He was sitting off in the trees, watching us when we walked by."

"The Vagabond?" I turned to face Abi, confused by why she thought that guy had anything to do with Papa Mac's or our hideaway. Or why we should be wary of him. "He's been wandering around here since we were little kids. My dad says he's harmless."

None of us knew the real name of the Vagabond, so nicknamed by the local kids for his tendency to pop up randomly around Amberton and the obvious fact that he had no permanent home. Rumor had it he bathed in creeks, slept on park benches, and wandered the roads at all hours of the night. And then there had been the night Jack and I saw him at my kitchen door, found the bullet on the counter. But as far as we knew, he'd never actually hurt anyone.

"It was…just a little creepy is all." Abi's lips moved again, almost imperceptibly, but nothing came out. I sensed there might be more to the story, but I knew Abi well enough to know that whatever it was, she wouldn't tell until she got good and ready. Suddenly perky again, she hopped on the three-wheeler and patted the stringer of fish on the back. "Let's get out of here. Daddy thinks I've been out rolling yards with the girls, but it's really late, and you've got fish to clean."

"Well, I'd say fishing with a friend is more wholesome than tossing toilet paper in people's trees."

Abi poked me in the ribs playfully from behind. "I'll let you tell Daddy that when you drop me off."

In my haste to show the Hideaway to Abi before we had to leave, I forgot to chain the boat back to the tree, so I had to ride back out the next afternoon. And I'm not sure why I even walked up the hill to the Hideaway again, but I did it almost unconsciously, like a kid who gets a shiny new bike for Christmas and can't help going outside every thirty minutes just to look at it.

Our fire pit had been used.

New ashes and partially burned wood fragments sat where green grass had been the night before. Who had been here? The Vagabond? A chill rippled through me. Had he been there watching Abi and me fish in the lake below? I kicked the ashes and coals to see if I could tell whether any part was still warm, although I wasn't sure what I would do with that information. Something hard collided against the toe of my boot, and I heard a clank of metal against rock. Pleasant surprise momentarily supplanted my unease as I dusted the ashes off of a beautiful knife, partially charred but remarkably undamaged overall. A six-inch blade with a deer antler handle, unlike any I had ever seen. The handle was fashioned from the base of the antler in such a way that a long brow tine arched from the butt back toward the blade, protecting the fingers and securing the grip on the tool.

I slashed the air a few times, fighting off another chill as it occurred to me the knife looked more like a weapon than a tool—and the owner of it knew exactly where our campsite was. I hung the knife on my jeans pocket by the brow tine. *Finders keepers, Vagabond, whatever your real name is. You better stay away.*

SEVEN

WE stopped at the end of Abi's driveway to survey the situation. Her two-story, brown brick home sat on a small hill, partially guarded by an ancient magnolia tree out front. Floodlights on each end of the house illuminated the front and side yards, and the faint murmur of music from the back wafted over the roof of the house and settled around us.

The walk had been short, but Jet and I both were perspiring—as much from nervous anticipation as exertion. "How do I look? I don't have sweaty pits, do I?" He raised both arms and pivoted toward the light for me to see.

I grimaced and pushed his elbows back to his side. "Since when do you worry about your appearance? And what girl are you trying to impress?"

"Tonight could be a big night." Jet pounded his fist into his other palm for emphasis. "Every fine girl from the seventh through tenth grade will be there."

"Well, you better hope some fifth or sixth graders show up for you to have a chance."

"Very funny. At least I'm not chasing someone I can't catch." He nodded toward the street where Lane's gold Jeep Cherokee parked on the shoulder might as well have been a flashing-yellow caution light.

"I ain't chasing." I punched him in the arm and quickly changed the subject. "Have you heard from Jack?"

"Said he was feeling better." Jet turned to walk up the driveway and motioned for me to follow. "Supposed to meet us here."

"I can smell your cheap cologne from here." The voice startled both of us before we recognized it. The magnolia giant shivered, and Jack emerged from its darkness.

"What are you doing, boy?" I asked. "The party is at the pool."

"Had a good seat on that low limb. Hated to give it up." Jack had been home sick most of the week, and I could tell he still wasn't himself. His voice was normal enough, but his tone matched a hollowness around his eyes and sounded forced, just like the grin he tried to give us. I patted him on the back and gave him a playful shove.

Starship's "We Built This City" met us as we went through the gate and walked around the pool. Jet smiled and sang along loudly, poking me in my ribs as he botched the lyrics. "Macaroni plays 'La Bamba,' listen to the radio." It amazed me how someone so smart could think that made sense, but whatever. I smiled and shook my head.

The pool house was a one-story wooden structure stained a mahogany brown and sitting off the back corner of the pool. The music pulsated from a boom box perched just inside an open window. A shallow porch protected a wrought-iron picnic table with various snacks set on it and a wooden swing hanging from its ceiling, where Abi and her best friend Rachel Hines swayed leisurely.

"Hey guys, come on up." Abi beamed. She jumped up and half walked, half skipped to us. "Everyone else is inside. Get yourself something to eat. Drinks are in the fridge." She changed her volume to a whisper. "No alcohol. My parents are home." She winked and gave an impish grin. Then her expression changed, and she paused, peering over my shoulder. I turned to see Jack staring into the darkness.

"Jack, are you feeling okay?" Abi's genuine concern made her even more attractive.

"I'm fine. Don't worry about me." Jack turned and forced a smile. He grabbed a brownie off Jet's plate as he walked by and went inside.

"Bless his heart, I can tell he still doesn't feel good." Rachel walked over to Jet and hooked her arm through his. "C'mon, let's go inside ourselves. Isn't this a *great* song?"

"I Can't Fight This Feeling" by REO Speedwagon was playing now. Did Rachel know more than I thought she should?

"What was that all about?" I asked Abi. "Rachel and Jet?"

"Well that could happen, you know. Jet's a really good guy. But no, she knew I wanted to talk to you. I've been waiting on you."

Each beat of my heart suddenly felt more violent than the last.

Abi sat down on the swing and patted the spot beside her. I complied.

"Where is Lane?"

"He's inside. Too busy talking about himself to worry about us out here, I'm sure."

"Did he say anything about us fishing?"

"No, he doesn't know. But we've been having ... problems."

Now it seemed clear to me. Disappointing, as I expected. She wanted some advice. "Well, I'm sure he—"

Abi stopped me with her finger over my lips. The smell of her perfume aroused me. "I don't want to talk about Lane. I want to talk about us, about the other night. I just want you to know, I've been thinking about what you said, how you answered my question. I'm confused about some things right now, but I don't want anything to interfere with our ... our ... friendship."

I turned now to look at her.

Her piercing blue eyes darted back and forth, looking into each of my eyes individually, seemingly searching for a glimpse inside me, then settling, as if she had found what she was searching for.

She understood my feelings for her, and it was exhilarating. "What do you think I meant by my answer to your question?"

She looked away. "Well, I think I know. I hope I know."

I continued to look at her, and her gaze matched mine, unwavering. Abi's hand was beside mine on the swing, and our fingertips had accidentally found each other. She subtly, ever so gently, intertwined our fingers.

My chest verged on exploding. "What are we doing here, Abi?"

"It looks like we're doing what I've wanted to do for a while," she whispered, and turned her face toward me, leaning in.

"Well, well, well. What do we have here?" A strange, obnoxious voice.

Abi quickly pulled her hand out of mine and scooted a couple of inches away from me on the swing. Two people I didn't recognize were walking up.

I glanced at Abi to see if she knew them, and her look of dismay told me she might.

The one who had spoken approached me, and I stood to meet him. He was about two inches taller than me but more slender. His beige linen suit, pastel blue T-shirt, and shoes that looked like house slippers told me he was either new to town or visiting. His hair was combed straight back and cemented in place with hair gel. "Who you got here, Abi?"

Before Abi could answer, he turned to me and stuck out his hand. "I'm VJ. Short for Vance Jr. My friends call me VJ. You're not my friend, but you can call me VJ. As in MacIntosh." He snickered toward his pal, amused at what he somehow thought was a clever comment. "And this here is my friend Blake."

Blake was huge. Born to play offensive tackle if anyone ever was. I didn't think I knew him, but he looked local—stone-washed blue jeans, gray sharkskin boots, Ocean Pacific T-shirt.

I shook VJ's hand reluctantly but firmly. "Case Reynolds."

"I don't recall inviting you guys," Abi said.

"You didn't. Lane did." VJ turned back to me. "We've gotten pretty tight since I moved to town. In class together."

So far I had learned three things: Papa Mac's son Vance apparently had a Junior, this VJ was most likely a sophomore, and most importantly—I didn't like him. I shrugged to emphasize my disinterest. *Like I care to know about you and Lane.*

"Case Reynolds. How do I know that name?" He pretended to think about it a moment, but clearly he knew more about me than I did about him.

"I doubt you and Case know each other," Abi said. "Why don't you get some food and go inside. Lane's in there."

VJ ignored her and snapped his fingers. "I know, you're the guy my Papaw says is supposed to be helping him 'watch the farm.'" He simulated quotation marks in the air with his fingers. "Well, I hate to tell you, but Papa Mac, as you call him, is sick, and he won't be getting better. My dad and I have moved from Memphis to this godforsaken hellhole to take care of him. And there's gonna be some changes around here."

"Changes?"

"That's what I said. When the farm is ours to manage, we ain't gonna let the local scum traipse all over it, getting in the way. Gotta get it ready to either sell it or develop it. You know, sell all the timber, tear down any old buildings, all that."

The stranger named VJ sucked all the oxygen from the space between us, but I held my ground, staring him in the eye, hoping he didn't see me trembling. Was it anger, fear, or something else? "Look dude, I don't know what your problem is, but I haven't bothered you. Never even met you before." I reached for Abi's hand. "C'mon, let's go inside." I'd get Dad to call Papa Mac later to sort this out.

VJ stopped me with the back of his hand on my shoulder. "Gonna hold her hand like you was doing earlier? How would Lane feel about that?"

My plan was to shake him off and walk inside anyway, denying if Abi wanted me to, being honest if she didn't. Instead, Jack walked out the door with Jet right behind him, and relief washed over me. As far as I knew, Jet had never been in a fight, but if this came to a scrap, Jack could even things up in a hurry. I had never fought him myself but knew I never wanted to. He was tough as nails and mean as a starving yard dog if you made him angry, which was actually hard to do—unless you messed with his family or friends.

"Well, hello," VJ said. "Jack Masterson, son of Stone Perkins. I'm VJ MacIntosh. You don't know me, but I know you. I'm actually sick and tired of hearing how much trouble your daddy—no, it's your stepdaddy, isn't it? How much trouble he is in with my father."

Jack looked at me, an unfamiliar expression in his eyes. I expected him to step up to VJ and ask if he wanted to settle the problem right then and there. Instead, he just looked down at the ground and walked away, around the pool, and out the gate. Jet followed him.

"Coward like his stepdaddy, I guess," VJ said.

I was more bewildered by Jack's behavior than VJ's nonsense, so I began to move in the direction my friends had gone.

"I hate my Rottweiler almost ate your daddy for supper that day," VJ said, louder now.

I froze in my tracks then looked over my shoulder at him. "That wasn't my father. It was Jet's."

"Well, whatever. Either way," he sneered, "I sure hate I accidentally let him out of the car on you guys. Could have been a real mess."

I wheeled and marched up to face him. He let that dog out on purpose. He wanted me to know it, and he wanted me to know it was meant for my father.

"Case, please don't. He's not worth it."

I took a step closer to VJ. "What's your problem?"

"What were you doing at my grandfather's house that day, anyway?"

At least Papa Mac hadn't told him about the Hideaway. "None of your business." I scowled.

"Maybe I make it my business." VJ pushed me backward, hard.

I stumbled into the four-by-four post on the porch, hitting my head. Not hard enough to do damage, but hard enough to hurt. And to infuriate. I grimaced, grabbed the back of my head with my left hand, and crouched slightly like I was going to sit and nurse my wound. Then I exploded from my coiled position with a right hook that hit VJ square in the jaw before he could even widen his eyes in surprise.

His knees buckled, and he stumbled backward, tripping over a pot of begonias and landing on his back. Before he bounced once, I was on top of him, ready to hit him again if he needed it but mostly to make him know there was more where that came from. But before I could draw back a fist, something grabbed me, crushing me, expelling my air like a used up swimming pool float. Blake had me in a bear hug, and not the friendly kind. Sounds blended together into something indiscernible, like the noises one hears when underwater. Was there shouting? Screaming?

Then just as suddenly, Blake and I were on the ground, entangled with someone else. "Stop it. Stop it right now!" The giant released me, and I staggered to my feet, gasping for air. Lane Buckley stood between us with his arms extended, hands on each of our chests. "What's going on?"

VJ rose from the dead and stumbled over to us, holding his jaw. He gestured at me. "I caught Loverboy here trying to make a move on Abi, and he just up and hit me."

Lane tensed, and I braced myself. The Amberton High backup quarterback would be a much more formidable opponent than VJ, and with Blake on standby to crush me like a paper cup and my two best friends gone AWOL, I didn't stand a chance. But I would not back down from VJ's lies. I balled my fist and tried to step around Lane. "You lying sack of—"

A familiar soft hand grabbed my arm, and I stopped mid-sentence. Abi inserted herself between Lane and me. "Case, no." She had tears in her eyes. "You need to go."

Her words hit me like the blast from a fire extinguisher. My anger died as quickly as it had ignited, and a feeling of stark abandonment took its place.

Lane taunted me as I walked away. "You stay away from Abi, or I'll take care of you myself."

———

Alone in the dark, wandering the streets circuitously toward Jet's house, I tried to make sense of what had happened, but it was futile. In the span of an hour I had somehow managed to alienate the girl of my dreams, likely get kicked off Papa Mac's farm for assaulting his grandson, have my innards nearly squeezed through my eyeballs, and get deserted by my closest friends. And I couldn't for the life of me figure out where exactly I had gone wrong.

I walked faster, my feet pounding the asphalt, skin burning like my blood might suddenly boil through it. I envied Bruce

Banner and his curse, his ability to transform into the Hulk, destroy something, blame it on a mutant alter ego, and move to the next town. Instead, all I could think to do was run. Somewhere—anywhere—leave my frustration in the dust. I veered off the road to the right and hopped the ditch onto a three-wheeler path that meandered through a series of wooded lots. Dense clouds diluted the moonlight, but it didn't matter. I could handle these trails with my eyes closed. My feet suddenly lighter, I coasted over the packed earth, cooled by the breeze of my movements, deftly taking each turn and leaping over exposed roots that studded the paths I knew so well.

Then a tree shifted positions. Or was it the shadow of one? On the trail in front of me, like something had moved out of my way. Something upright. I stopped dead still, desperately trying to calm my breathing, to hear whatever it was. Was there movement again, maybe a twig snap? Was there someone there? I had never been afraid of the dark, but suddenly I knew I was not alone, and it terrified me. I lunged ahead, reaching full speed by my third step. The trail turned right but instead I dove left, off the path, toward the flickers of light filtering through the trees from the street. Briars and low-hanging limbs tore at my face and clothes. Just as I burst into the clearing by the road, I stumbled and fell face-first in knee-deep grass, moist with dew. Before I could jump to my feet, someone grabbed my shoulder.

"Ahhheyyaa!"

Jack jumped back at my outburst, wide-eyed at first, then laughing. "What are you doing, you nutcase?" he said.

"Dangit, Jack. That's not funny. Shouldn't do a man like that."

"What were you running for?" Jet stood a few feet closer to the road.

"I was just mad. Mad about everything. Needed to blow off some steam."

"I'd say you definitely blew something off with that scream." Jet chuckled.

I tried to slow my breathing and gather myself. I wanted to slug Jack and Jet both just like I'd done VJ but knew the night didn't need to get any worse. "Thanks for your help back there at the party."

"What happened?" Jet asked.

"What happened is Papa Mac has a hoser of a grandson named VJ, who showed up and just lit in to me—and you too, Jack, in case you weren't paying attention—for no reason, and I slugged him. Then that gorilla bodyguard or boyfriend or whatever he was almost killed me." I detailed Vance's plans to sell the farm, or at the very least raze it, once Papa Mac died. How VJ let the dog loose on purpose, how I flattened VJ. And how things ended with Abi.

"So you really laid him out?" Jack asked. "Sorry I walked off. I really didn't think it would end in a fight."

"Well it did." I glared at Jack for a second, then walked over and sat on the edge of the street to rest. They followed suit, waiting on me to get over my anger.

"Case, listen." Jet's was tone suddenly more serious. "Jack has something he needs to tell you."

"I'm listening." I was still angry.

"Okay ..." Jack paused, clearly having difficulty with the words. Then, he looked up and spoke with a matter-of-fact tone. "Stone left us."

"What do you mean? Left, as in, moved out?"

"No, more than that. He grabbed a bunch of his stuff and drove off and said he's never coming back."

"Wow." I took a moment to process the new information. "You know he'll come back. People get mad all the time and walk out, rethink it, then come home."

"I don't know, man. He took his pistol, a couple of suitcases full of clothes, some other random junk, that's it. Some car I've never seen before pulled up, he got in, and they took off. He sold his truck a week or two ago, I think. I heard him and Mom arguing about it. I figured he'd buy something else, but he never did."

"Well, remember what he told you that day," Jet said. "That he might leave."

Jack shrugged. "Didn't think he would really do it though. Mom was at work, and him and Michelle got into it about her grades and how she wasn't ever gonna amount to nothin' good. Michelle said it was none of his business, that he wasn't her father no way, he was just a sorry drunk. He started yelling, and I took her side, then he just stopped. He went to the back of the house, made a phone call, packed up some crap, and left."

"Who was in the car?" Jet asked.

"No idea. Couldn't really get a look. Brown two-door, I think. But he's been been constantly whispering on the phone lately with somebody. Michelle and me think it's another woman, but we didn't say nothing to Mom. She probably knows."

"When did it happen?" Jet asked.

"Last week."

"Dude, why didn't you tell us?" I asked.

"I was embarrassed, I guess. Embarrassed about being upset about it after hating him and wishing he'd leave for so long now. Anyway, now you know."

"How's your mom?" Jet asked.

"About the same as me. She's been a wreck for a while now anyway. Working and arguing with him, arguing with him and working, that's all she's been doing. Maybe she's relieved, but I hear her crying too. I bet she's worried about money. And maybe she

cared about Stone once, before he went crazy. It's hard on her …
with, you know, with …"

"What happened with your father," I finished for him.

"Yeah, I mean I was only two when he died, but I've heard
Mom talk about how rough it was."

I patted Jack on the shoulder. "Hey, y'all are better off. Stone
was warped. Tell your mom to be careful with her bank accounts
and credit cards though. I've heard Dad talk about people taking
off and clearing out all the money, running up big credit card bills,
stuff like that."

"She's been working on that this week," Jack answered. "Heard
her tell Michelle he had gradually cleared out a savings account.
Anyway, now I'm ready to try to move on." He pointed forward
with both hands.

"Wish I could have seen you nail that VJ guy," Jet said.

"He pushed me."

Jack finally showed a full smile. "He doesn't know you very well."

"Or maybe he does. Getting me to cold-cock him may be the
best way possible to get us kicked off his granddaddy's farm." I
thought about the possibilities. VJ had admitted to me about sic-
cing the dog on us that day, but no one but Abi and Blake were
there to hear it. And as best I could tell from how she sent me
away, Abi had switched to the dark side. If we tried to tell anyone,
it would be my word against VJ's, and he could twist the fact that I
had punched him any way he saw fit, with Blake Frierson there to
corroborate whatever story he chose to tell.

One other thing bothered me. What had VJ been talking
about when he'd said that Stone was in trouble with his father? I
didn't know if we'd ever know that answer, but I figured now wasn't
the time to burden Jack with discussing it.

We all three stood and brushed ourselves off to head home.

"Boy, I wish I had a picture of your face when Jack grabbed you," Jet said.

"That wasn't cool, scaring me back there on the trail like that."

Both boys stopped and glanced over their shoulders into the darkness. "Hey Bud, we didn't go on the trail," Jack said. "We were standing on the road when you came blasting out of the woods like your butt was on fire."

My heart skipped a beat and flipped in my chest, and I quickly followed their gaze, searching the trees off the road for evidence of human-shaped shadows lurking on the trails. I wanted Jack to be joking. But the look on his face told me he was not.

EIGHT

Six months later

Meet me after school at the railroad trestle

THE note was penned in black ink with a calligraphic flourish, on paper from a spiral bound notebook with the jagged edge neatly trimmed away. Abi touched my waist lightly before she slipped it into my hip pocket, walked away with a teasing smile, and awakened a flutter of butterflies in my stomach—with an eight-word sentence that could mean just about anything.

I was irritated at how she affected me. I had wanted to stop caring about her, to erase from my mind the look of disappointment on her face when she had asked me to leave her party. We had been sitting on a swing, poised for a kiss, and only a few moments later she had thrown me off her property for getting in a little fight. With a punk like VJ MacIntosh? She had heard how he talked to me. How could she possibly have taken his side?

Now who did she think she was, essentially giving me a command to meet at the halfway point between our two neighborhoods after we had barely spoken for months? I snorted aloud as I read the note again, incredulous at its presumptuous tone and insulted that she thought so little of my resolve to hold a grudge that she believed I would show up.

Then the butterflies returned, and I couldn't brush them away. Abi wanted to meet me. Alone. But why? Maybe she was so sick of my shows of indifference toward her that she planned to embarrass me somehow. Maybe she would stand me up, and there would be a crowd of kids waiting to mock the look on my face when I realized it. Deep down, I knew that wasn't Abi, though. She might have turned away from me that night at her party, but she was not a vindictive or petty person. If she asked me to meet her, she would be there.

Even though I wanted to stay angry, I had begun to struggle with it on a daily basis. I missed our friendship, and I yearned for an explanation as to what happened that night. I had no choice but to go.

She was indeed waiting on me, alone. Beneath the trestle, dangling her feet over the edge of the creek, her heels bouncing against the gray rocks. A bluebird sky suggested warmth, but the long afternoon shadows and a harsh chill on the breeze foiled any attempt to imagine spring was very near. She wore jeans, a sweater, and pink leg warmers. Abi patted her hand on a rock beside her, similar to how she had done that night on the swing. The look on her face told me it was not a command but an invitation.

I sat down beside her. "You misspelled trestle."

"No, I did not." She playfully rapped me on the leg with the back of her hand. "Looked it up to make sure. Two weeks ago."

"Two weeks ago?"

She wrinkled her nose sheepishly. "Yeah. Been trying to get the courage to give it to you. You've been a bit harsh the past few months."

"I don't forgive and forget easily. I'm told I need to work on it."

"Yeah, well …"

I remained silent, giving her the opportunity to say what she came to say. This was her show, not mine.

After a pause, she finally realized I wasn't going to comment. "At my party. That whole thing just caught me off guard. I was ashamed I got caught—we got caught—"

"So you were ashamed of me."

"No, please, just give me a chance to explain. I don't think it's right to cheat, and that's what I was doing, or about to do, sort of. I was ashamed of that, not you. After you left, I lied to Lane, and felt even worse about that. I think he suspected, but he promised to be better—to do better. And he made me promise to stay away from you. So he tried for a while, and I tried, but …."

"But what?"

"But he was just the same old Lane. Lame, as Jack likes to say. He started back hanging out with the same losers as before. I should have seen it. I'm sorry."

"Is that it?"

Abi studied my eyes the way she had that night on the swing. "And I missed you."

Butterflies again. Actually, this time they felt more like birds, maybe the chimney sweeps I had watched at Papa Mac's house back in the fall. "So you're saying…"

"I broke up with Lane three weeks ago. If you'd have let me talk to you, you would have known. I didn't exactly advertise it. Lane is telling all his friends he dumped me. Whatever."

"Well, I'm, I'm glad to hear it. If you know what I mean. Glad about you missing me. And being sorry. Not that you're a sorry person, just sorry about us. Not about us, about what happened with us. Or almost happened."

"Case."

"Not that there's an us, but there was—sort of. You know what I mean."

"Case."

"Well, okay, maybe there wasn't an us, but there almost was. I think."

"Case, would you just shut up, please?" Abi grabbed my hand. I turned my face toward hers, and we kissed before I knew what was happening.

I always wondered if Jack had planted the idea, just because most off-the-wall schemes, good or bad, could usually be traced back to him. But it was Jet who claimed it, and Jack seemed as surprised as I did.

"I've had an epiphany."

Jack tried to whistle with a mouthful of oatmeal cookies but instead spit a crumb onto his kitchen counter. "Sounds awful. Take some antibiotics."

I frowned, both because Jack had just poured the last drop of milk and because it was impossible to tell when he was joking. "Let me guess, da Vinci, you're replacing the Pythagorean theorem."

Jet slapped a piece of bologna between two slices of bread dripping with mayonnaise and took a bite. "C'mon, guys. What do we think about more than anything else?"

Jack grimaced. "First of all, that much mayo is nasty. And second of all, *we* don't think about the same things. But since this is your epitome, I'm going to say, quadratic equations?"

"Epiphany." Jet held both hands palms up, expecting us to guess, but finally gave up. "Girls, of course."

I imitated the sound of the buzzer from *Family Feud*. "BONK!

Girls is not on the list of common thoughts for the one hundred nerds surveyed."

"You're such a loser." Jet's voice dropped almost to a whisper. "Let's get the girls to campout with us at the Hideaway."

And there it was. The idea of ideas. The past several months with Abi had been a seesaw, and I needed a way to steady it. For six months we had barely spoken, then suddenly one day we kissed on the railroad trestle. Still, I sensed my position with her was precarious at best. After the kiss, she had confused me again by expressing concern about romance ruining our friendship. I could make no sense of it, but I had no intention of giving up, and Jet's idea might be just the opportunity I was looking for. I stood from my barstool and sauntered into Jack's living room area. "Where's my favorite chair? What's your mom call it? Sacco? I need it."

Jack's brow wrinkled. "That old red chair? Finally had to get rid of it. Seams broke and beads started falling out."

"I did my best thinking in that chair," I grumbled. "Fit me perfect."

"It fit everybody perfect," Jack said. "That's the point of those kinds of chairs. Who cares? What about Jet's idea?"

Jet had told me once that resolve was my quiddity. I didn't know if that was an insult or compliment at the time, but after I had studied on it, I decided he was mostly right. I was usually nothing if not determined. Maybe hardheaded was a better word, but I chose to see it as an asset rather than a detriment. If Abi and I did not wind up together, it would not be because I yielded to self-doubt or irresolution. And I was confident that Abi's feelings for me mirrored mine for her. She would be unable to deny it if given the right opportunity.

"You have my attention," I said finally. "Do you have a plan?"

Jet grinned broadly. "Actually, I think I do."

"Sounds like you've been around Jack too long."

Jack winked at me with a conniving smile of his own.

———————

It was impossible to identify the source of the footsteps moving toward us along the edge of the soybean field. The night was dark. Pitch black, I'd heard it called, though as far as I knew, I had never seen pitch to really know its color. To me it was just black dark, the kind when the moon takes the night off, clouds cover the stars, and you get far enough away from streetlights to feel the real weight of it.

"That's them." Jack hissed.

"C'mon." I moved from the edge of the tree line and walked along the dusty road at the edge of the field, toward the footsteps.

I heard faint whispers but couldn't make out any words at first. Then, louder, "Hey, Case. Is that you?" Hearing Abi's whispering voice was a relief. Three shadows materialized into female figures immediately in front of me.

"Yeah, it's us. Did anybody see you?" The plan had been for them to pretend to be camping in Rachel's back yard before sneaking away.

"No, we're good," Rachel said. "I'm sure my parents have been asleep since five minutes after the ten o'clock news went off."

"Are we gonna stand here being scaredy cats all night, or are we gonna have some fun?" A new voice, the third member of the female trio.

Jack poked me in the ribs from behind. "Case, have you met Chrissy?"

"I suppose I have now." I had been hearing Jack talk about Chrissie Tunsil for the past week. She was Rachel's first cousin, visiting from Haughton, a town on the other side of the county. To hear Jack talk, she was something of a free spirit—a perfect match for him, he was certain. I couldn't really see her yet but could tell she was petite, much shorter than Abi or Rachel. According to Jack, she was supposed to be blonde with brown eyes, cute but not gorgeous. He said Rachel had refused to give him her opinion as to whether she had nice legs or not, which he thought likely meant she did and that Rachel was slightly jealous.

"You haven't met her either, Jack," Rachel said.

"I know, but you've told me about her, so I feel like I know her already."

I was sorry I couldn't see Abi's face better. I was smiling, and I could imagine she was rolling her eyes with a there-he-goes-again look.

"Come on, ladies, we'll show you the Hideaway," Jet said.

The question of revealing our secret spot to the girls had been a point of contention, the only resistance to the plan when Jet introduced it. Since the whole thing had been his idea, Jet of course had no problem with it, but Jack had been against it and suggested we go somewhere else. I had been the tiebreaker, and because, unbeknownst to them, I had already taken Abi to the Hideaway, I saw it as a way to make that particular secret more obsolete. Jack had acquiesced when Jet offered a guaranteed date with Rachel's cousin as an inducement.

"Once we get around this corner up here, we can turn our flashlights on," Jet continued. "Nobody can see us from the neighborhood then."

"You got a neighborhood watch that's gonna arrest us or what?" Chrissie asked.

"No, but we're not exactly supposed to be camping out here. The landowner doesn't want us here, and we believe he'll *prosecute* us if we're caught." Jack's voice was laced with dramatic inflection.

"Plus, we've already gotten sideways with the sheriff, but he let us off with a warning. So we could get in a *lot* of trouble. But it's worth the risk."

I coughed to hide my chuckle, and Jack elbowed me. I could hear Abi's muffled whisper of incredulity, and I eased closer to her for a conspiratorial elbow also, mine much more gentle than Jack's.

"Ooh, we all may be on the FBI's Ten Most Wanted list by morning." Chrissie's voice was thick with sarcasm.

She was right. There should be no legal consequences to getting caught by Vance MacIntosh. Papa Mac would see to that if he was still able. Still, I hated to think about what would happen if my parents found out what we were doing. I was generally allowed a lot of freedom as long as I didn't abuse it. But I was fairly certain that including girls on a campout would be considered abusing it.

Our fire at the Hideaway had burned down to only glowing embers, and Jet stoked the coals with a charred oak limb as we all found a seat around it. Clusters of sparks danced upward on rising waves of heat and smoke before disappearing as if pinched by invisible fingers.

Jack stood and paced, staring upwards. The clouds had broken, and the stars had come to life as if awoken from a slumber. "What are you doing?" Abi asked him.

"Jet, where is the hunter? Orion? You know, the dude with the three stars in a row for his belt. Remember, we were looking at that a few months ago."

"Yeah, I remember. That was back in the winter. Orion disappears in the warmer months. Why you wanna know?" Jet asked.

"I was gonna show him to Chrissie. You know, the greatest hunter of all. Kind of like me. Orion is my boy." Jack hit his chest with his fist, smiling.

"Yeah that is a *lot* like you," I said. "Myth-ology."

"I don't really like hunting," Chrissie said. "Seems cruel to me."

Jack's eyes widened, and he looked at me with alarm. Maybe she wasn't his soulmate after all.

There was a brief awkward silence before Jet finally came to the rescue. "Well, the key is not overdoing it. You know, taking only legal limits, eating what you harvest. The story of Orion is pretty cool. Has a moral and everything. There are several different versions, but I'll tell the one I like."

"Jet, we don't want a Sunday school lesson or an astrology lecture." Rachel sighed but smiled.

"Astronomy. And I'm mostly talking about the mythology part anyway, so just hold your horses. I'll make it short. Jack's the one who brought it up, not me."

"Yeah, let him tell us," Jack said. "I like this stuff."

"We would love to hear the story, Jet," Abi offered.

"Okay, here goes. In Greek mythology, Orion was the greatest mortal hunter of all. He became friends with Artemis, who was daughter of Zeus, king of the gods. Artemis was a hunter herself, protector of all wild beasts. One day while hunting with Artemis, Orion began to boast and said that he was so skilled, he could kill all the animals on the Earth. Artemis was offended, but Mother Earth herself became furious. She sent a giant scorpion to teach him a lesson. They had a battle for the ages, but the scorpion finally killed Orion. Zeus was so impressed he put the scorpion into the heavens as a constellation to honor it for killing the mighty hunter, and also to teach mortals to respect nature and avoid being boastful. Artemis talked Zeus into putting Orion into a constellation as well, but Zeus kept them separate so they wouldn't continue trying to kill each other. So they're never seen in the sky together. Orion is best seen in winter, and Scorpius in summer."

Jet stood and walked a few feet behind us, pointing over Snake

Lake to the south, where the water met the horizon on the far side at the levee. "There is Scorpius right there. Just over the edge of the water. See the red star, there? That's Antares, the heart of the scorpion."

We had all stood up to surround him, peering in the direction he pointed. I could see Antares. I wasn't sure I saw a scorpion though. I'd have to look that up later, if I thought about it.

"I thought it was Scorpi-o, not Scorpi-us," Jack said.

"No, Scorpius is the constellation. Scorpio is the name in astrology. You know, the twelve signs of the Zodiac. Hmmm...Case, I believe you are the only Scorpio among us, actually. Born November tenth, right? Know what the characteristics of a Scorpio are?"

"I do." Abi said. "Know the characteristics of a Scorpio, I mean. Determination and loyalty." Abi smiled at me and walked in front of me, leaning back and grabbing my hands. I let go and put my arms around her waist. The smell of her was intoxicating. "I'd say that fits you to a T," she whispered over her shoulder to me.

"So, Jet." Rachel looked at Jack. "You'd say the moral of the Orion story is not to brag and do stupid stuff to impress a girl, right?"

"Ha, ha, ha." Jack smirked. "I'd say the moral is just to make sure if you talk the talk, you better be able to walk the walk."

"Well somebody told me once I am an Virgo but act like a Sagittarius," Chrissie chimed in. "I don't know Sagittarius from Sacagawea, but I know standing around here having school is boring me to death. I see water down there. Let's go skinny dipping."

"You're crazy. Do you know the name of that lake?" Jet asked. "Snake Lake. We call it that for a reason."

"Aww, snakes won't mess with me. I'll splash around and stuff. Gotta have a little faith." She skipped down the hill toward the water. "Who's going with me?"

Going along was no temptation for me on this night. First, I knew Abi would never consider it. And second, there was no way I was getting in that water in the dark, with or without clothes. I looked at Jack. "Man, that's your game to play. Sideline for me."

He shrugged as if to say, "What am I supposed to do?" Then he turned to follow her. "Hold on a second, Chrissie."

I looked at Rachel. "Your cousin is about to become water moccasin bait."

"I told Jack she was wild as a buck. I've known her my whole life. If I try to stop her—and Case, I know you, if *you* try to stop her—she'll do something even crazier. Maybe Jack can talk her out of it, or maybe she's so crazy, she'll scare the snakes away."

I briefly reconsidered going with Jack to help save Chrissie, but Rachel's warning and Abi's presence put an end to that. Jack was on his own. Whatever happened, happened. I figured one way or another, our time on Papa Mac's farm was limited anyway, and it might be my one and only chance to be share a night with Abi at my favorite place in the world.

"Well? What now?" I looked at Jet and Rachel, who were holding hands. I still had my arms around Abi's waist and was resting my chin on her shoulder.

"I'd like a starlight tour, please," Rachel said playfully. "Say goodbye to your friends."

"*Arrivederci,*" Jet rolled flamboyantly as Rachel pulled him away.

"Looks like we're alone." Abi turned around and grabbed my hands in hers.

"Yes, we are." I leaned in and kissed her. A brief brush of lips at first, then deeper, longer.

She touched her fingers to my lips, separating us. "What are we doing here, Case?"

"I know what *I'm* doing. You know how I feel about you. You tell me what *you're* doing."

"Let's not overthink this. Let's just enjoy the night."

I searched the darkness, trying to see her face clearly. Her gaze was locked on mine, and I was disappointed I couldn't see the brilliant blue of her eyes. "I wish I could see your face better."

"It certainly is dark out here."

"Are you scared?" I teased, pulling her close to me. I was surprised when she pushed away.

"I don't scare easily, you know." She smiled.

"Oh, is that right? What if I walked away and left you here by yourself?"

"We both know that's not going to happen, don't we?" She gave me a quick peck on the lips.

"What makes you think I won't walk off and leave you?'

"I don't *think* you won't, I *know* you won't."

"Oh, do you now?" I replied.

"Yep. Girl's intuition." She smiled and tugged my hand. "C'mon, let's walk."

"Fine with me." I grabbed a light out of my pack and took her hand.

"What's down there?" Abi pointed down the trail opposite the direction Jet and Rachel had gone.

"I can show you. Good opportunity to find out if you're as brave as you say you are." The last time I had visited the old horse barn, back in the fall while rabbit hunting, it was severely dilapidated and overgrown. After six months more of deterioration, on a night this dark, I imagined it to be much more foreboding than anything Abi had in mind. *You talk the talk, Abi, but can you walk the walk?* I smiled to myself at the thought of her being frightened and having to eat her words.

Soon the barn loomed ahead in the wide yellow beam of the flashlight. Vines and thorns had only engulfed it more since the last time I last saw it. In the partial light, the entrance could have been the mouth of a cave, swarmed by cobwebs and thorns in a mountain of greenery.

"What is that?" Abi asked.

"Your worst nightmare."

"Ha, ha. No, seriously, what is that?"

"Well, it used to be a barn. I'd say now it's a good place for a wild animal to live. Or a ghost. Word is, it's haunted."

"Whatever."

"Seriously. It's a slave child from the old MacIntosh Plantation. Drowned in the lake down there, some people say maybe murdered. Used to haunt the other buildings on the place, but they are all gone except this one, so she lives there now."

"That's ridiculous," Abi said. I thought my story was a good one, but if she was buying it, she hid it well. "You think I'm afraid to go in there?"

"Actually, yeah. I'd say I think you're afraid to go in there."

"Hmmph," Abi grunted. "Shine the light over here." She picked up a dead limb and hacked at the cobwebs blocking the entrance.

"You're really going to go in?"

"If you'll shine the light for me, I will. Unless you're scared." She stood with hands on hips, huffing a bit from her effort. I assured her that I was not and helped her clear the remaining limbs blocking our path. In short order, we had an opening wide enough to slide through sideways in a stoop but without having to crawl. We both swatted mosquitoes as they buzzed around our heads. The breeze off the weather front had kept them under control outside, but inside the old barn, where the air was stagnant, they were much more active.

As we stopped and stood to our full height, we heard a rustling sound against the wall to our left. It ceased, then started again, then moved down the wall and disappeared through it.

"What is that?" Abi asked, a slight tremor in her voice.

"It's her." I gave my best imitation of a ghostly wail.

"Oh, stop it. What *was* that?"

"Probably her killer," I hissed. Then matter-of-factly, "Or, just some small animal. Rat, maybe. Or 'possum or coon."

"What's over here?" She moved to the right where a door opened to the other part of the structure.

"Nothing, really. A couple of stalls that connect to the outside. It's just an old horse barn. Hard to believe that not long ago, we used to come here and feed the horses, even snuck a ride on occasion."

I shined the light at Abi's feet and followed her into the adjacent room. She stopped just inside the threshold, and I pulled her to me and turned off the flashlight at the same time. The adrenaline surge from the sudden impenetrable blackness combined with the feel of her against me made me tremble with excitement.

"What are you doing, mister?"

"This." I found her lips and kissed her.

She kissed me back then slid her mouth down my cheek to whisper in my ear. "That's nice, we should do it more often." Her breath poured into me like a desert wind and sent a hot shiver down my spine. I searched for her again, but she stopped me with her fingers between our lips, just as she'd done earlier. "Hold on. You know what else might be fun?"

I feared she could hear the pounding of my heart. "What?"

"This." Abi shoved me backward, grabbing my flashlight at the same time. She giggled and turned, hopping out the door and disappearing into the other part of the barn.

I was so startled as I stepped back that I lost my footing, tripping on something hidden in the musty pile of hay behind me. I fell backward, landed on my buttocks, and tried unsuccessfully to keep from rolling onto my back and head. "Owww!" Something hard and sharp jabbed my shoulder, not enough to break the skin but forceful enough I knew I'd have an impressive bruise later. I grabbed the object, trying at once to both identify it and make sure it was no further threat. "Ahhh!" I yelled again, this time from repulsion rather than pain. I jerked my hand away, not wanting to know more, only wanting to exit as rapidly as possible.

I jumped up and groped in the dark for the door, felt my way through it, then saw the flashlight beam bouncing off the walls of the other room.

"Are you okay?" Abi's silhouette leaned into the entrance from outside the barn.

"No, I'm not okay." I growled. "You could have killed me. I fell into a, uhhh, a—"

"I don't think it almost killed you, but I didn't mean for you to fall."

I stormed out of the barn, ignoring the thorns scratching my face as I brushed past her. "Well, I did fall. What was that about anyway?"

"I was just having some fun. I was just gonna run out with the flashlight. Aren't you Mr. Tough Guy?" She brushed off hay and picked broken briar twigs from my clothes.

I shooed her hand away. "Didn't scare me, it just wasn't my idea of fun."

"I'm sorry. What did you say you fell into?"

"Oh, nothing. Let's go back and find the others."

I had no intention of telling her that I was almost certain I had fallen into a pile of bones.

NINE

WE found Jack at the Hideaway, sitting cross-legged on the ground watching helplessly as Chrissie pretended to surf atop his three-wheeler, one foot on the seat and the other on the back equipment rack. She was singing a Beach Boys song and doing a poor job of it. It was painful to listen to, but one positive was that she still had her clothes on. Plus, the look of sheer bewilderment on Jack's face was absolutely priceless. I only wish I had been in a better state of mind to fully relish it.

"What is she doing?" Abi asked Jack.

"She's surfing. Been doing that for the last fifteen minutes. Before that, she was skinny dipping, then climbing trees, then gymnastics. But the singing has never stopped."

"Did you swim with her?" I asked Jack with a wink.

"Thought about it. But no sooner'd she go in then she popped out like a jack-in-the-box, put her clothes on, and shinnied up that big willow."

"What's wrong with her?" Abi asked.

"Apparently for the last couple of hours she's been sipping on some Jägermeister she snuck from her father's liquor cabinet."

Abi shot me a confused look. "Yager what?"

"Jägermeister," Jack said. "It's some kind of German liquor. I tried a little. It's nasty. She said she picked it because it had a pretty green bottle."

Chrissie continued with her performance, swaying unsteadily and pointing at Jack as she sang, seemingly oblivious to my and

Abi's presence. "I'm pickin' up good vibrations. He's giving me excitations, I'm pickin' up good vibrations. Oom bop, bop, good vibrations. He's giving me excitations."

"You're giving her excitations, Jack." I snickered.

Jack huffed. "Well I ain't giving her nothin' else, I'll tell you that."

Abi put her hand on my shoulder. "You need to go find Rachel."

I said nothing and stomped off dutifully in the direction Jet and Rachel had gone earlier, listening behind me to Chrissie complaining vigorously to Jack and Abi that she didn't need help getting down, and why didn't anybody ever like her singing?

What a disaster. I had wanted to spend several hours alone with Abi, confident she would see things my way, that we were better together as a couple than apart as close friends. I knew she was just being playful when she pushed me, but good grief. Why couldn't she have just been content to stand there and kiss me in the dark?

Instead, I had fallen onto what I knew with only a shadow of a doubt to be a carcass, a skeleton of some sort, and I would have a bruise tomorrow to show for it. I wasn't a great biology student, but the words "ball-and-socket" had immediately come to mind when I grabbed the shaft of the bone beneath me and slid my hand down to its rounded end. The disturbing thing, aside from landing on a skeleton in the first place, was the size of it. This was no raccoon or stray cat. It was a larger animal than that. But what was it doing in the barn? I couldn't explain why it mattered to me, but I knew I had to go back and take a look.

Jet and Rachel were snuggled up when I found them, pressed against the trunk of a massive red oak at the end of an overgrown, barbed wire fence row, a tangled jetty in a sea of knee-high soybeans. I heard their giggles from a distance and considered sneaking up to grab them from behind, but thought better of it. I didn't think Jet was carrying a gun but wouldn't put it past him. Plus, I just wasn't in the mood.

"Jet." I hissed. "It's me. I'm walking up."

"What has Chrissie done?" Rachel asked, before I could even show myself.

Abi and Jack had coaxed Chrissie into a lawn chair by the time we got back. She was jabbering nonstop, but more slurred now, as if she were a toy that would soon need to be rewound. "I sure've had fun tonight. Have you 'ad fun tonight? I like dancin', do you like dancin'? You see me dance on that surfin' motorcycle? I can sing too. Good, good vi-bra-shuns. Y'all said there were snakes in that lake. Snake rhymes with lake. Is 'at why it's Snake Lake, so it'd rhyme? That's funny. I didn't get bit. Maybe it's a *fake* snake lake. That's *real* funnnny. I sure have had fun tonight."

"Chrissie." Rachel marched up to her like a mother prepared to send her child to the corner. "What have you done?"

"I'm just havin' a little fun."

"She drank this." Jack raised the bottle of Jägermeister, then turned it upside down to emphasize its emptiness.

Jet grabbed it from him and flipped it upright to read the label. "Jägermeister. You know I'm pretty sure that translates to 'hunting master,' literally. How ironic is that, Mr. Orion, the mighty hunter?" He tossed the bottle back to Jack. "She selected that especially for you." He chuckled.

Chrissie reached up, grabbed the bottle, and threw it backward over her head into the bushes. "Uh-uh," she slurred. "I told you I don't even like hunting."

Jet and I both burst into laughter.

"Very funny." Jack kicked at both of us, now laughing a bit himself. "We've got to do something with her."

"I need to get her back home before she hurts herself out here," Rachel said.

Jack reached to help Chrissie up from her chair. "Let's go."

I grabbed Chrissie's other arm and helped her stand. "You guys all go on and head that way with Chrissie." I gently pushed her toward Jet and Rachel. "Jack and I will catch up in a minute. We've, uh, got to check on something here first."

Jack shot a what-are-you-talking-about look but didn't disagree. "Yeah, we'll catch up."

Abi gave an exasperated sigh. "I'll go with them." I didn't know if she was flustered that I was not being more empathetic toward Chrissie's plight or that I was influencing Jack not to tend to his date himself. Or was it that I obviously wanted to talk to Jack alone and was leaving her out? Regardless, I had to go see what was in that barn. I wasn't sure if I was avoiding telling Abi what I had in mind because I was still irritated at her for pushing me, or if I thought I was somehow protecting her. But I had to find out. Tonight. Right now. And I didn't want to go alone.

"What's the deal?" Jack asked, as I led him down the road toward the barn.

"Not sure, but we gotta go look at something."

"Down there? What's down there?"

"It's in the barn. I'll show you. I'm actually not sure what it is."

Jack stopped in his tracks and started backpedaling. "I'm not going in there. That place is an overgrown mess. Gives me the creeps. What were you doing in there with Abi anyway?"

"Get your mind out of the gutter. We were goofing around, I was trying to scare her so we walked in there. She may have been less afraid than me, actually. But there's something in there."

"Whatever it is, I ain't gonna find out. You're lucky it didn't bite you."

"What I found ain't biting *nobody*."

"What are you talking about?"

"It's probably no big deal. I fell on it. Felt like, like some bones or something. But it's big. It'll be cool to see what it is. Real quick. Then we'll catch up."

"Bones? You can go yourself. I'm gonna catch up to the others." He turned around.

"Since when did you get to be such a sissy?"

Jack wheeled to face me. "I'm no sissy, but I'm not stupid either. Some things are better left alone. Give me a dude to fight or a cliff to climb, but dark, deserted barns and dead things ain't nothin' to mess with."

"I'm going to look. If you don't want to come, fine. I'll go by myself."

"Whatever. Let's go be horror movie morons." Jack huffed and marched down the narrow road. By the time I reached the barn, he had already crawled in through the tangle and was standing inside with his arms outstretched. "Okay, what now, Indiana Jones?"

"Dude, why are you being such a punk?" I stood to my full height and brushed off my jeans with my hands. "I just wanted to show you something. Forgive me." I pointed my flashlight beam through the dark doorway to the stall where Abi had left me in a panic on the floor. "It's in there." I eased toward the opening. Halfway there, I realized I was tiptoeing and corrected it. No reason to sneak. Whatever was in that heap of moldy hay wasn't going anywhere.

"You sure you want to go in there? Why can't you leave stuff alone?"

"Jack, we're here. Let's see what it is. You know I've got to find out."

He sighed deeply. "Yeah, I know."

I turned the corner into the small room and shined my light back to the right, where I had fallen into the mound of hay. At first, I couldn't tell much. I could see something white—no, more of a pale, ashen color—protruding from beneath the clipped swards of grass, but I could not make a clear identification. I glanced over my shoulder at Jack, who stood quiet and stolid, calmer than I anticipated, given his reluctance to enter.

To that point, I was uncertain as to why I had been so preoccupied with what was in that hay, why I felt such a compulsion to find out. What was the big deal with an animal, perhaps a deer or large dog, wandering into that old barn and dying, or maybe being dragged in there by another animal?

But as I stared at the single bone protruding from the hay and contemplated the others I had felt hidden beneath, the reason suddenly jumped at me like the resurrected ghost of whatever creature was hidden there. Those bones were *under* the hay, not on top of it. Whatever was in that hay had been put there intentionally. It had been buried.

I almost turned and left at that very moment, but that would be futile. I would just come right back. Instead, I gathered myself and crouched to get a better look. The exposed bone looked to be over a foot long with a dingy amber hue up close in the light. A few small, shriveled particles of dried flesh clung to its rounded end. I shuddered and thought I might be sick. Neither of us said a word as I reached to move the hay and see more clearly what it covered. My hand trembled as it hovered over the task, and

I quickly clenched and opened my fist to fight the dread.

"Just do it," Jack whispered.

I took a deep breath, set the light at my feet, and swept the hay to the sides with both hands. The shock of what I saw almost caused me to fall for the second time that night. I lurched backward, tripping on Jack's feet and entangling myself in his arms and legs.

"Whoa. It's a person. It's human. Jack, it's a body!"

Jack pushed me off him, stepping forward to get a better look. "Holy smoke," he said quietly. "I *knew* we didn't want no part of this."

I stepped up beside him, and we both stared, aghast. My heart raced, and I couldn't seem to get an adequate breath of air. The urge to turn and run returned much stronger than before, and my muscles contracted in preparation to do so.

The sound of another voice from the darkness behind us—only a trepid whisper, but a voice not belonging to Jack or me nonetheless—startled me so badly I almost collapsed.

"I know who it is," it said.

Jack and I both whirled, cursed, and searched frantically for the source.

My light found her face first. Abi stood in the doorway, watching us, eyes wide and more black than blue, adrenaline-fueled pupils refusing to constrict despite the light.

I jerked my light to the grisly scene below as if something there might reach out and grab me if I averted my gaze too long. But Jack's never wavered. He remained locked on Abi. "What did you say?"

"I know who it is." Abi's voice was only slightly stronger now. She walked up to stand beside us.

"What are you doing here?" I was miffed at her intrusion, yet intrigued by what she had said. "And what do you mean, you know who it is?"

"First of all, I don't need your permission to be here. I knew you were up to something by the way you acted earlier, and the way you and Jack looked at each other. And I wanted to know what, so I told Jet and Rachel to go on. They didn't need my help anyway. And second of all, I think I know who that is."

"So are you going to tell us or not?" I asked.

"Yes, if you'll give me a chance. Jack, you remember that guy who always wanders around town, with the shaggy hair and beard? You know, the dude who supposedly bathes in the river, all that stuff?"

He nodded. "You mean Vaga?"

It dawned on me what she was thinking. I remembered her suggesting months before that The Vagabond might try to use our Hideaway.

"I can't remember what Case said his name is … was."

"The Vagabond," I said.

Jack nodded again, more forcibly. "Vaga."

"His real name, I meant. Whatever. Anyway, yeah, that's him. Remember I told you, Case. Last year, about the time of my birthday party? Rachel and I saw him that day in the neighborhood, right at the edge of Papa Mac's place. He waved at us. Seemed friendly, but kinda creepy too."

"You think it's him?" Jack asked.

"I asked Daddy about him. Apparently, he and some others from church tried to help him, but he turned them down. Supposedly a brilliant guy, but Daddy said he just wanders around, living off the land, sleeping in the woods and stuff like that."

"What's your point?" Jack said.

"That day, when we were walking away, somebody pulled up in a truck and hollered at him, told him to get lost or he'd regret it, something like that."

"Why didn't you tell me that before?" I said. "Who was it?"

"I … I don't know. Couldn't tell. But think about it. When's the last time you saw him?"

"It's been months at least," Jack said.

I couldn't recall the last time I'd seen him either. "You thinking that guy killed him?"

"I didn't say that. But I know he disappeared about that time. I know because I looked for him for a while after that. I was relieved that he'd left town before somebody hurt him. But now I wonder…"

Jack took a step back. "Who says somebody killed him? Maybe he was in here looking for shelter and froze, or was sick and died."

"Yeah, but he was buried." I poked at the hay with my foot. "Somebody buried him under the hay."

"Maybe he was trying to stay warm by getting under it. If a person killed him, don't you think they'd bury him in the ground?" Jack speculated.

That did make sense. Natural deaths were common enough in Amberton. Murders were not. But then again, neither were peculiar, scantily clad vagabonds, or skeletons under the hay in old barns.

"It doesn't matter," Abi said. "We got to get outta here and tell Mr. Reynolds about this. He's the investigator. He can figure it all out."

"Wait a minute, I'm not sure that's a good idea," Jack dissented. "Think about what happens if we go do that. You know they'll ask a ton of questions. My mom won't care, but Abi, you want everybody to know you was out here pulling an all-nighter with a bunch of guys? You want that to happen to her, Case? And if I know your parents, you'll be grounded for a year."

"Nobody has to find out about the girls. You and me and Jet can do the talking."

Jack cocked his head and raised an eyebrow. "C'mon, Bud. You know loudmouth Chrissie will sing like a parakeet as soon as this story gets out. I don't know much about her, but I ain't got to have Jet's brain to see she loves drama."

I hated to admit it, but he was making good points.

"Remember the uproar when Adam got caught by the cops skinny dipping with that girl, Lulu, at the Country Club? Her parents pulled her out and put her in a private school."

I remembered the story about the pool but never knew what happened to Lulu Dodds. Rumor was, she wasn't the first or the last girl Jet's older brother hopped the fence with though.

"Well, I'm not going to stand in the way of a murder investigation." Abi hissed. "I don't care if I do get in trouble."

"Always so dramatic." Jack waved a dismissive backhand toward Abi and moved toward the entrance as if to leave before pivoting to come back and stand over the skeleton. He pointed toward the heap at his feet without taking his eyes off of us. "You both know that most likely this guy hunkered down in here last winter and died. Ain't nobody's fault but his. If you want to make believe it's more than that and get caught up in all that drama, then leave me out of it."

I certainly did not want my father finding out about our little campout. Even though it had ultimately been fairly innocent, their assumptions and the punishment that ensued might not be. Even more importantly, I did not want Abi to get in trouble or have her reputation smeared. This had been the boys' idea, after all. But another thought was brewing in my head, one that ultimately mattered even more to me. "Guys, something else. Even though I agree with Jack that this probably isn't a crime, what happens if others think it might be? Until they figure it out? There'll be cops wandering around all over the place here, maybe even reporters.

Plus, Vance will get called out to see what's happened since Papa Mac isn't able. He doesn't know about the Hideaway. He doesn't know about our boat, our little firing range where we target practice, all that stuff. We're flying under the radar now, but according to VJ, he already wants to flatten this place one day. If he's half the jerk his son is, I bet he'd do it even quicker just for spite."

"So what are y'all saying?" Abi's eyes widened, and her jaw dropped "Just leave it here and pretend nothing happened?"

Jack shrugged.

"No way. I'm not going to be part of that." She shook her head emphatically. "He may have family looking for him."

The three of us stood silently, toeing the packed earth and loose hay strands at our feet. "I may have a better idea," I finally said, softly.

TEN

JACK came home with me the next morning, both of us hoping to get a nap after a night of no sleep. We stopped short in the kitchen, surprised to see my father sitting at the table nursing a cup of coffee, a somber look on his face. Blue jeans, a polo shirt, and penny loafers—atypical attire for a Saturday morning—told me he had somewhere to go.

"Son, we need to talk," he said.

My heart sank. How could he have found out so quickly?

"Dad, look, I can explain about the campout."

He shot me a puzzled look and held up his hand. "Unless somebody died, I don't want to hear it. You boys go clean up and get back here. We've got to go see Papa Mac."

A few minutes later we were in the truck, headed to Papa Mac's house. All that had been revealed to us was that Papa Mac had called and said he wanted to see Dad and me as soon as possible. I didn't know if Dad knew the reason for the visit yet, but I could think of a long list of possibilities, and none of them were good. Papa Mac found out about me punching his grandson VJ months before. Papa Mac wanted to lecture me in the presence of my father about coed sleepovers and premarital sex. Or worst of all, Papa Mac sold the farm. The only thing I was certain it would not be about was the skeleton. Only three people knew about that, and I trusted Abi and Jack with that secret even more than I did myself.

I sat in the middle, Jack against the passenger door. He leaned in and whispered, "Don't say nothing about that skeleton."

Out of the corner of my eye, I saw Dad look over at us, but he did not speak. I hoped the radio would drown out my irritated reply. "I ain't stupid."

Jack turned and stared out the window, concentrating as if he was taking a mailbox census.

Soon we were coasting up to Papa Mac's house, just as we had months earlier. Two or three cars were parked at odd angles off the shoulder of the driveway. The old, bluish Ford truck remained in its customary position under the huge pecan, but I didn't see the black Camaro. Still, I half-expected a rabid black dog to come charging around the corner. Dad turned the truck off but didn't open his door immediately. He turned to me. "Son, Papa Mac isn't doing well."

"What is it?"

"I am not sure how bad it is, but I know it's been coming on. Awhile back, his son Vance moved home to help take care of him for what time he has left. I don't entirely know why he asked us to come here today, but I owe that to him. Jack, when we go inside you can sit in the kitchen while Case and I go see him. I don't plan to be here long."

A bony wisp of a woman, with sunken temples and gray hair in a bun, opened the door before we could knock. She identified herself as Paul's sister and ushered Dad and me to the back of the house. The bare hardwood floor, its finish faded and scuffed, creaked beneath our feet as we walked.

I paused in the hall to study a framed black-and-white photo of a younger Papa Mac standing beside an old Ford truck with a petite beauty whom I knew to be his late wife, Matilda. The photographer had captured her mid-laugh while Papa Mac eyed her with a sideways glance and indulging grin suggesting simultaneous admiration for her and disdain of being photographed.

Was the old truck the same one stranded on blocks all these years in the front yard? Maybe it had sentimental value, or maybe Papa Mac just liked Fords. I remembered my grandfather telling me many times, usually in frustration with a wrench in his hand, that Ford stood for Fix Or Repair Daily—yet I never knew him to drive anything else.

"C'mon Case." My father beckoned from down the hall, waiting in a doorway. I could think of ten thousand things I would rather be doing at that moment, but I dutifully followed him into the room.

"Come in, men." Papa Mac's voice was clear and deep. He didn't sound sick, but his skin was gray like a gathering rain cloud, his eyes were hollow, hair disheveled. He sat in a beige recliner with pillows propped around him. Labored breaths, rumpled bedding in a hospital bed three feet from his chair, and an oxygen tank by his side suggested Papa Mac didn't stray far from his current eight-foot circle. Oxygen tubing clung crookedly to his face, missing one nostril.

Dad squatted beside the old man's chair and gently straightened the tubing, then clasped Papa Mac's right hand between the two of his. More than a cordial handshake. "How you hanging in there? You look a little stronger than last week."

I had no idea that Dad had been coming by.

"Rex, you never were a good liar." Papa Mac gave a weak smile. "Guess that's a good quality for an officer of the law." He gestured in my direction. "Is it okay if I talk?"

I stood several feet away, motionless and awkward but certainly within earshot.

"Yeah, he can handle it," Dad answered. "Almost a man, now."

"I don't know how much time I got, so I wanted to see you two. I got a mixed report yesterday. Bad news is my heart's done gone kaput, and the medicines they're giving me ain't working no more. Good news is I ain't short of breath too bad, and Doc says I'll go quick." He forced a smile and snapped his fingers. "There's worse ways to go."

I was not accustomed to much emotion from my father and was stunned to see tears in his eyes. After a swollen silence, he patted Papa Mac on the knee and stood. "We'll talk some more later. Call me if you need me. I know you wanted to talk to Case." Dad solemnly nodded his head at me and left the room. I think the look was intended to be reassuring, but it was not. This couldn't be good.

"Come over here, boy, and sit down." Papa Mac pointed at the vacant space on the rug between his feet and mine. I complied. "I'm sorry we haven't had more of these conversations. There's more'n a few things I'd do over again if I could. Your granddaddy would be proud of you."

"Dad says y'all were close, huh? Hunted together?"

"Your daddy and Vance used to hunt with us too. At least, until they—anyway, Hugh and I were best friends. Your grandmother was a jewel too. But Hugh and I were closer than brothers. Grew up together. Nothin' I wouldn't have done for him." He stared absently at a bare wall across the room for several seconds, each identified by the ticking of a mantel clock sitting atop his dresser. "I'm telling you all that to say this. Your granddaddy was a good man. Honest. And I miss him. And he asked me to look after you and Rex after he died. And to be honest, I've done a poor job of it. I didn't check on you like I should, so I'm sorry."

"Papa Mac." My eyes welled with tears. "You don't have to apologize to me. You let us stay out on your place all the time. That's enough. It's my favorite place in the world."

"I know you love it, son. And that's what I want to tell you.

My son Vance don't appreciate it like you do, never did, not like you and not like Rex did when he was younger. I've heard him talking on the phone about selling it or something. Makes me angry, but he's my son. And it'll be his one day. Soon. As long as I'm alive, you can do as you like out there. But I can't promise anything when I'm gone. I'm sorry."

"I understand, Papa Mac. Don't you worry about that." A shaky whisper was all I could muster, and I was ashamed of how I felt. This dying man was apologizing to a kid about him losing his hunting and fishing rights, of all things. I guess he knew it meant much more than that to me, but I felt no less guilty for my selfish feelings.

Papa Mac grabbed my right hand and stared intently at my knuckles. I said nothing, perplexed. "Just looking to see if it was made of steel." There was a twinkle in his eye. "From the bruise on VJ's chin awhile back, I thought it must be."

"Papa Mac, about that. I'm so sorry, I—"

"Shhh, don't you worry. Maybe he'll learn his lesson. Maybe not. I fear VJ is headed down the wrong path. Ain't all his fault, I guess. His no-good momma left him when he was a baby." He sighed a deep, long sigh and shook his head. "You go on now, I'm pretty tired. Tell your Dad thanks. For everything."

The Sandy Hollow Church of Christ, where Papa Mac had been a member along with his father before him, was a few miles northeast of Amberton, where the land began to gain elevation as it strained to touch the edge of the Appalachian foothills. It was a squat, red-brick structure set upon a small hillside, guarded on three sides by ancient post oaks, easily identified by their gnarly branches jutting out at odd angles as if they'd been trampled as saplings yet somehow survived. Two giant brick columns at the front steps seemed out of proportion to the size of the small church, yet the way the steps widened at the bottom, like the mouth of a funnel, gave it a welcoming feel, drawing in all comers willing to take the first step. I had been there once before and remembered the small cemetery was in back, spreading farther up the hillside.

Dad parked the car on the edge of the gravel drive that meandered in an irregular semicircle around the front of the church. Mom surveyed me as I got out of the car. "Stand still." She adjusted my tie and brushed something off the shoulder of my navy blazer as I fidgeted. "Relax."

"I'm fine, Mom. Just not my favorite thing." I had been to a few funerals before and hated them all. This one had the makings of the worst yet.

"Nobody likes funerals, but unfortunately, dying is part of living," she said.

As we trudged up the hill and gravel crunched beneath our feet, I pondered the name of the small country church. It seemed ironic that a church named Sandy Hollow would be on a rocky hillside. I asked Dad his thoughts on the matter, but he just frowned and shook his head.

The one saving grace was that there would only be a graveside service, and it would be short. Papa Mac had apparently told the preacher he would come back and haunt him if he turned his funeral into a sermon. I smiled at the idea of Papa Mac sternly lecturing the minister, but it died as I remembered the skeleton in his barn and wondered whether hauntings were a real thing.

I lingered at the outer edge of the growing crowd, figuring I'd wait until the minister assumed his position before I claimed mine near my parents. A meadowlark broke out in song nearby, perched on one of the twenty-foot cedars lining the edge of the cemetery, its yellow breast shining against the deep green of the conifers.

A memory stirred within me. What was up with the birds at this place? The last time I had been there was for Mat MacIntosh's funeral, what, seven or eight years earlier? I had only vague memories of Papa Mac's wife, but I did recall as a child visiting her and being fascinated with a wind-up birdcage she kept in what she called the parlor. Insert the key, crank it several times, and a beautiful yellow bird sang better than, and moved as well as, any living bird I'd ever seen. I would do it over and over, mesmerized. Wind, watch and listen, repeat.

"It's an antique," Mat had told me. "My mother brought it from Germany. Don't know if it's worth anything, but I like it. Your daddy used to do the same thing when he'd come over as a young boy." It was always hard for me to imagine my father as a little boy.

The memory might have been lost, but at her funeral a bright yellow bird with black markings, similar to the one from her cage, had lit on a branch near me and sung for a minute, darting his head back and forth as if he were looking for something or someone. I couldn't help but think of the bird as some of Mat's family, searching for her. I discovered later in my *World Book Encyclopedia* at home that it was a goldfinch in summer plumage. Mat had died in December.

The meadowlark was almost as out of place as the goldfinch had been. It was common for me to see them in prairies and fields such as those at Papa Mac's but not on wooded hillsides.

"What's up, hotshot?" The meadowlark flew away as I turned to see VJ leaning against another cedar behind me. He was dressed similar to the way he had been at the party, with a pastel T-shirt, light gray jacket, black jeans, and black loafers with no socks. "You taking up bird watching?" he sneered.

"Maybe. Cool-looking bird is all. Actually reminded me of that wind-up birdcage your grandmother used to have."

"That stupid old thing? Probably threw it away. Been cleaning out some junk from the house the past few weeks."

It pained me to contemplate how little regard VJ seemed to have for the things his family obviously cherished, from mechanical music trinkets to large farms. "Sorry about Papa Mac." I tried to take the high road.

"Papaw to me. Paul to everybody else. Nobody called him Papa Mac but y'all."

"Well, sorry anyway."

"I bet you are. Worried about my dad selling it, I know. Y'all ain't nothing but, what's it called? Squatters. Yeah that's it. Same thing you do when you take a dump. Squat." He laughed, amused at his own play on words. "Does your toilet belong to you, or do you just use somebody else's?"

"Look VJ, I'm not sure what I've done to cause you harm, but if you had a problem with Papa Mac letting us use the farm, you should have taken it up with him."

"Aw, really wasn't worth it, you know? Just bide our time and sell it when the time comes. Why fuss with a dying man? Matter of fact, why fuss with you now? Nothing you can say will change what's gonna happen."

I saw the minister walking toward the tent, and I caught the eye of my mother, who used two fingers to wave me over to her and Dad. "Whatever, VJ." I moved to pass him.

VJ grabbed my arm. "You know I'm not finished with you yet."

I squared my shoulders to him and yanked my arm away, clenching my teeth to contain my rising anger. "I'd say you're right about that, because I'm looking forward to us getting together again sometime. But if you mean you're not finished with me right now, then I'd say you're dead wrong because I'm walking away."

The service was short and efficient, and at the final 'Amen' I wondered if Papa Mac might be looking down and nodding in approval. Before I could petition my parents for an equally brisk exit, though, VJ and a man I knew to be his father sauntered up to us. The senior MacIntosh wore a three-piece, navy pinstripe suit and newly polished brown shoes, with a khaki trench coat draped over his left arm. I glanced at the sun and wondered if the coat was for looks or if he actually thought it might rain. "Vance MacIntosh." He reached out his hand. "I don't believe we've officially met." I looked him in the eye like I'd been taught, shook his hand firmly, and introduced myself.

"Son, you remember Vance, Papa Mac's son," Dad said, "and this is his grandson here, Vance Jr."

"Yessir, I know. I believe his *friends* call him VJ."

Vance turned to my mother. "Beth Anne. It's been a long time. You look stunning as ever."

Stunning?

Mom glanced toward the ground for a split second before looking up and eyeing Vance without wavering. She slipped her hand into the crook of Dad's arm. "It has been a long time, Vance. I'm sorry about your father."

"We are all sorry, Vance," Dad said. "He was a good friend to my father and to us."

Vance's eyes narrowed. "He will be ... missed." He tapped his index finger on his lips and then pointed it in Dad's general direction before dropping his hand to his side.

"Something else we need to discuss?" Dad was never one to beat around the bush.

"Oh, I don't think there's anything for you and me to *discuss*," Vance said. "I wanted to thank you all for coming. But perhaps there is something I should *tell* you. I know you and your boy have been using the farm for quite a long while. I don't know what all you do out there, and I'm not riding around out amongst the snakes and ticks to find out. He looked directly at me. "But I do want to tell you, all that could come to an end as soon as I get my old man's will probated. The sentimental old codger put a clause in there about letting you keep using the place as long as I owned it, but I don't know if it will stand up to a judge's review. No matter either way. I've got big plans for it, and if I don't develop it myself, I'm afraid when I sell it the new owners will likely run you off."

"Nobody has to run anybody off, Vance," Dad said. "I haven't been over there in years, but Case does enjoy it. But if you say the word, he will stay away."

I expected my days of using Papa Mac's farm to come to an abrupt end right then and there. I knew my father well enough to know that violating his promise given to another man under such a circumstance would not be an option.

But Vance backed off. "Nah, no need in that. Could take a few weeks, few months maybe. I'll let you know. Just don't mess anything up." He stared at me hard for a second, then shrugged and looked away. "By the way—" he again turned to me "—has your friend, that Perkins boy—no, he's a Masterson isn't he? Has he heard anything from his stepdaddy, Stone? He and I have some serious business to settle. He ran off at, shall we say, an inopportune time."

Dad was having none of it. "You leave Case and all the other boys alone now, Vance. Jack has been through enough. I don't know where Stone ran off to, or why, but wherever it is has got nothin' to do with these boys."

"I'm pretty sure I know the why, I just need to know the where. Who knows, if you help me get what I need, maybe we can work something out on the farm." Vance winked at me then stepped closer to look Dad in the eye. Dad was about an inch shorter but more muscular. He was not intimidated and did not flinch. "Thank you for coming out. Be very, very careful going home. Winding roads up in these hills can be treacherous."

Once we got in the car, I expected someone to offer clarification as to what that had been all about, but Dad and Mom looked straight ahead and said nothing. Finally, I couldn't stand it any longer. "Dad, Papa Mac said you and Vance used to be friends but something happened. And Mom, why did Mr. Vance say you looked stunning? That was creepy."

My parents exchanged a look and remained silent for several moments. "Casey," Mom finally said, "I was once engaged to marry Vance MacIntosh."

ELEVEN

THE purr of the motor was the only sound as Jack and I rode his three-wheeler toward the Hideaway. I couldn't see his face, but I imagined it bore a somber look similar to mine. Unlike every other trip before, this was a business trip—unpleasant business, to say the least. Two sleeping bags, a small cooler with drinks, and two backpacks rode on the trailer behind us, along with an eight-by-ten tarpaulin borrowed from atop the woodpile behind our shed.

An airplane whistled above us, painting its linear signature in the azure afternoon sky, and I recalled a conversation with my Uncle Charlie, who had been a pilot in the Air Force and liked to talk about aviation more than I liked to listen. One discussion had somehow stayed with me, though, my interest piqued when he had mentioned almost running out of fuel.

"You gotta calculate the point of safe return and the point of no return," he had said.

"What's the difference?"

"Well, Case, the point of safe return is the farthermost point from which an airplane can safely return to the departure point using all the fuel available, and the point of no return is the point at which you can't."

"So they're the same."

"Essentially," he said. "The trick is knowing where the line is."

The three-wheeler hit an eroded depression in the field road and jolted me back to the matter at hand. Where was the line now?

Had we already gone too far by not reporting what we had found? Maybe not, but I knew Jack and I would fly right past the point of safe return by morning. Jack had readily agreed to my idea of moving the skeletal remains to a different location, but Abi had wholeheartedly opposed it. Her words of caution echoed in my head, even though she had reluctantly agreed to keep our secret.

Jack and I both knew that once we moved the body, we were committed to our course, wherever it led us. Was it worth it? To keep from getting in trouble for having a little innocent fun with our girlfriends? That really wasn't reason enough, but what about preventing damage to the girls' reputations? Maybe.

But it was more than that. The day we would be forced off of Papa Mac's was probably coming, but why hasten it by drawing attention to the place we cherished so much? Yes, Vance had said it might be weeks or months before he did anything with the farm, so one option was to do nothing and wait until The Vagabond's skeleton was found by chance. But we all knew Abi wouldn't wait that long to report what we had found. And I doubted I could, either. Even if he died of natural causes—and Jack's arguments had convinced me that was the case—Vaga might have family somewhere who cared about him and were wondering where he was.

Beyond that, a part of me believed there was a chance Papa Mac's and the Hideaway could be saved. The longer the destruction of the farm as we knew it was delayed, the better the chances that it might somehow, some way, be averted. If we could just hang on to what we had for a while longer, maybe Dad could figure out something. There had to be a way.

But why did I feel like there was something else driving me, some other nebulous motivation lurking like a shadowy reflection on the surface of Snake Lake, disappearing each time I tried to reach in and grab it? If only I could let the ripples settle, the image might become clearer again, but I couldn't seem to slow down long enough for that to happen. We would soon soar past the point of no return, but I had resigned myself to that and to what I imagined were the likely consequences of our actions.

———

Jack sat on a five-gallon bucket and gnawed a cold fried chicken leg while I stared at the glowing embers of our campfire. We didn't need the heat, but we never camped without a fire. Besides, the smoke kept the mosquitoes at bay. "So." He shook his head. "Your momma was once engaged to Vance MacIntosh?"

"Gives me the heebie-jeebies to think about. But yeah, in high school. They were going to get married right after graduation."

"And she never told you?"

"No reason to. Vance has never lived around here in my lifetime. Moved to Memphis after high school."

"So how'd they break up?"

"Dad. That's why Vance hates my family."

"But your Dad and Vance were friends, right?"

"*Were.* Vance didn't take it well when Mom broke it off with him and started dating Dad. Never got over it. Moved to Memphis, hooked up with VJ's momma, who ran off and left 'em after he was born. So Dad has been the enemy ever since."

Jack chuckled. "So I guess VJ thought if he let that dog eat your dad, Vance might get yo' momma back."

"Not funny."

My thoughts wandered to the other part of my conversation with Vance, how he had offered to let us stay on the farm in exchange for information about Stone's whereabouts. I hadn't mentioned it to Jack, mainly because I didn't believe Vance would live up to his promise, but also because my suspicion that Vance and

Stone were partners in something nefarious would just add insult to Jack's injury.

"Did I tell you what Dad told me about the Vagabond?"

"You *asked* him?" Jack's eyes went wide.

"In a roundabout way. Saw a homeless dude on TV, so I asked about homeless people in Amberton. He never suspected."

"So he knows—knew—Vaga?"

"Yep. Real name was Brendan Perry. Thinks he was from California but wasn't sure why he'd been living around here. Said he hadn't seen him in a while, figures he must have moved to another town like he does sometimes. Dad has arrested him a time or two for misdemeanors. Told me a story, though, about him getting accused of indecent exposure."

Jack made a face. "Pervert showing his junk to kids or something?"

"Naw, nothing like that. It's sorta funny. He answered an ad in the paper about buying a Harley. A woman had won it in a divorce settlement or something. So Vaga convinced her on the phone he'd have to take a test drive before he bought it. He showed up looking normal, but then he took the keys from her, stripped down and rode the bike all over town in nothing but his whitey-tighties."

"I'd have loved to see that." Jack cackled, then stopped abruptly and frowned. "Not him in his underwear. You know what I mean."

"Anyway." I laughed, shaking my head. "He came back to her an hour later, handed her the keys, said it wasn't exactly what he was looking for. Put half his clothes back on and walked off. Dad said they found him walking down the road about a mile away and brought him in. Decided not to charge him, though, since he did have his underwear on. Vaga told them he was just having fun, needed to let his boys get some air."

The laughs died after a minute, and we found ourselves staring at the fire again. "Name was Brendan Perry, huh?" Jack said.

"Yep. That's really sad, huh? To die alone like that."

Neither of us spoke for a time while we contemplated that, then finally Jack looked up. "So you think Goodsen's is the best place?"

"Yeah, I do, unless you have a better idea. I actually think it's perfect."

Miles Goodsen was a local cattle farmer who also dabbled in auto sales and scrap metal and was a minority owner of a fertilizer company. His farm, less than half a mile from Papa Mac's, seemed an ideal place to relocate the body, partly because it was close, but mostly because of its barrels. A few hundred 55-gallon metal drums, to be precise, some stacked in rows, others strewn about haphazardly. We supposed they had stored fertilizer at one time, but as far as we could tell based on our frequent trips there, no new barrels had been added in years.

My idea was to move the skeleton to the barrels. When we were younger, we had erected quite an impressive fort within them using tree limbs, plywood scraps, and broom sage, so we knew they could be used for shelter. It would seem no more unusual for the Vagabond to have tried to seek shelter there than in the barn on Papa Mac's. The way we saw it, his passing was natural, so what difference did it make where it had happened? Or, at least, where we made it *look like* it had happened. If it kept folks away from the Hideaway, the outcome should be the same.

"What if we get caught?" Jack inquired. "We will be screwed."

"That we will. But think about it. All our trips back and forth from here, around the neighborhood, at all hours of day and night, with our little trailer full of junk. Ain't nobody ever stopped us."

"True."

I reached into my backpack and pulled out the antler-handled knife I had found in the campfire months before. I stepped to the edge of our clearing and, with a few hacks of the knife, cut a small hickory sapling to whittle on. I tested the feel of the knife in my hand, admiring how perfectly the antler handle fit against my palm, the way the tine at the end overlapped and protected my fifth finger, angling back toward the blade. I shaved a couple of hairs off my fore-arm to test its sharpness and marveled at how well it held its edge. I noticed Jack watching me. "Wow. Nice knife. Is that an Old Timer?"

"No, it's a Case." I smiled, and Jack rolled his eyes at my pun. "I think it's custom made. Here." I tossed it toward him, flicking my wrist slightly so the blade would flip slowly back toward me. He didn't flinch, reaching out to snatch it from the air perfectly by its handle.

"Where'd you find it?" Jack rubbed the charred part of the handle with his thumb.

"Who says I found it?"

"Okay then. Where'd you *get* it?"

"I never told you?"

"If you told me, I wouldn't be asking you now."

I frowned at Jack and gestured vaguely past Snake Lake. "Found it down there in the bottom awhile back." It wasn't hard to come up with reasons not to tell Jack I'd found the knife in the campfire. For one, Jack might think it morbid for me to knowingly be carrying a dead man's blade. And I had to admit, it probably was. Then there was the fact I had broken our pact and used our boat with Abi right before I found it. Jack and Jet still didn't know about that. Plus, Jack was being a wise guy.

"What will you take for it?"

"I don't want to sell it. This is a cool knife. Never seen one like it."

"I know, that's why I wanna buy it from you."

Even if I had wanted to sell it, I didn't want to sell it to Jack. His mom was back working two jobs again, and I knew money must be tight. "Tell you what. Just take it. We'll work out a deal later. Consider it yours for now." What he didn't know wouldn't hurt him. I felt better already.

"Suit yourself." He hurriedly slid the knife into his backpack and walked over to the Hideaway. "I'm going to sleep. See you in a few hours. Set the clock, will ya?"

"Got it." I pulled the windup alarm clock from my bag and set it for 2:00 a.m., though I doubted I would even need it. The prospects of finding sleep seemed remote at best.

"Case. Case! Wake up!" I forced my eyes open, startled. Jack was kicking my lawn chair. For a moment, I was disoriented to place and circumstance, and worst of all, time—confused by the beams of amber light filtering through dense foliage to our east and the calls of shapeless birds still hidden in the grayness of dawn.

"What happened?" I rubbed my aching neck, struggling to clear my head and process what was happening. My watch said 6:56, but how was that possible? An hour past sunrise? It seemed like only minutes before I had been staring at the fire, the idea of sleep unfathomable. Somehow I had not only fallen into a deep slumber but also managed to mess up the alarm.

"You tell me. It's too late now."

"Hang on, hang on. Let me think." Jack paced nervously while I rubbed my forehead and pondered. "Maybe it's actually perfect."

Jack stopped in his tracks. "Are you trippin'? It's daylight."

"I know, but think about it. We've never been stopped before, so why would we now? Plus, in the middle of the night we look suspicious. In the daytime, we look like kids just messing around on a Saturday morning."

Jack paced again, and it was my turn to study him. His reluctance was out of character, and it fueled new doubts in my mind. What about the embarrassment that getting caught could cause my father, given his position with the sheriff's department? I remembered what Sheriff Turner had said about Dad running for sheriff one day, and that thought took root. Maybe we should leave well enough alone and just go home.

Before I could say anything, Jack stopped pacing suddenly and eyed me with a resolute glare. "Let's do this. Nobody will ever know. Gotta protect what's ours."

And that was that. Without a word, we drove to the barn.

Surprisingly, at first glance, the scene was not much different than what I envisioned it would look like in the daylight—a conglomeration of upturned hay, bones, and leaves blown in over time through a hole in the tin roof. I couldn't help but shudder, though, not from fear of being caught but because of the very *idea* of what we were doing. Were we really going to gather up the remains of a human being—a real person we knew, not some Neanderthal fossil at an archeological dig—and move them?

Jack answered my unspoken question by unfolding the tarp, and I helped him spread it beside the skeleton. We had already discussed our plan—just get it over with. Although we did not want to leave any evidence to be easily discovered later, there was no point in being overly methodical. The bones would not be in any type of anatomical arrangement, as animals had likely scavenged the body at some point. In fact, we figured it probable that some parts had been dragged out of the barn into the surrounding tangles of Johnson grass and Chinese privet.

I couldn't remember how many bones were in the human

body and briefly wished Jet had come, because he would know. No matter. If things went according to plan, any bones in the bushes could remain there forever, especially if it was never known that someone had died nearby.

I was afraid that deep in the hay we might find tissue remnants, but thankfully that was not the case. Some of the bones were still joined, though. Were they ligaments or tendons? I couldn't remember and felt a surge of guilt for even trying, as if this were just a homework assignment and not a real person. An unfortunate, miserable person who had died alone in a rotten barn.

Then something caught my eye. Clearly out of place. A small white bead, the size of a pea but almost perfectly spherical, lying amongst the debris. Further inspection revealed four or five more, each identical to the first.

"What do you make of these?" I asked, holding them in my hand.

"No idea. What difference does it make?"

"Just looks out of place is all. Nothing else here like that, nothing manmade. Have you noticed there's no clothes here?"

"Yeah, but you know he did that. Remember the Harley story?"

"Yeah, but out here?"

"Maybe animals drug them out of here, or maybe they got wet or something and he was trying to dry them out but never made it back to wherever they were. Or maybe he was crazy as a run-over road lizard. Who knows?"

"Could be, but you'd think we'd have found them somewhere around. Maybe they rotted already over the winter. But why these white beads?"

"Man, I don't know," Jack said. "All I know is I want to get this over with."

"Okay, let's finish. That's all the obvious stuff. Kick the hay around and make sure we didn't miss anything. Anything outside will get overgrown eventually, and anyone other than an anthropologist will assume what they find is just part of a wild animal or dog or something."

I stuffed the white beads into my jeans pocket, my uncertainty as to why I felt compelled to save them equaled by certainty that I did not like having questions without logical explanations. Unfortunately, Mr. Brendan Perry would never be able to provide us that information.

———

POSTED: NO TRESPASSING VIOLATORS WILL BE PROSECUTED.

"Great." Jack slammed the chain and padlock against the aluminum gate. "Just our luck."

The access points to Papa Mac's farm had always been either unlocked or unobstructed, but the neon-orange-lettered sign on the other side of the creosote post reminded us that Papa Mac was dead, Vance MacIntosh was in charge, and the rules had obviously changed. Our trailer with its macabre contents was only thirty feet from the road that would take us straight to Goodsen's, but we might as well have been five miles away.

"Now what?" I leaned on the gate and clutched it tightly as if my angst might cause it to magically open. I shook it in frustration. "We should've checked first. Our only choice is to go all the way back around to the other gate. But even if we can get through the mud hole and get out the gate, we'll have to drive right through the middle of two neighborhoods."

"We can get through the mud hole," Jack said. "I'll drive this bad boy through it like a monster truck. Bigfoot ain't got nothing on me."

Just as I turned away from the gate, a vehicle passed on the

road, then came to a sudden stop. Windows down with stereo blar-
ing, its sub-woofer thumped so loud I looked for the pines around
us to tremble. The engine slowed, then revved. Backing up.

"Hurry up," Jack hissed. "It's VJ."

I glanced over my shoulder as I hustled to the three-wheeler
and could see that Jack was clearly correct. Vance Jr.'s black Camaro had backed up and was now turning left off the road to pull
up to the gate, at first spinning the gray slag gravel behind its back
tires, then crunching it beneath them as it pulled to a stop.

Two car doors slammed, then VJ called out. "Hey girls, where
you headed in such a hurry? Looks like your rig don't know if it's
coming or going."

I then saw that Jack, in his haste to back up and escape, had
jackknifed the trailer behind the three-wheeler. "You talk to him
while I get us turned around," he whispered to me.

I turned back to face VJ and noticed Blake Frierson standing
beside him, as vacuous and gargantuan as I remembered him from
our last encounter. Peering across the horizontal bars of the gate,
I contemplated the irony. Today the bad guys had the good guys
locked up. "We're just out taking a Saturday morning ride."

"Looks like you've got quite a load there. Stealing from my
property?"

"VJ, unless you've recently taken up camping, you'll know
none of that stuff is yours."

"I'll be the judge of that. What you doing camping on my land?"

"You know your dad said we could. You heard him at the funeral."

"I heard him tell you he might let you keep hanging out here
if y'all would come up with some useful info about where Stone
got off to. He owes us money, needs to settle up. But far as I know,
you guys haven't told us diddly. So I'd say you've about worn out
your welcome."

"Well, I'll let your dad decide that. Hey, maybe *he's* got something to do with Stone leaving, huh? You know what they say about a stink—the smeller's the feller." I looked back to see that Jack had straightened the trailer and backed it off the field road, perpendicular to it so he could go either direction, through the gate or back the way we had come. Jack was off the three-wheeler, walking our way. What was he was up to?

"Well, well, well. Loser number two, step right up. It's your turn to play get off my land and give back whatever it is you're stealing."

It suddenly occurred to me that we hadn't really even needed the trailer. We could have wrapped the remains up and crammed them semi-inconspicuously onto the equipment rack of the three wheeler with little difficulty. Jack had suggested putting it all on the trailer, and I had never considered otherwise. *Too late now, dummies.* I wanted to kick both of us.

"I heard Case tell you, we ain't stole nothing. Just moving our camping stuff. But since you're into game show make-believe, then how about *Let's Make A Deal?*"

"You ain't in no position to make a deal." VJ cocked his head back warily.

"Wrong, I think we are. Here it is. Behind door number one: You leave us alone, and we'll turn around and go back the way we came. If you try to follow, it'll take you a minute to open that gate, and we'll be gone. But if you come anyway, I'll gun that Big Red, trailer and all, and take it through every mud hole and ditch on this property. Feel free to try to follow in your freshly waxed Camaro if you want to, with those slick street tires on fifteen-inch wheels. Your other option is door number two: You open the gate and let us through, and we'll show you what's in the trailer before we go on our way."

"Jack." I grunted, under my breath. He winked, and I knew

he had a plan. I just hoped this one was better than some of his others.

Without saying a word, VJ pulled out a single key from his pocket and unlocked the gate. "Make sure they don't pull in here," Jack muttered to me, walking back and climbing astride the three-wheeler while I watched VJ and Blake warily.

VJ let the chain and padlock dangle from the creosote post and nodded at Blake, who dutifully swung the gate open.

Jack slowly pulled the Big Red through the gate and stopped it when it was even with the front door of the Camaro. "Mighty obliged, sir." He nodded to Blake with a sarcastic smirk.

I stood beside Jack while VJ and Blake made their way to the sides of the trailer. "What are you doing?" I growled, softly enough so VJ could not hear but emphatic enough to be sure Jack understood my apprehension, which by this time was nearly unbearable.

"Be ready," Jack whispered.

Ready for what?

VJ reached down into the trailer and shifted some of its contents around. "Ahh, what do we have here?" He smirked, reaching deeper.

I fought a surge of panic that either Jack's plan had failed or he had lost his nerve and given in, but it was short-lived. "Drive." Jack hissed through clenched teeth as he yanked me toward the three-wheeler and dove through the passenger window of VJ's car.

"Hey! Get out of there!" VJ hollered, running alongside the trailer toward the car. I had instinctively hopped into a driving position the instant Jack had cleared the three-wheeler, and I shifted it quickly into gear as I pressed the throttle. The trailer lurched forward, and VJ dove to the side to get out of the way, rolling in the gravel.

I understood what Jack was doing and swerved the three-wheeler to the right, around the back of the car, the trailer barely missing the rear bumper. As I expected, at that moment Jack scrambled out the driver's side, rolling on the ground but in one motion regaining his footing and leaping onto the back of the trailer as I veered sharply to the left and sped forward.

I drove another sixty feet or so and stopped in the road, looking back. Jack stood triumphantly in the back of the trailer, gloating at VJ sitting dejectedly where he'd landed on the ground. VJ's car keys dangled from Jack's index finger. "I told you that you could see what's in the trailer. I kept my word. You saw all you need to see. Nothing there but camping equipment, but that's beside the point. It's none of your business. Now, have fun. You'll find these behind door number three." Jack threw VJ's keys as far as he could into a briar thicket off the side of the road.

Jack jumped off the trailer and started my way, then stopped suddenly. His eyes widened and his face contorted. I sensed a change in my surroundings and knew what I would find before I even turned around. Blake's behemoth shadow hung over me, his huge paw gripping the handlebar of the three-wheeler, knuckles white from the pressure. His face gave away nothing—impassive almost. Just doing a job. "You can't go yet," was all he said.

"My, my, how the tables have turned." VJ sauntered up to us with newfound confidence and a ridiculous, exaggerated swagger that reminded me of something I'd seen from John Travolta's tough-guy-wannabe character in *Grease*. "I think I'll have a better look at that trailer now. In fact, no, I think I'll just *take* that trailer now. Unhook it and leave it here. You can reclaim it later at a time and date of my choosing."

"Let go." I gritted my teeth, my adrenaline surging. I wasn't exactly looking forward to it, but if a fight was what they wanted, a fight they would certainly get.

"Or what?" VJ jeered. "Blake will break you in half."

Sitting on the three-wheeler, I was not in the best position to gain any advantage on Blake, but I thought if I could get at him from above I might be able to leverage him to the ground. If I stunned him, anything could happen. I knew I couldn't beat him, but if I could slow him down enough, then maybe I could get back on the three-wheeler and speed away. I hoped Jack had my back and wouldn't take long with VJ.

In one motion, I flexed my right hip to get my foot on the seat and leapt up toward Blake's head, bringing my other foot down hard on his hand still clutching the handlebar. I grabbed at hair, shirt collar, whatever I could grasp, and came down behind him, hoping to use gravity and my momentum to pull him backward. He did not budge, so I dangled from his back, holding his collar at first, then managing to get my arm around his neck. Meanwhile, he continued to maintain his grip on the three-wheeler and pummel me over his back with his other hand.

"Stop right now!" Jack's voice roared, a booming authoritative sound with an enraged timbre to it I had never heard from him. Jack had VJ by the shirt, holding the knife I had given him to VJ's throat.

TWELVE

BLAKE froze, and I slid down his back to the ground.

Jack's eyes were wide and maniacal, with the whites showing around both irises. His nostrils flared, and his jaw jutted forward to reveal his lower incisors like a wild beast. "We are going to get on this three-wheeler and drive away," he snarled. "Neither of you is going to bother us again. I am sick of your meddling, and it ends here, or somebody is going to get hurt. I have had all of it I am going to stand. Now Blake, step away before I cut this lizard."

I held up both hands and took one step toward him. "Whoa, Jack."

"Shut up, Case. I'm sick of it. I'm sick of it!" Jack was screaming now.

"Blake, please let us go." I touched his hand, coaxing him to release his grip on the handlebar. "I don't want anybody to get seriously hurt here. Please. It's not worth it. Let me get him out of here and figure out what is going on. Please."

"Blake." VJ whimpered. "You heard him."

Blake let go and stepped back. Jack shoved VJ away and hopped on the seat behind me, brandishing the knife the entire time.

"You're going to regret this!" VJ yelled at our backs as we drove away. "I don't forgive or forget."

———

I turned off the road, slipping out of sight down the overgrown driveway of a long-abandoned shotgun house. Its roof was collapsed on one side, and a gum sapling grew out one window.

I stopped the three-wheeler and jumped off, turning to face Jack. "What are you doing? You can't go around trying to stab people."

"If I'd tried to stab him, he'd be dead." Jack stared at the ground, eyes rimmed with tears.

"You know what I mean, Jack." My voice softened. "I'm worried about you, dude. I know you don't take crap off nobody but back there you, you just weren't yourself."

Jack wiped his eyes with the back of his hand. "I'm okay. I wasn't gonna do it. But I just had to get us out of there."

"Well, we're in for it now. Wait'll he tells ole Daddy Vance what happened. May even try to prosecute for attempted murder or something, who knows? And I think he saw something in the tarp."

"First of all, it's VJ's word against ours, and I doubt it's the first time somebody's pulled a knife on that punk. Second of all, what he found was *this.*" He walked back to the trailer, managing a smile as he reached down and pulled out a box of donuts. "I think he got excited about the ones with the sprinkles."

I chuckled out loud before I realized the implication. "Hey, you had those last night and didn't even offer me one?"

Jack shrugged sheepishly, his grin growing as he held up the box. "Want a donut?"

———

A barbed wire fence with a single locked gate surrounded Miles Goodsen's property. The ten acre plot adjacent to it was hidden by a row of thick cedars and had no locked gate, so we could park unseen from the road and close the distance we'd have to drag the tarp.

I dismounted the three-wheeler and opened the fence gap for Jack to drive through, then closed it behind him. The pasture was devoid of cows and had not been cut in many weeks. Dogfennel, like mini evergreen trees, loomed everywhere above the uncut Bermuda and Bahia grass, its woody stems yanking at our feet and snapping in two as we drove through the high weeds. An aroma suggestive of sour parsley filled the air, and I understood why the juices of the fern-like plants supposedly repelled mosquitoes.

Two minutes later, we stopped at our destination, and Jack killed the engine. "This is it."

"This may be a bad idea."

"Yeahhhh." Jack dragged out the word for emphasis. "Remember, this was your idea. But you're right, we don't want Vance all up in our business."

"Point of no return now."

"Yep."

I checked the twine that bound the tarpaulin at each end and confirmed all was secure before we each grabbed an end and slid it under the barbed wire. A constant survey of our surroundings showed no one in sight, yet as we drug it, I was still glad the tarp was gray and not a conspicuous bright blue like so many of them were. The only brief delay was crossing a narrow but deep ditch that transected the property. Even though our bundle wasn't heavy, the ditch's steep, slippery banks made for an awkward obstacle.

"Now what?" Jack asked five minutes later as we both caught our breath from the run.

"Now we make a shelter. It's gotta look like he was tryin' to get warm or hide or whatever here, but hidden so nobody knows we just now built it." I turned toward a double-stacked section of barrels behind me and motioned for Jack to follow. I wriggled sideways between two barrels, turned left and maneuvered between several more, dropped down on my hands and knees to slide under one lying horizontally across two others, and stood up to my full height in an open space approximately four feet by six feet. Jack was three seconds behind me. "I seriously doubt Mr. Goodsen has been in here," I said.

"Wow, I like it. How did you know about this?"

"Jet and I were hunting over here last year. Nothing was happening, and we got bored. Found it just goofing around."

We crawled back out and scrounged around to find a scrap piece of tin and a jagged, partially rotted piece of plywood. Soon we had a serviceable roof partially covering the hidden space.

With less difficulty than I anticipated, we manipulated the polyethylene bundle through the maze and dropped it in the center of the void. I pulled out my pocketknife and cut the twine, sliding it through the grommets to release the bound edges. "I hope he didn't suffer too much. You know that's got to be a hard life. Just wandering around, no home, no family. Dying alone. You know, Dad acted like he was a pretty okay dude. I feel so bad—what if he has family somewhere, wondering about him?"

Jack lifted a corner of the tarp. "Dude. c'mon. We've already discussed this a hundred times. He's been gone this long. A couple more weeks ain't gon' matter. Even Abi agreed to that."

I glanced around us as if to make sure no one was eavesdropping and immediately felt ridiculous. Only fifty-five-gallon barrels could be seen in every direction. But why did it feel like they were watching me? *Don't be ridiculous.*

In grim silence, we dumped the bones randomly in the space, and I used a cedar bough I had broken off on the way to sweep away our footprints. Jack pulled the tarp out, and I backed out after him, dusting our path as I went.

When I finally popped into the open and stood up in the

bright sun, a wave of relief washed over me. I took a deep, liberating breath and wiped a glaze of perspiration from my forehead. The heat had become stifling inside there. The sun was too high for the barrels to offer much shade, and lack of a breeze made it worse. More than that, though, anxiety had begun to close in on me like a pressure cooker. I just wanted it all to be over. *Only a week or two more.* Then we would make an anonymous call, and that would be the end of it.

Suddenly, before I could digest my last thought, Jack grabbed my arm. "What was that?" he whispered.

"What was what?" I whispered back, not sure I wanted to hear the answer.

He hissed through gritted teeth. "I heard a sound. Right there, up in the barrels." He gestured slightly to the left of where we had just emerged, twenty feet away.

And then I heard it too.

THIRTEEN

S OMETIMES, if a stout wind is blowing just right, one cannot hear a person shouting from twenty feet away, much less discern what is being said. On the other hand, if the air is calm enough and one is still enough, even the whispered murmur of viscera can be distinctly clear from the same distance. It is a sound you don't spend much time thinking about and seldom notice, except maybe in church, or when you're quiet late at night in the bed. And, when you are mistakenly convinced you are alone in a place and circumstance you desperately want to keep secret. Then, the cause of the sound you never really thought about before becomes as obvious as the source of the morning light. Jet would tell me later that *borborygmi* is the medical term for a stomach growl. *Disaster* was the word that came to my mind when I heard it. Someone was watching us.

"Somebody's there." I broke left to try to get a glimpse of the perpetrator who had been watching us, but instead I only saw a fragment of a shadow. Jack dove into the midst of the barrels where we had just been, and I heard empty drums clattering against each other with a sound like distant thunder as he struggled to find a way to the spy. To Jack's left and in front of me, the sound of disappearing footsteps scratched the packed earth, but I heard no barrels banging. *He's running on a path in there.* I hurdled over the first drum I found that didn't have another stacked upon it, not knowing where I'd land, and was relieved to indeed find an open space beyond it. There, a narrow corridor between the barrels led away from us.

"Jack, circle around to the south and cut him off!" The barrels created a veritable maze, and what appeared a straight path at first became ten different possibilities. I decided our best chance was out in the open, so I took what looked like the easiest way out. I burst into the open pasture and scanned every direction, seeing nothing.

Jack emerged at nearly the instant I did. The terrain sloped upward to my left and downward in front of me and to the right. If our unwelcome visitor had gone left, I would already be able to see him above me, so my natural instincts took me at a forty-five degree angle to the right, running as fast as I could while still being able to survey my surroundings. Jack was right beside me. Suddenly, just ahead where the terrain dipped even lower, I glimpsed the top of a person's head bobbing above a patch of broom sedge as he ran. The head disappeared as quickly as it had appeared. "There he is!"

Jack and I doubled our pace, dodging the spiny leaves and purple blooms of musk thistle, hurdling the ubiquitous cow-patties, and fighting through clawing branches of pervasive briars, all the while bracing ourselves for whatever was about to happen when we overran our target. After surging forward seventy-five yards or so, we checked up and stopped, chests heaving.

"You see him?" Jack had his hands on his knees, breathing heavily. The sun was high now, merciless in its onslaught. Drops of sweat covered Jack's face and slid onto his already-drenched shirt. I was faring no better.

"No, but this is where he was. Right here." I kicked at a clump of sedge, or sage grass as we called it.

"He couldn't have disappeared. There's nowhere to go without us seeing him."

Then it hit me. "Aw, no. No. Hold on a second." I turned to my right, sprinted past Jack through a thick patch of sage and dropped into the deep ditch we had crossed on the way in. It ran parallel to the direction Jack and I had been running, and we had failed to factor it into our pursuit.

I climbed back out and gazed as far as I could see behind us, past the barrels toward the road. "Look, Jack. He doubled back on us." Approximately three hundred yards away, a figure climbed out of the ditch and moved toward a group of trees between it and the road. I was almost certain he stopped, looked back, and nodded at us before turning and melting into the shadows.

"You guys are crazy. I want noooo part of this." Jet toed the grass of the open lot behind his house, staining his shoe. He looked around suspiciously and hissed through clenched teeth. "You can't just go moving dead bodies around. Unbelievable."

"I know, Jet, it sounds crazy," I said. "But it's not like we killed the guy. Poor dude just wandered in there and died. We're just trying to stay *out* of trouble, not get *in* it."

"That's the stupidest thing I've ever heard. If you'd just left it alone a week or two nobody would have known. Now you're *making* trouble."

"Well," I said, "it would have brought Vance and VJ and my dad and a dozen other cops right in the middle of our stuff. Innocent or not, you know what would have happened to our Hideaway."

"C'mon, Jet. Help us," Jack pleaded. "Just take a look at it and see what you think. We wanna know if you see anything we missed that will get us in trouble when we call it in anomalously."

"Anonymously."

"Yep, what I said."

"I'm not a forensics expert, you know."

"You're an expert on everything else. Why not this?" I chided.

"I just don't know." Jet turned and looked past me. "What do you think?"

I pivoted to see Abi standing behind me. She had become upset, furious even, when she found out that we left her out of the moving of the bones. I couldn't believe she would have wanted to participate in that horrid job to begin with, but no amount of reason could make her understand our logic behind leaving her out—not just to spare her from the detestable nature of the act, but to protect her in case we ran into trouble. Virtuous motives or not, our folly was not consulting her on the decision, and I knew it.

I had asked her and Jet both to meet us, but she had told me hell would grow icicles before she helped us. Apparently, she had changed her mind. I suspected Jet had something to do with that. I thought it curious that he appeared to be resting his decision on her counsel above all others.

"I think we should just report the body, but Jack and Case are seriously having a cow about it. And maybe they have a point. A week or two isn't that much time, and I guess it doesn't matter much where he's found. So I'm not going to be a traitor. It has to be all of us or none of us."

Jet frowned and shook his head. "I had a feeling you'd say that."

———

When we reached Goodsen's place, Jack and I circled the barrels once to look for secret visitors. They had no reason to suspect otherwise, but we had chosen not to tell Jet and Abi about our encounters with VJ and whomever it was that had spied on us. That could come later, but Jet was already on edge, as we knew he would be. We feared he would bail if he found out how close we were to being discovered.

Once satisfied that all was clear, I showed Jet where to go. I'd already seen enough of a human skeleton to last me several lifetimes, so I left him with it and stood guard outside with Jack and Abi.

"How did you know about this place?" Abi asked neither of us in particular.

"Been playing and hunting over here since we were little kids," I said.

"By yourself, with guns?"

"Naw, rubber bands," Jack said sarcastically.

Abi rolled her eyes. "So if you come here a lot, don't you think you'll be a suspect?"

"Suspect for what?" Jack asked. "Not giving help to a homeless man who didn't want help?"

I tried to sound more confident than I felt. "Only crime is moving the bones, and nobody will ever know." *If only that were true.*

Jack stuck his head into the crawlspace between the barrels. "Hurry up, Jet. You're slow as Alaskan molasses."

When Jet finally emerged, his saucer eyes and ashen face made it clear that something was wrong.

"What is it, Jet? Tell us," Abi implored gently.

"Fellas," Jet said finally, taking a deep breath. "It wasn't an accident. We have a murder on our hands."

FOURTEEN

"WHAT are you talking about?" Abi asked. "What do you mean, murder?"

Jet nodded toward the barrels. "Come see for yourself."

"You guys go," Jack said. "I'll keep a lookout."

Jet turned and walked back in without further discussion, and Abi and I followed. She shot me a look of either contempt or worry, I wasn't sure which. I could only shrug and shake my head, too confused to dwell on it at that moment.

Jet was holding a triangular-shaped bone and poking it with a stick when we caught up. I remembered seeing two of them but had given them only a passing glance before. "This is the scapula," he said. He reached and dug into my back, grabbing a bony prominence to the left of my spine and curling his fingers under it toward my chest cavity, into my rib cage.

"Ow."

"Right here." He ignored my protest and touched Abi in the same place, more gently. Then he relocated his fingers slightly higher up her back and traced a bone out to her shoulder. "This is the same bone here, and the ridge I'm touching on you, Abi, is the same one on this part of the victim's scapula. So this is the back of his shoulder blade." He used the stick to point it out on the ground.

"Okay, thanks for the anatomy lesson," I said. "So?"

"So, look right here." He took the stick and inserted the tip into a small hole near the tip of the triangle. I had not noticed it before, but I knew immediately what it was. A sense of dread suddenly engulfed me.

"Is that what I think it is?" Abi's eyes were also wide and knowing, darting from Jet to me. Hoping one of us would discredit her fear.

"Bullet hole." Jet turned the scapula over and showed another hole, from which the stick now protruded. It was about twice as large as the opposite side where he had inserted the stick. "The hole is larger there."

"That's the exit side." I had dressed enough deer to know the exit wound was always larger than the entry, and I had heard my dad discuss cases enough to know what it meant.

"Meaning?" Jet asked me, rhetorically.

"Meaning he was shot in the back," Abi whispered, before I could get it out. She looked squarely at me, tears now glistening in her wide eyes. "What have you done?"

Abi covered her mouth with her hand and slipped out like a wisp of smoke. I staggered out behind her, evading the sudden feeling the barrels were closing in on me, ready to suck me into their belly with the remnants of fertilizer they once stored. Jet was not far behind.

"Not good?" Jack asked as Jet and I rose to full height. I inhaled deeply, doubting the air quality was any different but knowing it felt better on the outside nonetheless. Abi had stepped several feet away and stood silently, looking away with her arms crossed.

"You could say that," I said. "Somebody killed him. He has a bullet hole through his shoulder blade."

Jack frowned. "How we know he didn't kill hisself?"

"Well, I didn't find a gun," I said. "Did you? Kinda hard to shoot yourself in the chest, then get rid of the gun."

"Maybe he shot himself, and it took him awhile to die, and he left the gun wherever it happened. Or maybe a hunter shot him by mistake, and he wandered in there afterward."

"C'mon, Jack. He was shot *in the back,*" I exclaimed. "And even if it was a hunter, it's still murder, and who do you think they'll suspect first if it gets out he was on Papa Mac's? The only people who are out there hunting or firing pistols every other weekend. Us." That fact made me glad that we had moved the remains to a different location. After all, our whole plan was to keep our involvement incognito.

But knowing we had destroyed a crime scene also cut my emotions in the opposite direction. Besides making my father's job to find the killer more difficult, our actions had the potential to irreparably damage his reputation. And he might just kill me when he found out.

"I think he died quickly," Jet said, softly. "I'll have to look at some anatomical drawings, but from what I recall, the tip of that scapula sits behind the heart. The bullet angled in from the left side toward the middle of the chest cavity. Right towards the heart, in other words."

"That's just great, Sherlock," Jack said. "But I don't recall you having a degree in crime scenes. So who knows if that's right."

"It's called forensics, and I already acknowledged that up front. But I knew enough to know which bone that was, and I have hunted enough to know which direction the bullet went."

I looked at Jack and gestured for him to calm down and give Jet a chance. "Jet, how long ago you think this happened?" I asked.

"Like Jack so aptly stated, I'm not a forensics expert. But I have read that bodies decompose a lot faster above ground than under. I think if it happened four or five months ago in the dead of winter, there'd be a lot more tissue left on the body, since we had an unusually cold winter. For the bones to be as clean as they are, I think it had to happen before winter when it was still pretty hot and the decomposition would set in real quickly, before it got cold. So I bet at least nine to ten months or longer."

Abi turned back around. "Nine months." We stared at her, waiting. "September. That's when I had my birthday party. When I saw Vagabond in the neighborhood."

"Brendan Perry," I said.

"Huh?"

"We found out Vaga's real name is Brendan Perry."

"Okay, whatever," Abi said. "Seriously. Any of you seen him since September? I told you guys somebody threatened him."

"You said somebody told him to get lost," I said.

"It was more than that. He did actually threaten to kill him. Told him if he ever saw him around the neighborhood again he'd kill him."

I remembered Abi that night we'd gone fishing, how she'd hinted at something else but checked up. Now I knew what had been on her mind. Why she had kept that a secret then, and later in the barn, was a mystery to me.

"Wow," I said. "You should have told us that. Might have changed our plan."

Abi clutched her head between her hands and slung them back down to her side in frustration. "Both of you said he died of natural causes. And I believed you."

I tried to remain calm. "Okay, but still, why didn't you tell us he said he'd kill him?"

"Because I hoped it didn't matter." Abi was crying now. "Because of who it was."

"Abi? You know who it was?" Jet asked.

Abi locked her eyes on Jack. "I didn't want to hurt you more."

"Just spit it out, Abi," Jack said, holding her gaze.

"Okay … it was Stone. Stone Perkins threatened to kill him."

Jack was speechless, which was unusual for him. But more than that, I could tell he hurt, like his emotional wounds had suddenly been salted. After the initial shock of Stone leaving, Jack had actually seemed relieved at times, but I knew that the very thing that gave him and his family peace also tormented him. The only father figure he could remember had abandoned them. It was surely a painful paradox. I hurt with him, and I could tell Abi did too.

"I'm sorry, Jack. Stone may not be the one who did this, who knows? Doesn't matter for us anyway. The police can sort it out." She turned to me. "Your dad can figure it out."

"Yeah, we're in over our heads," Jet interjected. "The police should handle this. I've been doing some reading. There's a new forensics technology that uses DNA in criminal cases. It's not widely available yet, but who knows, maybe they can use it on this case."

"DNA?" Jack said.

"Yeah, you know, deoxyribonucleic acid. The building block of the genetic code. They can match the DNA on the skeletal remains to DNA known to belong to a suspect—hair samples from a brush, cells on a toothbrush, something like that."

Jack's gaze met mine, and I knew what he was thinking. "There's something Jack and I didn't tell you guys." I paused for effect. "Yesterday when we moved the, the uh, remains over here, we had some, uh, some complications. As we were leaving Papa Mac's, we got stopped by VJ and Blake at the gate. They suspected—"

"Whoa, whoa." Jet cut me off. "They saw what you were doing?"

I replayed our encounter with VJ and Blake, leaving nothing out, even the donuts. Jack remained silent but affirmed my retelling with intermittent nods of his head.

"Okay." Abi's angry glare confirmed the response I expected

her to have to our secret. "So they saw you with a trailer but never saw what was in there, and you rode off and left them behind, and they don't know where you went. So what?"

"Well, they may have followed us. Or something. When we were in there—" I pointed toward the barrels— "someone watched us. Spied on us. He was in there with us, and we didn't know it." Once again, I explained every detail, hoping two of the most intelligent people I knew could offer some insight into the possible identity of the unwelcome snoop.

"So you think it was VJ?" Abi asked.

"Couldn't get a good look, but maybe," Jack said.

I shook my head. "I doubt VJ would have the guts to do it alone, and if he had Blake with him, why would he run?"

"Good grief, this is terrible." Jet said. "So whenever this gets reported, whoever it was will point right to you guys."

"Maybe not," I said. "I've been thinking about it. Couldn't sleep last night. Why aren't the police here already? I was a nervous wreck all night waiting on the call to come to Dad. But it never did. So whoever it was either doesn't fully understand or has some ulterior motive. And I think we need to find out what that is."

"I don't see how he *wouldn't* understand," Abi said. "You said yourself he was right there listening to you guys talk."

"Exactly. So I don't think that's it. For some reason, he hasn't spilled the beans yet. I just don't know why. Maybe it was VJ or Blake, but it just didn't *seem* like it. It has to at least be somebody connected to them though, doesn't it? One of Vance's people?"

"It doesn't matter, guys," Jet said. "You've got to report this. You're not seriously considering anything *else*, are you? It's a murder." He knew me well enough to know I had something on my mind, and he didn't like the direction it was taking me.

"Let's not do anything just yet," I said. "We need some time to sort this out. If we get ratted out, so be it. Nothing we can do about that, it is what it is. But it'll just be on Jack and me. We'll leave you two out of it and just tell the truth about why we moved the skeleton, and plead ignorance about it being a gunshot. But if we don't get turned in, we need to wait a couple of weeks to sort this out. It's been nine months. Two more weeks won't matter, right? And we just might be able to figure out what happened in the meantime.

"Vance was harassing Stone. Stone threatened Brendan Perry, who showed up dead, where else but on Vance's property. Stone disappears, and now Vance is still trying to figure out where he went. You see the circle? It's all connected, but how? You know Vance isn't searching for Stone out of the goodness of his heart because he thinks he hurt Perry. And whoever knows we moved the body isn't telling, but why? If we can figure out where Stone is, then that will lead right to who killed Perry. And that's all that really matters. Nobody will care about some dumb kids messing up the crime scene if the killer is caught. But if it gets reported now, we'll get drug through the mud along the way while they sort it out. The first thing they will do is check ballistics on every gun our families own and question anybody who's ever seen us back and forth here and at Papa Mac's too. And we'll be guilty until proven innocent."

I stopped and took a breath, trying to analyze their expressions and body language to see if my persuasions were winning any supporters. Abi and Jet appeared indecisive if not somewhat dazed. Jack was the only one who looked the least bit resolute. "There's no doubt we need to wait," he said. "I don't know about all this find-the-killer stuff Case is saying, but I definitely think we need to lay low for a while. We could have just reported it and acted like we found the bones while we were over here goofing off, but now there's a witness who knows what we did. Like Case says, he's not telling for a reason. We need to see if we can figure out why and convince him not to tell on us. What y'all think?"

"I see your reasoning," Abi said. "I'm just not sure it's worth the risk. But I'll go along with it since you feel so strongly about it. Jack, you may not like what you find, you know?"

"I don't think what comes out can be worse than what I already know."

I wanted to ask Jack what that meant but also didn't want to know. His life with Stone likely included some dark elements that he'd never share with me, things he'd rather forget about and certainly didn't want to talk about. I would respect that.

We all looked to Jet, and no one spoke for several seconds as we awaited his verdict. "Jack," he said finally, "if we can somehow find out what happened to Stone and that helps get to the bottom of what happened to Perry, and by some miracle helps keep us all out of trouble, then I guess I'm in too. Friends stick together, right?"

A nod of our heads was all that was needed. "Looks like it's settled then," I said. "We have a team."

———

Seeing the white four-door GMC truck parked in Jack's driveway, I let off the throttle of my Honda 250SX and prepared to stop. The logo on the door panel read S&S Heating and Cooling, same as the one I remembered seeing on Stone's work shirt months before.

Jack never checked up, yelling as he zoomed down the road past me. "Don't stop!"

I didn't listen and instead coasted into the driveway of one of his neighbors.

Jack looked back over his shoulder and wagged his head when he saw I had stopped. He slowed and motioned futilely for me to come on, then hammered the throttle through every gear in frustration as he raced back and braked hard beside me. "That's Stone's boss, Walter Simpson."

"What's he doing here?"

He revved the engine. "Who cares? Let's go talk to Abi like you said."

"Don't you wanna know what Stone's boss is doing at your house?"

"Not really. Ain't nothin' new."

I looked around to make sure no one was within earshot, since I had to speak loudly to be heard over the idling motors. "Really? Is he … your mom … are they?"

"No, dummy. He drops in to check on us."

"Nice, but weird," I said. "Let's go see if he's heard anything about Stone." Jack shook his head in protest, but I insisted. "C'mon. We're getting nowhere. We've heard nothing for a week. Time to put up or shut up. Maybe he can give us a starting point."

"Fine." Jack shifted his three-wheeler into gear, lurched out of the driveway, and accelerated toward his house. He was irritated, but I wasn't sure why. I had given up on trying to understand his moodiness.

The owner of the white GMC had emerged from the house and was leaning against the driver's side door, arms crossed over his chest, eyeing us as we cruised to a stop beside him.

"Hi, Mr. Simpson." Jack's tone was flat and unwelcoming.

From radio commercials, I knew that Walter Simpson's late father had built his company from a single used truck and a plumbing license to what was apparently a multi-million dollar business. "The best to beat the heat and scold the cold" according to their familiar jingle. Simpson was a large man, probably six feet three inches. His upper torso was out of proportion to his lower half, which appeared to belong to someone much smaller. He was thick and broad-shouldered but not necessarily muscular. Striking silver hair stood out above a red-complexioned face, like a man familiar with alcohol, the sunshine, or both. His look was stern but not unfriendly. "Hello, Jack," Simpson said. "Any information for me?"

"No sir, any for me?"

"You'll be the first to know. Who's your friend here?"

I walked over and introduced myself, extending my hand. His thick paw swallowed mine.

"Oh yeah, Rex Reynolds's boy. Tell him I said hello."

"Yessir," was all I could say. I was distracted. *What information?*

"You call me now, like we talked about." Simpson turned and climbed in the truck. He backed into the street slowly without taking his eyes off Jack. I marveled at how he was able to do so without backing into the ditch.

"What was that all about?" I asked Jack.

"Nothing. Let's go."

"Bullcrap. I want to know what he was talking about."

"It's no big deal. He comes by wanting to know if we have information about Stone. He's afraid Mom won't tell him if she finds out, so he asks me to keep my eyes and ears open."

"Why does he think you would tell him if your mom won't?"

"Because he offered to pay me a hundred dollars."

"Seriously? And why does he want to know so bad?"

"He says he just wants to help. Says Stone is in trouble, and he can help get him out of it or keep him out of it. Something like that. He won't say what kind of trouble. He says it's not for us to know, and that's it. It's all confusing, why he and Vance both keep asking about Stone."

He and Vance? "Is Vance MacIntosh coming by looking for him too?"

Jack hesitated and shuffled his feet, avoiding my stare.

"He is, isn't he? Why didn't you tell me?"

"Because it's *my* business. He's coming by *my* house." Jack whirled and kicked a three-wheeler tire. "I don't *have* to tell you everything."

"That's true, and I don't have to help you find out about what happened to Stone. Maybe you don't want anybody to think you care, but I know you do."

Jack suddenly looked uneasy. I had hit a nerve.

"It's complicated, Case."

"Tell me."

Jack sighed. "Vance, he, he says Stone owes him and that certain people might have to take it out on the family if it's not cleared up."

"Vance threatened *your family*? That's low, right there, Jack. You need to report that."

"No." He took a deep breath and lowered his voice. "There's nothing to prove it, and do you really think we need the cops swarming around here? I don't, and Momma don't. Not with Michelle and her … habits."

"Still, that's serious. They won't do anything to Michelle. She's a victim too."

"No, Bud. If he intended to hurt us, he'd have done it already. No offense to your dad, but no cops. Now you see why I didn't tell you?"

"Stone has gotta be hiding somewhere. Seems like the people who might've wanted to hurt him are all lookin' for him. Is there anybody else who might have a grudge, looking for him? Maybe there are others we don't know about."

"All I know is what I saw that night he left. Let's just stick to our plan. No police, though. Let's figure out something on Stone, and it might help with our *other* issue."

"Other issue? What kind of *other issue* you losers got?"

We whirled to find Michelle standing six feet behind us.

FIFTEEN

ICHELLE Masterson's stringy, light brown hair was matted flat against her head. She was barefoot and wore a short, white tank top and cutoff jeans. What appeared to be a new tattoo on her left lower abdomen peeked just above the waistline, partially hidden by her shirt. Part of it looked like a blue flower, but the edges were still an angry crimson. She squinted at us from hollow eye sockets, but I wasn't sure if it was because she was contemplating what we had been talking about or because she had a hangover.

"None o' yo business, sis," Jack said.

"You're in my driveway talking about me. Pretty sure that's my business."

"Simpson just came by again."

"You was talking about something else though. I heard you say police. Something about an issue." She stepped up to Jack and eyeballed him hard, hands on her hips. "What you hiding?"

Jack seemed amused by his diminutive older sister craning her neck to challenge him face-to-chin. "Quit being paranoid. I know when you hear the word 'cops' you wet your pants and automatically think it's about you. But for your information, I was telling Case why we weren't calling the cops on MacIntosh." He put his hands in his pockets and bumped her playfully with a shoulder. "But if you want, we'll get them over here ASAP. Send them back to your room for a search."

She rolled her eyes and stepped back. "Shut up. I didn't say I wanted to call no cops. Use one of them holes in the side of your head for something besides a wax factory."

"Chill out, Michelle," I said. "It's none of my business. I just happened to be here when Mr. Simpson came by, so I asked what was up. I ain't gonna say nothin'."

"What *issue* are y'all talking about, Jack? I heard you say it. You tell me right now. I ain't playin'."

"Don't push me, Michelle," Jack said, his voice lowering. Serious again. "You *know* I am *not* your enemy."

I suddenly had an idea. It was worth a shot. "I suspect Jack has the same issue you do, Michelle. What is Simpson paying you? You know, to sell out your family."

She narrowed her eyes at me, then settled her stare on Jack. "I haven't heard nothing to tell him."

"Maybe," I said, "but maybe he gave you a down payment? You know, a retainer fee?"

Michelle said nothing, her face locked in a scowl.

"Michelle?" Jack said, dismayed. "Drugs? Money?"

She stared at the concrete between her feet.

"Okay, then, it's settled," I said with a tone of finality. "Jack's issue is none of your business, and your issue is none of his. C'mon, Jack, let's get out of here."

Jack decided to ride with me, and I drove my ATV for several minutes in silence before he finally spoke to me over my shoulder. "I never even thought about him paying her."

"Technically, she didn't admit to it. Look, you can sort all that out later. Last thing we needed, though, was for her to be suspicious of us. Now let's go talk to Abi."

I parked near the Rossinis' garage, and we walked through it to the door. Abi's mother opened before I could even knock. The resemblance to her only daughter was striking, but Martina Rossini was more handsome than beautiful. The angular lines along her nose and chin were not as soft as Abi's. Her dark hair, almost black like Abi's, was straight and cut short. Her smile revealed pearly white teeth with a slight space between the front two on top. "She and Lane are out back, by the pool. I took some cookies out earlier. Just go through the side gate."

Lane? Forget the gate, I wanted to crash through the fence. *Lane Buckley, so help me....*

Jack chuckled as I quickened my pace. "Go get him, Rocky."

"Shut up."

Jet and Abi were sitting on the edge of the pool, feet dangling in the water. She had on a turquoise bikini and had obviously been sunbathing. Her bronze skin glistened with tanning oil. The bottle sat beside a beach towel-draped lounge chair a few feet behind her. Jet wore cutoff jean shorts, unraveling at the bottom, and a Great Smoky Mountains T-shirt. They were laughing about something.

"That's the craziest story I've ever heard." Abi was still unaware of our presence.

Jack interrupted. "Are you two telling calculus jokes again? The very thought of a-squared saying that to b-squared is just hilarious."

Jet turned around. "Very funny."

"We talk about all kinds of stuff," Abi replied. "You just never know."

"Well, I'm glad it was you, Jet," I said, turning to Abi. "Your mom said Buckley was here. I was ready to lay somebody out."

"Lane? You must have misunderstood."

I looked at Jack for backup. "Nope, she said Lane," he confirmed matter-of-factly.

Abi waved her hand. "Mom mixes names up all the time. Jealousy is not a good look for you, Case. You knew Jet was coming."

"Yeah, but I didn't see his three-wheeler."

"Always looking to fight somebody." Abi stood and pulled some khaki shorts over her swimsuit.

"Not true. They look for me, I think." I winked at her. "Hey, some things are worth fighting for."

Abi rolled her eyes good-naturedly and wiped off with her towel before slipping on a plain white shirt. "Moving on."

"Okay, what are we going to do?" Jack grabbed a cookie from a plate on a side table and tossed me one.

"I have an idea," Abi said. "Go back to the original crime scene. The barn. Look for clues that might have been missed the first time."

After talking with Walter Simpson, I had a better idea. "Hold that thought, Abi. We may need to do that, but we learned today that Stone's old boss is looking for him too. Jack, what's the name of that guy you said Stone worked with, hung out with some?"

"Dude named Elbert Dale."

"That's him, I kinda know who he is." I crammed most of the peanut butter cookie in my mouth and continued. "Lives out on Goatweed Road. What if we call him? See if he'll talk with us since Simpson won't. He may know why Simpson is looking, what trouble Stone was in, whether he had a girlfriend. It's a starting place at least."

Jack would have to make the call, as it would not make sense coming from anyone else. He was skeptical to say the least, but he finally agreed. After we spent several minutes rehearsing what he would say, Abi found the number in the phone book and dialed from the pool house.

"Mr. Dale? This is Jackson Masterson ... Yes, Masterson. My

father, uh, was, umm, is Stone Perkins ... Yessir. He talked about you a lot, and I was, we were, my mother and sister and I were wondering if you had any idea about what might have happened to him. Like, where he went and why he ran off ... Yessir. That's how it happened. He just took off with somebody ... I didn't get a look really ... No sir, we haven't heard from him. But some people are asking about him and ... But I don't understand. Can you tell me anything at all? Mr. Dale? Mr. Dale?"

Jack slowly placed the phone's handset back on its cradle. The coils of the cord swung rhythmically against the table for a few seconds and slowed to a stop while we waited for him to speak.

"Well?" Abi asked.

"He told me to leave it alone. Said Stone would come back or he wouldn't, but he had nothing to say to me about it. Told me if I knew what was good for me I'd drop it."

SIXTEEN

JACK said he was afraid his walls had ears. My mind raced as I rode toward the dead end of Mathis Drive. What was so important—and secretive—that he couldn't tell me over the phone? "It's what we've been waiting on. Jet's on his way." That was all he would tell me.

We had spent the better part of a week on high alert, nervously watching the news and surreptitiously listening to our parents' conversations. We jumped each time the phone rang, our hearts skipped a beat each time we heard the static click of the school intercom, and we measured the glance of every adult we encountered with suspicion.

The few words Elbert Dale had spoken to Jack had piqued our interest and confirmed there was much more to Stone's disappearance than just a man disgruntled with the work-and-family grind. But it appeared neither Elbert Dale nor Walter Simpson would give us any information, Jack insisted Stone had no friends, and we had no idea who Stone's mystery girlfriend was—if she even existed— much less where to find her. So unless we could find another source, that left only the MacIntoshes, and the last thing in the world we wanted to do was initiate a conversation with Vance or VJ. We had thought about trying to learn more about Brendan Perry but couldn't figure out how to do that without arousing suspicion whenever his remains were finally discovered. And we had absolutely no idea where to start trying to solve the other mystery of paramount concern: Who had spied on Jack and me at the barrels that day?

Whatever Jack had, I hoped it would give us answers. Or at least tell us where to find them.

The shadows were lengthening, not headlight-dark yet but enough that I picked up glimpses of Jet's bright yellow Yamaha snaking through the trees well before I saw Jack's red three-wheeler in front of it. Jack popped a wheelie as he left the trail and hit the raised edge of the asphalt road, and Jet repeated the move right behind him. They veered in opposite directions before circling back toward me and braking to a hard stop two feet from where I stood leaning against my back rack.

I waited for them to kill their engines before speaking. "Y'all fooled me. Though for sure yo' grandmas were driving, long as it took you to get here."

Jack ignored my insult and waved a white piece of paper in my face. "Read it." He turned the steering wheel slightly to aim his headlight at me and flipped it on.

If you won't to no more, be in front outside Dundees
Grill at 6:00 pm tomorrow   No cops, no parents
–E D

The note was scrawled in blue pen on the back of a dirty envelope. Jack said the message was stuffed into one of his tennis shoes and wedged into the space between the carport door and the outside screen door. Someone had rung the doorbell and disappeared.

"Dude knows he can't spell." Jet, still astride his ATV, laughed and pointed to his nose. "Or should I say, 'nose' he can't spell?"

I couldn't help but smile. "I doubt Elbert Dale attended Ivy League. And not everybody can be McKinley County Spelling Bee champion."

"I was not the champion. I spelled 'discombobulated' correctly,

142

but the judge misunderstood me. Said I skipped the *e*. That's absurd. Maybe the *t* and the *e* ran together a little bit, but I said it. What kind of idiot would leave the *e* out of discombobulated? Can't believe Lou Ann Seldinger beat me."

"Focus, please," Jack said.

"I'm just saying, I didn't leave out the *e*."

"Lemme see that again." Jack stood up on his footrests, leaned forward, and grabbed the envelope from me, studying it for himself as if he didn't already know what it said. "Why do you think he wants to meet me at Dundee's?"

"Because your mom works there? Figures you can make up some excuse to get there somehow, maybe," I said.

"I'm surprised he wants to meet in public, though," Jet said.

"Maybe he thinks I might kill him." Jack sounded only half-joking.

"Or maybe he's afraid you'll chicken out if it's in a dark alley somewhere," I countered.

Jack grunted and cranked his three-wheeler. "He don't know me very well then."

Dundee's Grill had once been Dundee's Drive-In, built in the 1950s when Amberton was booming in the years after World War II. Back then, pretty carhops dressed as cheerleaders took orders and brought food to the customers while they waited in their cars. As drive-ins were replaced by drive-thrus, Dundee's Grill was born. The food was good enough that customers stuck around, even when they were asked to come inside to dine. The original metal canopy remained out front and probably helped business. Customers could park beneath it and get inside without getting wet, even in the most torrential downpours.

"Craving the Thursday night special, huh?" Janice Masterson pointed us to a table in the corner before heading to the back for her shift as a cook. "I'll send a waitress out."

Jack and I both ordered the chicken and dumplings special and sweet teas from a waitress with black army boots, cargo pants, and the physique of a Mississippi State linebacker. I told Jack I wished Dundee's had kept the cheerleader theme, but I otherwise struggled to divert my thoughts from the task at hand. The idea that we were meeting with a total stranger for information about a possible murderer who disappeared after most likely killing a homeless guy was overwhelming if one dwelled on it too long.

My thoughts diverted to Jet, who had lost a rock-paper-scissors contest to decide which of us would come with Jack. "Bet Jet hates he's missing out on dumplings."

Jack nodded toward our waitress. "Is that what he calls her?"

I laughed hard into my drink and had to wipe my mouth with the back of my hand. "Speaking of dangerous, did you decide to bring a weapon?"

"My pocket knife."

"Not what I'm talking about. That's like asking if you have on underwear."

Jack cocked his head and widened his eyes. "You never can tell. Remember when you borrowed my shorts last weekend?"

I grimaced and chose to believe he was kidding.

Jack's expression grew serious again. "Dude isn't going to shoot us here in broad daylight."

"He wanted you to come alone."

He waved a finger in the air emphatically. "The note said no cops, no parents, but it didn't say nothing about best friends."

"Truth." I nodded. We had discussed that technicality many times already. "Some crazy people in this world though."

We picked at our food in silence. I anxiously studied my watch every few minutes while Jack stared at the wall behind me. At 5:55, I was just about to suggest we walk outside when Jack said, "Let's go." When I stood and turned around, I realized he'd been watching a clock on the wall behind me the whole time.

Neither of us were sure what to do when we left the restaurant. Nervous glances in every direction revealed nothing, so we finally sat down on a bench at the end of the canopy. It faced the highway away from Dundee's, like a traffic observation post at the end of a rusty metal colonnade.

Six p.m. came and went, and absolutely nothing happened. Jack and I studied every movement around us between shared glances of uncertainty. Nothing. Nobody. Not even a regular customer parked and went in. We marked every passing car and saw nothing suspicious. None even slowed down.

Ten minutes later we decided we had either been tricked, or Mr. Elbert Dale had backed out. "I bet me being here scared him off," I said.

"Trust me, ain't nobody gonna confuse you for a cop."

"Shhhh."

"What?" Jack asked impatiently.

"Shhhh. You hear that?" A soft ringing sound, almost inaudible to us because of the din of the highway. I stood, turned, and scanned every direction. A hundred feet behind us, a pay phone mounted to the brick around the side of the restaurant was ringing.

"There, Jack, get it. That's it."

Jack leapt up and raced to it. He grasped the black handset and froze, looking back at me as I trotted up.

"Answer it!"

The ringing stopped before he could answer. Hoping we had not missed our opportunity, we both stared at the phone but still jumped when its shrill ring erupted again.

Jack grabbed the handset before the first ring ended. "Hello?" I put my ear to his so I could hear what was said.

"You a little slow there, boy. Are you alone?" A gruff, unfamiliar voice.

"Yes … yessir."

"Don't lie to me. I should hang up on you right now."

Jack's eyes widened. He pulled his face away from the phone and mouthed silently, *"How does he know?"*

I shrugged and pointed at the phone insistently, telling him, *"Talk."*

"Sorry sir, no I'm here with my friend Case. He's my partner on this."

"Any cops there?"

"No sir."

"You lying?"

"No, sir. I swear. Just me and Case."

"Why are you kids asking me questions about Stone Perkins? How come yo' momma or the cops ain't asking me?"

"Um, because, uh, Mom really don't care that he run off, and he didn't do nothing illegal so the cops don't care either, and I just kinda wanted to know for myself."

I gave Jack a thumbs up, then pulled it down as it dawned on me that Elbert Dale was probably watching us.

"It ain't true that nobody cares he ran off. Some folks want to know real bad," Dale said. "You need to leave it alone."

"Yessir. We've had some guys come by to ask, threatened us kinda. That's partly why I wanna know."

"Trying to be the man of the house, huh? I can respect that. Meet me at the end of Seder Lake Road the night after tomorrow. Nine. You two come alone or you'll never see me."

"Okay, we'll be there."

"Hey, boy."

"Yessir?"

"It don't make you less of a man if you decide to leave this alone and not show up. Tell the cops yourself somebody is threatening you."

"No, I'll be there. We'll be there."

Jack hung up the phone and broke into a grin. Either he did not share my feeling of foreboding, or he was choosing to ignore it.

"What are you smiling at?"

"Aw, I ain't really smiling. But I do have a plan."

Seder Lake Road was a dead end blacktop off the main highway, running the length of the lake and stopping abruptly alongside the point where the levee dropped off to a shallow spillway. The lake could be seen from my neighborhood but was not accessible by automobile from that side. ATVs and bikes, however, usually did just fine.

This was a night for tennis shoes though. Stealth was required, especially for Jack's plan to work. We knew the Seder Lake area almost as well as we knew Papa Mac's, so our plan was to sneak in early and hide Jet out of sight, so he could listen. Jack figured three sets of ears were better than two, especially since Jet's memory was like a bank vault. I couldn't say I disagreed with the plan. If Jet was never seen, what Elbert Dale didn't know wouldn't hurt him.

What surprised us was when Abi showed up at my house, too.

"Didn't expect to see you here." I looked at Jet and back to her again.

"No, I guess you didn't," Abi replied. "Especially since you didn't tell me about this."

"This was Jack's plan. Supposed to be a secret."

"Oh, okay, another secret? I guess Jet is the one I should trust to keep me informed."

"Sorry, I didn't mean it like that," I protested. "Elbert Dale wanted us—told us—to come alone. Jet was one extra already. What was I supposed to do?"

Abi glared at me. "I'll let you figure that one out." She stormed off down the street, saying she would meet us there.

I caught up and tried to hold Abi's hand while we walked around the block to our destination, but she was having none of it. Efforts at conversation didn't go much better. She didn't ignore me, but her answers were curt. I finally apologized again and told her to let me know when she wanted to talk, I wasn't going to beg.

By eight-thirty, we were sneaking across Brandt Colby's property to get to the head of the trail that led through the woods to the Seder Lake levee. At the end of the driveway, cedar trees loomed large with brushy, low-hanging limbs obscuring the trail from anyone who didn't know it existed. I remembered misspelling 'cedar' in a story I wrote for school when I was younger. I had argued with my teacher about it, adamant that it was spelled 'seder'—why else would all those type trees be around Seder Lake? I was quite perturbed when my mother later explained that Seder was the name of the man who had built the lake a quarter century before, and the cedar trees were a coincidence.

"Why are we here so early?" Jet asked. "Not gonna take me and Abi an hour to hide."

"We're not early," I whispered as I ducked beneath a cedar bough. "Dale is gonna meet us at nine."

"No, Jack told me nine-thirty."

"He told you wrong. I heard Dale say it myself. Ask Jack."

Jack nodded quietly. "My bad. It was nine. We gotta hurry."

Jet stopped and grabbed Jack by the back of his shirt. "I thought it was nine-thirty. You said nine-thirty."

"I *know*. I got it mixed up," Jack said. "Who cares? Come on."

We had one small flashlight but had decided not to turn it on until we were several yards beyond the edge of the Colbys' backyard. We knew the trail's every dip and turn by heart anyway. Still, it was surprising how the blackness of the night deepened when we stepped into the trees, how so little moonlight survived the shadow of the canopy above us. Mosquitoes buzzed around me, and perspiration dampened my clothes.

The trail was packed earth, devoid of vegetation from frequent travel. It turned sharply back to the left, dropped down several feet, then climbed steeply until it evened out on the levee of Seder Lake. A line of trees rose from the slope of the levee abutting the lake, overhanging the edge of the water. The largest was a huge willow. Wooden steps nailed to its trunk and a knotted rope dangling from a thigh-sized limb marked our favorite swimming hole. We affectionately referred to it as the Seder Tree. The crescent moon and a single cloud appearing to glow beside it reflected perfectly on the still water of the lake, the only disturbance being random tiny ripples caused by the weeping of the willow.

"That's beautiful, huh?" Abi whispered, reaching out and stopping me with her hand to look.

"Yeah, it is. The water sure is calm, but a breeze sure would be nice to keep these skeeters away." I swatted at invisible tormenters around my head.

"Hurry up." Jack hissed.

We fell in line behind him, making very little noise as our tennis shoes padded along on the bare earth, only occasionally stepping on a random twig or leaf. Suddenly I became aware of a series of crunching sounds to my right, down in the brush, almost paralleling our footsteps. The hair on my neck stood erect, and a chill rippled down my back, despite the heat.

Something—or somebody—was following us.

SEVENTEEN

"STOP," I said. "Did you guys hear that? Jack, shine your light down there." I pointed in the direction of my suspicion, and Jack did as instructed. Trees and brushy undergrowth with murky shadows beyond them were all we could see.

"You're hearing things, dude. Nobody's following us," Jack said. "Let's go."

Jet dropped back beside me as we started walking. "Did you hear something?"

"I don't know, but it sure did sound like it." I had an idea. I leaned over and whispered in his ear. Jet nodded, turned and whispered something to Abi, and kept walking.

I dropped to my knees without a sound while they walked on ahead. My heart pounded in my chest. I couldn't help but recall a story my grandfather had told me from his boyhood, growing up on a farm in Arkansas. Late for supper one winter night, he had taken a shortcut through the woods to get home from a friend's house. He heard something following him, so he picked up his pace, but it did the same. Soon the thing following him began screaming like a terrified woman. He broke into a dead run, certain of being overrun any moment. The creature was only a few feet behind him when his stepfather, who had heard the screams of the animal and knew the boy might be coming that way, stepped from behind a tree and grabbed him up. The mountain lion fled, but the next day it was hunted down and killed less than 200 yards from the house.

I knew there were no mountain lions in Amberton, but what I didn't know was what I had heard. Or even if I had heard anything at all. It was probably just a raccoon, or 'possum, or even a dog, I tried to convince myself, yet I could not suppress the urge to try to find out. Every fiber in my being told me we were being followed. I squatted motionless for several seconds while my group went ahead. Silence prevailed at first, all except the sounds of their feet, which were ever diminishing as they increased the distance between us. Then I heard it. Footsteps ahead, off to the right. Moving toward me.

Why did we bring only one light? And why didn't I have it? Knowing it would be foolish to tear into the bushes blind, I turned and raced up the trail to catch up to Jack, Jet, and Abi. In a few seconds I was upon them. Jack turned quickly, shining the light on me. "What in the—"

I snatched the flashlight from his hand and jumped off the levee to the right, into the woods, toward the sound of our unwelcome accompaniment.

"Who are you?" I said, loud enough to be heard by someone close by, but not loud enough to carry across the lake and be heard by anyone in the neighborhoods. "I know you're there."

Silence again. Not a peep, save the hum of crickets, locusts, and mosquitoes. I shined the light in every direction but saw nothing but tree trunks surrounded by tangles of honeysuckle and privet bushes. And whatever they hid within them.

"Case, you're losing your mind," Abi said. "Get back up here with that light. We gotta go."

Jack concurred. "C'mon, quit playing games. It's time to be there."

I knew it was useless to protest and couldn't help becoming skeptical about whether I had even heard anything.

Five minutes later, we stood at the small spillway separating the levee from the road. Beavers had built a rudimentary dam with intertwined sticks and small limbs, each with its end chewed into a semblance of a point. Water no deeper than our ankles trickled down the shallow spillway into a narrow ditch below. We crossed to the other side, having no trouble finding high spots to avoid getting our feet wet.

"You guys hide right here," I whispered. "There's brushy cover, and it's in the shadows where you won't be seen. Hurry and *be quiet*. We *cannot* let him see y'all."

Jack and I stood in the middle of Seder Lake Road at the dead end. A house about a hundred yards up the road, the only one in the immediate vicinity, was devoid of light or evidence of other activity. Jack checked his watch and told me the time was 8:57. He stared back up the road, anticipating the headlights from whatever Elbert Dale would be driving. Jack said nothing else, which I thought was unusual for him. I welcomed it though, as I strained my ears for sounds betraying the presence of the intruder I had heard earlier. I suspected that Elbert Dale might have been the culprit, in which case he had figured out that Jack and I were not alone and was likely already headed far away from Seder Lake.

In a few minutes, though, we both heard the unmistakable sound of footsteps coming from a direction we did not expect— across a grassy field at the end of the road—and not from the lake levee trail or the road itself. I supposed it could be the person I'd heard earlier, but because it was coming from a completely different direction, I seriously doubted it.

A tiny orange light glowed in front of us, then a figure smoking a cigarette emerged from the grass. Jack shined his light on the person, revealing a rangy man, about six feet tall but not weighing much more than 150 pounds. A sparse goatee was beginning to show a little gray around the edges, and he wore a red Hogsbreath Saloon T-shirt with blue jeans and boots. He looked to be mid-forties, but something about him made me suspect he was actually younger. He must have parked a quarter mile away, somewhere off Longpepper Road, and walked through the woods before coming out in the small field. "Cut that light off, you idiot," the man said to Jack. "We don't want the whole world knowing we're here."

"Mr. Dale?" I wanted to ask him if he was back in the bushes along the levee earlier, but since he had actually shown up, I knew in all probability it couldn't have been him. Plus, I was afraid if I mentioned it he'd either want to search, in which case he'd find Jet and Abi hiding, or he'd spook and just drop the whole thing. So I didn't bring it up. "Where'd you park?" was all I said.

"Don't worry about where I parked. Had to make sure you boys was alone." He pointed to me. "You said your name was Case?"

"Yessir."

"Case who?"

"Reynolds." I suspected he already knew and was testing me.

"Yo' Daddy work for the sheriff?"

So he did know. I worried about where this was headed but knew there was no point in lying now. "Yessir, he's an investigator."

Dale blew a puff of smoke toward the moon. "What, he got his boy out doing his investigatin' for him?"

"No sir, he don't know nothing about this. If he did, I'd be in *big* trouble. Jack's trying to figure out some things for his family. No cops. So I'm trying to help him."

The man scratched his goatee and scanned his surroundings cautiously. "See, if I was doing something illegal, this would be a no-go. But since I ain't, I guess we're okay. What I do need to know, Jack, is who else'd you bring with you this time?"

Had he seen Jet or Abi, or was he bluffing? "Nobody," Jack

said quickly. Too quickly, I thought, but Dale didn't look as if he suspected anything. "Just us. Just like you said."

"Yeah, okay," Dale said. *Good call, Jack.* "So what do you wanna know?"

I slapped a mosquito boring into the back of my neck. "Why so secretive? Meeting out here?"

"Because I know where you boys live, and it's the best place we can meet within walking distance of your house. I don't want no parents getting on me."

"Do you know where Stone is?" Jack asked. "You were his friend at work."

"No offense, but not friends exactly. He didn't have a whole lot of friends. But we hung some at work, yeah. Listen, you boys don't need to be messing with this. Grown-up stuff."

"Please just tell me something," Jack pled.

Dale discarded his cigarette stub and ground it into the asphalt with his boot. "Shouldn't tell you kids none of this, but you're trying to be a man, and I get that. Plus, you said some folks was messing with you and your mom, and that ain't cool. So Stone was in some kind of trouble, I think. I know he had a gambling problem. Gambled all the time. Some MLB, but mostly football. He'd be nervous as a nun on a stripper pole every Friday before a football weekend. He talked to his bookie all the time, I mean, *all the time.* Got real antsy every time he talked to him. Every time he talked *about* him, actually. I started hearing him saying stuff like, 'I promise I'll get the money, it's coming,' stuff like that. He told me once his bookie wasn't nobody to mess with, that he'd send somebody to cut your nuts off if that's what it took to get what he was owed." Dale grabbed his crotch in a protective gesture.

"The other thing was," he continued, "some equipment disappeared from the company, from S&S. I think a lot of folks, maybe even Simpson himself, suspected Stone, but nobody could prove nothin'. It was *several* thousand dollars' worth. Power tools, welders, copper tubing, even some cooling units, all kinds of stuff."

"So why are you so scared about telling us this?" I asked.

"Because I don't want nobody to know I'm involved in any way. Fact is, I ain't involved. I told you what I know, which ain't much. But I don't want anybody to *think* I'm involved. Frankly, I'd like to keep my nuts."

I had to admit, that sounded like a good reason to me.

"Did Stone ever mention anywhere he might go?" I asked. "Or who the girl could have been that he left with?"

Dale chuckled smugly. "I didn't know he had no girl. I mean, he talked sometimes like he was a ladies' man or something, but we all thought it was a bunch of bull. He mentioned his old lady sometimes." He paused and looked at Jack. "No offense. But I was shocked when folks said he left with a chick."

"What you know about his bookie?" Jack asked.

"You crazy? I don't gamble, didn't wanna know his name. I think he was out of New Orleans, though." Dale pulled out another cigarette and stuck it between his lips. He brought his lighter up and cupped his hand around it, but something changed his mind before he struck it. He abruptly stuffed both the cigarette and lighter into a back pocket. "You boys should leave this alone if you know what's good for you, I'm telling you." And with that, Elbert Dale turned and disappeared the way he had come without another word.

"That went well," Jet whispered as he emerged from the shadows. "He didn't kill you or even assault you. Plus, I heard you got a little bit of info."

"Let's get outta here," I suggested.

"Hold on," Jack said. "It's just now nine-thirty. We could go swimming or something while we talk it over."

"Wanting to show off your Superman Underoos?" I joked.

"Nah, commando." Jack smiled. "Forgot my pocket knife too."

"Uggghh," Abi said, "coulda lived my whole life without that mental—" The sight of headlights coming up the road stopped her from finishing.

"Abi, go hide," I said. "Back where you were." To my surprise, she did so without protest.

"Let's go." Jack said. I agreed with him, and we turned to hide as well.

"Hold on." Jet stopped us. "Maybe old Elbert thought of something else to tell and didn't wanna walk back over here again. Just drove over here since he thinks you're alone."

"Could be, but I really don't think he's had enough time for that yet. I bet it's somebody else," I said. "Jet, go back where you were, just in case."

Jet slipped back into the bushes where he'd been hiding. I decided to see what was coming. I had no reason to be worried about anyone out on a leisurely drive, and I wanted to know if it was indeed Elbert Dale. Jack stood with me off the shoulder of the asphalt at the dead end and waited. I fully expected the vehicle to stop at one of the last houses, or at the very least turn around in a driveway and reverse its direction, but the black Lincoln Town Car did neither. It slowed to a stop directly in front of us, and the passenger door opened first.

Out stepped Vance MacIntosh.

EIGHTEEN

"HELLO, boys." Vance smirked. "Surely I haven't missed the party?"

"No party," Jack said. "Just out walking."

"Oh, so you boys are just hanging out here at this dead end at night for no reason?" MacIntosh motioned in the general direction of the car, and the driver side door opened. A younger man I did not recognize emerged. Marginally taller than MacIntosh but much more muscular, he wore boots, jeans, and a black Henley shirt. A Cardinals baseball cap was pulled low on his head. "We were under the impression," MacIntosh continued, "that there would be an exchanging of information occurring at this very spot, at this very time. Information that might be useful to us."

My mind was racing. I could not figure out why Elbert Dale would have told Vance MacIntosh about our meeting. Dale was the one with the information. What did he have to gain by telling us what he knew, warning us to leave it alone, and turning us over to these two yahoos? "I'm not sure where you heard that," I said. "We were just leaving. Have a nice night."

The man who had been driving rushed around the car to intercept us as we moved toward the levee trail. "We're not done here." His voice was somewhat hollow, higher pitched than I would have guessed by looking at him. "I came a long way to help get some information, and we're not leaving here empty-handed."

"I told you, we don't have any information to *tell* you, and we sure don't have anything to *hand* you," I said, mocking his choice of words.

"Ah, you think you're a wise guy, huh? Well if your brain is as smart as your mouth, you'll start talking."

"I've told you over and over, Mr. MacIntosh," Jack said. "We don't know nothing. Why don't you tell us what y'all want with Stone?"

MacIntosh stepped toward us. "Liar. You and baby Reynolds here know something that will help me find out where Stone Perkins got off to, and that's *all* you need to know. Now I know you were meeting somebody here. Did he not show up? Did he leave already? You tell me what you found out, and we'll leave you alone." He turned to me. "Reynolds, what would your Daddy think about y'all sneaking around in the dark like this? Maybe I should tell him."

"About the same thing he'd think about you harassing a bunch of kids, not to mention Jack's family. Maybe *I* should tell him."

MacIntosh's menacing glower was unmistakable despite the shadows.

I should have stopped there, but I couldn't resist. Another thought had occurred to me. "Maybe *you're* the one who is hiding something. Maybe *you* did something to Stone, and you're snooping around to make sure nobody is figuring it out, or to make people think you had nothing to do with it."

Jack broke in. "We're outta here. C'mon, Case."

Before Jack or I either one could take a step to leave, the man in the Cardinals cap reached out and grabbed me. With a grip like a vise, he balled the front of my T-shirt up in his fist and pulled it upward, under my chin, lifting me on the tips of my toes. I grabbed his wrist and tried to pull myself away but could not loosen his hold.

"You listen here, you little piss-ant," he growled, his voice much lower now. "Vance here has been nice, but I don't play by his rules. I hear yo' daddy is some Barney Fife deputy or some such, but I don't care. It's time to start talking, or somebody is gonna get hurt. It might be you tonight." He paused to use his free hand to gouge his thumb under my collarbone, forcing a muffled whimper I couldn't suppress. "Or somebody in your family next week, next month, whatever. Give us some useful information, and you won't have to wonder which it is."

Cardinal Cap had his back turned to the shadows of the trees and bushes by the lake, so he could not see what I could. He must have read my eyes, though, because he tried to turn and look behind him. It was too late. Abi hit him with a bat-sized sapling picked up from the spillway, swinging it like a softball player hitting for the fence from the cleanup spot. It caught him right across the back of the thighs, and he buckled like his legs had been kicked from under him by an ornery mule.

Cardinal moaned and let go of my shirt to reach back and brace his fall. I fell forward, almost on top of him, but caught myself and scrambled to get away. As I stood, he rolled slightly to one side and reached to grab something strapped to his back. The source of the moonlight flash off stainless steel was unmistakable.

"Run. He's got a gun!" I kicked his hand, knocking the revolver eight or ten feet away, buying us some time.

Abi stood in the same spot where she'd swung the stick, her eyes wide and mouth agape.

I grabbed her arm as I ran past. "Come on!" I looked over my shoulder to the left to see Jack leaping off the road like an Olympic long jumper. When he landed, his foot hung in a vine, and he sprawled face-first, our only flashlight bouncing away from him and going black. He regained an upright position and raced straight ahead, dodging trees and feeling his way through the vegetation to get to the trail.

As we raced by Jet, still squatting in his hiding place, I hesitated. Was he just going to hide and hope he wasn't detected? Or was he panicked and frozen? Either way, he couldn't stay put.

Cardinal was on his feet now, pistol in hand, limping but clearly coming in our direction. On a mission. Vance MacIntosh was yelling something to him that sounded like a protest or admonishment, but he did not check up.

"Jet, come on!" I cried. His hesitation, and therefore mine, cost us. It was probably less than two seconds but seemed like an eternity. Jet finally started running, but I was afraid with his speed, or lack thereof, we would never get away. I feared shots might start ringing out at any moment. Despite that, we had no alternative but to run. Maybe, maybe if we could get across the spillway and up to the levee trail, we had a chance. There, some of the moonlight, sparse as it was, would partially light our path of escape. The down side of that was the probability we could be seen if we were unable to get far enough ahead of them. Off the levee though, beneath the canopy of the trees, the darkness would be blinding.

Our first bit of good fortune was the blow Abi had delivered. Cardinal was slow to get going, and it was difficult for him to navigate the uneven footing of the spillway behind us. That gave us a paltry bit of extra time, but at least it was something. Unfortunately, even with that, by the time the four of us converged on the levee trail, he was scarcely forty yards behind us. If we all ran together, he no doubt would catch us. Cardinal on one good leg was almost certainly faster than Jet on two.

Jet knew this better than anyone. "Y'all go on." he said. "I'll be fine."

I grabbed him and jerked him along. "No." I knew if we split up, even if only one of us got caught, it might as well be all of us. This guy was unpredictable and made a pretty convincing case that he had no qualms about hurting us. Would he kill somebody? Common sense told me surely not a kid, but common sense seemed to be in short supply, and why else would he have pulled a gun? I had no intention of Jet or anyone else getting shot, not if we could help it.

The last option was to hide, but the odds of that working seemed less than negligible. We had no light, and I could see behind us that our pursuers had found one.

Our second bit of good fortune came out of nowhere. Off the levee, below us to our left, a shadowy figure suddenly appeared in the underbrush. "Come here! Now, if you want to get away!"

We all four scrambled down the slope of the levee and plunged into the darkness.

NINETEEN

"THEY were just here. Right here on the levee."

"Put that gun away, you idiot. We're not shooting anybody tonight," Vance MacIntosh said.

"Maybe, maybe not. I got a case of self-defense. Got a ruined leg to prove it. Either way, they got some pain comin'."

"Put the gun away, and let's see if we can find them. They're scared enough now to talk."

"Oh, they'll talk alright. Amazing how tongues start wagging when the pain comes."

"Couldn't have gone far. They don't have a light."

We cowered in our hole like hunted animals, pressed to the back of an erosion in the side of the levee, hidden in the shallow cave by a curtain of honeysuckle foliage. After we slid off the trail into the underbrush, our mysterious benefactor had ushered us into the hidden space, lifting the interwoven vines just enough for us to crawl under. I strained to see the man's face but could see nothing but shadows and vague shapes. Nothing distinctive. It was just too dark. "Get in there." he had hissed. "Don't get out for fifteen minutes, then get out of here." The space might have been large enough for two people. We had crammed four into it.

My right leg ached beneath me, twisted awkwardly and already going numb from Abi sitting on it. Jack and Jet were faring no better, wedged in beside Abi among a tangle of vines and roots. Jack whispered a complaint about Jet sitting in his lap, then something about bad breath, body odor, and fat butts.

I strained to hear Cardinal and MacIntosh's angry jabbering above us on the levee. MacIntosh's dissuading the use of firearms was only mildly encouraging, since his partner didn't sound convinced. The talk of inflicting pain only made my heart pound harder. I was certain that anyone nearby could hear it thumping against my breastbone.

Abi clutched my hand, and she trembled against me.

Then, to my left came the unmistakable sound of our pursuers clamoring down the edge of the levee. Their flashlight beam bounced around, searching. For a few seconds, it settled on our location. Sprinkles of light darted like yellow lasers through the vines and came to rest on us, illuminating a piece of skin, a patch of blue jeans, the white of an eye. I feared Abi's light gray shirt was standing out and betraying our location. I fought back an urge to burst from cover and run and hoped the others would do the same. I dared not even breathe. Abi was so still I knew she must be holding her breath as well.

The light disappeared. I breathed a sigh of relief but still was afraid to move.

"Over here," MacIntosh said. "They had to have gone this way."

A sudden cacophony of breaking limbs and rattling brush directly in front of us startled me. I jumped, and Abi did too, shaking the viney drape concealing us.

"There they are!" Cardinal yelled.

I tensed to run, thinking they must have seen us move.

"Go. Go!" MacIntosh hollered. I then realized no light was shining our direction, and the sounds of footsteps running through the leaves were moving away from us, deeper into the woods.

Then, silence.

"I think they're gone," Jack whispered. "Whoever that was decoyed them away."

"So who *was* that guy?" I asked. "And why did he help us?"

Equally nescient as to the identity of our rescuer, the four of us sat and said nothing for a few minutes before agreeing it was time to make haste toward safer ground. We hit the trail and jogged toward the place we started, in back of the Colbys' house.

"They may be here waiting on us," Abi said.

"I doubt it. They think we went the other direction." I nudged her gently with my elbow. "Or they high-tailed it home, scared you might have found a bigger tree to swing."

"Yeah," Jet said, "that was impressive."

We moved slowly out of the cover of darkness into the hazy glow of streetlights, seeing nothing threatening. We took a different route back to my house, skirting around and between houses rather than walking along the street.

"That was weird," I said as we gathered in my driveway. "How did those dudes know we were going to be there?"

"Dale must have told them." Jack grunted. "Sorry sucker."

Abi sat and removed a shoe, turning it upside down and shaking it. "Got a rock in here somewhere. Anyway, why would Dale do that? He could have just told MacIntosh what he knew. Makes no sense to bring us into it."

"I'll bet Dale thought we might have some information on Stone. You know, he tells us some, we tell him some," Jet said.

Abi slipped her shoe back on. "But that was Dale who shoved us in that hole, wasn't it? Why would he rat us out then save us?"

"Guilt," Jack said

I pondered on those possibilities a moment. "Why would Dale need information on Stone? He doesn't have any reason to want to know. And does anybody here remember him asking us any questions?"

"Only thing he asked was what *we* wanted to know," Jack said.

"Exactly." I was beginning to develop a sick feeling in the pit of my stomach. What I said next would change everything, and I knew it. "Jack, what time did you tell me we were meeting with Dale?"

"Nine. You heard him say it."

"And what time did you tell Jet we were meeting?"

Jack thought for a second. "Remember, I accidentally told him nine-thirty."

"So someone explain this to me," I said. "Why did MacIntosh say he understood there would be an exchanging of information, at that very spot, at that very time?" I paused, but no one offered an answer. "And exactly what time did MacIntosh show up, thinking he was going to be there to get in on our meeting?"

Still, no one said a word. Jack's eyes were locked on Jet, mine on Abi.

"Abi," I said. "when did Jet tell you we were meeting?"

"He called me yesterday and asked me to come. He told me nine-thirty." She frowned at me. "You don't seriously think I had anything to do with this, do you?"

"You tell me. I know Lane and VJ are big buddies. Maybe there's a connection."

"Are you *kidding* me?" Her eyes flashed like blue lightning. "You are so immature. Lane and VJ? Really? What would I gain by doing that? And why would I have *hit* that man if I'd asked them to come? I didn't tell anybody, and Jet didn't either. Tell 'em, Jet."

Silence.

"I don't think he can," Jack said. His eyes were still locked on Jet, whose face was a model of dejection. "I've known him too long. I can read him like a book. What did you do, Jet?"

"Jet?" Abi said. "Jet?" The dismay rose in her voice.

"Jet, is that why you volunteered to stay behind on the levee? Because you were their inside guy? Did you do this?" I clenched my fist, a tide of anger rising within me. "You tell me right now. We deserve the truth."

Tears gathered in Jet's eyes, and a single large one rolled down his cheek. "I'm sorry, guys." He lowered his head. "I never thought anyone might get hurt. Vance MacIntosh stopped me the other day when I was out riding around. He said if I didn't get him some information, things would be bad for my family. Said he'd make sure Dad never got another contracting job in this town. Said there's was a big construction project coming, he had some friends on it, and if I'd help him, he'd make sure Dad got in, might even get him a full time job."

"So you ratted us out?" Jack asked.

"No, I didn't tell him anything else about what all has happened. I didn't even tell him Elbert Dale's name."

"You ratted us out," Jack repeated.

"No I didn't. I mean, I did, but I didn't. I just told him there was a meeting, but I didn't know who it was with. What was I supposed to do? What difference was it going to make? You know, Jack, you never liked Stone anyway. Either way, you still would find out what happened to him. So what if MacIntosh does too? You get MacIntosh off your back, Dad gets a job, everybody wins, you know? It wasn't right, I know, but that's what I thought at first. So I called MacIntosh and told him when I found out there was a meeting. But that's all. I swear. I'm so sorry."

"You say 'so what if MacIntosh finds out'? *So what?*" Jack fumed. "That's not your call to make. Stone was—is—*my* family, not yours."

"Jet, how could you do that?" I asked. "MacIntosh has been threatening Jack's *family*. You almost got us killed."

"No wonder you were so eager to stay back and be a martyr for us," Jack growled, low and threatening.

"That wasn't it. I swear. He said he wasn't gonna hurt any-one, but he showed up with a gun, so then I thought I should be the one. I'm sorry." Jet was sobbing now. "I know I let y'all down, but you have to believe me. I'm just worried about my dad. He's stressed about money all the time, can't find work. The bank's threatening to take the house and Mom's car already. Do y'all know what that's like?"

"Yeah, Jet, actually I do," Jack said through gritted teeth. "Ac-tually, I do. My father died when I was two. And we barely got by before my mother married Stone, and now ever since he left. Isn't that—guess what, I don't need you to help me with this word—*ironic*? But I never hurt my friends because of it. So you take your sorry, no-good traitor, oversized brain and get on that three-wheel-er and get out of my sight. I never want to see you or talk to you again. You come around me, and you'll be sorry. I promise, you'll be sorry."

Jet turned to Abi. "Please, Abi. Can y'all please forgive me? I'll make it up to you somehow."

Abi had been silent. She lifted her head. She was crying too. She refused to look at Jet or me. "Jack, do you mind giving me a ride home?"

––––––––

Jack was slumped into his couch, flipping channels, and he didn't look up when I walked in the door. I turned to sit in my fa-vorite Sacco chair and caught myself when I remembered it wasn't there. "I still can't believe y'all got rid of my chair."

Jack ignored my complaint and kept punching the remote. "What's the plan?"

"You're the one who asked me to spend the night. You tell me."

"I don't know, man. I was just tired of sitting here by myself.

Michelle is staying with a friend somewhere, Mom is closing at the restaurant, won't be home until after midnight. She picked up a couple of movies at Movie Magic. Order pizza, whatever."

"That's cool, I don't care." I tossed my bag to the side and plopped down on the opposite end of the couch. "Look, we need to talk about some stuff."

Jack looked up for the first time. "Don't get all heavy on me."

"I'm not, but I need your help. I need you to call Abi for me."

"Me? Call her yourself."

"I've tried. She won't answer."

"You were sort of a jerk to her. Plus, it was stupid to think it was her."

"How was I supposed to know for sure? Had to be one of them."

"I thought you were smarter than that. Always choose the side of the girl." He frowned and cut his eyes toward me. "Especially the one who saves your butt."

"I know, I know. Look, will you call her for me?"

"What you want me to say?"

"Get her to come over so I can talk to her."

"And how do I convince her to do that?"

I raised up and leaned forward on the couch. "I don't know, use that silver tongue of yours. You know, the one that's always talked us into doing stuff we regret later."

"Hmmph." He rolled his eyes, clearly taking it as a compliment. He picked up the phone and dialed the number. "Abi? ... Yeah, it's me. What you been doing? ... Yeah, been kinda bored here too. I got somebody here that wants to see you real bad, wants to talk to you ... I know, he's a loser. He knows it too ... I don't blame you. Just give him a chance to explain. He deserves that at least, huh? If he didn't, you wouldn't have dated him in the first place, right?"

Jack could sell sand in the Sahara. No wonder he always talked me into stuff.

"We can come over there. Sure. Whatever works." Jack hung up the phone and began flipping channels again.

I hit him with a pillow. "Well?"

"Coming here. Parents had some company, and she wants to get away. Lucky for you."

"You th' man." I reached over and offered a high five, but he left me hanging.

"I did my part, but she's *mad*, dude."

"I know. I know. Maybe you can do the talking when she gets here."

Jack threw a threw the pillow back at me, Frisbee-style. "You really are a loser."

I let the pillow fall to the floor and studied it as my thoughts shifted to other matters.

"What?" Jack said. "I know that look. Getting heavy again."

"I think we need to talk to Jet."

"Why? You can. I got nothing to say."

"Fair enough. Maybe we should hear what he has to say."

"Maybe not. He's a traitor."

"That's debatable, but either way, nothing bad happened, and we've been friends too long to throw it all away for one mistake."

"I'll think about it." Jack stood and walked to a window. He parted the curtains and appeared to study the sky. "I got a question for you though. At Seder Lake, when you asked Vance if maybe he had done something to Stone. Why did you ask that?"

"I don't know, the thought just jumped in my head. That one was probably stupid too."

Jack nodded toward the door. "Here comes Abi."

I met her in the carport. Abi wore white shorts and a blue tank top that matched her eyes, all luminous against her bronzed skin. If she had any makeup on it wasn't much, but she was still stunning. "Hello, Case." Her tone matched her expression, flat and cold and void of geniality. She looked past me, as if she'd rather go inside than talk, but I held my ground between her and the door.

"Thanks for talking to me. I probably don't deserve it." I paused, hoping she'd disagree. She did not. "I just wanted to say I'm sorry."

Abi sighed and brushed past me to sit on the doorstep. "Why would you not trust me?"

I pounded my fist on the brick wall of the carport, feeling like I deserved the pain. "It just threw me for a loop, when I realized it. I was stupid, jealous of Lane as usual. I just don't want to lose you. Makes me crazy sometimes."

"You've got to get past this silly obsession with Lane. I can't make the past go away, and jealousy is not a good look for you."

"I'm sorry. I mean, I just didn't know what to do. I knew, uh, I thought, either you or Jet must have told, and I don't know why I picked you. I mean, I didn't *think* it was you, but I never really would have thought you *or* Jet would do something like that."

"You have a point about Jet. I never would have thought he would do that. I'm worried about him."

"So you forgive me?"

"Let's just say I accept your apology. We'll see how it goes. Have you talked to Jet?"

"Abi, look at me." I squatted down to face her. "Are we okay?"

"I love you, Case, I do, but you really hurt my feelings, and all this other nonsense has me pretty worried for y'all. For us." She tapped me on the cheek with her palm and stood up. "But yeah, we're okay. I am worried about Jet though. I called him yesterday. He sounded terrible. I'd say we should go over there, but he's out of town with his parents, going to help his brother move apartments at college or something."

An image of Adam swimming naked with beautiful college girls like he had with Lulu Dodds popped into my mind, and I almost joked about them needing to make sure they found him an apartment with a pool. But I knew Abi wasn't in the mood to appreciate any attempt at humor on my part. Instead, I stayed on topic. "Jack and I are gonna give Jet a call, see if we can straighten everything out." I hoped it would be the truth.

"Good. Now where are we going for supper? I'm hungry." Abi smiled, opening the door to go inside.

———

At that point in time I would have pulled Abi on my knees in a little red wagon down Main Street if she'd asked, so it didn't take much coaxing from her to convince me to ask Mom to take us to Pizza Inn where some friends were hanging out.

"Give me a second, and I'll be ready." Jack stood from his stool at the bar and moved past Abi and me sitting on the couch. "Gotta change outta this ratty shirt. You and Shaggy-Doo chill for a minute."

"Ha, ha. Yeah, there's one in the cabinet under the TV, I think," Jack yelled back. "Don't take any out to show at school! I'll kill you!"

Abi looked at me with a smile and an exaggerated look of incredulity. "Me?" she mouthed, hand laid across her chest.

"Yeah, you know you would." I retrieved the brown album with a faux leather cover. The layer of dust on it suggested no one had looked through it in a while.

Abi flipped pages of the album slowly. We laughed at photos of Jack in footed pajamas on Christmas morning, one of him showing off a car he'd whittled for a Cub Scout Pinewood Derby race, and another of him and Michelle laughing, wrestling in the living room floor.

"Awww, look at this little munchkin." She pointed to a photo of what looked like a five- or six-year-old Jack at the swimming pool. His hair was much more red then, freckles everywhere. He was smiling with his teeth clenched, sticking his tongue out as far as he could between the gap left by four missing incisors. "And who's that behind him with the crack attack?"

There I was in the distance, facing the other direction. I was half-mooning the photographer and everyone else around, oblivious to the fact my shorts had taken a dive at the same time I had.

"I was hoping you'd miss that part. Just showing how good my tan was." There was certainly no missing the demarcation between the brown of my back and the white of my butt cheeks. "How about we turn that page, before you really do try to steal a picture for show and tell." I turned the page, laughing as Abi pretended to try to remove the photo from the album.

Then I froze.

It was a photo I'd seen before. A long time ago, casually looking through photos like we were doing now. I hadn't thought anything about it then, had no reason to. But it was certainly significant now.

"Is that Stone?" Abi asked. "He looks so *young.*"

It was indeed a close-up of Stone with Jack and Michelle. Jack's mom was standing in the background, out of focus. They all looked happy. Jack appeared about the same age he had in the swimming pool photo. It was probably the same summer. They had been fishing, and Jack was holding a stringer of bluegill bream, giving his infamous gap-toothed smile. Michelle was slightly behind Stone, holding a Zebco 33 rod and reel in one hand and reaching around behind Stone with her other hand to cover one of his eyes. A human pirate's patch. He was smiling, something I'd rarely seen from him over the years, especially the last several.

But it was what Stone held in his mouth that stopped me.

It was a six-inch knife with a custom handle made of deer antler, with a brow tine at the end that arched back toward the blade.

TWENTY

IT was same knife I had found in the campfire that day after my fishing trip with Abi. The same knife Jack had acted like he'd never seen but wanted so badly for himself. The same knife he'd pulled on VJ and Blake that day. I now understood why he wanted it back, but why had he pretended not to recognize it? And how did it get in the ashes of that campfire in the first place?

"What's wrong?" Abi asked. "You look like you've seen a ghost."

"Nothing. Nothing." I blinked and gathered myself. "I just feel bad for Jack. Forgot they had some happy times."

"Yeah, looks like they did. I never saw that side of Stone." Abi slipped out a photo and started down the hall toward the back of the house. "Hey, Jack. I hope you're dressed. I gotta show you this. You remember that picture of Case at the pool with his pants down? Can I borrow it?"

Normally I would have smiled at the idea of Abi trying to show my naked butt to her friends while I tried to stop her, but I couldn't get the other photo and the disturbing thoughts that came with it out of my head. I remembered what Jack had asked me earlier, about me suggesting that Vance had done something to Stone. Was that what he was thinking all along, that something bad had happened and Stone was not just hiding? I didn't know exactly why Stone's knife was in the campfire that day, but to say I was getting an uneasy feeling about it was an understatement. The fact that a body had been found a few hundred yards away from that campfire was not lost on me. Jack must have thought something was odd immediately when he saw the knife, but why hadn't he pressed me about where exactly I had found it? I wanted to talk to him about it, but if I was wrong and he was not thinking along those lines, I didn't want to suggest the possibility to him. He was having enough trouble dealing with everything as it was. I didn't want to make it worse.

"Jack won't let me take the photo." Abi laughed, her voice breaking my trance as she and Jack walked back into the living room.

Jack winked at me, letting me know he was protecting me.

"Guess I'll have to come back and steal it sometime," she said.

"Careful," I said. "Show those sexy buns too much around school, and you'll have to fight all the other girls for me."

"Speaking of cheesy, let's go get some pizza." Abi slapped me on the butt as she walked by. "Your mom's here."

———

I opened my eyes halfway but wasn't sure why. Silent shadows danced on the walls, projected from the glow of *Soul Train* on the television. I couldn't remember the last thing I had been watching, but Jack must have turned down the volume after I dozed off. Then I heard the reason for my awakening—the wiggling of the kitchen doorknob. I first thought it must be Jack's mom trying to unlock the kitchen door. But then in almost the same instant I *knew* it wasn't. Too much wiggling for a person with a key. I looked at the clock. 11:45. She wouldn't be coming home for another forty-five minutes.

"Jack, wake up. Somebody's here." He had curled up on the end of the couch opposite me. I had fallen asleep still sitting up.

"Shhh. I'm awake," he whispered. "What do you think we need to do?"

I remembered a night from what seemed like another lifetime, at my house, when two little boys believed they had frightened away an intruder with cap guns. We didn't have any cap guns, but Jack had something better.

"Go get your shotgun." I said.

Before Jack could even stand, the wiggling of the doorknob stopped for a second. I briefly thought the would-be intruder had given up, but instead the door opened and two men stepped into the room. I recognized neither of them.

"Stay right where you are, boys. We appreciate you inviting us in," said the taller of the two as he closed the door behind him. He was fair-complected, slender but broad-shouldered, wearing khaki chinos and a red silk shirt which clashed with his thick, closely-cropped, copper-blond hair.

"Nobody invited you in," Jack said. "Who are you?"

"Our names ain't important," the second guy said. "What is important is that we are yo' special invited guests for the evening," His skin was as dark brown as the taller guy's was pale. He was short, not much taller than me, but thick. His tattooed forearms looked to be as big as my thighs and as hard as the barrel of a base-ball bat. "If you cooperate, we won't be here long."

"I think you are in the wrong house," Jack said. "You need to leave."

"No, we are exactly where we need to be," said the taller guy, obviously the leader of the two. "We thought nobody was home, but this may be even better. You boys might be of service to us."

I slowly backed up to the end table where the phone was, con-templating how to get a call out. I don't remember even looking at it, but the black guy growled, "Don't you even think about touch-ing that phone, boy."

"Now, let's get down to the nature of our visit," the tall guy said. "We think there could be something in this house we need, something that belongs to us. If it's not here, then clues to its whereabouts probably are. Now, we can do this the easy way or the hard way. If you know about a safe, or a special hiding place, or something like that, tell me now. If you don't, we'll just tear this place down until we find it."

"You're going to have to be more specific," Jack said. "Are you here for something about my sister or Stone?"

"Boy, I don't care about yo' sister," the tall guy answered. He rifled through drawers in the living room then lifted a bird print off the wall, replacing it when he revealed only bare wallpaper. "What, Michelle got some reefer hid up in here or something?" He paused to gauge our reaction to him using her name. "Yeah, I know who she is. But I'm not into that crap. This is about Stone."

Red moved down the hall. Jack started to follow him and spoke out in protest, but the black guy took three steps forward and told Jack and me both not to move unless we wanted to get hurt. The tone of his voice and the gun he pulled from his belt left no doubt he was dead serious.

The crash of furniture being overturned intermingled with strings of curses emanated from the hallway while Jack and I stood quietly, trying to appear brave but fighting the inevitable trembles of fear. After five minutes that seemed like an hour, our sentry called out to his associate in the back, "Hey Red, we gotta hurry up and get outta here. They momma will be home soon."

The taller man stormed into the room. "You idiot, no names. I've told you not to call me that, anyway. Why you gotta be so stupid?" Was the man's nickname an unwelcome reference to the color of his hair or what I considered to be his poor choice of shirts for the evening? I suspected the former.

Red turned to us. "Look here, you snot-nosed punks. We were never here. I know you gonna want to call somebody and think the police are gonna come over here and collect evidence and gather a posse and track us down, but that ain't gonna happen. Let me tell you why. First of all, they ain't gonna find evidence to connect us to this." He held up his hands and removed the pair of lightweight leather gloves he wore. He must have had them on when he picked the lock, and his accomplice had not touched a thing other than his own pistol.

"Second of all, we knocked on the door, and you invited us in. Not the wisest move, you know? I can't believe Stone didn't teach you no better than that. Third, we ain't committed no crime. The back of the house is a bit messy, but teenagers act crazy sometimes, huh? Fourth–is it fourth? Wow I'm running out of fingers to count on here. I got more reasons than I thought. Fourth, if you know what is good for you and your family, you clean this mess up before yo' momma gets home. A police search will likely find that dime bag of weed your sister has hidden in her room, not to mention whatever hard stuff I might have stashed away somewhere you don't know about.

"And last, I think this is the last one, this is the one you *better* listen to." He pointed a long, crooked finger at us. "There have been people who have crossed me before, who didn't do what I said, who didn't live to tell about it, if you know what I mean. So if you like your family, if you don't want nothin' bad to happen to 'em, keep your mouth *shut.*" He emphasized the last word and poked the finger deep into Jack's chest. Red then looked at me, making a gesture like he was sealing his lips, followed by a slashing motion across his throat. "You too, Reynolds."

"We gotta go. Now," the black guy said.

Red used his index finger again but pointed it upward. "Now, one more thing. I figure you don't want bad things to happen to your family. And I figure you want us to go away and stay away forever, instead of dropping by to see if, if we need to apply more … pressure. So, if—no—*when* you get some information we can use, when you find what we're looking for, you call me." He handed Jack a scrap of paper with a phone number written on it, then looked at me. "Don't think you gonna give it to the police and have them track me down, either. I'm too smart for that, smarter than they are. And remember, I ain't done nothin' wrong, nothin' that nobody can prove. Just dropped by to check on an old friend. *So* disappointed he wasn't here. Maybe next time."

"Sir?" I asked, speaking for the first time.

"What?"

"Are you working for Vance MacIntosh?"

The man called Red laughed mockingly. "That's funny. Vance MacIntosh is an amateur. He's just a dog turd I hope I don't step on but know how to scrape off if I do." He shook his head and looked at his partner. "Me, working for Vance MacIntosh, that's funny right there."

I interrupted the shorter guy's snicker. "Can I ask one more thing?"

Red stared at me but didn't answer immediately, so I said nothing. After all, his friend did have a gun. "Hurry up. What you want, a handwritten permission slip?"

"Okay. How does Jack know if he finds what you're looking for?"

"From what I hear, you boys are smart. You'll know it when you find it."

———

Jack and I stood in stunned silence after the intruders left. "Who was that?" I finally said.

"No idea."

"What do you think he is looking for? Something Stone left behind, or something he might have hidden here?"

"Case, I don't know. I just don't know. Stone took everything he had when he left. I never knew of any secret place he would hide something."

"This is getting ridiculous. Every time you turn around there's somebody else asking about Stone, threatening. I need to talk to Dad."

"No. You promise me right now you are not going to tell anybody about this. You heard what he said. I can't bear the thought of somebody else in my family getting hurt if I can prevent it."

Someone else in my family getting hurt. Jack's words and my recent discovery about the knife were like an alarm clanging in my head. But why didn't he say something about it? Did he think that could have been Stone's body we moved from the barn? Did he really not know what all these guys were looking for?

On the other hand, maybe that wasn't it at all. The other thing the photo of Stone with the knife showed was a time when Jack had a father figure who spent time with him, took him fishing, laughed with him. The trauma of Stone disappearing combined with the tragedy of his biological father dying when he was small, had to be devastating. And now he had multiple people harassing his family.

"Case, you promise me right now." Jack's eyes were pleading.

Whatever the truth was, I felt sorry for him. "Okay." I nodded.

"Now we got to clean up before Mom gets here. You gonna help me?"

I looked at the clock. It was 12:15. She'd be home any minute.

TWENTY-ONE

I crossed the living room three times before I finally sat down, attempting to appear nonchalant. I wasn't afraid of my father, but his uncanny ability to recognize lies and unravel them was unnerving. I had too many questions and far too few answers, though, and I suspected that if anyone could help me, he could. The trick would be getting what I needed without raising suspicion.

"What's eatin' at you, son?" Dad asked.

I was ready with my answer. "Nothing much."

"That's not true. Something's bothering you. It's written all over your face."

"Well, I'm just worried about you a little bit."

"Worried about me? Why in the world?" Dad kicked down the leg rest of his leather recliner and sat upright.

"Well, you know, my friends and I talk sometimes about what our fathers do for a living. And I've realized none of them really have dangerous jobs like you do."

"Dangerous? What makes you think my job is dangerous? Did somebody say something?"

"Well, you deal with criminals all the time. You can't tell me none of them want to hurt you."

"Aww, most of them are pretty harmless. They don't bother me."

"But you do investigate murders and stuff sometimes, huh?"

"That's true, but not very often around here," Dad said.

There, the segue I was hoping for. The guy whose partner had called him Red had implied that he had killed one or more of his adversaries. I assumed that since he wasn't in jail, he had either gotten away with it or served some time and gotten out. My gut told me it was the former. "But when you do get a murder case, you put them away. So they can't hurt anybody else?"

"We try, son."

Now ask the question. "Have you had any murder cases go unsolved?" I eyed him closely.

Dad's expression hardened. "Not many."

"But you have had some?"

"Not enough for you to worry about."

He clearly did not want to talk about this topic, but I thought I might be on to something. "Not enough" meant the number wasn't zero.

"C'mon, Dad. I'm fourteen. I'm not a little kid anymore. Can you tell me *something?*"

He sighed and stared past me, as if studying the horizon through the wall. "Believe it or not, there's really just one. I'll tell you about it, and I'll tell you that you don't need to worry about me. There was a case a few years ago. A case that most everybody thought was an accident but it wasn't."

"What do you mean?"

"Just that. Most everybody thinks the death was an accident, but it wasn't. I mean, it's not a complete secret. The papers reported an accident, but our investigation lasted too long for it to have been an open-and-shut case of accidental death, so rumors flew and a lot of people figured it out."

"Who was it, Dad? Anybody I've ever heard of?"

He didn't say anything for a time. The thin line of his mouth spoke of conflict, of a reluctance to share the details of a dark moment straining against a desire to honor my plea and give me a glimpse of his world, to treat me as a young man. I felt guilty for my deceit, but there was no turning back now.

"You remember Sheriff Hall?" Dad finally asked.

My mind raced back to my meeting with Sheriff Turner several months earlier. What had he said about his predecessor who was involved in department corruption but died before he could go to trial? His death occurred under "mysterious circumstances?" Could the man named Red have had something to do with that?

"Yessir, I remember him. I thought he got killed while he was out deer hunting or something?"

"Yeah, that's right. It was 1982. He was deer hunting. An accident. Shot himself with his own .30-06. At least that's what most people thought. That's what we told the news media."

"He got shot, though, right? You're saying it wasn't a hunting accident?"

Dad clenched his teeth and studied the floor, then me, before speaking. "It was not, unfortunately."

"How do you know?"

"Because of the evidence. Sheriff Turner and I worked that case. Night and day for weeks, months. There are details that nobody else knows about but us. I'm hoping one day those details will help us catch the killer."

"Did you have any suspects?"

"Darn right. More than that, actually, more than that. We're pretty sure we know who did it. We just couldn't prove it."

"Who do you think did it?"

Dad frowned at me and shook his head. "You don't have to worry about it, son. He moved away, doesn't even live here anymore. He's no threat to me or anyone else around here." He kicked back in his recliner and crossed his arms, suddenly intent on watching TV. I wanted to ask the name of the suspect, but I knew my father well. This discussion was over.

I certainly hoped he was right about the person no longer being a threat, but based on the way things had been transpiring lately, I had my doubts that was true. In fact, I feared that even though Dad hadn't told me the name of Sheriff Hall's killer, I already knew what he looked like.

The Longtown Memorial Library was just down the street from Amberton Junior High. I had once asked why Amberton's only library was named after another town, but apparently the library had been started a half century before by a Mrs. Berrylean Longtown, who was not only its benefactor but was the only librarian for thirty-plus years until she died. Fortunate for me, even though I despised math and only tolerated science, I was an avid reader, so it aroused no suspicion when I asked Mom to drop me off there the next morning.

The library was a single-story, red brick building with an unassuming front entrance at the top of two concrete steps. A plaque affixed to the brick beside the forest green front door detailed the building's construction in 1933, made possible only by donations of both money and historical documents from Mrs. Berrylean Longtown, especially remarkable in the midst of the Great Depression.

The squawk of protesting hinges and a two-tone bell ring greeted me as I pushed open the heavy front door, and I decided that whoever was in charge could have saved money spent on the bell if they weren't going to grease the hinges. The unmistakable yet welcoming aroma of glue and paper met me next, followed quickly thereafter by the movements of a short elderly lady struggling to slide her chair back from a desk at the end of the vestibule. She pushed herself up and moved to greet me. Even though her hunched posture and unsteady gait suggested she needed a cane,

I'd never seen her use one, and I feared she might sprawl prone onto the floor if she teetered forward any more.

"Hello, young man." She greeted me with an infectious smile, showing teeth that were perfectly straight.

I remembered commenting on my grandfather's straight teeth when I was a little kid and being startled when he abruptly flicked them out of his mouth with his tongue. Hers must be dentures, too, but they looked nice nonetheless.

"What can I help you with?" She cocked her head slightly to the side to look at me because I was much taller than her, and she couldn't extend her neck far enough straight back.

I considered telling her the real reason for my visit to save time but hesitated for fear she might know who I was and say something to Mom later.

"You're Beth Reynolds's son, aren't you? Is it Casper?" She seemed to read my mind. I would have to be careful. I looked for a name tag to remind me of hers but did not see one.

"Case, like the knife. Can you tell me where the fiction section is? It's been awhile since I've been in here."

"Well, we've rearranged everything anyway, so it's probably changed. Follow me." She turned and led me down a center aisle then pointed to several shelves on the left. "Those eight rows right there, arranged by author's last name. And if you want the newest releases, they're up by the front door, close to my desk. What kind of books do you like?"

I was preoccupied thinking about the purpose of my visit and drew a blank. "Uhh, I, uhh, read a little bit of everything. The last book I read was *Lord of the Flies*. It was good, even though it kind of freaked me out a little bit." I smiled, trying to be cordial.

"Ah, William Golding. You should take a look at *Fahrenheit 451* by Ray Bradbury then."

"Okay, I'll just look around a bit, then. Thanks, Ms., uh ...."

"Holst. Like Holster without the er." She pretended to draw a pistol from an invisible holster and fire it at me.

I shot back at her playfully, and she pretended to be shot, feigning a stagger step backward. I almost panicked that she'd fall, but she caught herself, smiled, and tottered back up the center aisle toward her desk.

"Let me know if I can help you," she said over her stooped shoulder. She was a little odd, but I liked her.

I piddled around in the fiction section for a few minutes, quickly picking out *Fahrenheit 451* per her recommendation. I actually didn't care for dystopian novels, but getting it was easier than explaining why I hadn't. I then grabbed *Rumble Fish* since I knew Mom would expect me to come out with at least two books. I wandered back up to Ms. Holst's desk, pretending to be bored.

"Did you find anything? Oh, very nice. S.E. Hinton is very good. I like *The Outsiders* better, but that's nice too."

"Well, I think I'll try these."

She opened the back covers of the books and stamped the due-back date on the appropriate line of the cards glued inside, below where it said 'Property of Longtown Memorial Library.' I looked at my watch. I had only been there fifteen minutes and knew Mom wouldn't be back for at least thirty more. I pretended to look through a front window toward the street where she'd let me out of the car, then turned and said, casually, "I thought she might be back by now, but she's not. Can I just browse around?"

"Certainly, Mr. Reynolds. If you're interested, we have a display of Native American artifacts on the other side." She gestured to a doorway behind her.

"Actually, I just thought of something. Where do you keep newspaper articles?"

"Any particular newspaper? We only subscribe to certain ones."

"*The Amberton Advocate.*"

"Oh, yes. You know it comes out weekly. The last two issues are in the back." She pointed to a corner of the library. "Hanging on that wooden rack with the *Tupelo Daily Journal* and the *Jackson Clarion Ledger.*"

"Perfect." I took two steps in that direction then pretended to think of something else. "What about old newspaper articles? From years ago?"

She began walking toward the back of the library, and I followed. "Well, we should have every one since the paper began in 1938. We also have copies of the old *Amberton Advertiser* articles too. You know, it went defunct in 1935 or so. Didn't even have a paper for about three years there. Anyway, most of it is on microfilm."

This was starting to sound complicated. "Microfilm?"

"Yes, microfilm. It's a photographic media to keep copies of the newspapers and other documents on film without hanging on to all the original newspapers. You know, this is a pretty small library, so storage space is at a premium. We'd run out of room rather quickly if we hung onto all those papers. Plus, the papers decay over time. Come back here, and I'll show you how to use the machine. May have to change the bulb. Seems like it blew last time we used it. And the motor can be cranky. Wants to advance but not rewind sometimes. I'll bet we can get it to work though. I'm so glad you came in. Not many folks come in here wanting to see that very often. What did you say you wanted to look at?"

I had about decided I should abandon this idea. I was going to run out of time before Mom came back at the rate we were going, and there appeared to be great uncertainty as to whether Ms. Holst could even show me what I needed. A lot of hoopla was the last thing I wanted. "Aww, just wanted to look back at some old newspaper stuff. No big deal. I can try later."

"I guess I should clarify. *When* did you say you wanted? What year?"

I knew exactly what year I wanted, but I didn't want it to look like I was looking for anything in particular. "Oh, I don't know, early 80s?"

She laughed. "I thought you said you wanted to look at *old* newspaper articles, from *years* ago? The early 80s was practically yesterday, sonny. Depending on how early you go, what you need may be in this filing cabinet right here. We keep copies of the papers for five years before they get copied to microfilm." She had stopped walking and now rested her hand on an upright gray filing cabinet. Each of the five drawers was labeled with a year, 1982 through 1986.

Bingo.

I wasn't sure exactly what I was looking for, or if it would even be in the newspaper from 1982, but I knew anything I could learn about the circumstances surrounding Sheriff Hall's mysterious death might help me figure out who the suspect was that Dad spoke of and whether or not he was the same person who threatened Jack and me in his living room. How that information could or would help me ascertain how he connected to Stone Perkins was another mystery altogether, but it was a starting point if nothing else.

Mrs. Holst ambled off, and I dug through the contents of the file drawer labeled 1982. Sheriff Hall was deer hunting when it happened, so it had to be during the hunting season, either January, November, or December of that year. I remembered being in the fifth grade because my teacher, Ms. Harrison, had been related to the sheriff somehow and had lectured us *ad nauseum* about gun safety in the weeks following his death. That narrowed it down to either November or December. Since deer season always started the Saturday before Thanksgiving, the first paper I checked was the next issue after that, Wednesday, November 24, 1982.

The *Amberton Advocate* was not a lengthy publication, nor had it been in 1982. Two pages of local news, a national and world news page, a two-page sports section, an editorial page, and the classifieds were about it. So it didn't take long to determine that Sheriff Sykes Turner had been speaking the truth when he told me his taking over as sheriff in the wake of Sheriff Hall's resignation had been controversial.

One editorial from November 1982, written by a man whose name I did not recognize, essentially accused him of stealing the special election by cooking up false charges on members within the sheriff's department as well as other possible competitors. It spoke about what a shameful condition the county was in when certain special interest groups were able to hand pick a candidate and escort him right into office. No names were given. I was no expert on journalism, but it seemed such a vague and shoddy if not slanderous piece that I couldn't believe the paper had printed it.

The next few issues contained nothing about Sheriff Hall but did mention some drug busts, DUI arrests, and an investigation into a robbery of a pawn shop where the owner had shot at the perpetrator as he ran out the door. A photograph accompanying the last story caught my eye. There was Dad, watching while another man used a dog to search a field. I could see Sheriff Turner, out of focus in the background, pointing in a different direction. The next week's paper had a front page story about the man being found half a mile away by the dog, hiding under the shell of a child's turtle-shaped sandbox. Nothing about Sheriff Hall though.

A search of the remainder of the 1982 newspapers revealed nothing. Had I missed something? Dad had said it happened in

1982, and I knew what grade I was in when it happened, so it *had* to be there. I glanced at my watch. I was running out of time. Mom would be back soon, and I had no idea how to explain what I was doing. I started back at the beginning, rapidly but carefully flipping back through the six issues, and had no better luck.

Then, I had an idea. I left the 1982 issues on the table and quickly opened the 1983 drawer. The first issue, on January 5, had it on the front page:

Former Sheriff Killed in Hunting Tragedy

Former McKinley County Sheriff Alton Hall was found dead Saturday, December 31, 1982, on his family farm in the Willow Grove community. The retired sheriff's family became alarmed when Hall, who was hunting alone, failed to return home Saturday night. After a brief search, his son-in-law found him dead near his truck, the apparent victim of an accidental self-inflicted gunshot wound.

"We lost an important member of our community today," newly-elected Sheriff Sykes Turner said. "He served this county honorably for twenty-six years, and it is tragic this has happened. The prayers of the department go up for his family and close friends."

Hall resigned from the sheriff's department in April amid controversy and accusations of corruption within the department. He was charged with embezzlement and drug trafficking, and his case was scheduled to be presented to a grand jury in February.

Sheriff Turner, when asked if foul play was suspected, responded, "It is against department policy to comment on ongoing investigations. As with any unexpected death, we will investigate the circumstances of this accident thoroughly and completely. At the present time, however, we are treating this as an accidental death."

Several other articles accompanied the front page story, detailing the sheriff's years within the department and the circumstances surrounding his resignation. The next issue of the paper had a three paragraph follow-up article about the accident, with a single quote from Sheriff Turner stating that "nothing has changed" in the department's investigation of the matter and no other mention of the possibility of homicide. Subsequent issues were silent. The frenzy over the death of Alton Hall had settled as quickly as it had begun.

The media had treated the death as an accident, just as Dad had said. But he was certain it was no accident and even knew who the killer was. Nothing I had read, though, put me any closer to knowing whether or not the person who had harassed Jack and me was somehow connected. What to do now?

I was at a loss and was out of time. I would have to find the information some other way. I folded up the papers from early 1983 and returned them to the appropriate drawer. As I began folding up the 1982 issues, a familiar name in the print caught my eye. It was from the article about the capture of the pawn shop robber. The name Reynolds jumped out at me, as one's own name will often do from a list. Out of curiosity more than anything, I read to see what it was saying about my father.

"Give credit where credit is due," chief investigator Rex Reynolds said. "Our canine unit was the key to breaking this case. That dog is pretty special. He is a Belgian Malinois, just like the Secret Service uses. I can't deny it. Deputy Redmond Patridge has done a nice job with him."

I read it once, then again to figure out what bothered me about it. Did Dad sound reluctant in his praise for the deputy, or was I reading too much into it? Where had I heard the name Patridge, or had I? I stared at it for several seconds before it hit me. That was the name of the man Sheriff Turner had warned me about that night in his patrol car, the man who had his heart set on the sheriff's appointment when Hall resigned and who had launched a smear campaign against my father in an attempt to steer the supervisors' votes in his favor. After Turner had been appointed sheriff in a surprise move by the supervisors, he had fired Patridge sometime later, apparently in late November or December 1982.

My heart rate quickened. I grabbed the previous week's newspaper, turning to the photo I'd seen of the man with the hound. I had not paid much attention to him when I'd perused the photo the first time but now planned to study it more closely. My hands were trembling, so I spread the paper on the table to steady the image.

He was wearing a dark, sheriff's department cap pulled low on his head, and his face was not in clear focus. And I could not discern the color of his hair since the photo was in black and white, but he appeared to have a pale complexion. Despite the poor image quality, I was fairly confident I recognized him as the same person who had come into Jack's house looking for information about Stone and threatening us. The man who had alluded to killing others who crossed him. The man who, I thought now, had almost certainly killed Sheriff Hall.

I tried to calm myself. The photo was a bit blurry, after all.

What if I was jumping to conclusions, trying to make the facts fit my conclusions instead of the other way around? I pointed to the name on the page, tapping it, certain I was missing something.

Suddenly, as if a tiny spotlight switched on to illuminate a shadowed memory, I again recalled what the man's accomplice had called him that night at Jack's. My finger stopped tapping and just trembled, pointing at the name on the page. The stocky black man had called him Red.

Not a meaningless reference to the color of his shirt or his hair like I'd thought.

His actual name was Red.

Redmond Patridge.

TWENTY-TWO

"**W**HAT are you doing, Casey?"

I jumped at the familiar but unexpected voice behind me. Hoping Mom hadn't noticed my startle or the photo I had been studying, I stood and snapped the paper closed as I turned.

"He's looking at old newspapers." Ms. Holst wobbled up and stopped slightly behind my mother.

"Oh, I thought you were here to check out a book to read." Mom arched a suspicious eyebrow.

"I, uh, was, well, I uh, did check out a book. Wait, no—two, actually." I held up my two selections with a triumphant grin, but Mom's still-raised eyebrow made me falter. "And then, you weren't here, and so I, uh…"

"And so I suggested he look at the old newspapers," Ms. Holst interjected. "I thought he might see an old photo or two of himself from Little League, you know, he might get a kick out of that. And knowing how he'd been reared the right way, I knew he wouldn't mind helping me by putting them in order as he went. We are getting ready to put them on microfilm, and they are all out of order. Two birds with one stone, you know?"

My mouth dropped. Ms. Holst winked at me.

"Yes ma'am, I'm sorry, but I just got started, didn't get much accomplished."

"No problem, young man. Maybe you can help me next time. I appreciate the effort anyway."

"He can stay awhile longer if you need him to." Mom's eyebrow fell into a broad smile, and her tone lightened. "He is a pretty good helper when he wants to be." She gently tickled my back with her fingernails.

"No, you two get out of here. He has books to read," Ms. Holst said.

Mom nodded and headed toward the front of the library.

Ms. Holst put her hand on my shoulder, pulling me down where I could hear her better. "I don't know what you were doing there, but that's your business. When somebody comes in my library, what they study is their business and nobody else's. You come back anytime." She patted me on the butt like a football coach ushering a player into the game from the sideline.

I jumped, wondering if she had meant to hit me there or just missed low because she was so short. I faked a smile, muttered a "thank you," and almost jogged ahead to where Mom was browsing some of the new releases by the front door.

"Don't forget your books." Ms. Holst stopped us at the door and reached out with both books balanced on an unsteady hand. She winked again and flashed her perfect dentures.

I smiled back, grabbed the books, and made a hasty exit.

Mom drove, and I stared out the window, where questions swirled like debris in a tornado. I thought of the scene at the beginning of *The Wizard of Oz*, when Dorothy was being carried by the twister, looking out the window and trying to understand why her aunt was knitting in her rocker, the farmhands were riding the wind in a rowboat, and her rude, bicycle-riding neighbor was transformed into a witch on a broom. My unanswered questions darted in and out like misplaced familiarities, more confusing with each appearance.

What was the identity of the skeletal remains we had found, the significance of the white beads with it? Was it the Vagabond—Brendan Perry—and if so, had Stone, the person who had threatened him, killed him? Was that why Stone ran off?

Or could the body have been Stone Perkins himself? If it *was* Stone, then what had happened to him after Jack saw him leave that day? Who was the female he'd left with? If Stone was dead, then why were Walter Simpson, Vance MacIntosh, and Redmond Patridge *all* acting as if he was hiding from them? What was Stone's true connection with Redmond Patridge, my father's former nemesis, who also happened to be Sheriff Hall's most likely killer?

If the body Jack and I had found *didn't* belong to Stone, then why was Stone's knife found a few hundred yards away, and why was Jack hiding the fact that it was Stone's?

Who was the person that spied on us at the barrels that day, and was it the same person who'd rescued us at Seder Lake? And why was he not reporting the body hidden in the barrels to the authorities?

Last but not least, it appeared that Jack was hiding at least one thing from me, and Jet had betrayed us as well. Who could I even trust now?

I was nearing the point where I had no choice but to tell my father what was happening. Trying to delay the inevitable end of our days at the Hideaway and Papa Mac's farm and avoiding whatever minor discipline we'd face for moving a dead body seemed trivial in the face of whatever serious complexities—and crimes—lay at the foundation of our dilemma. But Jack had made me promise not to divulge what was going on, and given the family crises he had faced, I felt obligated to honor that, to a point. I just wasn't sure where that point was. Was Jack trying to protect Stone? Did he actually know where he was? Was it all about trying to protect Michelle because of her substance abuse issues?

"Are you okay, Casey?" Mom's voice broke my train of thought. We were home, and she had already turned the car off.

"Yeah, sorry, Mom. Girls." An incomplete version of the truth, but not a lie.

"Ahh," she answered. "You and Abi having troubles?"

"Nothing we can't handle." I forced a smile as I opened the door and got out. "Just the usual ups and downs." The truth was, I had no idea where Abi and I stood as a couple. I had been rude and distrustful. She seemed to have forgiven me, but how could I know for sure? I wanted to repair the damage but couldn't find the energy to think about that with all the other problems raging around me.

I couldn't slow down the tornado of my questions enough to answer any of them, but I knew what I needed to do. I walked to my room, picked up the phone, and dialed the number.

"Hey, Jack. You won't believe what I found at the library. We need to meet. I have an idea."

JACK cranked the three-wheeler, and we left his house in silence, in the dark. Through Papa Mac's farm, down Highway 16 for a half mile, left onto a well-worn yet nameless gravel road, until we stopped before a yellow metal gate.

Jack turned off the engine and whispered over his shoulder at me. "This is nuts, you know that? I know I have come up with some wild plans over the years, but nothing like this. You're gonna get us killed."

"You want to find out what happened to Stone, right?"

"I guess. I mainly want all these jackasses to leave us alone."

"Well, we're gonna get this guy to mess up and tell us something that will help us figure out what's going on," I said.

"But I don't see how this is going to help us. We don't have any, anything that gives us an advantage."

"Leverage."

"Yeah, leverage. We don't have any."

"Well, we do know about him killing Sheriff Hall."

Jack spoke in a hiss through gritted teeth. "Exactly. Did you hear what you said? *Killed* a sheriff. That's not something I really want him knowing that we know. What keeps him from killing us then?"

"He's not going to kill a couple of kids. We don't have any real proof anyway. What we know is the same thing my father knows. Plus, we have something he wants."

"We do?"

"As far as he knows we do. Look, just trust me on this. We'll get to the bottom of this."

The gate bore a weathered wooden sign, its painted white letters faded yet still clearly legible: Clifton "Tiger" Townsend Sports Complex. Jet had told me once that his great uncle or a cousin or something had donated the land for the sports facility. I had no reason to doubt him. Townsend wasn't exactly a common name in Amberton.

I jumped off the three-wheeler and fished around beneath a cinder block lying inconspicuously among some weeds behind the gate post. My fingers curled around a small, bronze-colored key, and soon I had the gate open. I considered it a minor miracle that the key was there, but then again, I did every time we searched for it.

For those who knew where to find the key, "The Tiger" was a favorite nighttime hangout for teenagers. Four baseball fields and two softball fields at the end of a mile-long gravel road, with a huge parking lot in between, woods all around, and no other civilization in sight. It was a common gathering place for groups to hang out and for couples to park for more intimate entertainment.

The unwritten rule was the opposite of what one might expect but made perfect sense for those of us who shared the secret. If the gate was locked, it meant either no one was there or someone was who didn't mind company. But if it was dummy locked, with the padlock oriented to appear closed when it wasn't, you'd best try again later. More than one guy wanting to be alone with his girl had been known to deliver a skull bashing on the spot for a violation of the code. For those less inclined to violence, a more embarrassing, calculated payback later was not only considered fair game but was expected.

Tonight the gate was locked. I closed it, dummy locked it behind me, and replaced the key. I couldn't see a clear image of Jack's face in the dark as I got back on the three-wheeler behind him, but he shook his head as we started down the gravel road past the gate. Jack did not want to be here and had questioned my sanity more than once in the past three days.

I can't explain how I felt. I was scared out of my mind yet driven to proceed by the very adrenaline surge that sprang from my fear. I had no idea if what we were doing was the right thing or not, but I would not consider turning back now.

The parking lot was empty when we arrived. We pulled over to one edge and killed the engine. In the center of the complex, a lone streetlight perched above the small building that housed the concession stand and bathrooms. The outer reaches of its illumination barely penetrated half the surrounding parking lot and none of the ball fields. We stood in the shadows and listened to the distant bark of a dog for a time before Jack finally spoke. "Your dad would kill us if he knew what we were doing."

"Probably," I replied. "We're lucky your mom is working late, so we can sneak out and nobody know."

"What time is he supposed to come?" Jack asked.

"Any minute now. Hey, let's go over to field number two." I pointed at the field nearest us. "We can sit in the dugout at least."

"It's dark though. Shouldn't we be here in the light where we can see?"

"No. Let's stay out of the light."

Jack gave me a questioning frown. "Whatever you say, Bud."

By the time we walked onto the dark field, we heard the crescendo of gravel crunching beneath the tires of a slow-moving automobile. A late-model, two-tone Dodge Ramcharger approached at a deliberate, menacing pace and stopped beside our three-wheeler. After an excruciating wait that was probably less than a minute, the Dodge's motor turned off and its lights followed suit.

Redmond Patridge, silhouetted by the streetlight but instantly recognizable, stepped out from the driver's position, and his short, stocky partner slid out of the tall vehicle from the other side.

"You boys alone?" Patridge asked.

"Yessir. We don't want no trouble," I said.

Patridge and his accomplice strode quickly toward us and onto the field to where we stood near the first base dugout. The shorter man shined his flashlight erratically in each direction like a lighthouse beacon gone awry. "They don't want no trouble, they say," Patridge said mockingly in the direction of his friend. "I have to doubt the veracity of that statement considering these two boys have the balls—or is it stupidity—to come out here in the middle of the night to meet up with two men they don't even know who broke in their house and waved a gun in their face just a few nights ago. Reckon can we trust anything they say?"

"I don't know, boss. I ain't liking this."

I fought back a surge of panic. What did he mean by that? Was he suspicious of something or remorseful for what he was about to do to us?

"Check 'em," Patridge said.

The pat-down didn't take long. Anything more than jeans, a T-shirt, and tennis shoes would have been unbearable in the summer night's oppressive heat. "Yo' heart 'bout to beat out of yo' body, boy," Patridge's accomplice said to me as he palpated my chest area.

I didn't say anything. Was Jack as scared as I was? I couldn't get a good look at his face, but his chin was raised, jaw set in a defiant posture. Whatever fear Jack had before was gone now. Either that or he deserved an Oscar.

"What y'all doing standing in the middle of this ball field?" Patridge asked. "Let's go over by the concession stand where there's some light."

"We thought we could sit in the dugout here, out of sight. You know, in case somebody drives up," Jack said.

"Well that's about the dumbest thing I've ever heard," Patridge said. "My truck is out there, and so is your little three-wheeler. Anybody drives up, they'll know we're here. I want to be able to see what's going on. I ain't talking here."

This was not going according to my plan at all. "I, I, uh, really think we should just get this over with right here. We can sit down and be done with it. I insist."

Patridge erupted into a vicious laugh. "You insist? You insist. You ain't in no position to insist nothing, boy." He paced around. "You got this here dugout bugged, *boy*? You got somebody hiding here?" He grabbed the light and shined it all around, in every corner and crack of the dugout, much more deliberate than his partner had before. He scrambled up the fence across the front of the dugout and scanned the top of it.

I thought my knees would buckle, but they didn't. I froze, waiting. What had seemed like a good idea suddenly had the makings of a calamity.

After a few seconds, he hopped off the fence and walked over to glare at me. He leaned down, six inches from my face. The reek of cigarettes and alcohol forced me to turn my head before he even spoke. "I guess you're telling the truth. No bugs here. But we're moving over there—" he pointed toward the meager glow of the single streetlight— "where I can see what's going on around me. I ain't asking."

My plan had fallen apart, and I knew we needed to abort or risk a catastrophe. "This has just been a misunderstanding. We were just clowning around. Sorry to waste your time."

Patridge rumbled like a threatened, slough-bottom alligator protecting its territory. He spoke slowly, each word growing in volume and intensity. "There is no such thing as a misunderstanding with me. You told me you have something for me, now we gonna go over here, and you gonna fork it over and tell me where you got it!"

"I told you, we don't have—"

Jack craned his neck forward and stopped me with an incredulous stare, as if I had just suggested the four of us pair up for double dates. "Case may have lost his mind, sir, but I haven't. We do actually have something for you. Sort of."

"Both of you, shut up for a second." Patridge gave us each a shove. "Now move it, we gonna get over there in the light."

The soft sounds of the night were interrupted by the hoot of a great horned owl from somewhere across the parking lot. "What was that?" Patridge's friend asked.

"An owl, dummy." Patridge replied. "City boy ain't never heard an owl before?"

"Sounds spooky is all."

"Spooky?" Patridge said. "Did you just say spooky? Go get a tampon out of my truck if you need it."

I smiled to myself. Great horned owls were harmless. We often imitated their call when turkey hunting to locate a gobbler. The sudden sound of a crow or hawk or owl would sometimes initiate a shock gobble from an otherwise silent tom.

Patridge and friend marched us off the baseball field and toward the light by the concession stand. Plywood shutters covered the front windows. The shorter partner walked around back and confirmed that all the doors to the little building were locked.

"Now," Patridge said, "let's get down to business. You boys called me and said you had some money for me."

"We have something for you," Jack said. "A deal."

"A deal? Unless this deal includes you handing over some money for me, we ain't got no deal. But I'm listening."

"Well," Jack continued, "Case and I did find a backpack that was Stone's. It had a little bit of cash in it, but I bet it's not all of what you were looking for."

"How much and where is it?" Patridge motioned toward his friend, who walked toward our three-wheeler, obviously to search it for the backpack.

"Five hundred dollars."

Patridge snorted. "Five C-notes? That all? Son, you wasting my time. Give me the money, and call me when you really got something." He pushed Jack in the chest.

Jack caught himself as he stepped back. "There's more."

"What you mean?"

"The backpack had a key in it." I said. "We think we know

what it's to, where you'll find your money."

"Quit playing games with me, *boy*. Hand it over."

"We can't right now," I said.

"I'm sick of your games. Quit leading me along, and tell me what's on your mind before I give your dentist some work to do." He balled up his fist and crammed it in my face.

"Okay, just hear me out. Jack and I want our cut. Not much, just the five hundred we found. Consider it payment for leading you to the key and the box it unlocks. You can have all the money the key leads you to. After you get it, you leave Jack and his family alone. Deal?"

Patridge burst out laughing, and again addressed his friend who had walked over after coming up empty with the three-wheeler search. "You can't make this stuff up. The stepson of Amberton's biggest con and the son of McKinley County's finest are teaming up to try to scam a scammer. That's priceless right there. I mean, what a treasure.

"You know, it's funny how life comes full circle. I been messing with these two pukes since they were just outta diapers. Snuck in Reynolds's house and left good ol' Rex a memento so he'd know I'd been by. These two snots about crapped their pants. Popped a cap gun or something and went screaming down the hall for Daddy Rex."

My heart jumped in my chest, remembering a .45 cartridge left on my kitchen counter years before. Remembering the look on my father's face, telling me the shadowy visitor in our home had been someone far more sinister than a new homeless guy around town looking for food. "That was *you*?"

"Ha. Always wondered, didn't you? My way of telling your daddy to back off his investigatin' department corruption, as he called it. Now, I hate to change the subject, but enough of that.

Time for business. I'm just guessing you boys didn't bring the money *or* the key. Sort of your leverage to keep me from taking you out like I told you I was willing to do?"

Our silence answered his question for him. His eyes narrowed. "Let me tell both of you something. You don't know who you're messing with. You don't know what I'm capable of!" He was almost shouting now. He grabbed Jack by the neck with his right hand. "You don't think I've got the stones to take you both out right here, right now?"

I was still scared out of my mind, but at that point I had become something else as well. Mad. "You gonna kill us and make it look like an accident, like you did with Sheriff Hall?"

Patridge released Jack and whirled to me. "What did you say?"

"I know who you are and what you did."

"Ahh, you gonna be a little detective, too, you think? Or has your daddy been spoon feeding you his pack of lies? You don't know nothing."

"I know I don't want nothing to do with law enforcement. Too hard to make money, at least legally." Patridge's eyes bored into me like dark lasers, but I continued. "And I know Sheriff Hall somehow died from a .30-06 bullet from his own gun, but it wasn't no accident. You shot him with his own gun somehow. You probably killed Stone too."

"Is that what your daddy told you? Ha. You don't know squat then."

"What do you mean? I know enough."

"You think you're so smart. First off, I ain't killed Stone. Still trying to figure out where that imbecile ran off to. And I'm gonna tell you something else. And there ain't nobody here, at least nobody but dumb kids that'll as soon lie as look at you, to prove I said it. Your daddy knows this, or at least he should unless he's a moron and forgot it already. You think your daddy is telling you anything special about Hall, that fat, loudmouth, slob snitch? You can read what *you* know in the papers. Hall wasn't killed with no .30-06. Nah, was a .30-30 did him in. Close enough to not be able to tell the difference if the slug went all the way through him, but too much blubber on him for it to exit I guess. So they know it's a .30-30 and not a .30-06. Problem is, they couldn't find the weapon, so they got no case, you see? No case at all. That's the key. No weapon, no case. At least nothing that can be linked to anybody."

"Where did you hide the .30-30?" Jack asked.

"I swallowed it, ground it up in my gizzard, and crapped it down my toilet. Now shut up." Patridge drew his pistol. "There ain't gonna be no deals tonight."

TWENTY-THREE

"WE gonna take a ride right now," Redmond Patridge growled, "and you gonna show me exactly where that key is and what lock it fits." He waved the gun toward the Ramcharger. "Go get in."

I froze in uncertainty, and Patridge's face contorted in anger. He chambered a round and stepped toward me.

"Drop the gun." a familiar voice boomed from above us. "Nobody's going anywhere with you tonight, Redmond. Raise that gun a quarter inch, and I'll pump three holes in you and Melvin both before either of you hits the ground."

Melvin screeched an incoherent expletive and almost fell to the ground, covering his head with his hands.

Jack jumped, caught himself as he staggered backward, then froze.

Neither Redmond Patridge nor I moved a muscle. Patridge gritted his teeth and slowly tilted his head upward to glare at the source of the command he'd just received.

"Hello, Rex. Long time no see." Patridge sneered.

My father raised up from his perch on top of the concession stand where he had been hidden behind the short aluminum façade attached to the front eaves. He had his SIG Sauer P226, drawn down, unwavering, on Patridge. "I said drop the gun. Now. You too, Melvin. I know you've got a sidearm tucked in your belt there."

Both men followed Dad's instructions, dropping their pistols to the ground and kicking them away out of reach.

"I'm not sure what you think you're seeing here, Rex. You can't just go around stalking me and pulling a gun whenever you feel like a tough guy. Hiding out on top of Little League baseball buildings, using your son to try to entrap me? Pretty desperate for one thing, but more important than that, not legal."

Dad spoke into a handheld radio then clipped it back on his belt. "You let me decide what's legal and what's not, Red. You're not a cop anymore, so you have no say in the matter. I've got you on attempted kidnapping to start, and murder to finish. Son, you and Jack walk away, out toward the three-wheeler. Slowly. If something goes wrong, you ride away as fast as you can. Red, you and Melvin ease over here to the side where I can see you as I climb down."

"Dad—"

"Be quiet, Case. You've done enough already. Do what I said."

Jack and I plodded toward the three-wheeler, not saying a word, alternating between walking backward and sliding sideways to keep our eyes on the scene behind us.

"Did you say murder?" Patridge asked. "Ha. You've got nothing on me. Used your kids to entrap me is all you got."

"We'll see about that. Sounds like you're confused about what that means. Now, I'm going to hop down off of here, but my aim will not change. You make a move I don't like, and I promise I'll drop you like a blind date with body odor." Dad moved to the side of the building where the roof edge was smooth, motioning his captives along with his pistol to keep them in front of him. He held his .40 caliber steady on Patridge with his right hand as he swung his legs off the edge of the eight-foot roof, braced himself with his left, and gathered himself to hop down.

Dad's leap was effortless, but his right foot slipped on the loose gravel below. He stepped sideways with his left foot to balance himself, and it happened. The ankle—a veteran of one fracture, countless sprains, and two surgeries due to college football—failed him again, and momentum sent him hurtling to the ground. His grip on the gun was solid, but his arm flailed to the side as he fell, trying to catch himself.

Redmond Patridge was too quick for him. He sprung like a bobcat on a swamp rabbit, attempting to pin him with one foot while grabbing for the gun with both hands. Dad yelled, "Run, boys!" as he swung his left thigh over Patridge's back and rolled his whole body to the right, using Patridge's own momentum to sling him onto the ground on his shoulder.

I did as I was told for a moment but then stopped in my tracks. I was terrified, but I could not leave Dad behind. As I turned back, I became vaguely aware of what was happening in the other direction: Melvin picking something off the ground and running away while Jack headed for the three-wheeler as my father had ordered.

Just then Patridge grabbed at the gun, which Dad still held like a vise, and it flipped free, discharging with a brilliant orange muzzle flash and thunderous explosion of gunpowder that rattled the fences of the ball fields around us.

I was only fifty feet away, in full stride. I dropped to the ground and rolled on the rocks, never stopping as I sprung back onto my feet. If I had been hit by the bullet, I could not feel it.

Patridge and my father, both on the ground now, froze, wild-eyed and panting, each appearing to pause to see if his adversary had been hit and to make sure he himself had not.

In a blur, Patridge and Dad lunged simultaneously for the gun, sprawling forward. Both came up short, pulled back by the other. Each rose to his knees, and Patridge swung at Dad, who ducked and then connected with a right hook into Patridge's jaw. A left jab from Patridge at the same time caught Dad in the nose, spewing blood.

I searched the ground in front of the concession stand frantically for one of the pistols dropped by the criminals. *Where? Where? They were right here.* It couldn't have been more than a couple of seconds, but it felt like a lifetime of searching, racing about frenetically in a fifteen-foot circle like a honeybee doing a life-or-death pollen dance for starving hive mates.

Then I saw it, abutting a scraggly clump of grass struggling to survive among the rocks.

The Beretta M9 felt at home in my hand. Dad had bought one just like it a few months earlier, taught me the features of the gun and let me fire at least two boxes of shells through it.

As I whirled toward the two men, pistol in hand, Patridge landed another blow that staggered Dad backward. He grabbed Patridge's shirt as he fell, but Patridge had the advantage now and lunged toward the SIG with Dad hanging on, wrestling futilely to hold him back. I fingered the top of the Beretta. The protrusion of the extractor head confirmed a round was already chambered. I flipped the safety lever upward and cocked the hammer. As Patridge strained toward Dad's pistol, I fired three quick shots. "Stop!"

Dust and gravel flew. Patridge jerked his hand back as if snake-bit and spun around. His eyes widened in obvious surprise to be staring down the barrel of his own weapon, loaded and cocked, with twelve more 9mm hollow points in the magazine. And held by a fourteen-year-old, snot-nosed punk.

Dad rolled away and grabbed up his pistol, checked it for damage and then pointed it at Patridge. "Case, put the gun down."

The gun, rock-steady in my hand at first, now trembled like the last withered leaf on a winter oak. The play in the trigger may have been the only thing that spared Patridge from my accidentally shooting him.

"Put the gun down. Now." Dad's command snapped me back. I lowered the gun to my side, where he eased it from my hand and flipped the safety lever to decock it.

"Thanks," I mumbled.

Dad said nothing to me, but the grave cut of his glance spoke volumes. His gaze settled again on his adversary, toward whom the aim of his weapon did not waiver despite him still panting from the fight. "Well there, Redmond. Looks like you just added resisting arrest, assault and battery of a police officer, and attempted second-degree murder to your charges."

Redmond Patridge scowled.

The sound of sirens broke the relative silence. Within seconds, two sheriff's department cruisers, blue lights flashing, burst into view from the gravel road and sped across the parking lot to our location. Both vehicles skidded to a stop, and Sheriff Sykes Turner leaped from the first one before it had completely stopped moving, asking Dad if he was okay as he approached Patridge from behind. The sheriff pressed a pistol hard into the man's spine. "On the ground!" he screamed in Patridge's ear, cuffing both hands as he complied.

"There's one more," Dad said. "Melvin Ware. You remember, that kid from down in Columbus that Patridge used to hang with. He took off running toward the road when things got crazy." He shot me the same cutting glance as before.

"Melvin's in my backseat," the second deputy said.

"Yeah, you don't have to worry about him," the sheriff said. "Deputy Sturgess here picked him up right after that other boy ran him down with a three-wheeler. Ran right over him, I'm tellin' you. Sturgess was coming in from the highway and saw the whole thing from a distance. Looked like that boy had chased him down the road a piece. Best we can tell, Melvin actually turned and shot his pistol at him, but the boy never wavered. Just ran him over. Melvin rolled over in the ditch and staggered into the bushes. Took us a minute to round him up. He's got some serious road rash and tire tracks on his face but nothing else hurt except his pride."

"Jack," I said. Sheriff Turner and his deputy turned to look at me but said nothing. "Jackson Masterson. That was my friend's name. Is he…is he…I mean, you said he got shot at? Is he…?"

"You mean did he get shot?" Turner said.

"I reckon he's all right," Sturgess said in a slow country drawl. "Rode over the top of that scumbag like a monster truck on a Volkswagen and never checked up. Got out of there faster'n a scalded dawg."

———

"What in the world were you thinking?" Dad slammed his hand down on the desk in his office, startling me. His quiet simmer to that point had suited me just fine, but now he was boiling, and the silence was over. He backhanded a stack of files on his desk to the floor, strewing papers everywhere. I leaned forward to pick them up, and he yelled again. "Leave them alone. I asked you a question. What were you thinking?"

A flurry of activity went on outside his door, where several deputies and other staff were busy with Sheriff Turner processing the two perpetrators and trying not to look at us. "Dad, listen, I was trying to help you."

"Help me? Help me by getting us both killed? I get an anonymous letter that Redmond Patridge is going to have a secret meeting that will *reveal some useful information*, and it turns out the message was from *you*? You and Jack are meeting with a murderer? How does that happen?"

My father appeared twice his normal size, pacing back and forth like a tiger on the other side of his desk. I slumped in one of his two chairs, glad the desk was there but not entirely certain he wouldn't leap across it.

I wasn't sure how much to tell him. I knew I'd best not lie lest it come back to haunt me later, but I couldn't reveal everything just yet. I explained how Patridge had come to Jack's house that night looking for something Stone left behind and alluding to the fact he had murdered those who crossed him in the past. I told Dad I had heard people talking over the years about Patridge trying to smear his reputation, and I knew he'd want to put him away if he could, but that he would have put a stop to everything if he'd known it was me. How we were afraid to do anything at first because of the threats, but then I thought of a plan to help Jack get more information about Stone, catch Sheriff Hall's killer, and avenge the slander of my father in one fell swoop. I decided not to tell Dad about Jack being unaware of my intent to give him the tip.

"That's what makes me so mad," Dad said. "I *did* want to get him. And I should have stopped the whole thing as soon as I saw it was you, but I didn't. I let it go because I wanted him *so* bad, and *I* put us all in danger." He kicked his garbage can across the room, and trash exploded across the floor. The bustle outside the door ceased for a second, then resumed as if nothing unusual had happened.

"Dad, it's okay. You did what you had to do. It worked. You got him."

He paced again for a minute. "How did you figure out who he was? And what he had done?"

I confessed about my library research, how I found a photograph of Patridge and figured he had to be the one Dad had alluded to as the prime suspect in Sheriff Hall's death. I chose to leave out the part about my meeting with Sheriff Turner, hoping that our street sign affair would remain forevermore a secret.

"So, back to Patridge coming to Jack's house. Do you know what this has to do with Stone Perkins running off?"

"We're not sure about Stone, Dad. We were—Jack was—hoping to find out something from Patridge about what happened to Stone. Maybe you can get it out of him."

"So where is this backpack you boys found with the money and the key?"

"We, uh, don't have it. We made that part up."

Dad stopped and stared at me, speechless.

"You made that part up?" Sheriff Turner's deep voice entered the conversation from the doorway behind me. I wasn't sure how long he had been there listening. Dad's eyes had not betrayed his arrival.

"Yessir. We just told him that. It was the best thing we could think of. He really didn't tell us he was looking for money, but we figured that had to be it."

"You made that up." Dad chuckled reluctantly. "Believe it or not, you boys were probably right about it being money he was looking for. Patridge has been working as an enforcer for a gambling ring out of New Orleans for a few years. At least that's what I'm told. So if he's looking for Stone, then I'm sure Stone owes him money. May be why Stone left town." That certainly matched what Stone's coworker Elbert Dale had told us. It didn't tell us what Vance MacIntosh's interest was though.

Sheriff Turner shook his head in disbelief. "This is crazy. Son, what were you gonna do if your Daddy hadn't showed up?"

"Well, I was afraid he hadn't shown up. I told him in the note to hide on top of the dugout, but he wasn't there. I'm not sure what we were gonna do. Guess we didn't think that out too good. But then I heard him give that owl hoot—nobody hoots quite like Dad—and I knew he was on top of the concession stand." I smiled at Dad, hoping to break the tension.

Turner took off his Stetson and rubbed his forehead with the other hand. "An *owl hoot*? Are you kidding me? Y'all watch too many Westerns. Rex, what I want to know is why were you there by yourself? You had Sturgess a mile up the road instead of close by for backup? And why did you not tell me about it?"

"I should have told you," Dad said, "but I truly thought it was most likely a hoax and didn't want to waste your time. But then I thought, what's to lose? Sturgess and I can check it out. The note was very specific about where the meeting would take place, and there was nowhere else at the ballpark to hide, really. Nowhere else to park the car closer without being seen or heard, and I wanted one of us to have access to wheels in case things went south."

He looked down at me. "Case, I didn't hide on top of the dugout for three reasons. One, I knew Patridge would never agree to a place someone else suggested. Two, I knew him well enough to know he would want to be in the open where he could see. And three, if it was a trap, I wasn't about to be where he wanted me to be."

"Sheriff?" I said. "I'm worried about Jack."

"I sent Sturgess to check on him and make sure he got home okay," Turner said. "He just radioed back that his three-wheeler is at his house, safe and sound. He didn't bother him though. We'll question him tomorrow."

"Case, let's get you home." Dad walked toward the door. "We'll talk more about this later. I dread trying to explain this to Mom."

"Yeah, Beth's gonna tear *both* yo' butts up about this." Sheriff Turner laughed, then he turned and disappeared.

We walked out of Dad's office down the hall, past the dispatch room toward the side entrance where his car was parked. Just as we turned the corner to leave, a voice called out, "Hey Rex, busy night tonight. Got another one here to process."

Dad stopped and took a step back so he could see down the hall.

"Fannie Fraunfelder found him asleep on her patio. Held him at the business end of a double barrel .410 until we got there."

"Just take his statement and let him go." Dad held up his hand, palm out, quelling a protest from his deputy before he even voiced it. "Just do it, Turnip. I'm sure Miss Fannie will rain her wrath down on me tomorrow, but I'll handle her. It's fine, he's harmless."

He's harmless. Where had I heard Dad say that before? I eased beside him so I could see down the hall myself. An overweight deputy I did not recognize led a man in handcuffs. The prisoner had long shaggy hair and a scraggly beard, and he was dressed in cutoff jean shorts and a raggedy T-shirt that had seen much better days.

I recognized him immediately. I wasn't sure if he knew me, or why he would, but as he passed us he nodded, first at my father and then at me. Then he winked at me.

Brendan Perry.

The Vagabond was alive.

TWENTY-FOUR

BRENDAN Perry was alive, which meant the skeleton we had moved belonged to someone else. But who? Stone Perkins seemed the next most likely *known* person, but now that I had seen firsthand what Patridge was capable of, my worry grew that it might be someone we hadn't thought about. And how did we know it wasn't a man we had never even heard of, who had absolutely nothing to do with the mystery surrounding Stone and Patridge and the others?

I needed to discuss it with Jack but couldn't get him to answer the phone. After a morning spent listening to endless ringing, I considered riding to his house after lunch and making him talk to me. Then I remembered the sheriff saying he would be going there to get a statement. *Nope, I do not want to be there for that.* Jack evidently needed time to cool down, and besides, I had another pressing matter.

I considered it to be an invitation to torture of the highest degree. Yes, I was the one who called her, but tagging along on an afternoon shopping trip with Abi and her mother was not what I had in mind. But I was desperate to remain in her good graces, especially since my other friendships were verging on the brink of collapse. So the afternoon found me surviving a marathon mall expedition, where I'm certain Abi tried on a few hundred outfits, only to wind up somewhere even less interesting—the arts and crafts department of Walmart. Abi was intent on restocking her supply of materials for friendship pins while her mother browsed elsewhere.

"I don't get it," I said. "It's just colored beads on safety pins."

"You share them with friends." Abi smiled. "Yes, it's a bit passé, but making them is still fun."

"I'll have to take your word for it."

Wishing I was in sporting goods but determined to stick close to Abi, I found myself wandering up and down the aisles, trying to entertain myself while she picked out the beads she wanted. Colored pencils and construction paper, paints and canvases, yarns and fabrics all failed to entertain me, but then something unexpected captured my attention. Styrofoam supplies. It wasn't the assortment of green cubes and cylinders for floral arrangements that caught my eye. It was the white balls. The spheres ranged from marble size to five or six inches. My thoughts jetted to the beads I had found on the skeleton in the barn. I had almost forgotten about them, but I suddenly knew that was a mistake. These were similar, only bigger. Was there some connection?

A store employee walked by me, and I stopped her. "Excuse me, ma'am? Do you guys ever carry these Styrofoam balls in a smaller size? Like about the size of a pea?"

"You mean like the itty bitty ones that go in stuffed animals?"

"No, a little bigger." I used my thumb and index finger to demonstrate the approximate diameter of the beads I had at home.

"Hmmm, no. No idea what that would be for. Sorry. These here are the smallest we sell."

I nodded and mumbled a thank you. What was I missing?

"C'mon, it's not *that* bad." Abi's voice interrupted my thoughts. "Frowning like a little boy at a lingerie shower." She just shook her head and waved at me to follow as she sauntered around the corner.

How bad was it? I didn't know yet. But I would find out. One way or another, I would find out.

———————

The phone rang twelve times before a female voice finally answered.

It's about time. "Hey, Michelle. Can I please talk to Jack?"

"Had a feeling it was you. Nobody else would let it ring that many times. You were the one who called all morning, weren't you?" She didn't give me time to answer. "I don't think he wants to talk to you. He told me what you did."

"What I did?"

"I reckon he can't trust nobody. Said Jet lied to him too."

"Just please let me talk to him. I can explain everything. Please? He's gonna want to hear what I have to say."

There was a period of silence. I didn't hear a click and assumed she was contemplating my request. "Hold on," she said. I could hear voices in the background. Arguing. Then Jack's voice.

"What do you want?"

"We need to talk."

"Nothing to talk about."

"Look, Jack, I'm sorry. I saw a chance to get revenge for Dad and solve a murder at the same time, and I honestly, truly thought we'd get some information about Stone. I still do. They are questioning Patridge and the other dude, Melvin. They'll come up with something."

"That's not the point, Case. I asked you not to tell anybody. You betrayed me, just like Jet did."

"Hold on a second." I got up and closed my bedroom door and locked it, then switched on the radio for some background noise. "In the Air Tonight" filled the air. I quickly turned the volume down, hoping Jack wouldn't be inspired by Phil Collins's vengeful lyrics. "I didn't tell anything, Jack. Not really. I just sent an anonymous note to Dad that Patridge would be having a meeting that he'd want to hear. That was it. The only thing he knows is that Patridge threatened us—you. That's it, unless you told more than that."

"Why would I tell? I gave you *my* word." His emphasis was meant to sting, and it found its mark.

"I said I was sorry. Nothing has changed as far as what's important in all this. And a murderer has been caught. Surely that counts for something."

"You coulda told me you were gonna do that."

"You're right, I should have." I tried to change the subject. "Hey, the deputy said you really flattened that Melvin guy."

"Yeah, I guess I did, didn't I? I chased him and don't know why he didn't run through the woods. Idiot just ran right down the road." It sounded as if he might be smiling a little, but I couldn't tell for sure. "On the other hand, I didn't know he had picked up his gun, so maybe I'm the idiot."

"He told the deputy that he wasn't going in them woods where wild animals were."

"Lions and tigers and bears, huh?" Jack said. "Shoulda been worried about Big Red."

I chuckled then fell silent and didn't speak until, as if on cue, Phil's signature drum sequence knifed through the void, compelling me to share the other reason for my call. "Jack, there's something else."

"What is it?"

"I was with Dad, at the sheriff's department. They brought somebody in."

"What do you mean?"

"Arrested somebody."

"Okay, so? I think that's their job, ain't it?"

"It was Brendan Perry. He's alive."

Jack said nothing for several seconds. "The Vagabond? You sure?"

"I'm sure. So you know what that could mean."

"What you trying to say?" His words were suddenly shorter and the pitch higher.

Now was the time to mention what I'd been suspecting as a possibility for several days and dreading as a probability for the past several hours. "Jack, you know who we have to consider that it might be."

"I'll tell you what we need to consider. That I'm sick of all of this, Case. All of it. I'm sick of sneaking around, I'm sick of all the lies. I'm sick of you playing detective. I'm sick of people playing by their own rules no matter what they've sworn to their friend. Jet's a traitor, then you. Of all people, I thought I could trust *you*. First you're using our boat with whoever you want, even though we swore not to. Then all this happens, and you sneak around like you're Magnum, P.I., tracking down murderers for your own selfish reasons, even if you almost get your best friend and father killed, not to mention yourself. And you got your dad involved even though you promised you wouldn't. Like what, you've got some special pass or something to do what you want because your dad is a cop? I'm sick of it."

"Jack, listen, it's not like I told the enemy. Dad is on our side. And you know it hasn't all been my idea. We've been in this to-gether from the—"

"I'm tired of talking about it, man. I'll talk to you later."

Jack hung up. I stared at the receiver in my hand for several minutes, trying to make sense of what he had just said. Finally, I reached over, turned off the music, crawled into bed, and closed my eyes.

Often a good night's sleep brings clarity and peace of mind, even if it does not bring resolution to a conflict that seemed insurmountable the night before. But sometimes sleep does not come. Jack's outburst had shocked me, but the more I tossed and turned, the more I realized I shared his sentiment, or at least part of it. I was also tired of it all. Months earlier, when we decided to move the remains of what we thought to be a poor homeless soul who likely died of exposure, who could have guessed we would later find ourselves running around meeting murderers and other criminals in the dark of the night, making deals for imaginary contraband, getting threatened and having guns pulled on us? We were just mischievous kids who had been desperate not to lose our connection to a place we loved to hunt and fish and camp, but somehow things had spun out of control and deteriorated into something much more serious, even sinister. Aside from the danger, the whole situation was, like an insidious cancer, eroding the bonds of friendships once thought by all of us to be inseverable.

Now Jack was angry at Jet and me both for our betrayals of his trust. He wouldn't even talk to Jet, and for all I knew, I was now in that same category. Besides that, even though Abi and I were technically still together, the strain of the situation and its secrets seemed to be pulling us apart with each passing day.

I pounded my fist into my pillow and sat up in bed. Trying to sleep was proving fruitless. I flipped on a lamp and grabbed a deck of cards from my bedside table drawer. Maybe a few dozen games of Solitaire would make me drowsy.

One thing I didn't agree with Jack on was his assertion that I had pushed him against his will into the events of the past few weeks. While I may have taken the lead most of the time, he certainly played his part with little hesitation. The fact that he now was withdrawing and trying to lay all the blame on me angered me a bit. Yes, I could partly justify it for him by self-admission of my misjudgment in bringing my father into the situation without Jack's consent, but I knew there was more to it than that.

Jack was not being entirely honest with me either. He had to believe that Stone Perkins was, at the very least, a likely candidate for the person we found in the barn, yet he was saying nothing. Stone had disappeared back in the fall, about the same time Jet had calculated the time of death. We had now ruled out the most likely victim, the Vagabond, Brendan Perry. Also, we knew the person was the victim of a gunshot wound, and it seemed that half the county had something against Stone Perkins. What we didn't know was, if it was Stone, which of the people searching for him had actually killed him, and why? Or was it someone else we had not even considered?

The cards spread across my sheets stared up at me, begging me to make a play. I hadn't flipped a single card since the original deal. Too many other moving pieces consumed me. Why was Jack acting so strangely? Why was he being so self-righteous, when he not only was a willing participant in most everything that had happened, but clearly was hiding things from me as well? Back in the fall, when Jet was out of town, Jack didn't answer my call, and I had asked Abi to go fishing instead, I had found Stone's knife near the scene. Months later, when I had pulled the knife out at the Hideaway, Jack must have known immediately it was Stone's and bargained to get it from me.

More troubling perhaps than that, his words from our phone conversation haunted me. *You're using our boat with whoever you want, even though we swore not to.* How did Jack know Abi and I took the boat out that night? I never told him or anyone else about it, and I had asked Abi not to either. There were only two possibilities, and I didn't like either one. If Abi had not broken her promise to keep our fishing trip a secret, I dared not think about how Jack could know. The thought sickened me.

I swept the cards across my room, barely noticing their flutter and fall. I flipped off the light and pressed my head into the mattress with my pillow, hoping maybe if I pushed hard enough, my head would stop spinning.

———

The next afternoon, I sat again on my bed and, much as I had done before calling Jack the day before, stared at the phone in my hand for several seconds before dialing. I almost hoped no one would answer, but I knew I had no choice. I had to ask the question.

Abi answered on the second ring. "Hello."

"Hey, babe. I had a good time yesterday."

"Which part? Watching me try on clothes or playing with fake flowers?"

"It's all good when I'm with you."

Abi huffed. "Yeah, right. You seemed a little distant. Or were you just bored?"

I had wanted to ask her opinion about the white beads at Walmart but had held back for some reason. Stubbornness maybe, or perhaps a misguided idea that I was somehow still protecting her. "It wasn't you, I promise. But I need to ask you a question. Please don't get mad, because I already know the answer, but I got to ask."

"Okayyyy."

"Remember last fall, when we went night fishing on Papa Mac's farm?"

"Yeah, we should do that again pretty soon, while we still can."

Her answer caught me off guard. What did that mean? I

pushed it out of my mind for the moment and pressed on with the purpose of my call. "You remember what I said about us using the boat? Keeping it a secret?"

"Yeah, it was silly but I remember. Don't tell Jet or Jack."

"Did you?" I said.

"Case Reynolds!" A scold using both names for emphasis.

"I told you I knew the answer. But I have to ask. Did you tell?"

"I'm not going to answer that. But you know I didn't."

Her answer was a punch in the gut. For once I wished she hadn't kept her word. "Just had to make sure."

"Why?"

"Don't be mad at me, please. But I can't tell you just yet."

"I'm so sick of this." Abi's tone turned contemptuous. "I gotta go."

"Dangit, I knew you'd be mad. I understand, but before you hang up, tell me something. Just a second ago, what did you mean when you said we should go fishing again soon, while we still can? You know something I don't?"

"I shouldn't tell you, since you won't tell me anything."

"Please, Abi."

Her sigh was loud and deliberate. "You know, Mom works as a realtor part time. I overheard her telling Dad about some group looking around Amberton. Some kind of tire manufacturing company."

"Tires?"

"Some German tire company. No, maybe Norwegian—starts with an R."

"Reisende?" I had seen the raised letters of that brand on my father's four-wheel drive, but that was the extent of my knowledge.

"That's it. They're wanting to build a plant in the Southeast, and none other than Vance MacIntosh's farm is a leading candidate for the site."

Another punch in the gut. At least now I knew what Vance MacIntosh had in mind for his farm. I had hoped he was just blowing smoke, but maybe not. Did that somehow tie in to his dealings with Stone? Did it help explain why Jack had been lying to me? I couldn't imagine how.

"Thanks, Abi. I owe you."

"Whatever, Case. Just let me know when you figure things out enough to let me in. I'm tired of peeking in from the outside." She hung up before I could respond.

Two nights, two phone calls, two hangups. Not a good batting average. I reached into my sock drawer and took out a small plastic bag. I dumped the five white beads into my hand and rolled them back and forth with my index finger, contemplating the significance of their presence among the bones in that barn so many months before. They were important, but how? The clerk at the store had asked if they were used for stuffed animals. Stuffed animals? That didn't seem like the answer.

I flung myself backward amid the pillows on my bed, sinking into them and wishing I could go to sleep, awaken from a bad dream, and smile at the absurdity of it. Beads. Bean bags. Pillows. *Chairs.*

I shot up as if I'd been stung by a hornet. I paced for a few minutes before sitting on my bed as the gravity of my realization took its toll. For a time I stared out the window, looking at but not seeing the sunset, much as one sometimes hears without listening.

When darkness fell, I told my parents that I didn't feel well and was going to bed early. I stared at the blackness of my ceiling for another two hours, then pretended to be asleep when Mom came to check on me on her way to bed. When all was quiet, I slipped on a pair of jeans, a T-shirt, and a pair of tennis shoes. I grabbed a flashlight, climbed out of my window, and stepped into the night.

TWENTY-FIVE

NORMALLY it might have been unnerving—a two-mile walk alone through the countryside in the black of night without a weapon. But not this time. I was so preoccupied, first with boiling questions, then with growing anger, that I thought little about what might be lurking in the shadows as I marched through Papa Mac's farm.

I arrived at Jack's doorstep shortly after 11:00. As I had guessed, his mother's car wasn't there. Working late again. Michelle's car was in the driveway, but I didn't care. She could hear what I had to say or not. I wasn't leaving without answers.

The lights were off inside. I slunk around to Jack's bedroom window and pecked on it several times, expecting the light inside to come on and him to peek out. Nothing happened. I tried again but got nothing, so I eased back around to the carport door and knocked, softly at first but then more loudly. Again, I expected a light to come on, either inside or outside, but none did.

Something had happened. I just knew it. Sure, Patridge was in jail, but his employers were not. Or maybe Vance and his deranged partner with the baseball cap finally had enough and followed up on their threats. And who knew who else was out there looking to find Stone? Instinct told me to run back home, but instead I hurried to the back patio and lifted a brick behind the air conditioner unit. The key was where it always was. My hands shook as if my pounding heart might burst through my fingertips while I fumbled to unlock the door, first the deadbolt then the doorknob.

I grasped the knob, but it flew out of my hand as the door was jerked open from within. A shotgun barrel stared me in the face.

"Don't shoot!" I covered my head with my hands.

"Case? What are you doing? I almost shot you, you idiot." Jack raised the barrel away from my face, but just barely.

"You could answer the door. Put that thing away." I shoved the barrel aside as I barged into the kitchen, my fear supplanted by resurrected anger. "We've got to talk."

"Dude, it's almost midnight." He leaned out the door and peered toward his driveway. "How did you get here?"

"I walked. My parents think I'm in bed. We've got to talk. Some things don't add up, and I think you've got some answers."

"Answers to what? Go home, Case, we can talk later. Mom finds out you snuck over here, you know she'll call your folks."

"I don't care."

Jack mumbled to himself as he closed the carport door then trudged over and closed the door to the hallway.

"Tell me what's going on, Jack. You've been lying to me."

"Lying? You've got a lot of nerve coming over here calling me a liar in my own house. What you talking about?"

"That knife I found at Papa Mac's. I know it was Stone's, and you know it too. But you acted like you'd never seen it before. Explain that."

"That's what this is about? A stupid knife? Yeah, I knew it was Stone's. But I didn't know how it got out there. I don't know why I didn't say anything about it. Didn't think it was important, I guess."

"Not important that I found it on the same farm where we found that body? Really, Jack? Well how about this? I found it in the campfire at the Hideaway. Two hundred yards from the barn."

Jack shrugged and dropped his head.

"You're not stupid. You know what that could mean."

He spoke softly but did not look up. "I knew it might be Stone. I hoped it wasn't."

"Okay, so let me ask you this. How did you know Abi and I used our boat in the Snake? I didn't tell, and she didn't either."

Jack stiffened and met my gaze, defiant now. "Yeah, Case. You know, we said we wouldn't let nobody else use it, but you did it anyway."

"First of all, Abi isn't just anybody, but whatever. So tell me how you knew. That was the same time I found the knife. Were you out there that night or something?"

"Did it ever occur to you that somebody else saw you and told me about it?" Tension rose in Jack's voice. "I know you think you're Sherlock Holmes, but you're not a ghost or a ninja or whatever. Just because you didn't tell nobody doesn't mean nobody saw you. I have my sources."

He was right, that thought had not occurred to me. One of the neighborhood kids could have been out there goofing around. Was I here accusing my best friend of something horrible that he had nothing to do with? "Okay, I'll play that game. But tell me who. Give me a name."

Jack's face burned crimson. "How dare you come up in here accusing *me*, after *you* lied to me about keeping things secret from your dad. Lied to me about the boat, too. Get out of my house, or I call your parents right now." He walked over and lifted the telephone receiver from the cradle.

Despite his indignation and threats, nothing Jack had said so far offered any real explanation, only deflections of my questions. But I had one more left. "Put the phone down, Jack. Let me ask you one more thing, and I'll leave. I swear."

Jack glared at me warily, the anger in his eyes now accompanied by tears. He stood motionless for a few seconds, then slowly replaced the receiver.

I pulled the little plastic bag from my pocket and threw it at him.

Jack caught it with one hand. "What's this?"

"You tell me."

Jack stared at it. I couldn't tell if he recognized its contents or not. His expression revealed nothing. "Am I supposed to know?"

"You and I found those with the skeleton when we moved it, remember?" I thought I saw a flicker of recognition, of understanding, but Jack said nothing.

"I know where those came from, Jack. Those are Styrofoam beads used to stuff things. Things like bean bag chairs." Jack's eyes darted, ever so briefly but most definitely, to the spot on the floor where my favorite chair, the red leather Sacco that conformed to my body so perfectly because of the beads within, once rested.

"Case, don't go there. Please." Tears streamed down his face.

"Don't go there? *Don't go there.* Jack. you tell me what's going on. Tell me right now, or *I* will be the one calling my father." I walked over and picked up the phone. "Stone was murdered, Jack. His knife was found close to the body. And beads from this room, from the chair that you told me wore out and had to be thrown away, were found on his body. And you've been hiding that all this time. So you tell me right now. Did you kill Stone?"

"No. I didn't. Please don't, Case." Jack's defiant posture melted, and his shoulders slumped. I had never seen him look so small. He held his hand out, palm down, urging me to put the phone down. "Please don't call, Bud. There are things you don't understand, things I can't tell you."

"We're all guilty, Jack." My voice softened as empathy replaced the anger. "But we've all got to stop the lying. You and me, best friends since forever. What's that worth if you—if we—can't tell each other the truth?"

Jack backed into the wall and slid to the floor, holding his head in his hands.

"Tell him, Jack," a quivering female voice said. "You're going to have to tell him everything."

Michelle Masterson emerged from the shadow of the hallway. She wore sweatpants with an oversized T-shirt and was barefoot. Her hair was disheveled, and her eyes were bloodshot with dark circles beneath them. My intrusion had awoken her, but no doubt there was more behind her dispirited appearance than that.

"Tell him, Jack," she said. "It's time. If you don't, I will."

"Michelle, no. I can't. Please don't ask me to do that."

Michelle said nothing, only nodded her head sternly toward me. She would not be dissuaded. Jack gave a guttural, crescendo growl, ran his fingers through his hair in a jerking motion, and threw his hands down. He stood and paced the room. Then, with tears in his eyes and an intermittent quake in his voice that he unashamedly did not try to hide, Jackson Masterson told me the story, with his sister filling in details when necessary.

TWENTY-SIX

KICKED back on the couch, Jack watched TV while his mother worked late, as was so often the case. He threw a pillow at Michelle, irritated by her obnoxious snoring from the red Sacco chair, more irritated by the fact that she didn't arouse. He was debating whether to throw something else at her or just give up and go to bed when lights from an automobile in the driveway flashed across the living room wall, followed by the loud roar of an engine and the squeal of tires straining against asphalt. Stone barged through the door, staggering, wild-eyed and on edge. He kicked Michelle's chair then turned and slammed the kitchen door, cursing under his breath.

Stone had been acting increasingly more bizarre in the preceding weeks. Gone for two or three days at a time with no explanation, then acting unpredictably when he did show up, his mood was volatile and antagonistic toward everyone in the family. On the phone at all hours of the night, talking in hushed but heated tones. Calls usually ended with him slamming the phone down, and although he had not yet hit anyone, he had smashed one phone to pieces and punched a hole in a bedroom wall. Screaming and yelling had become a constant in the house. Michelle had her own ideas about what Stone was doing on his nights away from home and had shared them with Jack.

"What are y'all looking at?" Stone growled as he took a beer from the fridge before slamming that door too.

Jack stood and leaned against the counter. "Who brought you

home?" He hoped to divert to a normal conversation, but he also wanted to know.

"You a nosy bastard, ain't you?"

"Where's your truck?" Michelle tried to rub away the fog from her eyes. "You get a d-designated driver tonight for a change?"

"Shut up. I sold it."

"Sold your brand new truck that you couldn't aff-afford?" Michelle pressed, her own words slightly slurred. "Sounds s-smart. Did you give the money to Mom?"

"I give your mother plenty. Why don't you get up and do something useful instead of sitting around like a bum?"

Michelle crossed her arms but didn't budge. "Why don't you tell, tell us where you've been? Have *you* been doing something useful?"

"Once again, none o' your business. Where've you been today? Huh? Out smoking dope or boozing it up? I saw you gorked out in that chair. Or maybe you just exhausted from whoring around all day."

"Don't talk to her like that," Jack said. "It's all your fault."

"My fault? My fault?" Stone gave a haughty laugh. He guzzled the last drop of his beer and crushed the can with both hands. "I'm out busting my balls trying to make some cash for this family, and y'all want to judge me? Y'all couldn't even pay the bills before I came around. Now you two just take, take, take, stand around expecting handouts. You have no idea what I go through for this family."

"I don't have to listen to this." Michelle stood and turned to leave.

"Yeah, just run away." Stone threw the crushed beer can at Michelle, hitting her in the back. "Run to your room, you little slut."

It didn't appear to hurt her physically, but his words already had. Michelle was in tears as she left the room, silent.

Jack's temper flared to a point it never had before. Stone's alcohol abuse, erratic behavior, and financial irresponsibility had led directly to Michelle's problems, both in school and socially. Because of him, their mother, who was the one loving constant in their life despite many imperfections and some questionable decisions, the foremost being to marry him, was working extra-long hours to pay the bills, was usually exhausted, and seemed depressed. And Stone berated Michelle constantly about her grades, habits, friends, and general existence. He did Jack the same way, but Jack was more apt to let the barrage of criticism roll off him than was his sister, who was generally more sensitive and even insecure. Always had been.

"There's no sense in that." Jack clenched his fists and brought them down hard on the counter. "I'm warning you. You'd best just leave us alone. Go back gambling or sleeping at your girlfriend's house or whatever it is you do. Go back to wherever you've been, and leave us alone."

Stone gave an amused smile. "Warning me? That's funny. Although leaving is a pretty good idea, and you may just get your wish. Oh, but you will miss me so much." He reached across and grabbed one of Jack's hands. "How you gonna know what to do without dear ole' Dad here to tell you?"

Jack jerked back. "You are not my father. You're not even a stepfather. Step-loser is more like it."

The perpetual scowl on Stone's face transformed into a flattened glare, a look almost devoid of expression save the unmistakable contempt leaping from his eyes, telling everything one needed to know about his emotions and his intent. He came hard around the counter, covering the few feet separating him from Jack in what seemed like one giant step.

"Stand tall and look me in the eye. Look at me! I can crush you,

you ungrateful little worm. You say you don't have a father? Fine! Then you're just a bastard kid. That's all you are." Stone grabbed Jack around the throat with one hand. He was not a huge man, but his grip felt like a vise as Jack struggled to separate himself from it, struggled to force a breath past the fingers compressing his airway.

Suddenly, Stone let go. He stepped back, staggering, his eyes wide again but with a different look now. A lifetime of looks, perhaps, compressed into a single moment. Dismay, sadness, terror, rage, hate, guilt.

Murder.

Jack thought he saw them all but acted on the latter. Instinctively, still gasping for breath but knowing Stone would be on him any second, he lurched toward a corner table fifteen feet away. There lay Stone's knife, where he often kept it and where it had been sitting the past three days. Jack grabbed the knife, unsheathed it, and whirled around, brandishing it at Stone. "You stay away from me! I swear I'll use it."

Stone was on him, grabbing his wrist. "Put that down, you idiot."

They wrestled for the knife, but the man was too strong and soon had it in his grasp. Jack had little doubt he was about to die. In a desperate attempt to neutralize Stone, Jack kicked him in the groin. Stone roared like a cornered grizzly, and his earlier, ambiguous look became one of certain, pure fury.

Stone came again at Jack, who frantically lunged and crawled across the room, searching for something with which to protect himself. He grabbed the only thing he could reach—the red leather Sacco chair. He picked it up and rose to his feet in one motion, turning with it extended in front of him to fend off the inevitable blow of the knife. As Jack expected, Stone hurled himself upon him just as a deafening explosion erupted.

Jack fell backward, the chair and Stone both on top of him. Confused and desperate, Jack struggled wildly to remove himself from underneath the weight on him.

The chair rolled away as Jack stood up, and he gasped. Stone lay on the floor, incapable of harming him. Limp, eyes wide but unfocused, his only movement was that of lips trying to form words that would never be heard.

TWENTY-SEVEN

ICHELLE stood across the small living room, frozen, with a pistol in her hands, still pointed at Stone's lifeless body on the floor.

"What? What have you done?" Jack reeled backward, stopped only by the wall behind him.

"He was gonna kill you." Michelle's tone was flat, her face expressionless. She stared at the body on the floor.

An overwhelming nausea consumed him. His vision blurred, and he rubbed his eyes with his fists to no avail. He staggered out the kitchen door into the front yard, collapsed to his knees, and vomited on the lawn. Breaths came in heaves as he tried to focus. He strained to listen for the footfalls and chatter of neighbors rushing to investigate the gunshot, for the inevitable crescendo of sirens bearing down on the scene. But he heard no such sound. Only the gentle summer's symphony of night creatures oblivious to the catastrophe, and the distant hum of a car engine, nonchalant, fading away.

Jack tried to calm himself as he walked back inside the house. Michelle sat on the floor, her head between her legs and the pistol on the floor several feet away from her. The telephone handset was off the receiver, its coiled cord stretched across the floor as if it had also been thrown in frustration. "You need to call the police," she said. "I tried ... tried. Can't ... get the number."

The handset began beeping in protest, and Jack hung it up. "Think, Michelle. What's gonna happen if the police come? What have you been doing earlier tonight?"

"What do you mean?"

"You're drunk, aren't you?"

She shrugged. "I was drinking a little."

"A little? What else?"

"A few pills."

"Don't you know what will happen if they come? You'll be charged with murder. It won't matter what our story is, you'll go to jail."

"He was gonna hurt you."

"It won't matter with you being messed up like you are. I've heard Mr. Reynolds talk about that kind of thing. Self-defense won't matter none."

She closed her eyes and held her head in her hands. "Just tell'em somebody else broke in and did it."

"That won't work. I think they can test to see who's fired the gun, all that stuff. They'll never believe us. They'll figure out we're lying, and then that'll make it look even worse for you."

She didn't look up. "I don't care. I just don't care. Call Mom. She'll know what to do."

"No. It will kill her. Michelle, look at me." Jack grabbed Michelle by the shoulders and shook her. "Look at me! You've got to snap out of it. We don't have much time. We have to do something right now."

"What you mean, do something? Do what?"

"I don't know. I don't know!" Jack paced and pulled his hair as if that would somehow extract a solution. He stopped after several seconds and turned back to Michelle. "Okay, look. Stone is gone. He tried to kill me, and you saved me. And there's no sense in you going to jail for that. You remember Stone hinting around that he was leaving?"

"Yeah."

"Well, he just left."

Michelle frowned, her expression changing to bewilderment as she understood what he was suggesting and the implications of it. "That's insane, Jack."

"Do you want to go to jail? Think about what that will do to Mom. I've got a plan."

Michelle's shoulders slumped, and she nodded as tears rolled down her cheeks. "Okay. Okay, but we gotta … we gotta get our story straight."

With very little further discussion, Jack went to work. His first job was to figure out where the bullet lodged. He had hunted enough to know he was fortunate the bullet hadn't passed through and hit him. A superficial inspection of Stone's body revealed that, sure enough, the bullet had passed through and come out his chest. The Sacco may have saved his life after all, not from a knife stabbing like he'd intended, but from a .40 caliber bullet. The chair had an entry hole but no exit.

In a rush, Jack used Stone's knife to cut open the chair and try to find the bullet within. Styrofoam beads spilled and scattered everywhere, and Jack gave up the futile search shortly after it began. They were going to have to get rid of the chair, so what difference did it make if the bullet was in it? If for some reason an investigation was launched and they were suspicious enough to look for a bullet, so be it. They'd go down anyway. Jack stuffed the knife in Stone's pocket in frustration and tried to close the opening he'd cut as best he could.

Michelle and Jack both ran to Stone's bedroom and gathered up as many of his belongings as they could. Clothes, shoes, bathroom supplies, pocketknives, an alarm clock. An old Bible gave them pause. Would Stone have even taken that with him? Would destroying it bring down God's wrath even worse than whatever was already to come? They decided to leave nothing. If Stone had brought it with him, he'd probably have taken it when he left. It was shocking how little he had, though. He had probably pawned off or sold most everything of value.

"What are we going to do with his stuff?" Michelle asked.

"*We* aren't doing anything. *You* are going to get rid of it. The chair too. Throw it all in your trunk. But you'll have to do it tomorrow. Can't drive until you sober up."

"Mom will freak out if we throw the chair away. She loves that thing. And what if somebody finds it all?"

"Nah, it's older than Methuselah, and she's been saying it was time to get rid of it. We'll say Stone kicked it, and it busted." Jack motioned at the beads scattered on the floor. "We got rid of it and cleaned up so she wouldn't have to deal with it. Nobody will find it. If they do, they ain't gonna be thinking it's Stone's. He ran off, remember?"

Michelle nodded. "Help me load my car." In short order, they had the clothes and other belongings stuffed in her trunk, along with the chair.

"You can't let anybody see you tomorrow." Jack put his weight on the trunk lid to close it against the bulky chair.

"Duh, you think I'm stupid? If either of us gets seen, we're both screwed."

Jack nodded gravely and walked toward the back yard. He pulled the three wheeler up to the door, and they set upon moving the body. A huge pool of blood had formed beneath it on the linoleum, and they had to abort the first attempt when Michelle saw it. She gathered herself and, after wrapping the body in an old sheet from the closet, helped Jack lift the body onto the three-wheeler rack.

"What about...?" Jack gestured toward the open door and the pool of blood visible beyond it.

"I'll take care of it." Michelle cut him off. Jack eyed her skeptically. "I'll take care of it," she repeated firmly.

"What if Mom gets back before I do?" Jack said.

Michelle, thinking more clearly now, was finally able to contribute. "I'll just have to tell her our story about how Stone left. You know, act like it just happened, like I was just about to call her. You got so upset you rode off, said you was going to Jet's house. She won't think nothing of that, and even if she comes looking, at least Jet's is the opposite direction from where you're headed."

Jack nodded and sped off, soon finding himself rumbling across the land that had called to him even before the spark of his idea had ignited into a discernable flame. He glanced over his shoulder at the dust boiling from the dirt farm road, a murky, brown steam obscuring the lights of the houses shrinking distant behind him.

The look was instinctive, an obligatory check to make sure no one was following. But in reality he wasn't particularly worried about being seen. The late hour had rendered the street desolate hours before. No, there was more to it than that. Something about seeing the lights fade to black and wishing the rotten memories would too. But he knew that wouldn't happen.

He whiteknuckled his grip against the jolt of each rut, worried the body might bounce to the ground, yet almost not caring. Almost. But he had to care. There was too much at stake.

He stopped a moment to examine the situation. Was there any blood dripping, leaving a trail? Did it even matter? If things went according to his plan, no one would be looking. Not for a long time, anyway. He kicked a tire and suppressed a frustrated yell. It shouldn't have had to be this way. He had warned Stone to back off! But all that was irrelevant now. Everything was irrelevant aside from the task at hand.

Centering his focus on the road ahead, he squared his shoulders and sped on his way into the night. Still, the spinning of the ATV wheels was nothing compared to the whirling inside his head, a tangle of questions for which he had no answers. Stone had it coming, so why should Michelle go to jail for what Stone did? Why couldn't Stone just leave them alone? Did it really matter if he didn't have any family looking for him anyway? Would he go to jail with Michelle if they got caught? Did they really think they could keep this a secret forever? Could he go to Hell for this? Did he deserve to? He was just trying to save his sister. Was there any other way? What if Case found out? Would Mom hate them or be thankful they kept Michelle from going to prison? What if she still loved Stone deep down? Could she forgive them? Could they forgive themselves?

If he had one question with no answer, he had a thousand. So much didn't make sense. The only thing that made sense was the plan. Stick to the plan.

———

Jack parked the three-wheeler at the Hideaway, both to pick up two concrete blocks left over from construction and to finalize his plan from a familiar location. He was not excited about getting into a boat alone in the middle of the night and was horrified at the reason for it, but he saw no other choice. The only place he had been able to think of to quickly hide the body, undetected tonight and undiscovered forever, was at the bottom of Snake Lake. It was a horrible thing to contemplate, much less actually do, but what were the other options? If he wasn't going to do it right, what was the point at all? He had seen enough crime dramas to think that all but the deepest buried bodies always seemed to get found. That was especially likely around here. There wasn't an inch of this property or the ones around it that he and his buddies didn't cover during hunting season, and he sure didn't have time to dig a deep hole. Two blocks tied to a nylon rope brought from home would sink the body, and no one would ever know.

Then he saw the headlight. Just a faint flicker through the undergrowth at first but soon growing in intensity, accompanied by the sound of a motor and unmistakable in its direction.

Someone was coming.

Jack wanted to vomit again.

He was afraid to stay where he was in case whoever was on the ATV was coming to the campsite. But he was even more afraid to crank up and try to move. He couldn't remember if he had left the headlight off or on, he couldn't see the switch to tell, and he was suddenly too panicked to remember whether up or down was the off position. Jack decided to shift into neutral and do his best to push the ATV and its grim cargo behind a tangle of honeysuckle.

He agonized from his meager hiding spot, desperate to tame his shaking and use its energy to plan his next move. Relief rushed over him when the ATV turned to his left, toward Snake Lake below. From his slightly elevated vantage point he could see silhouettes, partly obscured by vines and foliage, in the headlights of the other three-wheeler. Both voices were unmistakable. Case, explaining how safe the boat was and how it was a secret. Abi, not understanding entirely but agreeing not to tell.

He couldn't believe that Case was taking the boat. Their boat. The one they had vowed never to move, never to share. Now what? *Case, you sorry liar, you have fouled up everything.* His mind raced again, clearer now, searching for an alternate plan. He needed to get this done and get back home. Who knew what Michelle might do if left alone too long? The next best option came to him quickly. The one place on the property that, to his knowledge, no one had touched in the past few years.

The old barn.

Jack shifted the three-wheeler into neutral and pushed, hoping the sounds in the boat below would obscure the rustle of the tires as he navigated out of the campsite and down the road. With considerable but quiet effort, he soon faced the black entrance to the barn, guarded by tangles of briars and vines. He dragged the body off the ATV and fought his way into the dark, dilapidated building, if one could still call it that.

Jack was alarmed at how difficult it was to move the body. What he thought should take two minutes took fifteen. Under his breath, he cursed Case again for forcing him to change his plans. The sudden realization that getting the body in and out of the boat might have proven even more formidable did little to squelch his anger. It was the principle of it if nothing else.

His mother would be home soon. The clock was ticking. He had to hurry.

He set out to strip the clothes once he got the body where he wanted it. If discovered quickly, the clothes wouldn't matter, Stone's body would be easily identified. But if not found for months or even years, it might prove difficult to identify. He had heard of dental records being used, but Stone had an aversion to doctors and dentists—a paranoia about them in fact—and as far as Jack knew, he had never been to either in the years he had known him.

Jack shuddered as he frantically completed the task of removing the clothes, trying to avoid touching the cold flesh. As he removed the shirt, he inadvertently touched the back and felt an immediate chill. Something didn't feel right. *What is that?* Jack struck a match, and what he saw almost caused him to drop it.

Even in the meager glow, the huge scar across both shoulders was obvious. It was wide and raised, not like a cut. Maybe a burn? Stone had never taken his shirt off around Jack, and now he guessed he knew why. Sort of. What was the scar from, and why had Stone hidden it? Jack would never know. It didn't matter now anyway.

Jack buried the body in the hay and stood, staring, trying to think, for several seconds before he walked out. That would do for now. He could move it later. He was ashamed that he had no feelings for this man or his death. His eyes were dry. The space from which tears had flowed earlier now contained only emptiness. He asked himself if that made him a monster.

He stood at the entrance of the barn, staring into the night for what seemed like an eternity while he waited for the rumble of the other three-wheeler to begin and then fade away. He almost expected Case and Abi to decide to ride down to the barn for no particular reason. That's just the way the night had gone. Too exhausted to push his three-wheeler another inch, he resigned himself to whatever fate awaited should that happen. But they never came.

Once he was certain they had gone, Jack drove back to the Hideaway and walked down to the lake. At least the Snake could hide one secret for him. He hurled the gun into the center of the black water and startled at the splash. It was louder than he expected, like a beaver signaling danger with a slap of its tail against the water. As he trudged back up the hill, he replayed the sound in his mind and wondered if it was somehow a sign.

The last task was to destroy the clothes, and he knew just how to do it. His friends had often made fun of him, calling him a pyromaniac when he would insist on building a campfire at every opportunity, no matter the season, even when summer's oppressive heat was already almost unbearable. Something about campfires had always seemed magical to him. They weren't just a source of warmth but also of insight, their flaming tongues and beaming embers a kind of crystal ball for those who dared to seek the secrets they held. Jack found himself studying the fire this night as he had so often in the past, mesmerized by its destructive glow and what it represented this time, so very different from all others before it. But on this night, insight did not come. Only questions for which he knew there would never be answers.

The tick of an internal clock snapped him back into motion. He had planned to stay until the fire burned completely out, but he didn't have time for that. Jack rose, dusted himself off, and left quickly. It never occurred to him that he had absently set the antler-handled knife aside in the edge of the fire pit while he arranged the clothes atop the wood and squirted the lighter fluid.

TWENTY-EIGHT

"SAY something, Case."

I looked up for the first time in several minutes and saw that sometime during his confession Jack had slid to the floor again, back against the wall.

His look echoed his plea. "Please."

I sat stunned, trying to understand the implications his revelation posed me. For all of us. "Jack, I … I don't know what to say."

"You see why we did it, right? You understand?"

"What do you want me to say? Everything is okay? That I'm fine with the fact you've had me helping you cover up a *murder?*"

"I didn't—we didn't—mean for you to get involved." Jack said.

I frowned and cocked my head, incredulous.

"And it wasn't a murder," he continued insistently. "Stone was trying to *kill me*. Michelle saved my life."

"Then why did you try to hide it?"

Michelle sat beside her brother and put a hand on his knee. "I was messed up, Case. No matter what our story was, they woulda made me pee in a cup, and I'd have gone to jail."

"You don't know that."

She waited on me to look her in the eye before she spoke. "Would you have been willing to bet *your* life on it?"

Jack stood up. "My plan was to go back, move the body later, you know, sink it in the Snake. That's why I pretended to be sick and skipped school that week. But I had trouble getting up the nerve, and when I did go back days later, it was, you know, it was bad."

"Bad?"

He paced again. "The smell. I couldn't go in there. I just couldn't go back in there no more. No way."

I tried not to imagine what that must have been like.

"Jack didn't tell me about hiding the body in the barn," Michelle said. "I thought until just a few days ago that he had sunk it in the lake like he'd planned. I didn't know he had gotten you involved, Case. I'm sorry. I'm just glad it's you and nobody else."

I jerked my head upward to catch Jack's eye. His expression answered my question. He had not told Michelle about Jet and Abi's involvement.

"What about your mom?" I asked, turning back to Michelle.

"We told Mom the story about Stone leaving, and she really didn't act surprised. She seemed relieved, actually, at first. But then I'd hear her crying in her bedroom at night sometimes." Michelle turned her head away and wiped her eyes with the back of her hand.

"And nobody else has been suspicious?"

"No," Jack said. "That's the thing. It's like everyone who knew him *expected* him to disappear. Walter Simpson offered to pay me to tell where Stone went. Vance acts like he thinks he ran off for some reason. Patridge too. I can't make sense of it, but that's the way it's been."

"And Stone didn't have any other family?" I wanted to confirm what I had been told before.

"No, remember he moved from Pennsylvania. Was an only child, his parents both died before he moved down here. Never heard of no cousins or anything. If he had any, they must not have liked him. Nobody did."

"So why'd you go along with having a campout, knowing the body was just down the way?"

"C'mon, Case, what are the odds? When's the last time any of us went in there?" Jack's voice softened and he dropped his head. "And to be honest, after a while, it was just easier to pretend it never happened."

"And when we—when I—suggested we move the body to Goodsen's farm?"

"Well at first, I didn't know what to do. I just felt helpless. You didn't want a big mess on Papa Mac's place, and we didn't want the girls to get drug into it. Plus you thought it was just a homeless dude who died naturally, so I went along with it too. But then I realized it was a good idea. I'd be less likely to be a suspect, since that wouldn't have been somewhere I could have easily moved the body by myself without getting seen. And it would be about as unlikely to be discovered there as on Papa Mac's place. So I thought that even if one day someone figured out it was Stone, they wouldn't think it was us, as long as *you* kept the secret." Jack emphasized the last words, studying me, pleading silently with his eyes.

"Jack, I don't know. This is huge."

"Please, Bud. Michelle has problems, but she ain't a bad person. She saved my life. And Momma has been through enough. Ain't nothing nobody does gonna bring Stone back."

A flash of headlights shone through the front window. Janice Masterson was home.

"I was never here." I grabbed my flashlight and slipped out the back door, sneaking around the other side of the house to begin the long, confusing walk back home in the dark.

PART TWO

"Greater love hath no man than this,
that a man lay down his life for his friends."
—John 15:13, KJV

TWENTY-NINE

"HEY, I need you over here." Jack sounded breathless, almost anxious on the phone.

Three days and mostly sleepless nights had passed since I left his house in shock about the truth behind Stone's death, and I was no less confused than I had been the moment I found out.

"I don't know, Jack. I need some time."

"No, I need you here ASAP. Like, in the next hour. Then you can have time."

"You've told me all I need to know. I don't need to hear any more. Don't worry, I haven't said anything—yet."

"I got a phone call," Jack said.

"From who?"

"It was weird. Some guy named Spikes or Spright, something like that. Said he's an old friend of Stone's."

"What'd he say?"

"Said he had something for me and Michelle and my mom. Wouldn't say what it was."

"So why you calling me?"

"I don't know. I'm worried about what it might be. I ... I need you, Bud."

"Like you needed me to help cover up your murder?"

My jab was met with silence, and I thought Jack might hang up on me. But he didn't. "C'mon, man," he said finally. "Just come over here. Then I'll leave you alone. Please."

Jack smiled broadly as I walked in the door. "I knew I could count on you." He slapped me affectionately on the shoulder. It irked me that Jack had been furious with me until I caught him in his lie, and now that he needed me, I was his best friend again. Even so, it was hard to stay mad at him for long. That irked me, too.

"When's that guy gonna be here? And where's your mom?"

"Any minute now. And, Mom ... isn't exactly coming."

I narrowed my eyes at him.

"Don't be mad," he begged. "I just want to see whatever it is before she does. So I can decide what to do. And you can help me."

"So you lied and told him she'd be here?"

He grimaced. "No, I just didn't tell him she wouldn't."

"Good grief, man. You don't know when to stop do you?"

Michelle's voice broke in from behind me. "Case, at least see what this guy says, please? We're the only three who knows what happened to Stone."

I turned to answer and had to look twice to make sure it was her. She was dressed in slacks and a nice sweater. Her hair and makeup were perfect. She looked ten years older.

The sound of a car door slamming obviated my need to answer. "He's here," Jack said.

I heaved an exasperated sigh and moved away, but only as far as the couch. Far enough away to remind of my dissent but close enough to be complicit, since I would still be able to see and hear everything.

"Okay then." Jack flashed a thumbs up.

The man was dressed in a gray pinstripe suit, blue shirt with white collar, burgundy tie, and brown wingtip shoes. Round, gold-rimmed glasses completed the professional look. He had a receding hairline with a close cut, was average height, tanned with a bright smile. "Hello, I'm Timothy Speights. You can call me Tim. You must be Michelle." He extended his hand as she asked him to come in. "And Jack, right?" He looked at me.

"No sir, that's me."

Speights turned and found Jack to his left, on the other side of the counter. He smiled and shook Jack's hand eagerly, then glanced back at me.

"That there is my friend Case. He's pretty much family, too, though."

"Okay then, how about your mother?" Speights looked around the room expectantly.

"Mr. Speights, I'm terribly sorry to tell you this, but Mother had a delay at work and won't be home for several hours." Michelle used a shockingly sophisticated voice. I couldn't believe how authentic it sounded. "She called a few moments ago and apologized for being tied up. They had some type of emergency at the clinic. She just asked if you would discuss whatever it is with me, and I'll share it with her as soon as she gets home. Do you have a business card? I'll have Mother call you if she has questions."

Tim Speights raised his eyebrows with a skeptical-yet-impressed look, then produced a business card. "What clinic does your mother work in? You can see from my card there I'm in medical sales myself. Maybe I know her and didn't even know it."

I don't think Speights recognized it, but a moment of doubt flashed across Michelle's face. She recovered quickly, though. "Well, she works for a gynecologist," she lied as she studied the business card. "Do you sell those type products? You know, for pelvic exams and such?"

"No, no, no." Speights gave an uncomfortable laugh, took a

step back, and waved his hands in front of his chest. "No, ma'am, I sell orthopedic hardware. You know, plates and rods for fixing broken arms and such. I doubt the, uh, gynecologists use that type thing very much."

"No, I bet not." Michelle's businesswoman persona never wavered.

I thought Jack's eyes might pop out of his head trying to fight back a laugh. It was all I could do to keep a straight face myself.

"Now, sir," Michelle continued, "what did you need to speak to me about?"

"Okay, here's the deal." Speights turned to look at Jack, whose amused expression disappeared instantaneously like the image on a shaken Etch A Sketch. Speights's own expression clouded, and his tone became somber. He produced a brown envelope from inside his jacket pocket. "I have something for you two. From Stone. If I wasn't going out of town on business for a few weeks, I'd wait until your mother was available. But I want to put this behind me. She can call if she wants." He tapped his business card on the counter where Michelle had laid it.

"What is it?" Jack asked.

Speights handed the envelope to Michelle. "To tell you the truth, I'm not sure. I wanted to open it, but my attorney wife talked me out of it. And I guess she's right. I just hope whatever it is, it's somehow helpful to you. I need to ask you, though, do y'all know where Stone is?"

Jack and Michelle looked at each other but gave away nothing. "No, sir," Michelle said. "He disappeared."

Speights nodded. "That's what I heard. And I wish I could tell you where he went, but I really don't know. He and I weren't that close the last few years."

"Then how did you get this envelope?" Michelle said.

"I'm going to tell you something. Not many folks know this story. It's not necessarily a secret, but I just don't talk about it much." He paused and took a deep breath, clearly needing to gather himself before continuing. "I served in Vietnam with Stone."

"Wait," Jack said. "That's not right. My dad was killed in Vietnam, but Stone wasn't in the war. You've got them mixed up."

"Hang on, son. Listen to me. I'm not sure why he didn't tell you, but let me finish and maybe somehow, someday it will make sense to you. Stone *did* serve. I never got to know him that well, but we were in the same unit for a while, the 42nd Helicopter Squadron." He paused to let this sink in, but no one spoke.

"We were a rescue and recovery unit. After the Paris Peace Accords in 1973 that supposedly ended U.S. involvement in the Vietnam War, we still flew support missions over eastern Cambodia. One day, we went in to rescue an F-4 pilot who had been shot down but avoided capture. We took a hit from a MiG-21 in our tail rotor and had to crash land. Two of our five-man crew were killed instantly. The pilot and I were pinned in the wreckage, but Stone was not hurt at first, other than a few cuts and bruises. I had my leg caught beneath one of the landing skids and couldn't move."

Speights took a seat on a stool and continued. "I don't know how that son of a gun did it, but Stone somehow lifted the skid off me and dragged me to safety. It was almost superhuman. Seriously, there's no way he should have been able to lift it off, but he did. Then he went after the pilot, who was still alive. He climbed on top and tried to pull him through the shattered windshield of the cockpit with no luck. Smoke began pouring out of it, but he went around and climbed back inside the wreckage anyway. I was screaming at him to get out, but he wouldn't listen. Our pilot was a heck of a good guy, and we all looked up to him, Stone included.

He was determined to get him out or die trying.

"The smoke was pitch black, and I don't know how he saw to do what he did, but in a few seconds that seemed like hours, he rolled out of the cabin, dragging the pilot with him. I knew the thing was about to blow, but I couldn't help him. Both my legs were broken. Stone picked the pilot up in his arms and started running just as the helicopter exploded. He shielded him with his body and took second- and third-degree burns to his back in the process."

That explained the burns Jack had found on Stone's back. A glance from Jack told me he was thinking the same thing.

"What happened to the pilot?" Jack asked.

Timothy Speights had tears in his eyes now. "Another chopper came and hauled the three of us out of there, but the pilot died before we got to the hospital. Stone took it particularly hard."

"But that wasn't his fault." Jack's voice edged several steps higher than usual. "He did the best he could."

"Yes, he did. But Stone was always a bit … *different*." Speights bit off the word. "He didn't have a lot of friends. And the man he couldn't save was the one guy who always treated him fairly when maybe others didn't."

"Did you … did you know him?" Michelle's lip quivered. "The pilot?"

"Yes. Yes, I did." Speights tried to hold Michelle and Jack's unwavering stares but his eyes fell instead to his own hands fidgeting on the counter. "I knew him very well. In fact, we grew up together. His name was Michael Masterson. He was your father."

THIRTY

"NO! No! That's not right." Jack slammed his fist down on the Formica counter. "Stone didn't know my father. He just moved here from Pennsylvania with his job."

"Jack," Speights answered calmly. "I know it's a hard pill to swallow. I don't know why Stone never told you guys, and I'm sorry to be the one. I wasn't sure exactly where he was from to be honest, and I never asked. We never were that close, during or after the war. We didn't keep in touch. I lived in Texas for several years, and when I moved back, he was already here. He never was that easy to get to know, to be honest with you, and I did think it strange that he landed here out of the blue. But no doubt he saved my life, and I told him I owed him, to let me know if I could ever help him. He never did, until just recently."

Michelle placed the brown envelope on the counter. "This?"

Speights nodded. "He called me a few weeks before he disappeared and asked if I would still do that favor I owed him. I told him of course, I owed him a lot more than a favor. Anyway, he asked to meet me. He said he was in some trouble and would I hold on to that for him, and please keep it sealed. He wanted me to give it to you guys if he ever disappeared, but wanted me to wait several months first. I have no idea why, and he didn't say. Made me swear on my life I would make sure nobody but you guys ever saw it."

"He disappeared like, ten months ago," Michelle said suspiciously.

"To be honest, he was acting strange that day, and I wondered if I could even take him seriously. I was afraid he was having some mental problems and thought it might be some post-traumatic stress deal or something." He shrugged and adjusted his glasses in the same motion. "I told him he needed to see a doctor, and I'm ashamed to say I forgot about it until I found the envelope in my closet a few weeks ago. When I finally got around to asking around about Stone, I found out sure enough, he had run off back in the fall."

"And that's it?" Jack asked.

"What do you mean?"

"I mean, you just told us you and Stone were both with our father when he died, you've got an envelope to give us, and that's it?"

"I'm not sure what else you want, Jack. I thought the world of your dad, and I grieved for him for a long time. I really didn't want to relive that over and over, so that's one reason I stayed away after I got out of the war, and the main reason I stayed away from Stone when I moved back two years ago. From what I could see, he'd been dying in your father's place every day since Cambodia. He didn't need my problems, and I didn't need his."

Speights rose to leave. "Look, I've told you all I know. I'm sorry. Maybe whatever is in this will help." He tapped the envelope with his middle finger. "I promised him I'd make sure you two got it. But don't open it, just give it to your momma when she gets home. I'm not sure what she knows of that story. I would assume she knows it all. Tell her to call me if she needs to."

I had hovered in the background to this point, stunned by what I was hearing and reticent to inject myself into such a personal scene. But Jack had invited me for a reason, and something Speights had said bothered me. "Mr. Speights?"

The man blinked and cocked his head as he turned toward me, clearly having forgotten I was there. "Yes?" His toothpaste-commercial smile belied any attempt not to sound patronizing.

"You said *you two*. You said it twice."

He shook his head and contorted his face in a way that told me what his next words would be before he uttered them. "What are you talking about?"

"First you said 'I have something for *you two*,' then you said 'I promised him I'd make sure *you two* got it.' But then you told them to give the envelope to Ms. Janice."

Speights removed his glasses and pinched the corners of his eyes where they met at the bridge of his nose, but not before a fleeting eye roll gave away his opinion of my inquiry. He forced another smile and looked purposely at Jack and Michelle as he replaced his glasses. "Like I said, I didn't think Stone was thinking clearly that day. I'm sure he wanted *the three* of you to have the envelope." He held up three fingers and shot a glance at me then back to them. Again, I knew what he would say next. "*Three*, as in *you two* and your mom."

Timothy Speights opened the kitchen door, stopped and stared out, motionless for several seconds. Then he turned and spoke to Jack and Michelle once more. His tone was sincere. "I'm sorry about all this. Your father was one of the finest men I've ever known, and I would have given my life to save his if I could. I'm sorry about Stone too. Raw deal for you." And with that, he walked out, cranked his car, and drove away.

Jack and Michelle sat in stunned silence. Michelle was crying while Jack softly hit his fist on the counter repeatedly, like the drumbeat to a song abandoned by its music. I had no words of encouragement to offer either of them. What did it mean that Stone knew their father, that he had been injured trying, unsuccessfully, to save his life? Did that have anything to do with all the trouble, whatever it was, that Stone had been in before he died? "Guys," I said, "we need to see what's in that envelope."

Jack stopped beating. "Who cares, Case? It's all stupid and pointless anyway. Bad luck just leads to more bad luck for us. Just give it to Mom like he said."

"Jack, it sucks about your dad. Maybe Speights can tell you more about him one day. But right now, you've come this far, you might as well see what's in the envelope. And maybe I read more into it than I should have, but I think it's possible Speights got his wires crossed on who Stone sent that envelope to."

"Case, I think you're reading too much into that," Michelle said.

"Maybe, but there's one way to find out." I reached under the stove, pulled out a saucepan and filled it with water. I turned one of the larger eyes on HIGH and set the pan on it. No one said a word. "Give it to me," I said when steam finally rose from the pan. I reached out and took the envelope, which was padded with bubbled lining, making it impossible to tell what it contained. "I saw this on TV once. The steam melts the glue on the seal. Then you just glue it back with Elmer's or something and nobody can tell." I held the envelope over the steam and within a few minutes was able to open the seal without tearing the paper at all. I handed the envelope to Michelle. She hesitated only briefly, looked inside, then turned the envelope upside down to dump its contents into her hand.

It was a key. A single key, with a thin wire ring attached to a label. Written on the label, in lettering almost too small to read, was the following:

First Loyalty Bank, Amberton
Stone, Michelle, Jack on account
be smart

"Case, you were right." Michelle said.

"Ha." I smiled and held up two fingers. "A safe deposit box, with your *two* names on it. You can pay me my consulting fee later."

Jack's expression brightened too. "I knew I asked you over here for a reason. Looks like we're making a trip to the bank."

"Are we sure we need to do this alone?" Michelle turned her Toyota onto Main Street.

"We've been over this a thousand times," Jack sighed. "It's like Case said. Stone left Mom's name off this account for a reason. We need to know why."

"And y'all don't think we'll look suspicious?"

"There's nothing illegal about it," Jack said, "and if somebody asks later, we were just being nosy. Since when did you become a rule follower anyway?"

"Focus, people," I chimed in from the back seat. "I asked around to find out how this works, so listen carefully. You have a key, the bank has a key. You go in the vault with the bank person, put both keys in, and they pull the box out."

"Sounds easy enough," Michelle said, "if my genius brother doesn't foul it up."

Jack poked her in the ribs from his seat in the shotgun position.

"Stop." Michelle jabbed her elbow at him. "We're here."

The First Loyalty Bank looked like most any other small town bank. One story, light brown brick with a hip roof and cement columns supporting the portico guarding the entrance. I had never been inside but figured I'd passed by it at least a thousand times.

I was surprised at the paucity of activity in the spacious room when we entered. A single teller behind a counter to our left was turned away and talking to another teller at a drive-through window. Two empty leather chairs flanked a small table immediately on our right, and a tinted glass wall straight ahead hid what appeared to be three or four offices. Michelle, Jack, and I stood in the center of the room, uncertain where to go.

"Hey guys, what are you doing here?"

We turned to see Jet's mother coming through a door behind us and to the left.

"Hey, Ms. Maggie," I said. "I'm just, uh, here with Michelle and Jack."

Jack fidgeted uncomfortably. None of us had thought about Jet's mother working at the bank. I'm sure he was concerned about what Jet might have told her about their recent disagreement.

"I'm glad y'all came in." She smiled, giving no indication of hard feelings. "What can I do for you?"

"We want to access our safe deposit box." Michelle used a voice not as sophisticated as she had with Mr. Speights—Ms. Townsend would certainly see through it—but refined enough to appear to be a semi-responsible nineteen-year-old.

No doubt aware of Michelle's recent problems, the subtle lift of Ms. Townsend's eyebrows and downward curl of her lips suggested she was pleasantly surprised by Michelle's demeanor. She looked the girl over and broke into a broad smile. "Haven't seen you in a while, Michelle, but you look like you're doing well. I'm so glad." Her smile was genuine, and though her tone was somewhat patronizing, Michelle actually seemed to delight in the compliment.

"Thank you."

Ms. Townsend nodded and put her hands on her hips. Time to get down to business. "Who will be accessing the box today?"

"Jack and me," Michelle said.

"Okay, that's fine. Let me see your key to get the number. I'll be right back, just have to get our guard key and verify your signatures on the rental agreement." She disappeared around a corner.

"Signatures?" Jack hissed. "What is she talking about?"

"I have no idea." I shrugged. "Nobody told me about that part."

"Hey, Jack, don't you remember?" Michelle pointed at the far end of the counter. "Stone brought us in, and we signed some stuff right down there."

"Oh, yeah. That was what, a year ago? Is that what that was for?"

"I just signed like you did. Stone didn't like questions. I guess we're about to find out."

Ms. Townsend reemerged with a brass key in hand, similar to the one we had brought. She produced a bound notebook, set it on the counter, and opened it to the 'P' section, motioning Jack and Michelle over. I stepped back, hoping to hide my angst.

"I was sorry to hear about Mr. Perkins leaving awhile back," Ms. Townsend said. "Looks like he rented this box, but your names are on it also. Michelle, how old are you?"

"Nineteen."

"Good, you have to be eighteen to open it without an adult. Okay, if each of you will just sign right here, this keeps a record of who has accessed the box, and we match the signatures to those on the agreement. It appears that no one has been to this box since Mr. Perkins opened it two years ago."

Jack and Michelle did as they were told and signed the document.

"Yep, the signatures match." Ms. Townsend laughed. "Not that I had any doubt. Follow me." The trio disappeared into the bank vault where I could see rows of numbered boxes but nothing of what was going on inside.

Soon Ms. Townsend stepped out and approached me. "So, Case, I haven't seen you around much the past few days. Are you guys and John Edward okay? He hasn't seemed like himself, but he won't talk to me."

"Oh, yes ma'am, Jet and me, we're fine. Probably just some girl trouble." I lied, forcing a laugh. "I'll see him at baseball practice tomorrow."

"Are y'all getting excited about the district championship game?"

"Yes, ma'am. I think we can win it this year."

"I believe you can." Jet's mother nodded her head. "John Edward is so excited about it. I don't know if he plays because he loves the game like you and Jack, or if he plays because he loves being with you and Jack. Either way, I know he wants to win."

I barely acknowledged what she said, just shrugged and craned my neck as if trying to see in the vault. "What are they doing in there?"

"Oh, I don't know. I just use the guard key to get the box out, but I'm not allowed to stay in there while they open it. It's a little bit unusual though. Does Janice know about that box?"

"I don't think so, Ms. Maggie. She's been having a hard time with everything. They remembered it and wanted to check it to make sure there wasn't anything that would upset her even more. You know, Jack's trying to be the man of the house, and Michelle is trying to straighten herself out too."

"That's good, that's good." She diverted her eyes back toward the entrance of the vault, where Jack and Michelle were emerging. "Did you find what you were looking for?"

Michelle shrugged. "It was empty."

I already knew that was not true. Jack was stuffing something in his pocket as he walked out of the vault, and I could see the corner of a yellow piece of paper protruding where nothing had been before. From the direction of her gaze and the look on her face, I was certain Ms. Townsend had seen it too.

THIRTY-ONE

"COME on, man, tell me what you found." I slammed the car door and slid to the middle of the back seat, leaning forward between Michelle and Jack.

"We didn't find hardly nothing." Jack reached into his pocket and pulled out the yellow scrap of paper, tossing it over his back like a piece of trash. "I just knew there'd be some cash in there."

I retrieved the crumpled paper from the floor and spread it out. The words were scribbled in the same handwriting as that on the safe deposit key, though slightly larger:

See Chief Baker
CARE 11c

I flipped the paper over to make sure I wasn't missing something. Was that it? Could it have been any more vague? "That's all there was in the box?"

Michelle cranked the car and looked back at me. "Yep. That's it. Any idea what it could mean? Racked our brains for five minutes in that vault."

"Got no idea." I rubbed my temples. "Y'all be quiet a minute. I need some time to think."

I leaned back and turned toward the window while we rode. So many things didn't make sense. Why had Stone moved to Amberton in the first place, and why didn't he tell anyone he had known

Michael Masterson? Why had he put only Michelle's and Jack's name on the safe deposit box? What was Stone worried about? Was he planning to leave, or worse, do harm to himself? I looked again at the yellow note in my hand. What in the world did 'see Chief Baker, CARE 11c' mean?

Michelle deftly handled a sharp turn and accelerated into a straightaway, and I tried to sort out who knew what about Stone's death. It seemed like a drive to nowhere—infinite turns, each a dead end. Jack, Michelle Jet, Abi, and I knew that the body had been moved from the old barn on Papa Mac's to the barrels on Goodsen's place. But only the three of us in the car knew the deceased was not Brendan Perry or some other random victim. And beyond that, we also knew how Stone had died.

Yet Michelle didn't know that Jet and Abi knew what they knew. And last but not least, at least one other, unknown person—the man who had seen us at the barrels that day we moved the bones, who may or may not have been the person who saved us later at Seder Lake—knew something. Did he know the truth about what had happened to Stone? Who he was, why he was interested, and what he knew were anyone's guess. Just the questions themselves gave me a headache. And made me very nervous.

With no new answers, my thoughts turned to what to do. Should we just tell the truth and get this over with? I found it hard to believe that Michelle would be held responsible for her actions this many months later, but how to be certain? No doubt the police would be suspicious about why Jack and Michelle hid their actions, not to mention the fact that I helped them afterward. Their logical question would be that if Jack and Michelle had done nothing wrong by killing Stone in self-defense, then why cover it up? I fully believed Jack's story, and what kind of friend was I if I betrayed him now? On the other hand, what kind of person was I if I did not?

"Hey Bud, you figure it out?"

I looked up and saw we were turning into my driveway. "Huh?"

Jack gave me an exasperated frown. "You told us to shut up and let you think." He reached back over the seat and grabbed the note from my hand. "So what does this mean?"

I opened the car door and got out. "I don't know. But the day is young."

—————

"Case, are you sick?" Mom asked from across the kitchen table. "Spaghetti is one of your favorites, and all you've done so far is move noodles back and forth across your plate."

Dad rapped the table with his knuckles. "Better eat up if you're gonna get up to 150 by football season."

"I know, just not real hungry." I took a bite, wanting to be hungry but knowing it was futile. Too much on my mind. Among other things, I wondered if the investigation into Redmond Patridge's involvement with Stone might be shedding some light on what had Stone so anxious—and maybe even afraid—before he died. And if so, perhaps that might lead to answers about what Patridge's dealings with Stone had to do with Vance MacIntosh and Walter Simpson.

Finally, I couldn't stand it anymore. "Dad," I blurted, "has Redmond Patridge said anything about Stone Perkins?"

My father set his fork down on his plate and studied me while he chewed before taking a drink of sweet tea. "Son, you need to forget about Patridge. He is being charged with first degree murder for killing Sheriff Hall, not to mention the other charges that came from what happened with us. The judge thought he was a flight risk and denied bail, so he is still in jail."

"I know, I've been watching the news. But what did he have to do with Stone? Have you found out? Jack's been real upset about it."

"I can't say much, because it will come out in the trial. But it looks like Patridge was working as an enforcer for a gambling boss in New Orleans. Stone got in over his head with some gambling debt, and they called him on it. Nothing too complicated there. The guys in New Orleans are working that angle. We're just working on proving Patridge killed Sheriff Hall for now. Whatever Stone was into is on the back burner. We may get to that later. If we knew where Stone ran off to, we would probably focus on that a little more, but we don't have enough folks in our department to try to find him right now."

I already felt plenty guilty for deceiving my father, but another emotion burgeoned. Fear. Fear of what the legal ramifications would be if it was discovered we were concealing information possibly related to a separate murder investigation and an illegal gambling ring in another state. Fear of what would happen to my father's career, his aspirations to be sheriff, if it was discovered his very own son was involved. And probably most important to me, I realized, was fear of the disappointment my father would most certainly feel if he found out.

I suppressed my growing apprehension and forced myself to appear nonchalant, to hide the fact I was getting ready to lie once again. "Okay, that makes sense. Glad he's still locked up. On another note, can I ask another question? Mom, this one is for you too."

"Of course," she said.

"A friend gave me this clue. It's for a game, like a scavenger hunt, I think. I've got to, uh, come up with some ideas for what it could mean." I grabbed a napkin and wrote down See Chief Baker, CARE 11c on it, arranging the spacing as closely as I could to the original. I hoped against hope that this would not somehow backfire, but I was desperate to get this over with and thought if anyone could give me an idea, one of them could. "Any idea what this could be?"

"Hmm," Dad said. "Chief Baker. Naturally I think of police or fire chiefs, or it could be an Indian name. Or it could be just what it says, the head baker at some type of bakery. But we don't have one of those around here that I know of."

"No idea about 'CARE'," Mom said, "but the way it's capitalized makes me think it's not a verb, but a noun. An acronym for an organization, like ACLU or AARP, that type thing. Or maybe a place? 11c sounds like an apartment number. You could look in the Yellow Pages and see if any apartment complexes are named CARE."

After putting my plate in the sink, I grabbed a McKinley County telephone book from the kitchen desk drawer and headed to my room to contemplate a plan. I had very little hope of finding any answers in the book but even less in the way of better ideas.

The first thing I did was look through all the Bakers in the book. There were twenty-three of them. To no surprise, none of them had a first name of Chief, and none were otherwise remarkable to me. My next step was the Yellow Pages. My heart sank when I discovered 118 pages, each packed with individual listings as well as advertisements of different sizes. I found only eight apartment complexes listed, and the only one that even started with a 'C' was Coastal Apartments, which I thought ironic since the nearest coast to Amberton was 300 miles away. That could account for the 'C' and the 'A' in CARE, but what would the last two letters be? Somehow that just didn't seem to fit.

What else might have an identifier of 11c? I checked the Cs. Cabinets, cable companies, campgrounds, caterers, churches, contractors, convenience stores, the list went on. Nothing fit. I kept flipping pages, studying each listing and every ad closely, double-checking each page. I wasted tiny surges of adrenaline each time I saw the word for which I was searching. CarePlan debt relief company, KC's KidCare daycare center, and a car care center. I even found a beauty salon on page 11 where the slogan was "Where Blair will CARE for your HAIR." I made a mental note never to visit that place, and thought if nothing else useful came of my search, at least there was that.

After more than an hour of futility, I was disgusted, but I decided to give one final flip through the pages. Nothing new jumped out at me, but I paused to look at the section for Motorcycle and ATV Dealers out of my own curiosity. It was only then that I saw it just to the right on the opposite page, under the 'N' section.

Nursing Homes
Chestnut Acres Retirement Establishment
CARE.

My experience visiting nursing homes was zilch. But somehow I knew this one would have a room numbered 11c.

But who was Chief Baker?

"Do you two bozos have a plan?" Michelle questioned us again from behind the wheel of her Toyota Celica. We were a mile outside of town, off of Chestnut Road, a gravel road I had seen before but never had a reason to travel down, and parked in front of Chestnut Acres Retirement Establishment. A brick sign out front displayed the acronym CARE in bold raised letters, which explained why Stone had written only those four letters on the paper in the safe deposit box. The nursing home's full name was displayed much smaller beneath it, followed by the logo, "the CARE you deserve."

"We told you our plan," Jack said.

"No you didn't." Michelle countered. "You said you're gonna

go find room 11c and see who's in there. That's no plan."

"Well, it's the best we can come up with," I said. "I called and asked who was in room 11c. and they wouldn't tell me. So we'll just go see for ourselves. What's the worst they could do?"

"Call the cops on you."

I punched Michelle's seat from behind. "So you're not coming?"

"Uh, uh. Ain't no way, no how. First, those places give me the creeps. And second, I need to be out here in the car to help you clowns get away."

"You're chicken," Jack said, "but that's fine. Works better this way. You just park down the road a piece and pick us up if we come haulin' butt outta there."

"Whatever. But remember, you may think you're the Duke boys, but this ain't the General Lee, and I ain't no Daisy."

I laughed as I opened my door to get out. "Yeah, you ain't got the legs for it."

Jack and I tried to appear casual as we approached the front door. Chestnut Acres was a nondescript, single-story, blond-brick building with brown trim, shaped like a wide V and lined with rows of aluminum-framed windows in each direction. A shallow porch in the middle shaded a single entrance. Bird feeders and haphazard plantings of flowers were sporadically situated in front of the windows. Three or four elderly residents sat in rocking chairs and wheelchairs and monitored us with silent stares as we approached.

"You know, Chestnut is a good name for this place," I said.

"Why?"

"You ever seen a chestnut tree?"

"Not that I know of."

"Exactly. My grandfather told me some fungus killed 'em all like fifty years ago. They called it the chestnut plight or chestnut blight or something like that."

"So there's no more chestnut trees?"

"No, it didn't kill all of 'em exactly. There's a few left. But they're all old. Kind of like the codgers that live here. Maybe they named it to remind old folks of the old days when chestnut trees were all around."

"Or maybe they named it because it's on Chestnut Road and they could put the words together to make it say C-A-R-E," Jack said with a shrug.

"Acronym."

"What?"

"CARE. It's an acronym."

"I doubt that," he snickered. "You need to leave the deep thinking to Jet."

We stopped a few feet inside the doorway to get our bearings. Several residents perched in wheelchairs around a large open foyer, a dining room opened in front of us, and long halls sprawled to our right and left. The vinyl tile on the floor was remarkably clean and appeared freshly waxed, to my surprise. Women who I assumed were nurses milled around up and down the halls, tending to their work and paying no mind to us.

The place's odor fell somewhat short of putrid but landed squarely on unpleasant. Combined fumes from urine, industrial cleaners, feces, and a fusion of cafeteria smells dominated by some type of fried seafood painted an olfactory picture impossible to ignore.

"How do people work here?" Jack wrinkled his nose. "Smells like Mr. Clean ate too much fish and crapped his pants."

"You get used to it," a voice said from behind us. Startled, we turned to see a tall black female wearing what appeared to be a nurse's uniform.

"I, uh, just never, you know ..." Jack started, his face a deep crimson.

"It's okay." She smiled, amiably waving her hand in front of her nose. "You get used to it. When several have blowouts at once, though, it gets really rough." She chuckled as she dropped her hands to her hips, adopting a more business-like posture. "So, I'm Carol Treadway, the head nurse. What can I help you boys with?"

Jack looked at me with uncertainty. I decided to at least begin with a truth. "We are looking for room 11c."

"Room 11, on C Hall…" She looked up at the ceiling, appearing to try to form a mental picture of which resident occupied that room. She finally broke into a smile. "Oh, yes, that's Mr. Bill. He's a sweetheart." She began walking down the hall to our right.

"Mr. Bill?" Jack whispered in my ear as we followed.

"Let's just see. This has got to be the right place," I said.

Soon nurse Treadway stopped at a closed door labeled '11c– William Baker'. Jack elbowed me and nodded at the name. I frowned and nodded back to let him know I wasn't blind. The nurse opened the door slightly and tilted her body to peek in with one foot on the floor just inside the door and the other suspended in the air just outside it. She popped her head back out and frowned. "He may be having one of his days. Sometimes he's with us, sometimes he's not. You can try to talk to him but don't expect much."

"What's wrong with him?" Jack asked.

"I can't say much, but I guess it's no secret. He's had a stroke, and his doctor says he might have some dementia, so basically his brain has trouble functioning correctly sometimes, trouble remembering. I think a lot of it may just be his personality. Sometimes he doesn't want to remember. That's his prerogative though. Now, why did you say you were here to see him?"

"Just, uh, a family friend." I was unsure whether that was a truth or a lie.

She looked puzzled. "Okay, good luck." As we walked in the door, she spoke again. "Oh yeah, boys. One other thing. If he doesn't want to talk, just call him Chief. Sometimes that'll perk him up."

Jack shot me a conspiratorial smile, and in we went.

An old man sat across the room in a wheelchair, his features obscured by shadow, silhouetted against the light streaming through an open window. His back was turned to the door, and he did not move as we approached him from behind. We eased beside him and waited for him to acknowledge us, but he continued to neither speak nor move, only staring out the window in the general direction of a single sweet gum tree hovering over the edge of the front parking lot.

Chief Baker was mostly bald except for a scraggly strip of stark white hair low in the back. Deep wrinkles cut his cheeks and neck, and the dark spots splattered across his head reminded me of the ancient man who sat on the pew in front of me at church. He was clean-shaven, but his scalp and the area around his nose were scaly. Flakes of fallen skin stood out against the darkness of his navy shirt.

"Mr. Baker?" Jack said after a lengthy pause.

Nothing.

"Chief?" I said.

Again, silence. I looked at Jack and shrugged, unsure what to do. I took a second to survey the room, revealing only a few sparse furnishings. A small television topped a simple chest of drawers opposite the foot of the bed. On a shelf beside the bed stood a black-and-white photo of a young man and woman, arm in arm, presumably Mr. Baker and his wife on a day long since passed. I saw no other photos. A poster on the wall adjacent the television showed a scowling Pittsburgh Steeler appearing to watch over the room with a sideways glance. I recognized him easily, more by his missing front teeth than his number 58.

"Jack Lambert," I whispered to Jack with a frown and shake of my head. As an avid Dallas Cowboys fan, I thought Mr. Baker might as well have had a photo of Hitler on his wall.

The old man continued to stare vacantly into the window.

"What now?" Jack asked. "Looks like this was a waste of time."

I tapped the man on the shoulder and spoke loudly, in case he was hard of hearing. "Chief Baker, will you talk to us? Stone Perkins asked us to come see you."

The man jerked his head around and looked at us for the first time, almost as if he'd seen a ghost. His bottom lip quivered, and for a moment I thought he might either vomit or begin crying. "I can hear just fine, you don't have to yell. I'm going to need you boys to leave now. That will be all." He gestured toward the door with two waves of the back of his right hand. I noticed for the first time that his left hand and arm were contracted, drawn close to his body. He turned back toward the window, assuming his original posture and silence.

Jack and I stood there a moment before giving up and making our way toward the door. Just before we left the room, I reached out once more. "Mr. Baker, do you know Stone Perkins?"

The old man said nothing for a second, then just as we turned again to leave, he stopped us cold. "Of course I did," he said softly. "He was my son."

THIRTY-TWO

"WHAT ... what did you say?" Jack's eyes were wide. The old man sighed, as if a weight sitting on his shoulders made it difficult to inhale. "Sit down over here. I guess we'll talk."

We walked back in and sat on the bed, facing the back of the wheelchair. The old man made no attempt to turn toward us. "Did you, did you say Stone was—is—your son?" Jack asked.

"That's him. My son. He was." His voice was hollow, almost hoarse, like someone who had yelled at a football game all afternoon. Or who had spent a lifetime yelling. His persona suggested a reserved toughness, though. He didn't seem like the type who would have had to yell very much.

"How can that be?" Jack asked. "Stone's parents died."

"Yes, they did. But he was my son."

"Why do you say he *was*?" I asked. How could he know?

Finally, the old man moved. With difficulty, he used his good right arm to maneuver the wheel of the chair to turn toward us. A heavy silence followed, filled only with the sound of his labored breathing as he recovered from his effort and studied the two of us.

"Which one of you is Jack?" he asked.

Jack raised his index finger.

The man squinted, scanning him up and down. "He told me. He told me if you came, he'd be gone."

"Mr. Baker, we are really confused," I said. "Please tell us what you're talking about."

"Chief."

"Huh?"

"Everybody called me chief. I was the police chief."

"Here? In Amberton?" Jack asked.

"Amberton? Marbury, Pennsylvania. Where Stone grew up."

I looked at Jack to see if any of this was making sense, but he was frozen, locked in on Chief Baker, hanging on the next word.

"Can you tell us about it, sir?" I asked.

Chief sighed again and looked down, more frail than ever. He shook his head and closed his eyes, and I thought he was going to shut down and say no more. Then he raised his head, took a deep breath, and with a new look of resolve, told the story.

"Peter Perkins should have been a good boy. He *was* a good boy. His father was killed when he was five. Went to get a gallon of milk and got shot dead in a robbery of a quick mart. You know, the Smart Mart over on Hudson and Sixth. You boys been there, huh?"

Jack and I shared a look. The old man was confused about what town he was in. I didn't want to fluster him, though. "Yessir. I think I know where it is."

"Good part of town, too. Silly. Just an innocent bystander, killed by a scumbag I had arrested six months earlier, got off on a stupid tech ... techni ... what you call it?"

"Technicality?" I said.

"Yeah. Moron judge let him go the first time. Second time I caught him, but it was too late by then. Anyway, I was single, and I got to know Hilda while we were doin' the investigating. Married her a couple years later. Hilda was a good woman."

"Hilda?" Jack asked

"Peter's mother. She was a good woman. We got married."

"You got married when Stone—Peter—was seven?" I said.

"Yeah, about seven. Peter was a good boy. His daddy was a good man, so he kept his name. But I treated him like he was mine. He *was* mine. He was a smart boy. Good in sports, too, eh? I coached him in Little League." The old man studied the football poster on the wall. "Played football too. I taught him to hit like that guy. Lambert was a *football* player. Peter was a linebacker too, would hit you hard, and he was hard as a rock himself."

"Is that where he got his nickname? Stone?" I asked.

The old man smiled and held up his good right hand. "Hands of stone. Couldn't catch nothin'. Played defense like a champ though. Strong as an ox." Chief Baker turned his head to the side and stared out the window again. "Wish I had a picture of Peter up on the wall, but he wouldn't let me put up any of my family. Took 'em down if I put 'em up. Said something bad might happen to me if people found out I was here."

"What about Stone's mother?" I asked. "Hilda?"

He turned back toward us. "She died. When Peter was thirteen. Killed in a car wreck. Had been to visit her mother in Ohio and got killed on the way back. She was a good woman."

"Did Stone, er, Peter stay with you?" Jack asked.

"I told you he was my son. Of course he stayed. He was so strong when Hilda died." His lower lip trembled, and his voice cracked. "He was a good boy. Went to church and didn't get in no trouble. Vietnam just messed him up."

"Vietnam?" Jack didn't let on what he already knew about Stone's involvement there.

"Yeah, messed him up. Never was the same again." He grabbed the wheel of his chair and pulled it back to turn himself to the right. He awkwardly made his way to the chest of drawers, opened the bottom drawer, and shuffled through its contents. I was afraid he might fall forward out of his chair, but shortly he raised up with something in his hand. Jack and I sat on the edge of the bed, uncertain of what to do, but the old man gave no indication he needed or wanted help and said nothing until he rolled over to us. "Open it." He handed a cigar box to Jack.

Jack's hand shook slightly as he ran a finger down the edge of the top, like one might do on a present to see if it is taped or sealed shut some other way.

"It's open. If I taped it up, somebody would think I had some money in there and steal it." I shuffled my body closer to Jack's to be able to see the contents of the box. As Jack opened it, Chief spoke again, softly. "Peter told me to give this to you if you came. He said he thought it might be your mom or your sister, but he really thought it would be you. He said if you showed up one day without him, I would know he was gone."

"Gone, you mean, like run off?" Jack asked.

"Maybe. Or maybe gone to the next life. He never would say. Gone from me, either way." I expected him to ask what had happened to Stone, but he did not. Neither Jack nor I volunteered any information.

Jack lifted the lid of the box like he expected a fake snake or grenade to explode from it, but its only contents were several pieces of paper and two cassette tapes.

"Read the newspaper," Chief Baker said.

Jack withdrew a newspaper clipping from the box, from the *Marbury Dispatch*, dated March 20, 1974. "Perkins receives Air Force Cross for Heroic Efforts." There was a photograph of Stone receiving the medal, and a three paragraph, watered-down version of the helicopter accident that took the life of Michael Masterson and three others. It mentioned Timothy Speights but did not list any other names.

Jack rubbed his eyes, but the tears formed anyway.

I patted him on the back. "He won the Air Force Cross?" I asked.

"Yes. He was a brave boy. That's one step below the Medal of Honor, you know."

"Where is his medal?"

"I don't know. He never wanted to talk about it. I never did ask."

Jack picked through the box to examine the other contents. Several documents referred to Reisende Tire Corporation. As best we could tell on brief review, it was indeed a Norwegian company that had been expanding its footprint in the tire manufacturing business in recent years. The documents referenced global expansion initiatives and mentioned that McKinley County, Mississippi, was one of several sites in the United States being considered for a new $120 million factory.

Then Jack pulled out a white envelope. It was sealed, with a single word written on the outside: *Mastersons.*

"Open it." Chief Baker nodded. "He said for you to read it."

Jack looked at me with uncertainty. "Maybe I should save this for later."

"No," the old man said emphatically. "He said make sure it gets read right here. After that, I don't care what you do with it."

Jack took out a pocketknife and slit the top of the envelope, then removed a letter, handwritten on two pages of notebook paper, front side only. It was not dated.

To my family,

I'm not sure how to write this because I'm not sure who's reading it. But you'll get the idea. You've met Chief Baker. He was my father, the only one I really ever knew much. I knew my mother but she's been gone since I was a kid too.

They were my first family. You were my last. I am sorry I didn't do better for you.

I guess my friend Tim (tell him he don't owe me nothing, but thanks for the favor) told you about the helicopter crash. I tried to get Michael out, but I failed. It just didn't seem right that I got out but he didn't. Don't get me wrong I'm glad I lived but he was a better man than me I think. I thought I could help make it okay though. Well, not okay but better if I moved to Mississippi and could help his family like Chief helped mine after my real father was killed. But Chief did a good job. I guess I didn't. The way I turned out wasn't his fault, so don't blame him.

I just couldn't get that day out of my mind. Drinking was the only thing that made it go away. But then I messed up. Gambling. I thought I had a way to make the money back and fix everthing but it didn't work out and got myself in a mess. But I want my family to have some money not those scumbags. The tapes in that box will explain everthing. They ain't no wire taps or anything, just me talking. I just thought it was easier than trying to write it all out. Give it all to Rex Reynolds, and he can figure it out. I trust him. Like I said, though, be smart. Those tapes both say the same thing. Keep them seperate cause it will be dangerous if certain people find out about them.

I've got to go now. Literaly. I thought I might run off and try again. You know, start life over. But twice is enough so I don't know. I'm just to tired of it all. Got to many people chasing me. Got to many nightmares and bad habits chasing me too. None of them will ever leave me alone. So I'll just leave and they can all chase my memory.

I hope Jack will step up and be the man of the house.

Help keep a good foundation. I think it's in there if he'll just look. Maybe he should put it in a contract. Right, Jack? And I'm sorry for what I done to Michelle. It was the drinking. I hope she ain't too messed up. It's my fault.

Maybe I'll do better in the next life. I hope I get the chance.

-Stone-

p.s. I never told Janice about all this. I figured she wouldn't marry me if I told her. I planned to one day but never did. Maybe I should have. I want her to know I set out to marry her to make up for my failure, but I really did wind up loving her. She's a good person.

p.s.s. I'm sorry for the way I acted. I really ain't no bad person. Don't think nothing bad about yourselves for the way I acted. You deserved better.

p.s.s.s. I tried to take care of Chief. I should have done better making sure he's okay. Maybe theirs a way.

I read the letter twice before I realized Jack was crying. I've never been too good with tears—I don't think less of a person for having them, I'm just uncomfortable around them—so I didn't know what to do other than pat him on the back. He nodded his head to acknowledge my effort and wiped his hands across his eyes to dry them. Chief Baker had turned back towards the window.

"Do you want to read this?" Jack cleared his throat to hide the sadness in his voice.

"Nope. My last name ain't Masterson. Peter told me what I needed to know. If that piece of paper says different, I don't want to know about it."

"Okay, sir," Jack said. "I need to take this box with me?"

"That's the plan."

"What, what's going to happen to you? You know, if Stone doesn't come back."

"They said I'm running out of money to stay. Might have to go to the county home. But I'll be alright. These folks in Marbury know me. They'll take care of me. I'm old and used up anyhow."

I didn't know much about nursing homes, but I knew the McKinley County Home to be a government-sponsored facility for the indigent who had no other options. I had been in there once with my father. As best I could recall, Dad had said the workers there did their best with a scarcity of resources, but the quality of care was inevitably lacking. Nothing like that which places such as Chestnut Acres could offer.

"Yessir, I'm sure that's true," I said. "The people who know you will look after you." Of course, other than us in the room, it didn't look like a single other soul in Amberton *knew* him, who he really was, but I didn't see how telling him that would help. Confusion can be a good thing, I supposed.

"You boys go on now," Chief Baker said. "Tell me one thing, though, before you go."

"We'll do our best."

"Tell me now what happened to Peter."

I feared what Jack might say, he was so distraught by the contents in the letter. He took a breath to speak, but I reached out and put my hand to his chest to stop him. "We don't really know, Chief," I said. "He disappeared without a trace. But it looks like whatever he decided to do, he's in a place where no one is chasing him."

Chief Baker smiled and nodded his head, satisfied with the answer.

"I just don't know what to do now," Jack moaned. "Stone was trying to *help* us? Moved here to *help* us?" He paced around his bedroom, pounding a baseball in the pocket of his glove, trying to make sense of it. Michelle was long gone, having turned silent after we'd told her, before dropping us off and driving away without a word.

"I know, Jack. I know. It's a bad deal. I'm sorry, man."

"And have you seen our county home? It's a little craphole white shack in the middle of Podunk nowhere with retarded people and dirty old folks crammed in like sardines."

I nodded. "Jack, I don't have any new ideas, but I know someone smarter than us who might."

Jack eyed me suspiciously. "Don't go there, Case. I don't want him in on this."

"Why? He messed up, but how was his different than mine? Or yours?"

"He ratted us out to *Vance*. At least the person you told was your *father.*"

"Okay, what about *your* lying?"

"I was only trying to cover for my *sister*, to keep her out of *jail.*" Jack slammed the ball against the floor and caught it on the bounce.

"Dude, what has happened, has happened. We gotta put it behind us. You can't ignore him and pretend he doesn't exist forever. Plus, if we're gonna get through this, it's gonna take all of us working together." I picked up the phone and handed it to him. "Call him and tell him we're coming over."

———

"That's crazy." Jet shook his head. We were gathered with the door closed in his bedroom, where Jack had been explaining everything for the past fifteen minutes. Jet studied a world globe while he spun it, as if somehow the imprinted words and patterns might suddenly deliver some clarity to the confusion. I noticed his well-worn set of *World Book* encyclopedias on a bookshelf behind him. How many times he had read through them? "*Michelle* shot Stone?" he whispered. "And you've been hiding that all this time? This is bad, man. This is *madness.*"

"Jet." I stopped the spinning globe with my hand. "It's going to be fine, but we've got to figure out what to do. And we need your help."

"And Stone knew your father?" Jet shook his head, looking at Jack, who said nothing and glared at me. I ignored him.

I took my hand off the globe and sat down on the floor. "We need you to focus and help us. What are the chances Michelle gets in trouble now if we tell the truth?"

Jet tapped Australia absently with his index finger, staring over our heads while he pondered. "Okay. Well, it's gonna be hard to explain this far out why y'all hid it all this time if you didn't do anything wrong. But if you just say you got scared and panicked, it might be believable. That will still look bad for Mr. Reynolds, though, unless y'all can hide the fact Case was involved. But I'm still trying to figure out why Stone went to all that trouble to make sure it was months after he disappeared before his stepfather, what's his name—Chief Baker?—was discovered. And the letter and the tapes. Why not just produce those immediately? It seems like we're missing something. Have you listened to the tapes?"

Jack shook his head. "Stone's note says they're both the same. But no, I haven't had time." He paused. "And I'm not sure I can."

"Okay," Jet said. "Case or I can do that later. Let me see the letter."

Jack produced a partially crumpled envelope from his back

pocket. Jet studied the document for several minutes, flipping the pages to make sure he wasn't missing something on the back. I half expected him to pull out some forensics kit and analyze the type of paper or look for some invisible message, but he didn't. He handed the papers back to Jack. "You guys notice anything unusual about the wording in here?"

"He kind of rambled, I guess," Jack said.

"Yeah, but something else. Who is the letter addressed to?"

"His family," I answered.

"Yeah, but who is the only person he talks to specifically?"

"He talked to me," Jack said. "When he said, 'Right, Jack?'"

"Exactly. I think he's telling you something." Jet jerked the letter from Jack's hands, scanned it a moment and handed it back again. His words were quicker now, filling with excitement. "Look at the words before that part closely."

I looked over Jack's shoulder and read it again.

> Help keep a good foundation. I think it's in there if he'll just look. Maybe he should put it in a contract. Right, Jack?

"Holy cow," I said. "Jack, think about what a foundation is." I could feel my pulse quicken.

"It's what you build something on," Jack said, "but here he's talking about a family needing to keep a good base, like being strong together."

Jet saw that I was following his lead to the same conclusion. "I'm sure he means that, too, but what about a double meaning? Jack, look at the words. Foundation ... It's right in there if he'll look ... Contract. Think about foundation being a floor. Where is there a floor that maybe only you would know about, a floor that is hiding a contract?"

Jack drew in a deep breath with the sudden revelation. "The Hideaway. We hid that contract that your Dad signed under the floor. Stone, that sucker, must have found it somehow."

"He has hidden something there that he didn't want others to know about," Jet said. "And he wants you to find it."

THIRTY-THREE

JACK sped into my driveway late the next afternoon and skidded to a stop beside me. "What's that for?" I pointed to the small cooler he had tied on the rack of his ATV.

"Aw, I figured we might need to have a little campfire before we head back. Got some drinks and a few Polish sausages." He gave a mischievous grin.

"You and your fires. I like the way you think, though." I cranked my 250SX and raised my voice to compensate for its roar. "Where's Jet?"

"He's gonna meet us there. Said he was working on some unfinished business or some such."

We rode into the twilight, both more quiet than usual. I was contemplating the likelihood of finding anything hidden at the Hideaway and what to do with it if we did. I could only imagine what occupied Jack's thoughts during the times he grew quiet.

Would Jet already be searching the Hideaway? That question was erased when I saw a familiar brown ball of fur with a lolling tongue trotting down the field road toward us, leading a yellow ATV and its billowing dust cloud. "Hey, Mutt." I scratched him behind the ears when he reared and put his paws on my leg to greet me. His tail flailed about so hard it seemed to wag him. "Glad you brought him."

"As you can see, he kind of brought me." Jet smiled.

"Have you looked yet?" Jack asked.

"Nope, waiting on you."

We eased on into our campsite and killed the engines. It was obvious we'd have to do some cleanup before we did much camping once the weather cooled off. Weeds and briars were already trying to overtake the Hideaway, and a nest of red wasps lurked under the eaves of the roof on one side. For the first time ever, I sensed a waning allure about the place. I wondered whether we'd be back at all. Was that because we were outgrowing it or because of the secrets we kept? Either way, the realization both shocked and saddened me, like the feeling one gets when receiving the news that a lifelong friend is moving to a faraway place but hasn't yet gone.

The day we had forced Jet's father to sign the contract of secrecy and hidden it in the coffee container seemed at once like a lifetime ago and only yesterday. It had been less than a year, but the characters in the memory were much different from us. More immature, so much more naïve. So much had happened since then.

Jack eased into the building, pivoting his head back and forth as he watched for a threatening motion from one of the dozens of wasps that zoomed around the ceiling.

"Spheksophobia," Jet said.

Jack stopped. "Huh?"

"Fear of wasps. Spheksophobia. As opposed to entomophobia, which is fear of insects in general."

"Are you asking if we have it or telling me you do?" I asked.

"Well, I'm not saying I don't, is all," Jet said.

Jack frowned with a puzzled look and shook his head, then went back to the task at hand. He went right to the floorboard that had remained purposely loose on one end and slowly pried it upward. I expected some critter to scurry out, but none did. The Folgers can was right there beneath it, seemingly undisturbed.

"Is that all that's there?" I asked.

"Not sure," Jack said. "I really don't want to poke my hand

in there." Jet handed him a long stick, and he rattled it around in the space toward the back. I heard a different sound, something more synthetic and superficial than wood against wood or earth. "There's something there," Jack said, "but I can't get to it." I gritted my teeth and crawled in, hoping to seem innocuous to kamikaze stinger pilots. I helped him lift the partially detached board until it fully separated.

There it was, whatever it was, exactly where Jet had guessed it would be and sealed within a black plastic garbage bag wrapped in silver duct tape, about the size of a tennis ball canister. Jack grabbed it, and we scurried outside, miraculously avoiding any wasp stings. I hoped that was the beginning of better fortune.

"Jet, you truly are a genius," Jack panted.

"Well, what is it?" I asked. "Let's have a look."

"Don't get your panties in a wad. Gimme a second." Jack's hands trembled as he tried in vain to peel away the duct tape. I tossed him my pocket knife, and he made quick work of it.

Jet barely avoided the knife as he yanked out the contents of the bag. "Whoa, look at that."

Jack clutched a handful of green. "Who's ever seen so much cash?"

Stone had wrapped the bundle of money neatly in layers of newspaper. We found bills of all denominations, but mostly twenties and hundreds. A count and recount revealed a total of $43,120.

"Where did this all come from?" I said. "Did Stone rob a bank or something?"

"You're not gonna believe it when I tell you," Jet said.

"He told?" Jack asked.

"Every detail." Jet produced a cassette tape from his pocket. "This is your copy. I kept the other one. You better put this someplace safe until you decide what to do with it, and don't tell anybody. There's some serious crap on here. I'm talking felonies. Let's sit down and fire up some food, then I can explain. It's gonna take a while."

Jack wrapped the money up tightly and shoved it into his backpack. We built a fire and set out some chairs. Then we took an old grill top that we kept at the campsite for that purpose, balanced it across the fire, and cooked the sausages Jack had brought. Jet pulled out a can of beanie weenies and set it on the grill also.

"Dude, we got sausages. You eatin' weenies too?" I asked.

"Jack said he was bringing sausage, so I thought we needed some veggies, and this was all I could find."

"Hey, know what happens when a painter eats too many beans?" Jack said. He lifted a butt cheek and ripped off a loud one. "He creates works of fart."

"That's the worst joke I've ever heard," I said, moving my chair away from him.

"Yeah, it really stinks." Jack smiled. I just shook my head.

"Not many people know this," Jet said, "but the human body produces sixteen ounces of flatus every day."

Jack's eyes widened like he was staring at an alien. "Dude, you're so weird."

"I'm ashamed to call you my friend," I said. "You got any useful information? Like what you heard on that tape?"

"Yeah, yeah, okay. Stone was in a mess. A big mess. So convoluted I'm not sure I can retell it exactly right, but you'll get the idea. I had to listen to the tape three times to get it straight in my head." He paused and eyed us like he expected a comment, but we only nodded to tell him to keep going. I was trying to concentrate. If Jet had to listen three times, it must be complicated.

"So, first of all," Jet continued, "Stone had a gambling problem. A huge problem. That's where Patridge came in. He was the enforcer for some guy named Garcia in New Orleans. Stone owed a bunch of money and couldn't pay it back. So he had to come up with something. Well, lucky for him, or unlucky, depending on your perspective, he worked for Simpson & Son Heating and Cooling. He started stealing equipment from Walter Simpson."

"Stealing equipment?" Jack said. "What kind of equipment? And he just came out and said this on the tapes?"

"You can listen for yourself, but yeah, he just came out and confessed everything I'm about to tell you. I guess somebody will have to prove it, but I'm just telling you what he said. Anyway, the equipment was some tools and stuff, but also like air conditioner units, that kind of thing. He didn't say how he was doing it, or where he was unloading it, only that he did."

"Yeah, remember?" I said. "Elbert Dale said some stuff was stolen, and he thought Stone had something to do with it. I guess he was right."

"Well, there's more. A lot more." Jet scanned the foliage surrounding us as if he expected special forces agents in ghillie suits to burst out, seize the evidence, and lock him up at any second. "Stone's gambling debts exceeded his profits from selling the stolen goods. And he felt like folks were suspecting him, so he had to quit his little operation. So he had to find another way to make some money. Lucky again for him—or unlucky again, I guess—he had a friend from college who had become a big-dog executive in Reisende Tire. I looked it up. Yes, it's a Norwegian company, but their corporate office in the U.S. is in Pittsburgh."

"Stone grew up in Pennsylvania," Jack said.

"Exactly," Jet said. "So somehow Stone found out they were looking to build a new plant in this area, and like your uncle said, it turns out one of the places they were considering was Papa Mac's place."

"Wait, wait. Hold on," Jack said. "Why do they want Papa Mac's place? And how would that make Stone any money? He doesn't own any property."

"I didn't say they wanted it. I'm saying they were looking at it as a possibility. You know, we have the railroad and the waterway nearby, and land in this part of Mississippi is relatively cheap, so to somebody it looked like an attractive option. I guess Stone's buddy called him and asked if he knew any of the folks down here, if he knew the property, whatever. I'm not sure that's legal, but who knows? Now, if you'll hold your horses, I'm gonna tell you where the money came from."

"Isn't that insider trading or something?" I wasn't sure exactly what insider trading was, but I knew it had something to do with telling about a deal before it went through, and I knew it was illegal.

"No, that's different," Jet said. "That's only when a deal affects stock prices, and I think it was public knowledge that Reisende wanted to expand. The question was, where? So anyway, Stone decided he could possibly take advantage of the situation. He went to Walter Simpson and Vance MacIntosh to work out a deal."

"A deal?" Jack asked. "What kind of deal?"

"You are so impatient." Jet gave an exasperated grin. "Shut your piehole and listen for a minute so I can tell you."

"Hurry it up, then. You use ten words when two will do," Jack said.

Jet casually cut a piece of sausage and chewed it slowly, pretending he was savoring every morsel like he hadn't a care in the world.

Jack kicked his chair. "I'm going to shove that fork down your gizzard if you don't hurry up." He might have only been half-joking.

"Okay, okay. I'm just playing." Jet said.

"C'mon, man, tell the story." I was growing impatient myself.

Jet was relishing his opportunity to give us a hard time now, but I was ready to move things along. In the grand scheme of things, I just wanted to be a fourteen-year-old kid again, but it seemed like that chance was disappearing with every passing day.

"Okay. So, Vance had moved home to help with Papa Mac, and probably more than that, to figure out how to turn the farm into some money for himself once Papa Mac was gone. Somehow Stone figured that out. He then convinced Vance that he had an inside track to the corporate gurus at Reisende and could possibly influence them to build in Amberton, for the right price. Papa Mac's farm is worth a lot of money as it is—if you can find a buyer. But a guaranteed buyer like a big corporation, with the state possibly willing to pitch in with some tax breaks, maybe foot part of the bill, pay for access road easements, etc.? Then, the place can be worth a fortune. Millions."

"Millions?" I couldn't fathom those type numbers. But that would explain why Vance let us keep hanging out on the farm despite talking about having big plans for it. He had ambitions of million-dollar deals for the place. Kids kicking around were the least of his worries. "So Stone convinced Vance to try to bribe Reisende?"

"Yep. But Vance didn't have any cash. Papa Mac didn't have any real money to leave him when he died, so Vance was potentially land rich but cash poor. So they got the bright idea to go to Walter Simpson, who *is* rich. Vance and Stone convinced Simpson to put up the money for the bribes. Simpson would funnel the money through Stone to his buddy in Pittsburgh to try to influence the decision. Simpson would pay Stone a pretty penny to make the transaction, and the deal was that if the land sale went through, Vance would pay Simpson a hefty cut of his profit."

"Why Simpson?" Jack asked. "Just because Stone worked for him and knew he had money?"

"No. Because if that size manufacturing operation builds in Amberton, the contracts for the heating and cooling services, both construction and maintenance, would be worth a fortune by themselves. Simpson's company would make a killing on that, plus whatever cut he got from Vance."

"So what happened to the deal?" I asked.

"Vance and Stone both fouled it up. Vance decided what they were doing wasn't enough. He wanted to pay off some of the politicians, too, to get them to push harder for tax breaks and to put up the money to buy the land themselves if that's what it took to get Reisende to come. Eminent domain. Remember that from social studies?"

"C'mon, no history lessons," Jack moaned.

"Shhh." Jet hissed.

"Don't shush me, man."

"No. Shhh. Did you hear that?"

"Hear what?" I said.

"Something in the bushes over there." Jet gestured behind and to his right.

"Naw, dude, you're just paranoid. Nobody's out here," Jack said.

Jet listened intently for a few seconds. Evidently satisfied he'd heard nothing, he started again. "So, anyway, what was I saying?"

"M&M champagne." Jack smiled. "Or something like that."

Jet shook his head. "Eminent domain. Remember, the government can force you to sell your property if it's beneficial for the greater good of the population. Of course, in this case, Vance wanted to sell it."

"Okay, I got it. I'll put it in my notes for later," Jack quipped. "Keep going. How did Vance screw it up?"

"Somehow he figured out about Stone stealing the equipment from Simpson, and started blackmailing Stone. He was making

Stone pay him to keep quiet, and he was using that money for his own bribes to some influential politicians. So that put Stone in a real bind. He was having to pay his gambling debts and Vance both. He was skimming some of the money Simpson gave him all along, but when Vance started blackmailing him, he quit paying Reisende altogether and kept all the money for himself."

"How did he think he was going to get away with that?" I said.

"From what he said on the tape, he was going to just do it for a little while to get caught up, but he got deeper and deeper in debt. Then he realized he was in trouble that he couldn't get out of."

"So what about the tire factory?" Jack asked.

"I'm not sure. Stone didn't say on the tape. I think there's a lot more to those multi-million dollar deals than just a few thousand dollars sent to some local politicians and a guy in a corner office in Pittsburgh. Even if Stone had sent the money to his guy, you gotta figure the folks in Norway make those decisions."

Jack stood and paced the edge of the clearing, peering into the darkness behind where he'd been sitting. "Jack, what are you doing?"

"I thought I heard something too. It's gone now though. Must be an animal. I stepped in an armadillo hole when I was peeing earlier. About wet myself." Jack turned and returned to his chair. "So Vance MacIntosh and Walter Simpson were stupid to believe Stone could help them get what they wanted."

"Monumentally. MacIntosh especially," Jet answered. "He really messed things up when he got greedy and started blackmailing Stone. Killed the only chance he had, if he ever had one, when Stone stopped sending money to Pittsburgh. So it's no wonder MacIntosh is so hot to find Stone. They've figured out by now he cheated them, and they want their money back. Or retribution. Or both. And evidently, Stone wasn't caught up paying Patridge's guy Garcia either."

"So why did Stone hide the cash here?" I asked.

"He didn't come out and say anything on the tape about hiding money here. He expected Jack to figure it out from the letter, just like he did, I reckon. But he mentioned that he didn't leave stuff behind at his house or the lock box, because he figured it would get discovered. And I guess he worried if he left it at Chief Baker's, it would get stolen by some of the other residents or staff or somebody. And he had the lock box key delivered long enough after he disappeared to make it less likely also."

"So why didn't he put Mom's name on the lock box?" Jack asked.

"I've been thinking about that," Jet said. "Think about it. He got you to sign without knowing you were doing it, right?"

"Yep. Michelle and me both."

"But if he'd had your mom sign for it, she'd have gone straight to the box the minute he disappeared, right? But see, he wanted things to cool down for a few months before he sent you down the path to finding this money."

"Okay, I'd say that makes sense," I said. "And I bet he didn't want any of Vance's or Simpson's or Garcia's guys knowing anything about Chief Baker. He had hidden him this long."

"Exactly. I actually checked on Chief Baker. Made a phone call and found out who's in charge of him now that Stone is gone. I think they call it his responsible party."

"Who?" I asked.

"His doctor. Abi's dad, Dr. Rossini."

"So what's that mean?" Jack asked.

"It means I went over there and talked to Dr. Rossini about him."

"You told Abi about all this?"

"No, she doesn't know. I told Dr. Rossini that I had heard about him through a friend of a friend who was concerned about what might happen to him."

"And?"

"And he was aware that Stone was somehow kin to him, but he told no one because it was doctor-patient privilege, and Stone had told him to keep it secret. I could tell he wondered how I knew, but he didn't say anything. I asked him about Chief running out of money, and he said that he'd been told he'd be moving to the county home soon. But he also said he didn't have that long, like maybe he doesn't think he'll live very long. He said there was nothing we could do about it."

"Something's bothering me, though," Jack said. "If he was planning on running away, where is the money he was planning on taking with him? And why was he leaving money behind? What did he want *us* to do with it?"

"Jack." Jet shook his head, a pained look on his face. "Stone wasn't—he might have changed his mind you know, but from what he said in the letter, and what he said on the tape, he wasn't—you know, he hinted he wasn't planning on needing money where he was going."

Jack frowned and cocked his head to one side. "Bull. That's not right. He's got some more money hidden somewhere." He stood up and paced like he so often did when he was upset, like an agitated grizzly in a cage.

"I'm sorry, Jack. You know it's true."

"You think you're so smart. But you're wrong on this one."

Jet hesitated, and I tried to intervene. "Jet, it doesn't matter."

Jet shook his head. "No, he needs to hear the truth. Jack, what happened with Stone, it was going to happen anyway. The result would be the same. If Michelle hadn't shot him, he was going to do it to himself."

"You shut up!" Jack bellowed. He spun quickly, rage in his

eyes. Jack had a long fuse and rarely lost his temper, but when he did, it could be volcanic. He hit Jet with a violent, two-handed shove to the chest. Jet lurched backward, chair and all, feet flying upward, and hit the ground hard. Mutt, who had been resting lazily in the shadows away from the heat of the fire but still within the range of its glow, jumped up with a ferocious growl and lunged for Jack. I rose to get between them, but Jet beat me to it, scrambling on his hands and knees to grab Mutt by the collar, pulling him back.

"It's okay, Mutt." Jet stroked Mutt's coat as he growled reluctantly. "He's just playing."

Jack stood wide-eyed, appearing confused and displaced. "I don't need this." He stormed off into the darkness.

"Jet, to be so smart, that sure was stupid," I said.

"I just told the truth. It should have made him feel better."

"Sometimes the truth is best left unsaid. And if you think about it, you'll understand why."

I paused to read Jet's reaction. I knew Jack well enough to know why he had lost his temper, why the absolute realization of Stone's true plans that came with Jet's words tormented him above and beyond what he suffered already. Jet's logic had been that if Stone was going to die either way, Jack and Michelle shouldn't feel guilty for what happened. To Jack, though, Stone's plans represented the ultimate abandonment by the one person who had tried—and yes, failed for the most part, but that was beside the point—to be the father he never had.

Jet stroked his dog, saying nothing as he studied the fire for a time. Then he looked up at me and nodded his head before sighing and looking down again. Agreement mixed with apparent regret.

That was when we heard Jack's cry for help.

THIRTY-FOUR

THE yell came from below us, down near Snake Lake, piercing the silence and startling us into immediate action. Mutt jumped up and lunged toward the sound, barking incessantly, and a few reflexive expletives erupted as we sprang to our feet as well. My chair toppled over, and I tripped over it as I reached to grab my flashlight. Jet and Mutt beat me through the bushes down the trail toward the Snake, but I regained my balance and was quickly right behind them.

As we scrambled down the hill and the lake came into view against the glow of the moon, I realized Jack was running toward us down the bank to our left. "Get him, get him!" He was gesturing wildly but it was difficult to tell what he wanted in the dark. "He's getting away! Over there!"

Across the lake from Jack, a figure moved deftly along the shore, away from us. "Who is it?"

"I don't know," Jack yelled, frantically, "but he came from up there! He stole the money. Get him!"

As best I could guess, Jack had been walking around the lake to blow off some steam and had seen the other person sneaking down the hill from our campsite. Since he was on the opposite side of the lake and having to go the long way around because of a dense thicket blocking his path, Jack had no chance of catching the thief. It was up to Jet and me.

"Jet, you and Mutt follow him," I hissed, and turned to run back up the hill.

THE TRUTH THAT LIES BETWEEN

"Where you going?"

"Shhh, not so loud. Just follow him." Unless Mutt saw the guy and chased him on his own, there was no way for us to catch him from behind. We had one chance, and that was to anticipate where he was going and cut him off.

Knowing the farm like the back of my hand had its advantages. The lake shore where the shadowy figure was making his escape was relatively free of debris and brush, but only for so far. He would have to make his way away from the lake, and there was only one trail by which to do it, on the far end. The briars and underbrush were hazardously thick to each side, so I didn't think he'd get off it, especially if he thought we were way behind him. My plan was to race around the other way as quietly as I could and intercept him. I had no idea, though, what I'd do when I caught him.

Whether from anxiety or exertion, my breathing was loud and labored by the time I stopped at the intersection of the main field road and the trail leading away from Snake Lake. I struggled to control it. My internal clock told me I had beaten the man to the spot, but part of me hoped I had missed him or that he'd heard me and gone the other way.

I questioned my sanity as I squatted beside the trail in the darkness and backed into the reaches of a cedar tree for cover, letting its branches envelope me. Was I really gonna jump this guy, unarmed, alone, in the dark? I did not get to ponder the question or the appropriate answer for very long. Approaching footsteps erased my thoughts and replaced them with the crunch of dry summer grass beneath running feet.

A dark figure emerged on the trail in front of me. I was shocked by how close he was when I could finally see him. Without thinking, I lunged forward, shoulder lowered in my best form-tackling stance, and hurled myself into the man as he passed by. He was taken completely by surprise and let out a half scream, half roar as my shoulder crashed into him.

Since I expected him to be bigger than me, my intent was to use a spin tackle, where one uses momentum to twist the adversary to the ground, almost like an alligator's death roll. What I didn't account for was how my momentum could be used against me. My foe, while surprised, was strong enough and lithe enough to swivel his hips slightly as we teetered toward the ground, just enough to cause me to spin off him. The result was that, although I got him to the ground, it was with my shoulders pinned beneath his knees.

"What are you doing?" he growled. He smelled of wood smoke and body odor. I could not identify him by his voice, which was more inquiring and less ominous than I was expecting. His face was mostly hidden by the shadow of the night, but something about it was vaguely familiar.

The man jumped up, quick as a cat, and turned to run. I grabbed his ankle with one hand. He shook it free, but it slowed him long enough that I was able to swing my opposite leg around and kick his legs out from under him. He caught himself with his hands to keep from falling face-first, then rose to run again.

I was quick myself this time and stood at the same time he did. "Stop, or I'll shoot," I yelled, jabbing the butt of my flashlight into his back. The man froze in his tracks. "I swear it. I'll do it, you sorry thief. Don't move a muscle." I stabbed the flashlight into his flesh again, to reinforce the seriousness of my intent.

"Easy, there, buddy. Easy there. No need to hurt anybody. I ain't no thief."

"Sure could've fooled me. Jack saw you."

Rapid footsteps came up the trail. "You *caught* him?" Jack's voice asked, incredulous. He and Mutt materialized from the shadows, both huffing from the effort.

"Where's Jet?" I asked.

"I'm here." Jet gasped for breath as he ran up. "Jack passed me, surprise, surprise."

"Okay boys, you got me," the man said. "I don't want any trouble. No need to shoot anybody."

"Huh? Shoot anybody?" Jack said. "We didn't bring no...."

It was too dark for Jack to see my facial expressions and gesturing to shut him up. He realized his mistake at the same time the man did. I expected my quarry to either slug me, bolt down the trail, or both, and from what I had seen of his athletic ability, I didn't think any of us could catch him. Instead, he turned to face me, scrutinizing what I held in my hand.

"A flashlight, eh? Pretty clever."

I clicked the light on between us so I could see his face. He was smiling.

It was Brendan Perry.

THIRTY-FIVE

"RELAX, boys. You look like you've just seen a ghost," Perry said. "I'm not gonna hurt you." He was smaller than I thought, about Jack's height. He was thin, with long, light brown hair and the same scraggly beard I remembered from seeing him around town. He had on cutoff jeans, tennis shoes, and a long sleeve T-shirt, which I thought was odd given the hot temperatures.

He obviously read my gaze. "Helps with the mosquitoes."

I clicked off my flashlight, unnerved by his intuition.

"We thought you were dead," Jet said. "Well, once we did. Then we didn't. We haven't for a while. Thought you were dead, I mean."

I clicked my light on again. "I saw you getting arrested for trespassing."

The man winked at me like he had that night at the police station. "Ever watched the sun set over the river from Miss Fraunfelder's patio? Best view in the county." He put his hand over my light and turned to Jack. "But you never thought I was dead, did you Jack?"

"How do you know?" Jack said. "Wait. How do you know my name?"

"I know a lot of things."

"What are you, some kind of peeping tom pervert or something?" Jack asked.

"No, I just hear things. See things. You'd be surprised what you can learn just by being quiet."

"You were the one who saved us at Seder Lake that night," I said. "And the one who watched us at the barrels."

"Maybe. What if I was?"

"Then we'd want to know why you're spying on us," I said.

"Who says I was spying? Looked to me like I was helping. I haven't asked you why you've been doing the things you've been doing, have I?"

"What are you *doing* here?" Jack asked.

"I would ask you what you're doing here, but I already know. So to answer your question, I live here."

"Live where?" Jet asked.

Perry spread his arms wide. "Here. There. Everywhere."

"Okay, mister, you're not making much sense," I said. "What were you doing *here*, watching us *tonight?*"

"Y'all got any food left? Those sausages sure smelled good."

"Well," Jet said, "we got some beanie weenies, but—"

"Perfect."

Brendan Perry was quiet while we walked back to the Hideaway. He said a man couldn't communicate clearly on an empty stomach, and we didn't disagree with him. I noticed he didn't have Jack's backpack containing the money with him. Had he tossed it somewhere? But that question was answered immediately at the campsite. The pack was sitting right where Jack had left it. I picked it up and dropped it again, so Jack could see. He shrugged with a how-was-I-supposed-to-know look.

"That the pack I supposedly stole?" Perry didn't look up as he settled into a chair.

"We thought you might've," Jack said.

"I'm a lot of things, but a thief isn't one of them. Now, how 'bout some beanie weenies? I'm starving."

Jet tossed him a spoon, and Perry removed his shirt to grab the hot can from the fire. His wiry muscles rippled in the firelight, their sharp outlines beneath taught skin suggesting both a high level of fitness and an unfamiliarity with surplus calories. Jack handed him a Coke, and he devoured it all in short order. He wiped his mouth with the back of his hand. "Much better. Now, where were we?"

"You, uh, said you'd answer some questions," I said.

"Did I? Well alright, sure, we'll try that on for size. What you got?"

"Like I asked before," Jack said. "What were you doing here?"

"I saw you boys head this way, so I just sort of followed you. And I guess you could say I was eavesdropping, although technically it wasn't that, since the origin of the word for eavesdropping means standing under the eaves of a house, where the drops of water fall on you, in order to try to hear what's going on inside. And since you weren't in a house, and it's not raining, then maybe that's not the right word."

"But why are you spying on us in the first place?" Jet said.

"Spying. Maybe *that's* the right word. A wonderful question. That really wasn't my intent, I'll tell you. You actually came to me first. That day at the barrels, I was already there."

"Why?"

"First, you got to know a little about me. I'm not from here. I don't consider myself from anywhere, really, although I grew up mostly in California. I had a normal childhood, except I surfed a lot. You boys ever surfed? Guess not, living here in Mississippi. I'll bet you play baseball or something."

"Yessir, got a big game tomorrow. District championship."

"Baseball is cool too, but surfing, now *that* can be downright spiritual. You should try it if you ever get the chance. Hey, I'll teach you something." He held up his hand, curling his middle three fingers and extending only his thumb and little finger. "That is the shaka sign. Some people call it the hang loose sign. It's a surfer greeting that signifies friendship and loyalty. Try it." Jack, Jet, and I dutifully duplicated the hand gesture, and he nodded.

"Anyway," Perry continued, "I went to college, probably surfed more than studied, but I did okay. Dropped out, did some work in the communications industry. But some things happened, things changed." He took a deep breath and stopped as if deciding what to say next or whether to say any more at all. "I had to quit surfing, and I got tired of the grind. I decided I wanted to live my way, on my terms, where I wanted, how I wanted."

"So what are you doing living here?" Jack asked.

"Oh, that's just it. I don't live *here*. I live everywhere. I travel coast to coast, California to Florida and back again. Passed through here once and most folks were nice to me, Not all, but most, and that's about as good as it gets in my situation. So I keep stopping."

"So," Jack said, "you're just a, a vagabond?"

"Vagabond huh? I've heard that nickname. I'd consider myself more of a peripatetic."

"*Para* what?" Jack said. "I thought that was somebody who was paralyzed."

"Peripatetic," Jet interjected. "More of a wandering philosopher. Not paraplegic."

"Uh, huh. But, like, where do you sleep?"

"Wherever I need to. I find a place. Outside mostly. I don't like hotels and shelters, but I'll stay in one if I have to. I was looking for a place to set up camp for a while that day I saw you two at the barrels." He pointed at Jack and me. "I learned there you two were in a little bit of trouble. So I started keeping an eye on you when I could."

I stirred the smoldering coals with a stick as I contemplated his story and watched the sparks do their upward vanishing dance. "But why didn't you turn us in?"

Perry reached for the stick and stoked some dying embers on his side of the fire. "Why would I? I don't care much for many law enforcement officials, although I will say your father has always been fair to me." He pointed the stick at me. "And I know we need them to prevent anarchy, but sometimes they just don't understand. Anyway, why would I? I liked your spirit, your fight and determination, and best I could tell, you guys didn't hurt anybody."

"I guess you know who it is—who it was—the body?" Jack asked.

Perry shrugged. "I figured. I knew it wasn't me, and I knew Stone Perkins wasn't around anymore. Fact is, he was *not* one of the nice people around here I spoke of earlier. No offense, Jack. I figured however he got in that condition, he had it coming."

I gauged Jack's reaction. His eyes were locked on Perry. He was frozen, except for his mouth, which he moved deliberately as if molding his words into perfect form before letting them go. How it came out, though, sounded more like an impulsive blurt.

"My sister and I killed him."

Perry didn't move for a moment, then eyed Jack intently while he spoke. "You don't seem like the murdering type to me, and I'm a pretty good assessor of character."

"They didn't murder him." I gave the short version of the night Stone was killed, as Jack had told it to me. Jack was silent while I told the story.

"Well, like I said, I figured Stone had it coming," Perry said when I finished. "I believe that's what one calls justifiable homicide."

"You haven't told us why you followed us to Seder Lake that night," I said. "That was you following us, wasn't it? I circled around to catch you, but you disappeared."

"It was. I happened to be in the neighborhood—serendipitously for you, it seems—and I saw you boys sneaking down there.

Like I told you, I figured from what I saw and heard on ole Goodsen's farm that day you might be headed for some trouble. I wondered why those suckers were harassing you, but from what I heard tonight, I guess now I know."

"But why all the sneaking and hiding?" Jet asked.

"I don't like people up in my business. Wouldn't be here talking to you now if Lone Ranger here hadn't pulled his semi-automatic flashlight on me and figured out who I was. And if I hadn't smelled the sausages." He gave a crooked smile. "Now, I'd appreciate it if you leave me out of whatever story you tell about all this down the road. I'm sorry I bothered you. Let's just call it even and leave it at that." Perry stood.

"Wait," Jack said. "Can I ask you one more question? What do we do now?"

"Ooh, cool question. That's the one that steers our lives, really, eh? Day in, day out, what to do? But I can't answer that for you. You have to first figure out who you are and what you stand for, and that will tell you what to do. That's why I'm here and not in a high-rise office building somewhere. I figured it out for myself."

"That's it?" Jack asked.

"What did you expect me to say?"

"I don't know. Nothing I guess. That's just the usual grown-up mumbo jumbo."

"C'mon, Jack," I said.

Perry held his hand up and smiled. "It's okay." He sat back down and stroked his scraggly beard a time or two before speaking again. "Let me see if I can help you out a little bit. I can't tell each of you *who* you are. I just don't know you well enough. But I *can* tell you *what* you are. You boys are friends. Don't ever forget that or underestimate its importance, its power." He grabbed our wooden fire poker again but this time grasped it vertically with both hands and rested its point on the ground near his feet. "Let me tell you a story. A parable, really. It was inspired by a segment of an ancient, epic Hindu poem called *Mahabharata*."

Jack interrupted, "I bet even Jet can't spell that."

"Shut up and listen, dude," Jet said. "But you're right, I can't. Never heard of it."

"Like I was saying, a poem called *Mahabharata*, from over 2000 years ago. They actually made this part of the story into a *Twilight Zone* episode in the early 1960s, before your time. The story goes like this. A man is out hunting with his beloved dog, his best friend, really. They have an accident and both die. They head up the road together, looking for heaven. They come to a beautiful gate, and the gatekeeper tells the man that indeed, this is heaven, and he invites him right in. The only thing is, he'll have to leave his dog behind. It's not allowed. The man turns down the invitation, commenting that heaven can't be all that good if dogs aren't allowed.

"So, the man and his dog meander on down the road and come to a second gate. When he inquires about this gate, he's told that *this* is heaven, and indeed dogs *can* come in and are welcome. The man asks why he was deceived at the first gate. He learns the first gate was actually the gate to hell, and that there he had been given a test, for any man who would abandon his most loyal, best friend for selfish reasons is worthy only of hell."

"So, you're saying there's gonna be dogs in heaven?" Jack asked.

"Is that what you think it means?" Perry asked.

"No," Jack replied sheepishly. "I know what it means."

"Some days you're the dog, some days you're the man, but either way you're a friend," Perry said. "Look, I know you boys have been through a lot. Just remember this. Most of the time right and wrong are crystal clear, but sometimes the line between them is so blurred you can't tell the difference. That's when you must seek the truth that lies between." He paused and gazed toward the night sky briefly before looking hard at each of us, one by one. "Genuine friendship and the loyalty that comes with it, when you have that—and it can be a rare thing—when you have *that*, you have something. Put your focus there when nothing else makes sense, and you'll find your way. It's amazing what happens when you focus on your brother instead of yourself."

I wondered about this advice coming from a man who appeared to have few if any of the friends about whom he spoke, but something in his voice and in his eyes suggested his words rose from a deep hole he preferred to conceal. Was it a void caused by what had never been, or something once held and lost?

Perry stood again, and this time we did not try to stop him. He thanked us again for the food, started to walk away, then turned and spoke, almost as an afterthought. "One more thing. If you decide to come clean about where you hid that skeleton, do it together. But I would strongly recommend showing before telling."

Brendan Perry flashed a shaka sign, and with that, disappeared into the darkness.

THIRTY-SIX

"RARE back and rock, Jack!" Coach Grayson yelled from his bucket seat by the dugout.

Jack and I always got a kick out of Coach's familiar admonition, often wondering aloud what it actually meant to rare back and rock when one was pitching. Jack glanced in my direction, and we shared a smile as he fingered the rosin bag behind the pitcher's mound. Maybe we couldn't translate that expression into proper pitching terminology, but Jack and I and everybody else in the park knew what he needed to do—strike out the next batter. We were up by one run, but it was the bottom of the last inning, and Albany Central had loaded the bases with a two-out rally.

The problem was, Albany's batter was Carlton Bryan, who was as good a hitter as I ever played against, before or since. Jack was no slouch on the mound himself, though, and from my position at shortstop, I marveled at his calm but confident demeanor as the smile disappeared and he toed the rubber, eyeing his adversary like a boxer in a stare-down. Jack's first pitch was a curveball that looked like it dropped off a table. Bryan missed it by six inches. He gave Jack a spiteful smirk, but Jack remained stone-faced.

The next pitch was a high fastball that Jack hoped Bryan would chase, but he didn't. Then Jack missed again with a curveball low and away.

Two balls and one strike is a hitter's count. No pitcher wants to go to 3-1 if they can help it, especially in the last inning when a walk will tie the game, so pitchers will go to the pitch they can control the best, and hitters know it. I expected Jack to throw a fastball and worried that Bryan would expect it, too, and hit it hard. Instead, Jack threw one of the nastiest curves I've ever seen him throw, and Bryan didn't just hit it hard. He crushed it.

The pitch was low and inside, and Bryan, a left-handed hitter, turned on it. He lofted it high down the right field line, and my heart sank. Right field was Jet's position, and while he had a good enough glove and a decent arm, he possessed the speed of a caterpillar. Jet's legs churned like a mini locomotive toward the fence, and I almost felt sorry for him, reminding myself to compliment him after the game on such an admirable effort toward a lost cause.

Then suddenly, Jet had a chance. To this day, I don't know if a gust of wind held the ball up, Jet summoned a once-in-a-lifetime burst of speed, or if an angel intervened, but somehow the path of the ball's flight and Jet's plodding run intersected right at the fence.

Jet tore right through it. Literally tore right through the chain link fence. He somehow separated the fencing from the metal posts and rolled into the cow pasture adjoining the baseball complex. He didn't move for two or three seconds, then he raised his glove up.

Pandemonium ensued.

"Did he catch it? Did he catch it?" I screamed.

Jack had taken off on the crack of the bat and raced toward right field, step for step with the field umpire. Jet reached inside his glove, and sure enough, he removed the baseball. The field umpire gave the motion for an out, and Jack jumped up and down beside him, pounding him on his back with elation.

Coach Grayson, now off his bucket, yelled while searching for someone to high-five. "He caught it! He caught it!"

Albany's coach ran onto the field, hollering, "You can't do that! He was outside the fence. You can't do that!" He ushered the runners on base, including Carlton Bryan, to get back on the diamond and finish rounding the bases. "It's a home run!" he bellowed.

The home plate umpire, who was more than a bit overweight, lumbered into the outfield to confer with the other official, while Albany's coach ran alongside him, yapping incessantly in his ear. Meanwhile, players from both teams ran around like ants booted from an anthill.

"You did it! You okay? You did it!" Jack couldn't decide whether to hug Jet or check him for injuries, but when the rest of the team reached him that question became moot. He was mobbed by a pile-on of scarlet and gray. If Jet was hurt much, he didn't show it. We carried him on our shoulders all the way to the parking lot before putting him down. He got a cooler of water dumped on his head and hugs from every momma and most of the daddies. Carlton Bryan even came over and shook his hand. I had never seen Jet so happy.

Abi and Rachel were leaning on the fence waiting for us when the bedlam settled. They both gave Jet a bear hug and a kiss on the cheek, and each insisted on checking him for injuries.

"I'm fine, y'all," Jet protested. "A scratch or two, nothing serious. Tell 'em, Case."

"I don't know, man, they might have to strip you naked to make sure."

"I'll let Rachel handle that." Abi laughed. Rachel giggled and nestled herself under Jet's arm.

"Maybe I should have run through the fence too," I said.

"In your dreams." Abi winked and grabbed my hand. Her smile faded though, and she gave my hand a squeeze. "We need to talk." She pulled me to the side and lowered her voice. "Case, what's going on? We haven't talked in a week. Are you okay? Are *we* okay?"

"I was going to ask you the same question," I said. "It's not like you've called me."

"Well, you're usually the one who calls *me*. When you don't, I assume something is wrong."

"Nothing is wrong, baby. We've just been busy, you know, with *that situation* we have."

"Yeah, what's the status on that?" Abi asked.

I wanted to tell her about Jack's confession, about Stone, Brendan Perry, everything. But even though I knew I would likely regret it later, I kept it to myself. It was Jack's story to tell when he got good and ready. "We, uh, haven't heard much new. Probably gonna tell my Dad about it in the next week or so. Have you said anything?"

Abi gave me a hard look. "I told you I wouldn't say anything, and I meant it. You know that. Nothing has changed. At least not on that."

"What do you mean, 'at least not on that'?"

"I'm still not sure about *us*. You just haven't been yourself."

I took both of Abi's hands in mine. "Nothing is wrong with me, with us. I promise. I've just got a lot on my mind right now, but it has nothing to do with you. Okay? My feelings haven't changed. You know how I feel about you."

"Do I?" Abi smiled, cocking her head slightly to one side. A look I didn't see often, but when I did, it drove me crazy. "I'm having trouble with my memory. How is it that you feel?"

"You know."

"Nope. Can't remember."

"I love you, baby. How 'bout I show you too?" I leaned down to kiss her.

"Case. You're sweaty. And what if the parents see?"

"They're not watching, and I don't care." I grabbed her shoulders and pulled her to me. The kiss was brief but full.

"I love you too." Abi smiled and backed away, holding my hand until the last possible moment, sliding her fingers off mine slowly so our tips touched for one last second before separating. Then she turned and walked away. She and Rachel spoke a few words to Jet, then walked into the parking area.

I turned to look around for Jack and found him walking behind the dugout toward us. A figure emerged from the opposite side of the dugout and reached out to stop him. Jack's body language made it clear that he was irritated.

"Jet, c'mon," I hissed. We hustled to where the two were standing, and I grunted my displeasure when I realized who it was.

"Well, good," VJ MacIntosh spat, "The Three Musketeers all together. That's nice."

"What do you want, VJ?" I asked.

"To tell you the truth," Jack said, "I was only half-listening. Sounded like some psychobabble to me. Something about he wished he could play baseball but didn't quit sucking his mama until he was fourteen and couldn't understand why the other players laughed at him. I think some counseling might help."

"Oh, I don't think you want to go there, Jack. You ain't even got no daddy, and you're so pathetic you ran your sorry stepdaddy off too."

Jack's face turned the color of a habanero pepper, a sure sign the current arrangement of VJ's face was in jeopardy.

I stepped between them. "Listen, VJ. I don't know why you're here, but we got nothing to say to you. I've already cold-cocked you once, and I'll do it again if I have to, but why don't we just step away and all get out of here."

"Go ahead," VJ snarled. "Hit me." He looked to my left, and I followed his gaze. Standing off to the side was the man who had had the Cardinals cap on that night at Seder Lake. The man with the gun. This time, he tipped a Chicago Cubs cap at us.

"Who is that?" I tried my best to look unfazed.

"That there is my cousin Paulie. I believe y'all have met, huh? He came down to help, if you know what I mean. He's a bit different. Just let me say he doesn't think all the rules apply to him."

No doubt about that. He was willing to shoot kids. Plus everybody knew the Cardinals and Cubs hated each other.

"What do y'all want?" Jet asked.

"Well, brainiac, maybe you're not as smart as people say you are." VJ stepped sideways and put his face in Jet's. "Huh, fat boy? Who says you're smart? I have my doubts."

Jet didn't say a word, just glared at VJ, literally biting his lip.

"Leave him alone," Jack said. "Your problem is with me. Why don't you leave us all alone? You may have backup, but I bet I can have three teeth knocked out before cuz gets over here to help you."

"I don't think you want to try that. Look, my father needs Stone Perkins. And we think you know where he went. Now, Paulie ain't gonna do nothing with parents lurking around here. That's why I'm the one talking to you. You know, just an old school friend congratulating you on your victory. But I'm just telling you, *Jack*, things could get ugly if some info don't start turning up."

"It's funny you say that," Jack said. "Because maybe some info did turn up. Maybe some info about what your father's been up to lately, some bribes and blackmail and such."

VJ's expression twisted into one of surprise. I couldn't tell if he was surprised by the content of the accusation, the fact that we knew about it, or both. "So, *Vance Jr.,* take that and stick it up your butt cave. And *if* you leave me and my family alone, we *might* not give this evidence to the police. Go tell your father and uncles and knuckle-dragging cousins and whoever else is in your no-branch family tree *that.*"

I half-expected VJ to give the signal for Paulie to kill us. Instead, his face turned three shades of red, and he backed away. "Your time is coming! It's coming!"

Paulie grabbed VJ by the shirt from behind and shoved him toward the car, then turned back with a smirk and middle finger salute before walking away.

I took a breath for the first time in what seemed like several minutes, then couldn't help but smile. "Did you tell him to stick it in his *butt cave?*" I snickered.

"It just popped in my head. Gimme a break." Jack kicked some rocks beneath his feet. "I *hate* that guy."

"He's not *that* bad," I said. "Maybe he just needs a hug."

Jack rolled his eyes then turned to Jet. "Jet, why you let him talk to you that way and not even say anything? You got to stand up for yourself, man."

"Guess I'm a lover, not a fighter."

"Don't be a wuss."

"Jack, knock it off. He just ran through a fence to save all our butts. What more you want?"

"He did that, for sure." Jack patted Jet on the back. "Dangdest catch I ever saw. But I never doubted it."

"Bull," I said. "Nobody in that park thought he could get to that ball."

"Nobody but me and Jet," Jack said. "Why you think I beat everybody else to him?"

I remembered Jack running in stride with the field umpire to right field while everyone else watched, and I knew what he said was true. He had intended to be the first one to congratulate his friend for making the impossible catch, even before he had made it.

"There you go, then," I said. "Took a man to believe in himself enough to make that play."

Jack shook his head. "But that's baseball. I'm talking about life."

Jet looked at me, the hurt obvious in his eyes. I squinted and shook my head at him, a don't-worry-about-him-he's-just-being-stupid look. Jet just kept walking and said nothing.

THIRTY-SEVEN

THE day after beating Albany for the championship, several of us gathered at Jack's house, where his mom, likely feeling guilty for missing the game, ordered pizza and milkshakes from Dundee's grill. After eating, Jack, Jet, and I took a stroll around the neighborhood to discuss what to do next.

"Jack, what'd you do with the money?" I asked.

"It's under my bed."

"Under your *bed*?" Jet laughed.

"Yeah, I gotta figure out what to do. I thought about handing it over to Mom and telling her I just found it somewhere. I think she'd turn it over to the police though. And is that the best thing?"

"Whatever we decide, we need to get this over with before school starts back," Jet said. "I'm tired of worrying about it."

"Me, too," Jack agreed. "But how?"

"I don't think they'll do anything this long after," I said. "You just have to tell the story. I believed you. They will too."

"We'll *all* be in *some* trouble though for hiding it all this time," Jet said.

"I'm scared," Jack said. Words I had not heard him say very often. "Not about me, but Michelle. And what it will do to my Mom. Not just if Michelle gets in trouble, but just *knowing* what happened. You know what I mean? I think she can handle thinking he ran off with some slut better than knowing that her daughter *killed* him."

"You know, there might be a way to confess just *part* of the story," Jet said.

Jack's eyes widened. "What you talking about?"

"Maybe we get the tape anonymously to Case's dad, find a good way to use the money, and tell about how we just happened to stumble onto some skeleton on Goodsen's place."

"What do you mean, find a good way to use the money?" I asked.

"Y'all said Tim Speights' wife was an attorney, right?"

"That's what he said."

"And you said before they moved back here they lived in Texas? New Mexico?"

"Yeah, Texas."

"Well, I'll bet she has some old friends there willing to mail an item or two for her from an anonymous address. *And,* as an attorney I'll bet she handles setting up financial trusts and that type thing, you know, for people who aren't competent to handle their own finances. *And,* I'm just guessing that Ms. Speights might be willing to do a favor or two for the man who saved her husband's life, if she was convinced that it was for the greater good."

If there ever was a brilliant mind, I was looking at him. "Jet, you are a genius."

Jack patted Jet on the back. "I'm not sure I understand exactly what your idea is, but yeah, Jet, you're a genius."

Jet beamed. "I don't know about that, but I have a good idea every now and then."

The conversation stopped when a familiar black Camaro turned the corner just up the street from us and headed our way. It slowed to a crawl as it passed but made no motion to stop.

"Who's in there with VJ?" I asked.

"Hard to see through the tinted windows, but it looked like Lane Buckley, your best friend," Jack said.

"Hey, guys," a female voice called from behind us. Abi and

another of her friends, Lacey Parsons, were walking toward us. "Care if we join you?"

Jack waved them toward us. "Absolutely. Come on."

About the time the girls caught up with us, VJ's Camaro turned down the street toward us again.

"What is this guy's problem?" I said.

"*I've* got an idea now." Jack grinned wickedly. "Y'all done with your milkshakes?"

I knew immediately what he was thinking. "Aww, yeah. On three."

"VJ is gonna be *mad* at y'all." Lacey giggled.

As the car cruised past us again, all three of us reached back and hurled the remainder of our milkshakes onto the windshield. Strawberry and chocolate sweetness splattered, completely coating the glass with a milky film. We all hopped backward, howling with laughter as the Camaro screeched to a stop.

The passenger door opened, and Lane stepped out, furious. "You punks! You'll pay for that. That your idea, Reynolds?" Before Lane had finished his sentence, the car sped off down the street, windshield wipers slinging milkshake in both directions.

"Look, your buddy got scared and drove off," I said. "Tell him not to be worry, we're all out of scary dairy."

"Abi, you still running around with this juvenile?" Lane pointed at me.

"None of your business," she shot back.

"Leave her out of this," I said. "She's got nothing to do with it."

"Hey, just for the record, this was *my* idea." Jack stepped toward Lane.

"Oh, it was, huh? Then maybe I need to beat some sense into you."

"Jack, it's not worth it," I said. "Let's go."

"You crazy, Case? I ain't backing down from this punk. I am *done* with people threatening me."

"Mine ain't no threat, Masterson. I promise I'll hurt you."

"Let's do it then. Right here, right now."

"What, three against one?"

"No, my friends will stay out of it." Jack looked back from me to Jet.

"C'mon, Jack," Jet pleaded. "Don't."

"Stay out of it. Promise!" He pointed his finger at us without taking his eyes off Lane. Jet and I nodded. Jack's anger was at a boiling point, and I figured it better for Jack to fight Lane than for me to have to fight Jack. I'd stop it if it got out of hand.

"Case," Abi said. "You gotta stop this." She stepped toward Jack to intervene as he and Lane circled each other like bull terriers in a pit.

I grabbed Abi from behind just as Jack threw a punch.

"Let me go!" she screamed. "Let me go!"

I did, but by that time it was too late for her to do anything. Abi went silent, holding her hands over her mouth in horror as Jack and Lane went at each other, punching wildly. Lane lunged at Jack, who lowered his shoulder and tackled him. They rolled into the ditch, and Jack somehow maneuvered himself on top of Lane, pounding him relentlessly. Lane wriggled out or somehow threw Jack off him, and Jack hopped up and stepped back in the road to wait on Lane's next assault.

"Come on!" Jack bellowed. "Come on and get some more!"

I was vaguely aware of a car approaching and glanced back to see VJ's Camaro easing up the street toward us. I figured the coward would pull up about the time the fight ended and act like he was there to help, but I prepared myself mentally to take him on if he decided to get in on the action.

I turned back to see Lane lunge out of the ditch toward Jack with a roar. It was to no avail. Jack had worn him out, and just as he reached Jack, Jack sidestepped, kicked him across his shins, and shoved him face-first into the pavement behind him.

My vague awareness of the presence of VJ's approaching car turned to alarm. Why was it so loud? Too late, I realized VJ was bearing down on Jack as fast as he could go. Tires squealed as he caught second gear, but Jack was oblivious. Adrenaline surging, he was yelling at Lane to get up and come back.

"Jack!" I screamed.

A last-second look of surprise crossed Jack's face as he turned.

The body made a horrific thump as it smashed into the front of the car and flew over the top of it, landing with another awful thud behind it on the pavement in the middle of the street. The black Camaro sped away without checking up.

Abi and Lacey's horrified screams died in midair as everything slowed to a blurry, soundless crawl. I couldn't speak, I couldn't move, and the only thought I could muster was the importance of Jet. If anyone could offer first aid, he was the one. But Jet was not beside me, and I blinked hard to clear the haze because I knew that couldn't be. I spotted Lane off to the side on his hands and knees, wide-eyed and slack-jawed. But how was Jack on his stomach, looking back over his shoulder from the grass on the opposite shoulder of the road? The lightning flash of hope that my eyes had played tricks on me dissolved to despair when I saw the lifeless body lying in the center of the street.

It was Jet. John Edward Townsend, the smartest kid I knew. The bravest kid I would ever know. In the time it had taken me to blink, he had somehow pushed Jack out of the way.

His head was slightly turned to one side, motionless against the unforgiving pavement. One leg and the opposite arm were contorted in an unnatural, sickening way.

Abi rushed to his side and dropped to her knees. "Go get help! Go get help!"

I faltered, suspended in a nothingness between knowing I needed to get immediate help and an overwhelming desire to be with my friend. To be with him in what would surely be his last moments on this earth. To share this one last thing, like we had shared so many things before. Facing the certainty of everlasting regret if I left him bleeding there on the street and never got to say goodbye. If it wasn't already too late for that.

"What are you doing?" Abi glared up at me desperately. "Go get help!"

The force of her voice punched through my stupor of indecision. I blinked and turned to run but stopped short when I saw Lacey already standing on the front steps of the nearest house, gesturing wildly in our direction as she spoke to the woman who had answered the door.

"No, Jet, no! No!" Abi stroked Jet's hair, fighting back her sobs. Blood oozed from one of his ears. "I don't know what to do. I don't think he's breathing. Does he need us to help him breathe? We can't turn him over. What are we supposed to do?"

I had no answers. No answers for anything. Nothing in my world made sense. What were we doing here anyway? Why was my friend dying in the street? Over what? Nothing? How could it be nothing? I couldn't even remember.

In a lifetime compressed into an instant, I yearned for the days of rabbit hunts and tasting honeysuckle and jokes about slow base running. What happened to laughing at big words and camping and planning to save the world one day? How did that disappear into oblivion so fast, without warning or a chance to plan a farewell?

Abi petted Jet gently and whispered in his ear as tears streamed down her cheeks. "It's going to be okay, baby. It's okay. I'm here. We're all here. Your friends are all right here. You are going to be fine."

Jack's voice finally called out behind us. He spoke in an agonized whisper as he crawled past me and nudged Abi to the side, to get face to face with Jet. "Why'd you do that, Jet? Why would you want to die? You're supposed to be smarter than that. It should have been me. Not you. *Not you*. It should have been me. I'm sorry, I'm so sorry."

I dropped to my knees beside them and tried to see through the salty tears blinding me. I patted Jet's leg and tried to tell him goodbye and that I loved him and I hoped to see him again one day and that I was sorry for everything, although I've never been sure what words actually found their way past my lips.

Sirens in the distance infiltrated our huddle and grew in volume. None of us said another word. Jack hovered over Jet like a human blanket until the ambulance crew pulled him away.

PART THREE

"Those two times, therefore, past and future,
how are they, when even the past now is not;
and the future is not as yet?"
—St. Augustine of Hippo, *Confessions*

THIRTY-EIGHT

"Case, you got a letter," Mom called. "Something from the library."

I walked into the kitchen and saw she had laid it on the corner of the kitchen desk, like she usually did when mail was addressed to me. The plain envelope, with a return address from the Longtown Memorial Library, contained a typewritten note paper-clipped to a newspaper article.

Dear Mr. Reynolds,

One of my colleagues in California was kind enough to find the information you requested. Thank you for using the library services, and even more than that, thank you for your inquiring mind. I'm not sure what you're working on, but it's none of my business, and I'm happy to help. I hope this information is of benefit to you.

Sincerely yours,

Lucille Holst

The attached article was dated April 24, 1980, from the *San Francisco Chronicle*.

Communications Mogul Steps Down

Brendan Perry, CEO of CommUverse Corporation, resigned last week in a surprising move, the latest in a series of events that have shaken the rising communications company. Perry, along with lifelong friend and CFO David Elliott, dropped out of college to start the communications company in their garage, eventually building it into a multinational, multimillion-dollar corporation that took the Silicon Valley by storm.

Tragedy struck last year when Elliott, his wife Kathryn, and Perry's fiancée Emily Lancaster were all killed in an automobile accident near Sausalito. Perry, who survived the crash, took a leave of absence to recover from his injuries but indicated to the board of directors he planned to return and continue his efforts to build the company.

Despite that, upon his return, Perry had to negotiate what became a public dispute over efforts by some board members to oust him as CEO due to concerns regarding his fitness to effectively head the company. Perry then proceeded to not only return to his position, but to lead CommUverse to its most successful first quarter ever, increasing its earnings by 50% over the prior year.

Perry refused to comment on his reason for resigning, other than to say he planned to "pursue other interests."

THIRTY-NINE

M Y father slowed to a stop in front of Miles Goodsen's gate and threw the gearshift into park. "Why don't you boys tell me what it is we are going to look at?" Jack and I shared a glance.

"I just think it will be better for you to see it for yourself," I said. Brendan Perry's advice, to show before you tell, seemed reasonable enough, if for no other reason than to delay the repercussions, if there were to be any. Jack and I had convinced ourselves that it had been so long, no one would know we moved the body from the barn. They would surely figure out it was Stone, but since we thought Perry unlikely to tell on us, our part of the secret was also unlikely to be discovered.

VJ was in jail, and by all accounts having to be sedated, so it was unlikely that he would be able to link seeing us that day leaving Papa Mac's farm to the finding of the body. His gorilla-boy sidekick Blake Frierson seemed too dull to make the connection on his best day. And as for the likelihood of investigators figuring out how Stone got killed in the first place? Well, that was a question to which we didn't have an answer. That was what worried Jack the most.

"You boys have permission to be on Mr. Goodsen's farm?" Dad asked.

"Not exactly, but we haven't exactly been told to stay off either," I said.

Dad rolled his eyes and opened his door. "Okay, show me."

We crossed the fence and found that not much had changed since we had been there a few weeks earlier. We noticed no footprints, but a thunderstorm had hit two nights before. "It's in there." I pointed at the barrels.

Dad crossed his arms. "What have you been doing in there?"

"Aw, we just goof around, Mr. Reynolds," Jack said. "Explore and stuff."

"It's okay, Dad. Follow me." I slid between the two barrels at the opening, turned left for several feet, and stopped to wait at the point where we had to crawl under.

"Good grief." Dad fought to get his bulky frame through the tight space. "Gotta be skinny to fit in here. This better be good."

"Under here." I dropped to my hands, crawled into the opening, and stood to my full height. Dad and Jack followed quickly.

I could not believe my eyes.

The space was empty. Completely empty. My jaw dropped, and I looked at Jack in disbelief. My first instinct was to think I had gone to the wrong spot, but that wasn't it. What had happened was obvious.

"Well?" Dad said.

"Mr. Reynolds," Jack started, "we found some—"

"We found some, uh, some evidence that a person was living in here," I interrupted. Jack frowned at me. "We thought it might be a criminal you were searching for or something."

"What made you think that?" Dad said. "There's nothing here."

"Uh, there was an old quilt, and some food wrappers and stuff."

Jack raised an eyebrow but didn't say anything.

"Well," Dad said, "I don't see where anybody was building a fire or anything, so I doubt anybody was doing too much living here. Probably just kids playing around, like you were. Who knows?" He smiled and continued in a somewhat patronizing voice. "Look, boys, I appreciate your help, but y'all don't need to worry yourself. I know you're upset about Jet. That was tragic. And I know all that with Redmond Patridge was bad too, but those are once-a-career type things. We generally keep the bad guys locked up."

As Dad stooped to crawl out, he caught sight of what I had seen earlier and had tried to hide from his view. "Now, that's interesting. Behind you there, Case. You were standing in front of it. Somebody *was* in here. Did a little graffiti, if you can call it that."

Painted in white on one of the blue barrels. A hand, with the thumb and pinkie finger raised and the other three fingers flexed.

A shaka sign.

FORTY

"**Y**OUR dad came by today," Jack said. "Questioned Michelle and me. And Mom."

I closed the door to my room and pulled the phone into my closet, speaking in the softest voice I could without whispering. "So, he got the tape in the mail?"

"Yeah."

"Did he act like he had any idea where it came from?"

"No," Jack said. "He seemed completely baffled. Said Stone must have stopped in Texas and either lived there awhile or gotten somebody to hold it and mail it after he left. He wonders if maybe he went through Texas on the way to Mexico."

"So what about all the info that was on the tape?"

"He wouldn't tell us much. I figure he'll discuss it with Mom in private. He just said there was some very enlightening information that might lead to a lot of arrests once the investigation is complete. And he was embarrassed to ask, but he wanted to look at Mom's bank records sometime since he figures Stone had to have taken some money with him. Said he knows if he doesn't, the court will eventually subpoena them. Mom just laughed, said it would have been hard for him to take out money from accounts that didn't have any."

"Has your mom said anything else? You know, about the other?"

"After your dad left she sat us down and told us that an attorney had contacted her to tell her that Stone's father was alive, and that Stone had made sure he was taken care of financially before he left. She plans to look after him herself like Stone was doing, but we can't tell a soul, because the government might take his money away and send him to the county home."

I smiled. "Sounds like a secret you might want to keep. You said Dad questioned you. What did he want to know?"

"Asked us about the night Stone left again. And about the lock box."

"Safe deposit box."

"Whatever. It's a box, and it's locked."

"So they tracked it down, huh?"

"It's not like it was hard. Lock box in his name and our name at his favorite bank. And they saw where Michelle and I signed in and opened it."

"What did your Mom say about that?"

"She was mad that her name wasn't on there. Couldn't understand why it wasn't. And wanted to know why Michelle and I went to the box without telling her about it."

"And?"

"Like we talked about. We said we were trying to protect her, in case there was something hurtful there. And we didn't tell her about it after because it was empty, and we knew she'd be upset her name wasn't on it."

"What did y'all tell Dad about the safe deposit box?"

"We said it was empty."

"And?"

"And he said he had asked Ms. Townsend about it, since she was the one that opened it for us."

My heart skipped a beat. I remembered her seeing Jack stuff the paper in his pocket as he walked out of the vault room. There was no doubt she knew the box was *not* empty. "That's not good, Jack. I never told you this, but I was watching her. She most definitely saw you put that paper in your pocket."

Jack paused long enough that I thought we might have gotten disconnected. "Maybe so, but that's not what she told your Dad. She told him it was empty as far as she knows."

We couldn't stand not knowing. The answer to a question that seemed like it should make sense but did not, no matter how many times we turned it over in our heads.

After football practice one afternoon, I rode home with Jack, as I often did. We went straight to the Townsends' house, hoping to catch Mrs. Townsend coming home from work. She had been away from home a lot since the accident, but on this day we got lucky.

She opened the door shortly after the first knock. My heart ached for the days gone by when we knew Jet was home and would just walk right in, calling his name.

"Hey, Case, Jack. Come on in." She was dressed professionally as always, but red eyes and deep circles beneath them suggested hours of crying and sleepless nights, belying her attempt at a genuine smile. She guided us to sit at the kitchen table where we had sat so many times before.

"How are y'all doing?" I asked.

"Hanging in there. We just need time, I guess. And prayers. How about you boys? Y'all okay?"

"We're okay, Mrs. Townsend. It's just a bad deal, and we're sorry," I said.

"I know, I know. Don't be sorry. Nobody asked Jet to do what he did."

"We're sorry to bother you," Jack said. "But we just wanted to ask a question."

"Okay."

"I guess you know about the tape Case's dad got in the mail. And we heard that he came by and talked to you."

"That's right."

"That day we looked in the lock box."

"Safe deposit box," she corrected.

Jack cut his eyes at me. "Safe deposit box. You told Mr. Reynolds that you thought the box was empty." Jack's tone suggested half question, half statement.

She glanced at me, then locked her eyes on Jack. "Was it?"

"Uh, well, um…"

"Then it was empty. It's not my job to police what people put in those boxes, or what they take out. It's my job to take care of bank customers. Now, if I thought you and Michelle took something out that was dangerous, or criminal, or whatever, then it might be different. But I don't think that happened. Am I right?"

"Yes ma'am," Jack said softly.

Mrs. Townsend patted Jack on the arm. "Look. I don't know what you guys were up to, but that's not my job. Stone Perkins put your and Michelle's name on that box and no one else's. Y'all were within your rights to open the box privately. End of story. Stop worrying about that. Okay?"

"Okay."

"Now, on another note…" Maggie Townsend reached out again but this time let her hand come to rest on Jack's shoulder. "I'm glad you came to me, because there's something I've been wanting to say since the accident. I know you've been dealt a bad hand so far in life in a lot of ways, but let me tell you something. My son never saw you for what you *didn't have* but for what you *could be*. He always admired you. That's why he was so excited to tell me about you the day you befriended him when we first moved here five years ago. And nothing about that ever changed. What

I'm getting to is that there was a reason John Edward put himself in front of that car for you. I hope you will make that count for something."

Jack blinked back tears and nodded.

FORTY-ONE

Three months later

TENDRILS of poison ivy snaked up the walls of the Hideaway on two sides, fighting with hordes of other weeds for space and light. "Leaves of three, leave them be." The mantra taught me by my father normally spurred me to do just the opposite whenever I caught the contemptible vines invading my area. Over the years, I had dedicated more than a few hours to scouring the perimeter of our campsite for the tri-leaved intruders, hacking them into oblivion with a Kaiser blade.

"Better get to chopping or you'll look like a walking strawberry." Jack spoke as if he'd read my mind. He grinned back over his shoulder and stroked the despicable vines like a pet snake. He always got a kick out of my allergy to poison ivy and obsession with destroying it. He loved to grab it with his bare hands and tell me a real man should be able to do the same.

I gestured in his general direction dismissively. "Funny. Not much point in it."

Jack shrugged and ducked through the door. He emerged a couple of minutes later, dusting off a rusting Folger's coffee can. He held it up for me to see but didn't say anything.

I looked down at our fire, welcoming the growing contrast of its orange incandescence against the dying afternoon light. I wanted to stare into it until I forgot everything, let the flaming dancers of its unchoreographed ballet hypnotize me into a doze like they had so many times before. But that wasn't why we were there.

"Nothing like a good fire." Jack sat down across from me and planted the coffee can firmly between his feet. He reached into a backpack lying beside his chair. "Here." A flick of his wrist sent an object toward me, and the swirl of fire-glint and ivory arching over the flames told me exactly what it was. I snatched the knife from the air by the antler handle and remembered the satisfaction of its fit in my palm.

"What's this for?"

"It's yours now, Bud. I can't."

I switched the knife to my other hand and shook my head. "Naw, man. It's yours." I flipped it 180 degrees to catch the blade and thrust the handle toward him.

Jack waved me off. "You found it right here. Either I return it here and you keep it, or we throw it in the Snake. Nothing else seems right."

The unmistakable beat of footsteps to my right diverted my attention away from Jack's sentiment but not the object that spawned it. I rose to my feet and brought the knife to an attack position. "Somebody's coming."

We were supposed to be alone. Perhaps our benefactor Brendan Perry was back, but what if Paulie MacIntosh was coming to finish what his half-wit brother couldn't? Or maybe it was some of Redmond Patridge's gambling ring friends seeking revenge for the unexpected dike in their revenue stream. I took three steps toward the sound then eased to the edge of our clearing. If someone came charging in with a gun, maybe I could surprise him.

"No, Case."

I dropped the knife a few inches at Jack's admonishment but quickly brought it back up and didn't look back at him. There was no time for questions. The footsteps were upon us. Maybe he had lost his stomach for battle, but I would fight for both of us if I had to. The events of the past several months had done nothing to dampen my instinct for self-preservation.

Jack said something again, but I ignored him and focused on the hulking silhouette of the figure emerging from the darkness. Broad shoulders and a T-shirt struggling to contain surging biceps and pecs spoke of a man born to be big, who had refined his predisposition with hours of pumping iron. The cap pulled low was indeed reminiscent of our old friend Paulie, with his Cardinals versus Cubs fan identity crisis, but this was a camouflage hunting cap. And this person was much younger.

The light from the fire flashed across the young man's eyes as he stepped fully into our circle, and I understood. "Hey, Adam."

Jet's eighteen-year-old brother jerked to a stop and coiled back a fist. "Dang, Case. Scared the crap out of me." He relaxed and pointed to my hand. "Expecting someone else, I suppose?"

I dropped the knife to my side. "Sorry. Jack didn't tell me you were coming."

"I was trying to tell him," Jack said from behind me. "I think he thought you was either walking poison ivy or wearing a hockey mask."

Adam laughed and patted me on the shoulder. "You bad allergic to it too, huh?" He looked toward our cabin and scanned the remainder of our setup. "I see now why you and Jet always spent so much time here. Nice."

Jack spun an upside-down five-gallon bucket to a spot beside the fire. "Take a load off."

Adam gestured toward the lake below us as he sat. "Good fishing?"

"The best. Jet caught a six-pounder last summer."

Adam nodded, and the need for silence overtook us. We stared at the fire while the satisfying crackles and hisses of unseasoned wood reluctantly giving up its moisture filled the void between us.

Jack reached for the coffee can. "Thanks for coming, Adam."

"What you got on your mind?"

Jack produced a document from within the coffee can and handed it to Adam, who spun on the bucket enough to be able to read it by the firelight. A smile crept across his face as he read. He pointed to a line on the page. "Reproach and opprobrium? Jack, you come up with these words?"

"I think you know the answer to that."

Adam's smile widened. "No, I'd say this here page has my kid brother written all over it."

I spread my arms wide and made a circular sweeping motion. "You know they're about to destroy this place. Starting next week."

Adam's smile vanished. "Jack told me. I hate that."

"So we've got to end it the way we started," Jack said. "Official."

"And so why am I here?"

Jack cut his eyes at me, then back to Adam. "It wouldn't have been right, since Jet had, well, you know, and—"

Adam nodded and pointed at the signature line of the document. "And Dad is out of town."

Jack leaned toward the fire and suspended the piece of paper over it between two fingers. "Case, you want to say anything?"

I shook my head and thought it curious I had no inkling of tears. Had I become too numb to care because of everything that had happened, or was I simply resigned to the inevitable fate of Papa Mac's as it had developed in recent weeks? Maybe it was both. Move on we must, and move on we would. I hoped Jack's vision for closure would help us reach that goal.

Jack slowly lowered the contract toward the flames, but Adam reached out and stopped him. "Wait. I do want to say one thing."

He looked me in the eye, then Jack. "I just want to say thank you. Thank you for being Jet's friends." He clenched his jaw and nodded to Jack, who lowered the document enough for a fiery tongue to lick at the edges a few seconds before climbing rapidly toward his fingers. Jack dropped the paper, and we watched it flutter once before disintegrating.

"Got everything?"

I patted the rack on my three-wheeler with the stack of miscellaneous items strapped to it. "Got all I'm gonna get. The dozers can have whatever's left."

Jack scooted forward on his seat. "Ride back with me, Adam? There's room on the back."

Jet's brother nodded. "Yeah, Jack I believe I will. It was a peaceful walk in, you know? Trying to imagine all the fun you guys had out here. But it's getting late, and my bed is calling."

I reached to crank my ride, but second thoughts held me back. I needed to do one more thing before I left. I climbed off and dug around in my pack until I found what I was looking for. "Give me a second, guys."

Jack watched me and looked down at my hand but didn't say a word.

I turned and dropped off the hillside by the Hideaway and eased down to the edge of Snake Lake. I stood motionless for a time, taking it all in. Just one more long look. I didn't know whether the lake would survive or not. And even if it did, I wasn't sure I'd be back. I expected to see a ripple of a bass along the water's edge, or maybe a serpentine movement slipping across the glass of the surface, but the lake was perfectly still. As if it was patiently waiting for me to tell it goodbye. I hated to disturb it and wished my departing view of the Snake could be one of quiet, reflective serenity. But that was not to be.

Jack's eyes met mine when I crested the hill, and he nodded as I mounted my three-wheeler.

The knife was no longer in my hand.

Jack scanned the campsite before settling briefly on the now-smothered campfire. Then he cranked his ATV, kicked it into gear, and looked back at his rider. "Now Adam, while I drive, you got to tell me all about that time you got caught skinny dipping with that girl at the country club. What was her name? Lulu something or other?"

FORTY-TWO

"HEY mister. Hey mister?"

"I think he's talking to you, Jack," I say.

It is the younger of the two workers filling in Michelle's grave. It seems odd that he would be calling Jack mister, but he is a few years younger than us, probably only fifteen or sixteen. "Are y'all finished? We have to take down the tent and stuff, if it's okay. We, uh, finished covering the casket."

Jack glances around, no doubt looking for his mother. "Yeah, I'm not in charge, but I don't see her, so I guess it's okay. Nothing else for us to do here."

"Your mom seemed like she was doing okay," I say.

"Yeah, I guess. She has been through a lot, you know? My father, then Stone. Then she got pretty close to Chief Baker in the months she took care of him before he died. Now Michelle. I don't know how she's handled it."

"You've lost the same things she has, Jack. You're both strong."

"Am I, Bud? At one time I thought so, but I'm not so sure now. You know, things almost made sense when I felt like I was protecting both Mom and Michelle, and we even helped ole Chief with the secrets we kept. Maybe helped your Dad too, since he got sheriff. Even after Jet had his accident, it wasn't like telling about Stone would *help* anything."

"Yeah, it seemed like the right thing to do to me, too."

"This don't sound right, but I just kinda put it behind me. Did you? I hate to say forgot about it, but you know what I mean. I guess I sorta pretended it didn't happen. Played ball, won some championships, graduated, went to prom, started college, all that. But..."

"But?"

"But since Michelle got sick and we knew we were losing her, it stopped making any sense. And I can't make sense about why it doesn't make sense. Like I said, I can't get the thought out of my mind, if Michelle getting sick was somehow because of, of—"

"Because of what y'all did? What *we* did? No way, Jack. You gotta get that thought out of your head. People get cancer, Jack. There's no such thing as karma, even though as a baseball player, I know you get a little superstitious sometimes. Hey, do you still wear the same underwear every game when you're on a winning streak?"

I can tell Jack is in no mood to acknowledge my attempt at humor to lighten things up, but he can't let that one go. "It wasn't my underwear, you loser." He gives a wry smile. "It was my socks. And the answer is yes. Seriously though, man, I can't sleep. I started having nightmares again. Maybe I just need to give it time."

I've been having some nightmares too, but there's no point in mentioning it. "You've just been through a lot, Jack. What's done is done. Nothing we say now is going to do anything but cause more headache and heartache."

"You sure about that, Bud? 'Cause I'm having a lot more of both all of a sudden."

I don't know what to say. I feel guilty for not fully sharing his feelings. But then again, many more of *his* nightmares than mine are actual memories.

"Can I ask you a question, Case?"

"Shoot."

"You remember that day right after everything happened when we went to see Jet's mom?"

"I do."

"You remember what she told me?"

"Yes."

"Do you think I've done that? Have I made what Jet did count for something? Does what I'm doing with my life count for anything?" Jack's eyes glisten with tears.

"Sure you have. You were an all-state baseball player. All-district in football. Graduated, got a scholarship. And you're a good guy, Jack." I pat him on the back. I mean what I say, but the gesture feels awkward.

"Well, high school is long gone. I think I wanna quit baseball, and I don't feel so good about myself."

"Why quit baseball? You did pretty well this fall, huh?"

He shrugs. "Yeah, I don't know. Sometimes I just wonder what's the point?"

"The point is it's paying for your college education right now. Have you been going to church?"

Jack looks away. "No."

"Maybe that's a good place to start."

"How can I sit in a church with all the lies I carry with me?" He has a point that I usually choose to ignore. "Sometimes I think I just need to tell it all, get a fresh start. What would you say about that?"

What I think is that I'd rather not have this conversation at all. It is inconvenient to revisit the past, especially when it has been more than four years since that summer. What good will confessing everything do now? Nothing would bring Stone back—then or now—and he has no family hanging on the hope he will one day return. Jack's mom has not only survived but is more financially stable than ever, having worked her way up to be the office manager for a medical clinic and making enough to quit her waitress job. The criminals Stone was dealing with have been prosecuted and received their sentences. The cases were closed two years ago. The tire company never came to fruition, and the MacIntoshes lost the farm to bankruptcy. It has been taken in by a new four-lane highway.

Why go back to all that? Why not leave it all in the past and start fresh? But Jack has clearly been tormented by his role in what happened. I try to put myself in his shoes. *He* was the one who lived through whatever abuse Stone heaped upon them while he was alive. *He* was the one who watched Stone take his last breath. *He* was the one who cleaned up the mess and hid the body in the barn that dark night, panicked that he'd be caught and his sister might go to jail. And *he* was the one who watched that same sister, whom he'd tried to protect, rise out of the ashes of tragedy and turn her life around, only to get sick and succumb to cancer.

The more I think about it, the more ashamed I am in my judgment of him, given the difference in our perspectives. Jack's motives were always more noble than mine. He was trying to protect his family all along. I was merely trying to keep from losing a place to camp and hunt until I found out the victim had been shot, then only to keep from getting in trouble myself for moving the body. Inconvenient truths I have chosen to ignore for a long time.

"You just gonna ignore my question?" Jack interrupts my thoughts. "What would you say if I just came clean?"

"I'd say the same thing I told you way back then, I guess. I'll back you whatever you decide."

He reaches out to shake my hand, arm-wrestling style. "Appreciate it." He holds the grip until he's sure I'm looking him in the eye. "It's gotta be just me and you, though, Bud."

I nod in agreement.

Jack is suddenly distracted by something behind me. He breaks into a smile. "Look what we have here."

Ron Cervelo, Michelle's husband, walks up. He is shorter than both Jack and me, small-framed but muscular enough to fill out his suit, with a clean, short haircut, perfect posture, and a polished air about him. Jack has told me Ron is a captain in the Air Force, and he looks the part.

Ron is holding a small child, a girl, wearing a pink one-piece with footies, and a lavender bonnet. "I asked the baby sitter to bring her by before we have to head out. Figured you'd want to see her again."

The little girl's broad smile only reveals four teeth. She holds her hands out for Jack and babbles at him. "Tacky. Tacky."

I laugh. "Tacky? How appropriate."

Jack glows with pride as he reaches out and puts her on his hip and kisses her on the cheek. "Yeah, Michelle thought it would be cute for Janie to call me Uncle Jackie for some reason, but she hasn't learned her J's yet. So I'm Uncle Tacky. Ain't she cute?"

"Janie, huh? I like it. She's a doll." I thrust my hand out to Ron and introduce myself. "I've heard about you but haven't met you. I'm very sorry about Michelle."

"We all are. She was a great girl. Great mother." Tears try to form, but Ron blinks them back and holds his chin up. "Can I talk to you guys about something real quick?" He motions for a lady who appears to be in her fifties to walk over and get Janie.

"Bye, Janie baby." Jack blows her a kiss, and she giggles, then she mimics him by placing her hand to her mouth and pulling it away in an exaggerated sweeping motion.

"What's up, brother?" Jack says to Ron once the lady has walked away with the baby.

The smiles Ron had in his daughter's presence are replaced by a more somber look. He reaches into a briefcase that I only now notice and produces a brown envelope, from which he removes a stack of papers clipped together. The dimensions are smaller than standard letter, only six-by-eight inches or so. "These are from Michelle's diary. I never read any of her things. They were private, of course. But before she died, she asked me to read these and give them to you. I guess you probably know what's in here."

"Wow. I never knew she kept a diary," Jack said.

"She did for years, apparently. I don't think she wanted anybody to know. I can't look at all of them right now. One day maybe I'll be able to, and I'll share it with you and Janie if I can. These pages are the only ones I've read, and only because she made me. She said these are the only entries that talk about what happened, you know, with Stone." Ron glances around as he finishes the last sentence to make sure we are still alone.

"We're both in there?" I ask. "Jack and me? You know, what all we did?"

"Yeah, just you two. And Michelle of course. If there were others, she didn't write about it."

"What do you plan to do with that?" Jack asks.

"It's taken me awhile to wrap my mind around what I *should* do, but I've thought long and hard, and I plan to give it to you, Jack, just like your sister asked me to. Hey, you're eighteen, almost nineteen now. You can make your own decisions. What you decide to do with this is your business. I'm sorry all that happened to you and Michelle. She didn't like to talk about it much, but from what I gather, Stone was not a good guy, at least, not at the end. Maybe there was no other way. I'll tell you this, though. Michelle obviously was able to turn her life around after that, and I am lucky to have had her for the time I did. I've got a beautiful baby as a result. That's all that matters to me. Nothing in here can change or diminish that. The past is the past."

Ron hands the stack of papers to Jack and pats him on the shoulder. "I've got to get going, but you call me if you ever want to talk. You and your mom come up to visit us in the next week or two maybe. Janie will be missing her Tacky." He turns to me. "Nice to meet you, Case. You be a good friend to Jack, eh?"

"Yes, sir." I salute him and immediately feel silly for doing it, but Ron laughs, returns the salute, and walks away toward his car.

FORTY-THREE

"THAT was unexpected," I say.

"You can say that again."

"What now?"

"I don't know. Gotta do some thinking." Jack folds the envelope and shoves it into his inner coat pocket. "Hey, you see who else is here?" He points in the direction of a group of people who had been talking but are now dispersing to their vehicles. A young man and woman are leaning against the side of a dark Volvo sedan, not leaving like the others. Waiting to talk to us.

"Yeah, I saw them earlier."

"Have you talked to them?"

"They were across from me, talking to some other folks, so I didn't get to."

"Uh huh, I'll bet. You still love her, don't you?"

"Doesn't matter if I do or if I don't. Things worked out for the best. We grew apart, she moved on."

The couple rises to meet us. He is broad shouldered, just slightly shorter than me, wearing gray slacks and a black coat. He appears strong but stiff and walks with a pronounced limp. The woman's blizzard blue eyes appear almost fluorescent against her tan skin and the black dress that nearly matches her hair. Her smile is reluctant, just barely revealing her perfect teeth. Happy to see us, sad for the reason why.

"Thank y'all for coming," Jack says.

"We wouldn't miss it. You know that." Abi gives Jack a hug.

"I'm very sorry about Michelle."

Abi's eyes catch mine briefly, and we both look away for a second before our gazes lock again. "Hello, Abi. You look nice."

"It's good to see you, Case."

I turn and smile at her companion before shaking his hand and pounding him on the back affectionately. Genuinely happy to see him for the first time in three or four months. "Hey, Jet. How you been?"

"Doing great, man. Miss you guys. Too bad we couldn't all stick together for college."

"How's the back and the leg?" Jack asks.

"The same. As good as they're going to get, but that's fine. My leg still doesn't want to follow my instructions sometimes, but luckily I really don't have much pain."

I am not sure I believe him. It has hurt me just to watch him try to get around ever since the accident.

"I've got it figured out though," he says. "I just compensate for my lack of velocity with deceptively poor acceleration."

We all laugh. Jet has handled his accident and recovery re-markably well. Two weeks in a coma, four surgeries, and another three weeks in the hospital, followed by six months learning to walk again in a rehabilitation hospital in Jackson, did nothing to dampen his spirits. Despite missing most of one school year, he somehow managed to not only catch up and graduate with the rest of his class, but to be valedictorian. Only Jet could have pulled that off.

"Case, can I talk to you a second?" Jet asks. He and Abi share a look, then he hobbles past me, walking down the gravel road that meanders through the cemetery.

I fall in beside him and match his pace, hands in pockets be-cause of the cold, walking slowly. "What's up?"

"I just wanted to see if, you know, if things are okay. We haven't really talked about…"

"About you and Abi dating?"

"Yeah, that. I know, it was end of senior year, then starting different colleges, but we just haven't talked. You don't seem like yourself."

"I'm fine, Jet. It's no big deal."

"It *is* a big deal. We were best friends. I never meant to mess that up. I'm sorry."

"Dude, don't *worry* about it. Abi and I grew apart and broke up. I know you were in love with her before then—don't say you weren't—but that's not your fault. For crying out loud, she doted over you and nursed you back to health as good or better than any nurse or therapist ever could. She couldn't *not* do that. I know that. That's just *Abi*. I lost her in the process, but it's nobody's fault. She couldn't help eventually falling for you any more than you could her."

"Maybe so. I owe her a lot." Jet stops walking, glances back toward Abi, then forward again, now staring off into the distance. "I just want us—you and me, I mean—to still be friends. No matter what."

I pat him on the back. "We are, Jet. I promise. Nothing can change that." I sincerely mean that, but I am desperate to change the subject. "School going well? Still planning on medical school?"

"That's the plan right now. I'm majoring in biological engineering so I'll have a backup if something changes, you know, if I can't get in. What about you?"

"Jet, that sounds like a *terrible* major, especially since there's no chance you *don't* get in. Now, majoring in English like me, *that* sounds much more sane."

Jet laughs, then his expression becomes serious again. "How

do you think Jack is doing? You know, with Michelle?"

"He's okay. Having a hard time reconciling things."

"The person he was protecting is gone."

I don't answer for a time, gathering my thoughts. Jet has turned and is looking at me, waiting. "Jet? No matter what happens, you know, if someday stuff comes out about that, about Stone..."

"Yeah?"

"You guys don't owe Jack or me anything."

"What do you mean?"

"I'm saying, there's no point in associating yourself with what happened. It serves no purpose. Just keep quiet and move on."

"You think something's going to come out?"

"I don't know. I just don't know. But you and Abi stay out of it, okay?"

Jet looks conflicted. "Case, we were complicit in it by just knowing what happened and doing nothing. We share some guilt too. Plus, it was a long time ago, and I don't think they would do anything—"

"Jet, promise me. You don't owe Jack anything for sure. He owes you his *life*. And me, if you owe me anything, it's a promise to take care of yourself and Abi too. I just want you guys to do well. Who knows what little thing in somebody's past might keep them from getting into medical school or whatever. I need you to promise me you'll look after Abi and keep both of you out of it."

"Okay, Case. I promise. You and Jack don't do anything stupid."

"It's up to Jack. I'm just along for the ride."

FORTY-FOUR

JACK rides with me from the cemetery. The silence between us is heavy, weighed down by more than Michelle's death. I have been with Jack for much of the past four days, and he seems different now somehow. I suspect—I know—it is because of what is in the breast pocket of his jacket. It is unlikely that the pages of Michelle's diary contain any new information. But the fact is that memories, good and bad, can gradually lose their potency over time, becoming more nebulous and indistinct. Now, it is as if the evanescing vapor of painful recollections from Stone's death have suddenly been condensed and crystallized onto pages of paper. Like sheets of ice sitting against Jack's heart.

I know this, because I know my friend. Still, I don't know what to say, so we ride in silence for a bit.

Jack reaches into his side pocket and pulls out an object. He hands it to me and asks if I know what it is. It is a medal—a bronze cross with an eagle in the center, surrounded by a green wreath. The ribbon is blue with stripes of red and white at the edges.

"Stone's Air Force Cross?"

"I found it the night it happened. When we threw out his stuff. I didn't know what it was. For some reason I kept it and nothing else. Been keeping it in my pocket a lot lately."

"The person who won that medal wasn't the person who died that night, Jack."

"Can I tell you something, Case?"

"Tell me."

"I've never told anyone this before."

"Okay."

"No one. Not even Michelle."

"Jack, you know I won't say anything."

"That night that Stone died?"

I wait for him to continue, but he doesn't. Like he needs my voice to trigger him to speak again. "Yeah?"

"You know, Stone was attacking me."

"Yeah. He came after you with that knife, and Michelle saved you."

"Yeah. Stone wasn't gonna kill me."

My instinctive emotion is sudden anger. Four years of lies? Was it all a lie? Surely not. Surely. Then clarity. I calm myself and drive on. "What do you mean?"

"I mean, I saw it in his face. He attacked me, and I think at one point he *was* going to kill me. Then his face changed. It was suddenly ... sad. Like regret. Terrible regret. But it was too late."

"Michelle shot."

"Yeah, she shot, and it was all over."

The weight of this revelation settles heavy between us for a minute before I finally speak again. "It wasn't your fault, Jack. Stone did that to himself. It wasn't anybody else's fault. Michelle couldn't have known."

"I know. I never told her. You know, she was like a bird released from a cage after Stone died. He ... affected her."

We ride in silence again for a minute.

"Case?"

"Yeah."

"I try, but I can't get that look on Stone's face out of my mind."

I am sorry that I don't have cures for the memories that haunt Jack. Soon I turn my Ford Ranger into Jack's driveway and pull to a stop. "What are you gonna do? You asked me what I would do if you decided to come clean."

"I heard your answer back there at the cemetery. But that was before Ron gave me the diary."

I sit silently for a moment before I speak, mulling over the implications of the diary's words and trying not to again relive in my mind the events that inspired them. My thoughts come to rest on the memory of a strange wanderer we called the Vagabond, on the irony that his words made as much sense as any I'd heard in the past five years. "My answer is the same, Jack. I'm with you. You remember the story Perry told us? The man and his dog, looking for heaven?"

"Yeah, I remember."

"Well, I reckon we gotta stick together till we go both go through that second gate."

Jack smiles. "Truth."

FORTY-FIVE

THE aroma emanating from the paper sack on the truck seat beside me exacerbates my hunger pangs. Returning from a fast food run, I stop my truck at the end of my driveway and wait for the mailman to finish depositing his delivery in our box so I can pull in. He's the same mailman we've had for years. A familiar face, but I don't remember his name. He gives a short, courteous wave before driving his white, box-shaped USPS Grumman LLV to the next house.

There really is no need in getting the mail. Mom always stops on her way home from work and checks it. I decide to grab it anyway, in case there is something I need to see before I head back to Mississippi State. The stack of mail seems thicker than usual. I don't check the mail enough to know. Is there usually more of it on Friday?

It is my last Friday of winter break, which has been much less enjoyable than I had anticipated. I loathe the thought of starting classes again in two days but don't think another month off would help me. Michelle's funeral was disconcerting, to say the least. Was it seeing Abi again? Was it Jack? He and I made a half-hearted attempt or two at hunting but have not revisited our conversations from after the funeral. Clearly, though, he has not been himself, and the more introspective I am, the more I realize that neither am I.

I throw the collection of papers on the kitchen counter and focus on my late lunch, a burger and fries from Dundee's that I hope is as good as I remember. A fry and first bite of the burger both disappoint. Nothing tastes as good lately.

As I chew my food, one piece of mail catches my eye. A brown envelope, slightly smaller than letter size. My hands tremble as I separate the envelope from the others. It is addressed to Sheriff Rex Reynolds. The return address is for Jackson Masterson. I measure the thickness of the envelope with my thumb and index finger and weigh it with both hands, as if to gauge its contents, though I don't have to open it to know what is there.

My mind races. First I think about how easy it would be to burn the envelope, destroying it and its contents before Dad gets home. Then I wonder if it's possible that Dad might just slip the pages into a secret file, as if they never existed, to focus on other, less inconvenient infractions with more temperable outcomes. I know this possibility to be an impossibility, and I am suddenly comforted by the realization that I am not alarmed by it.

I ponder whether Jack will have a conversation with his mother before Dad calls her, and I imagine that he will. Then I contemplate whether Dad will just show up at my dorm or call and ask me to come home. Will he speak to me with the concerned tone of a father or the authoritative voice of a sheriff? I don't know which I prefer, but I am prepared for either.

I scribble Dad a note on the envelope while savoring the last bites of my burger and fries. Soon I pull my truck onto the street, make two left turns, and as if on autopilot, cruise slowly along Amberton's newest four-lane highway, traversing what was once a farm where young boys lived adventures about which most could only dream.

I notice the afternoon sun seems to shine a little brighter today. I hope my friend Jack sees it too.

THE END

ABOUT THE AUTHOR

W. D. "Dwight" McComb graduated with a degree in chemical engineering from Mississippi State University before deciding that a career in medicine was his true calling. He received his Doctor of Medicine degree from the University of Mississippi, then earned board certifications in Internal Medicine and Pediatrics as well as a specialist certification in wound care. He has been practicing medicine for the past fifteen years in northeast Mississippi, where he lives with his wife and three children. When he's not treating patients or writing, he can often be found on the sideline with the local high school football team, roaming the woods of the Buttahatchie River bottom, or tossing batting practice to his kids. *The Truth That Lies Between* is his first novel.

www.wdmccomb.com

Author photo by Parish Portrait Design

Book and cover design by David Provolo

CPSIA information can be obtained
at www.ICGtesting.com
Printed in the USA
FSHW011450291219
65193FS